SHIELD OF FIRE

A RELIC HUNTERS NOVEL

KERI ARTHUR

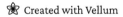 Created with Vellum

With thanks to:

The Lulus
Indigo Chick Designs
The lovely ladies at Hot Tree Editing
Dominic Wakeford
The ladies from Central Vic Writers
Julie from Cover Craft for the gorgeous cover

CHAPTER
ONE

DEATH SLIPPED THROUGH THE NIGHT, AS ETHEREAL AS A GHOST BUT as powerful as the storms rumbling overhead.

And it was coming for us.

I opened my eyes. Deep shadows wrapped the loft, making it difficult to see anything that lay more than a few yards away. Not that I really needed to see—aside from the fact I'd been here often enough now to be familiar with the layout, I was an Aodhán pixie. Wood song, whether it came from trees or floorboards, could guide me through darkness in ways eyesight never could.

But the soft song that spun through the loft remained unchanged, and that meant there was no one else in Cynwrig's apartment, either up here or downstairs, attempting to find the concealed entry point into this area.

But the sense of danger continued to build, and unease stirred. Whatever—*whoever*—it was, it stood apart from the storm and the icy blast that formed within it. Stood *opposite* it.

I frowned, not understanding the insight. Which, to be

honest, wasn't really surprising. Second sight might be a family gift, but it was a talent I'd come into only recently.

I hesitated, then carefully pulled away from Cynwrig. He stirred but didn't wake, which wasn't really surprising. For all their legendary stamina, not even a dark elf could go days on end without sleep. Between mopping up the aftermath of betrayal by some of his kin, helping his twin sister run the Myrkálfar empire for his ailing father—who happened to be their king, although that was a term they could no longer officially use—and his bevy of women, the man had had little time to rest.

Of course, if he'd been awake, he'd strenuously object to my use of the term "bevy." According to him, that implied he was seeing ten or more women, and apparently, even *he* couldn't cope with *that* many demands on his time. He *had*, however, admitted to seeing six others.

Unfortunately, one of those six included the lovely Orlah. She was the tall, dark-skinned elf with long, curly black hair and to-die-for figure who'd briefly interrupted our dinner at an upmarket and very expensive restaurant recently and had made it patently clear she had her sights set on marriage. With him.

And while I was painfully aware our relationship was destined to be short term rather than long—highborn elves, whether light or dark, didn't marry outside their race —I simply wasn't ready for it to end.

But I had no intention of wasting the next ten years in a relationship destined to go nowhere, either, which was precisely what I'd done in a previous relationship with an elf.

This time, I was also seeing someone else. Another pixie, in fact.

He might not set my heart and soul alight, but the relationship was still very new, and he was at least a "safe" option.

"Safe" being relative only when compared to a dark elf.

I slid from the warmth of the bed and the man and padded naked and barefoot toward the sliding glass doors directly opposite. The loft was surprisingly large; the pitched roof had been raised, and the dormer windows that lined the Watergate Street side of the building gave the area a bright and airy feeling in the daytime. It was divided into two distinct areas by low storage cabinets: a bathroom and office lay in the front half, and an enormous bed and small living area in the other. This was his den—his home away from home. Few of his bevy made it up here, apparently, which I guess made me special.

It was just such a shame I would *never* be special enough...

I shoved the thought away and stopped in front of the sliding doors. The night was dark, and the moon hidden behind a storm about to unleash her fury. The balcony, like the loft, lay wrapped in shadows, but streetlights glimmered on the streets below, forlorn stars whose light was about to be muted by the icy rain sweeping toward us.

It was the sort of night in which the Annwfyn loved to hunt.

Whether they *could* now that Rogan, who'd been my brother's boss at the National Fae Museum, had successfully stolen Agrona's Claws—three ancient artifacts that had the power to destroy a world—from us and taken them into Annwfyn, remained to be seen. His goal had been to forever end their threat in revenge for them erasing his entire family, and he'd given his life to achieve that aim.

And while there'd been no reported attacks in the five

days since that cataclysmic event, no one was sure how long the peace would last.

Not even the goddess responsible for the Claws' existence.

Energy surged across the night yet again, but this time, it was filled with an unworldly—perhaps even ungodly —heat.

I opened the sliding door and stepped out. The wind hit me immediately, running chill fingers through my short red hair and sending goose bumps skittering across my skin.

I was tempted to go back inside and grab a coat, but the rising sense of urgency had me padding across the patio instead. The yellow glow of the streetlights below puddled across the wet tarmac, highlighting the emptiness while casting the areas beyond into deeper shadows. The old city wall dominated the other side of the street, and beyond it lay one of the world's oldest racecourses.

Whatever I sensed wasn't hiding within the track's confines, however. It was on the street below somewhere, hiding in plain sight, and that usually meant a shadow shield was being used. If it was, they'd be standing well away from the lights, which could shred a shield instantly. Unless, of course, they had one able to operate in both dark and light situations. They were generally very, *very* expensive, though, and technically illegal, although *that* had never stopped anyone from using them before now.

I narrowed my gaze and studied the street, but couldn't see the airy shimmer that sometimes indicated a shield. He —or she—was there; I could feel it, but I was simply too far away to spot him.

A thick coat holding a musky, earthy, and very manly scent dropped lightly around my shoulders, then arms slid around my waist and pulled me back against a body that was warm and muscular. Lips brushed my neck, a feather-light caress that sent desire leaping through me. I leaned into Cynwrig's warmth and said, "Sorry, didn't mean to wake you."

"It wasn't you so much as the cold air whipping in from the open door."

His voice was deep, velvety smoke, and the urge to turn and kiss him was fierce. Like most dark elves, he was blessed with not only magnificent looks, but an inner magnetism that made him nigh on irresistible. Light elves might be divinely beautiful beings, but dark elves were sex on legs. And very fine legs these ones were, too.

"Sorry," I said, though a large part of me wasn't. Standing here encircled by his warmth was a much nicer option than standing alone.

He laughed softly, his breath brushing enticingly past my ear. "Most would consider it a crime to be sleeping when they had you in their bed. I take you didn't come out to commune with the storm?"

"No."

Though I technically *could* if I wanted to. I might be an Aodhán pixie, but my father had been a minor god of storms and lightning, and I'd inherited some of his abilities. Of course, just like the second sight I'd gotten from Mom, I was still very much a novice when it came to using the power that was mine by birth.

The old gods certainly weren't offering much in the way of help either, even though they were demanding *I* help them. As for my father, well, he was obviously aware I existed and had even pushed some help my way, but he'd yet to come see me. And it wasn't like I could question Mom about him, because she was dead. Murdered.

Tears stung my eyes, and I fiercely blinked them away. I

would not—*could* not—allow myself to grieve her loss. Not yet. Not until revenge had been had. To do anything else might well break me.

Not that I take justice into my own hands—shedding blood in any way *other* than self-defense always went badly for us pixies—but deep down inside me, there was a darkness, an anger, that certainly *wanted* to.

Once my emotions were under control, I quietly added, "Something down there doesn't feel right."

"In what way?"

I hesitated. "I can feel an energy source, a powerful one, but I'm not sure if it's magically based or something else."

He didn't answer for a second, but his tension rose. "There's someone standing in the deep shadows under the arch."

I didn't question his certainty. He was a dark elf and could not only command stone and earth at will, but use it to glean information in much the same manner as I could wood.

"Is there just one person?"

"For the moment, yes." He paused again. "The distribution of weight suggests a male, but there's a lightness to his stance that makes me suspect he's not human."

"Elf?"

"Or shifter."

"A bird shifter wouldn't need to use a shadow shield." Especially when there were plenty of trees lining the far side of the old wall. A shifter could roost in any of them with no one thinking it odd.

"A rat shifter wouldn't need one either, but I suspect that's not what we're dealing with. Shall we go down to investigate?"

"I think we should."

Because that caress of power was sharper, and I had a bad feeling we didn't want to be in the vicinity when it was unleashed.

Cynwrig caught my hand and led me across the patio. Once inside, I hurriedly dressed, then pulled on my socks and boots, glad I'd listened to instinct and gone with water-proof comfort over glamor earlier tonight.

"Ready?" His smokey, silvery gaze swept my length and came up heated. "You should go braless more often. Your breasts are too magnificent to be caged."

I snorted. "Says the man who never has to hold down unleashed breasts when running or risk black eyes."

He laughed, a sound as smooth and as rich as honey. "A truer fact has never been uttered, but that does not void the observation."

I rolled my eyes and motioned toward the stairs. "You can lead."

He raised a dark eyebrow, his eyes gleaming with amusement. "So that you can inspect my magnificence in the same manner as I just did yours?"

"What's good for the goose is good for the gander, remember."

He laughed again, then spun and sauntered toward the stairs, moving with a grace and power that would draw the eye of anyone with a pulse.

It didn't hurt that he had wide shoulders, arms that were muscular without being overly so, and a classically beautiful V-shaped body. And, from behind, a butt that looked magnificent in jeans.

Or, indeed, out of them.

I resisted the impulse to race him back to bed and followed him down the old stairs whose song was faded but still filled with joy. When Cynwrig's family had renovated this building long ago, they'd obviously done so with the aid of a pixie, because there was no tale of destruction to be heard in that song. The same could not be said about many other redeveloped buildings within Deva's old walled city. The council might have strict rules in place for all heritage-listed buildings, but that didn't mean they understood or even cared about the wooden bones of those buildings.

Cynwrig unlocked the door at the bottom of the stairs then ushered me into his main residence—a large room containing a luxurious kitchen to the right, a dining area on the street side, and a big old sofa and four comfortable chairs in the middle facing the fireplace and the TV above. It was a comfortable, if little used, space, at least when we were together. Given past comments, the opposite was true when it came to the bevy.

I walked across the room to grab my woolen jacket from the cloak closet, pulling it on as I followed him out the door and down the stairs. No sound came from the other apartments—there were two on each of the three floors—but that wasn't really surprising given the amount of sound insulation installed. The foyer was large and ornate, the front door a wide expanse of old oak that hummed harmoniously with the rest of the building.

We didn't use it, however. Cynwrig caught my hand and tugged me to a rear fire exit that wasn't visible from the front door. He pushed it open and followed me through, but didn't let the door close, holding it open with his fingertips instead.

The storm I'd felt earlier had started to unleash, the rain more like sleet as it splattered across the already wet concrete.

I hastily did up my coat, then shoved my hands into the

pockets, gaze scanning the immediate area but still not seeing the danger I sensed. "How do you want to play this?"

"I'll head out the front door and draw their attention. You come in from the side."

"What if they run away?"

Amusement twitched his lovely lips. "They won't get far."

"Unless we *are* dealing with a bird shifter."

"Then you can use the wind to leash the bastard."

"Fair point." I rose onto my toes and brushed a kiss across his lips. "Be careful."

He laughed softly and lightly touched my nose. "I'm not the one with a long history of getting injured during quests."

"I wouldn't call it a *long* history," I replied, amused. "I've only been doing this whole relic-hunting, bad-guy-chasing thing for a few weeks, remember?"

"And that's what you think is out there? A bad guy?"

I hesitated and then nodded. "They intend harm."

What form that harm would take was a question I couldn't answer, but I wasn't liking the gathering heat. Thunder rumbled overhead, an uneasy echo of the dread growing within.

"Then let's move," Cynwrig said.

He stepped back inside and quietly closed the door. I walked down to the end of the lane, then paused and scanned the street. Lightning flashed in the distance to my right, her power echoing through me, sparking something deep within. Just for a heartbeat, it altered my vision, allowing me to see the air in the same way I could see the golden rivers of life that pulsed through trees or wood when I touched it. These currents were neon bright, however, and filled the darkness with a seemingly endless range of color, allowing me to see objects otherwise hidden from normal sight because of distance or darkness.

The flash faded, and so too did that river.

I drew in a deep breath and released it slowly, uncertain whether I should be excited or fearful of this new development. Granted, it might be a very useful gift on relic hunts, but I knew there'd also be drawbacks. There always were when it came to psychic or magic gifts, even if inherited from a father who was a minor god of storms.

I crossed the street and went left. I couldn't see the arch itself from this angle, but there was a small, orb-shaped section of turbulence hovering several feet off the ground just before it. It was neither a shadow shield nor a natural occurrence, but it was very definitely the source of danger I sensed.

Cynwrig appeared out of Watergate Street, the hood of his black coat drawn low over his head and his body hunched against the rain, an action that somehow made him appear less of a threat.

The heat and sense of danger nevertheless spiked within me, and its source wasn't that turbulent mass of air up ahead.

We were no longer alone in the rainy darkness. Others were out here now, even if I couldn't immediately see them.

Thunder rumbled overhead, an ominous sound I felt through every fiber of my being. Once again, I briefly became one with that storm, as incandescent and as bright as the lightning that spun through her. Sparks danced across my skin and drifted away into the night.

One of those sparks briefly caught the gleam of a golden eye.

A man, coming at me, moving so fast he was little more than a blur.

But no man—no *human* man—could move like that. Not unless he was a shifter or had magical assistance.

He leapt high into the air, then twisted around so that the soles of his thick black boots were aimed straight at my face. I swore and dove sideways, hitting the rough patch of ground between the pavement and the wall hard enough to tear skin from my hands. Pain slithered through me, but I ignored it and scrambled upright. The air whispered with movement, and without thought, I twisted around, lashing out with a booted foot, hitting the stranger hard enough to knock him off-balance. Before he regained it, I lunged forward, grabbed his wrist, and growled, "Stay still and make no sound until I command otherwise. Understood?"

That last bit was rhetorical. All pixie women—no matter what the size, be they full height or half—were blessed with the so-called six gifts of womanhood: beauty, a gentle voice, sweet words, wisdom, needlework, and chastity. While the women in *our* particular branch of the pixie tree had successfully avoided most of them, we did have a variation of "sweet words" and could enforce our will on all others—except elves, for reasons unknown—with a mere touch.

As the man froze, the wind whispered of more movement.

I turned and saw a thick metal bar with a wicked, pointed hook at its end coming straight at my face. I swore again and flung air between us, catching the crowbar inches away and forcing it straight back at my assailant. It smashed it into his forehead and split it wide open. He dropped like a stone to the ground and didn't move. I scrambled over and pressed two fingers against his neck.

Alive, thank gods.

While the pixie curse thing never applied in cases of

self-defense, I really didn't want the weight of any more deaths on my conscience. There was more than enough already.

I thrust to my feet and moved on. The orb was now the size of a basketball, with snake-like tendrils of fire flicking back and forth across its surface. The heat it emitted was now so fierce it vaporized the sleet long before it could hit the ground.

At any moment now, it would be unleashed, and the destruction would envelop us all.

I didn't question the certainty. I just ran toward it.

Beyond the orb came flickers of movement—Cynwrig, fighting three men. Another two lay unmoving on the ground near his feet.

Seven men to protect one.

Or, perhaps, seven men to protect the *intention* of one.

But what was that intention? Who was their target? I doubted it was Cynwrig—the hood of his coat had fallen away during the fight, so if he'd been their mark, he'd probably already be dead.

Besides, the orb appeared to be aimed at the building rather than the man, so it was either another resident, or maybe even... The thought died as something—some*one*—cannoned into my back and sent me sprawling to the ground. My breath left in a whoosh, but before I could react, a heavy weight dropped onto my back and a hand wrapped around the back of my neck, holding me down, holding me still. A pinprick of pain flared briefly—a needle being inserted, perhaps—and I tried to shift, move, with little success. I reached for the wind, but before I could unleash her, two knives tore into my shoulder and a heated wave of agony swamped me.

Only it wasn't knives.

It was teeth.

It hurt—gods how it hurt—but I bit back my scream and reclaimed my grip on the wind, wrapping it around the shifter's body in a desperate attempt to remove him. But his teeth were lodged deep in my skin, and as the wind ripped him away, it tore my shoulder apart. Warmth flooded my back and side, and my arm went numb. It didn't matter. Nothing did right now, except preventing the chaos about to be unleashed.

Because the orb was now screaming, and it was an ungodly sound of utter fury.

I gulped back bile, flung my attacker at the wall hard enough to knock him out, then struggled to my feet and raced on toward the arch.

Only to hit—and bounce off—some sort of block.

The stranger wasn't *just* using a shadow shield. He had some sort of magical perimeter boundary set up.

Fuck.

My knives could have shredded such a barrier, of course, but I hadn't thought to bring them with me. And while I *could* call them to hand, that took concentration and energy, and right now mine was flowing away as fast as the blood pouring down my back. I sucked in a deep breath that did little against the gathering wash of weakness, then caught the wind and once more flung it forward.

Not at the orb, nor even the man who hid behind his barriers, but at the nearest streetlight. It bent like butter against the wind's force, its light spearing into the arch, ripping the shadows away from the figure there.

It was an elf. A *red*-haired, dark-skinned elf holding a stone that glowed with an unnatural fiery light.

Just for a second, our gazes met. The recognition that

stirred through his eyes echoed through me, though I didn't for the life of me know why his features seemed so familiar.

He smiled, gave me a polite nod, and then unleashed hell.

Straight at Cynwrig's building.

CHAPTER
TWO

With an almighty whoomph, the building exploded, the force so great it knocked me off my feet and sent me flying. I hit the old wall hard, dropped to its base in a heap, and curled into a ball to protect my body against the thick rain of brick, glass, and wood filling the night. The air was putrid, every breath laden with gritty particles that caught in my throat and made me cough. I breathed as shallowly as possible, fear pounding through my body as I waited for the deadly rain to ease.

When it did, the screaming began, a solitary voice that rose from depths of destruction.

A harbinger of what was yet to come.

I shivered, braced my good hand against the wall, and pushed upright.

There was almost nothing left of the beautiful old building.

All that remained of the two street-side walls were a few ragged bits and pieces little more than a foot or so high, while the back and side walls had partially collapsed. The internal structure was now little more than jagged fingers of wood and plaster that reached forlornly toward stormy skies, as if pleading for help against the flames that now crackled, unnaturally bright, through the remnants of the ground floor.

Strangely, the destruction *hadn't* extended to any of the nearby buildings. Whether that had been intentional or merely a fluke, we wouldn't know until we caught and questioned the bastard behind it all... My gaze went to the arch. The elf was gone. No surprise there, I guess. Only a very stupid man would hang around to gloat, and there'd been nothing in the elf's demeanor to suggest stupidity.

I couldn't see Cynwrig, but three of his attackers were partially buried under building rubble. Where the others were, I had no idea, nor did I really care at this point.

I pushed away from the wall, intent on looking for him, but had barely taken more than a few steps when the woman's screams intensified. I stopped. I couldn't walk away from her. If I did, she'd surely die, killed by the flames or the collapse of her floor into the rubble and fire below. It couldn't be holding on by much; not given the devastation that lay all around it.

That same devastation made it dangerous for anyone to go into the building, but thankfully, I didn't really need to. I sucked in a deep breath, then reached for the wind again and directed it into the building. Pain pulsed through my brain, a warning, perhaps, that I was reaching the end of my strength, be the cause blood loss or simply overuse of a very new skill. But nearing the end didn't mean the tank was empty, and if I didn't at least attempt to save that woman, I'd hear her screams in my dreams for the rest of my days.

I had some idea of her location, but a general "fetch"

order would not work, as it might well grab the very thing that was keeping her floor upright.

I warily deepened my connection to the storm and lightly drew down its power, letting it infuse me as it had earlier. Once again, that network of neon air appeared again. The building's remaining framework all but disappeared, becoming nothing more than black spots around which the neon rivers flowed. The fire glowed a ghostly green that was unhindered and untouched by the currents. As I'd suspected, there was nothing natural about those flames.

My gaze swept across the various neon streams, and, after a few seconds, I spotted the small shadow huddled in the jagged junction of two walls. I wrapped a finger of wind around her and gently lifted her up. Pain pulsed through my brain, and just for a moment, the wind slithered from my grip and the woman dropped. I caught her before she could hit the floor, but it was warning enough that I was not only reaching the end of my strength, but perhaps also pushing the limits of my control.

I sucked in a breath and then raised her again. She was no longer screaming, and her body was limp. I hoped she was unconscious rather than dead, but it was hard to tell from this distance.

I lifted her free of the building, past the piles of debris littering the road, and deposited her on the grass near the old wall, close to where I'd first been attacked... Fuck, my prisoner—was he still alive?

I couldn't see him, but it was possible the force of the blast had sent him tumbling, just as it had me.

I hoped he'd survived, though not because I felt responsible for what might have happened to him. It was simply nigh on impossible to get answers from the dead.

I released the woman, then turned around. As I did, a figure emerged from the shrubs lining the left side of the road past the old streetlight, and my heart leapt.

Cynwrig.

There was a ragged cut on his cheek, and he was favoring one leg, but he was alive, and that's all I cared about. He looked up, saw me, and even from this distance, the relief that swept his features was evident. I walked toward him; he met me halfway but didn't say anything. He just wrapped one arm around my waist and, being very careful of my torn shoulder, pulled me close and held me tightly. I closed my eyes and let his warm strength wash over me, momentarily chasing away the pain and weariness.

"How many people were in the building?" I asked softly.

"Impossible to tell at this point, but all the apartments aside from Treasa's were leased. She hasn't used the apartment in months, though, thank gods."

Treasa was his twin. "Couples or families?"

Please, don't let there be families.

"Elven families rarely live outside the encampments, as they prefer to keep close to relatives so there's always help with the kids. Aside from one elderly Ljósálfar couple, the tenants were all single businesspeople."

I wondered if the woman I'd saved was one half of the couple. I hoped not, for her sake. Light elves might be emotionally remote beings—when it came to love, anyway, because they certainly did the whole hate and vengeance thing *very* well indeed—but they were very long-lived. It would surely hurt to lose someone you'd spent at least three or four centuries with.

"Were they all elves?" I asked.

"Yes. My father prefers not to have humans or shifters in his more expensive properties."

He kissed the top of my head, then pulled back. That was when I noticed the people streaming out of the nearby buildings, heard the wail of approaching sirens, and saw the blue flashes of security lights as building alarms sounded all over the area.

"We'll need to give Sgott a call," Cynwrig said. "The IIT will have to deal with this mess, not the regular force."

The IIT—or the Interspecies Investigation Team, as it was more formally known—dealt with all police events involving non-humans, and had both a day and night division. Sgott Bruhn was in charge of the night division, but had also been my mother's lover for over sixty years. In very many ways, he was the only father I'd ever known.

"I'm afraid my phone is buried under that rubble somewhere," I said. "So, unless you have yours, we'll have to borrow one."

"I'll see if one of the bystanders has one, then head over to what's left of the building to see if I can detect any life under all that rubble."

I touched his arm. "Be careful. That fire isn't natural, and the building could collapse at any moment."

He smiled. "All the more reason to go over there—I can shore it up and protect anyone who might, by some miracle, still be alive. In the meantime, you need to get across to that ambulance and have your shoulder looked at. You're bleeding heavily, and there's a large strip of skin hanging down your back."

The pain radiating from my shoulder immediately intensified, and a cold sweat broke out across my skin.

Cynwrig cupped my elbow, obviously sensing the wash

of weakness. "You okay? Would you want me to help you over there?"

"No, I'm perfectly fine."

He snorted softly. "From what I've seen, you'd say that even if you were stepping through death's door."

"Death wouldn't have me. We Aodhán pixies are too ornery for the likes of him."

He raised an eyebrow, amusement briefly muting the concern in his expression. "Says who?"

"Says death himself. Or so Gran once said."

His amusement increased. "And how did she know this?"

"She had a fireside chat with him once, apparently. And no, I don't know the details. It was an off-the-cuff comment she wouldn't explain."

Of course, death—or the devil, as humans preferred to call him—not accepting us didn't mean we couldn't die. It just meant our souls couldn't enter his realm. And to be honest, that wasn't a bad thing. Hell, from all reports, was not a fun place to be.

I rose on my toes and kissed him, tasting dust and weariness and strength. "To repeat, be careful in that building."

He nodded, lightly touched my cheek, then turned and walked over to the gathering crowd. I sighed and forced my feet to move in the opposite direction, heading for the ambulance pulling up behind the two cop cars blocking access to this section of the street.

Two paramedics jumped out of the ambulance, one running to the back of the vehicle while the other darted across the road to the woman I'd pulled from the rubble. He knelt beside her, felt for a pulse, and then snapped directions toward his partner.

She *was* alive.

The relief stirred so fiercely that my knees threatened to buckle.

A second ambulance pulled up behind the first, this one marked as an ASP ambulance, meaning there was an elven healer on board to deal with both human and non-human species. Which made sense, given the building would have been flagged as elven-owned when the destruction reports came in.

I walked toward it. The paramedic took one look at me and immediately grabbed my arm, ushering me into the back of the vehicle. Obviously, I looked every bit as bad as I felt.

He took my vitals, tsked over the various cuts and bruises, then cut away my jacket and sweater to examine that wound more closely.

"I take it a shifter did this?"

"Yes." I paused, briefly debating whether I really wanted an answer before asking, "How bad is it?"

"It'll need to be fixed at the fae hospital," he said. "He's torn through muscles and damaged the bone, and it'll take a specialist to repair and knit everything back together."

It was a common misconception that all elven healers could heal any wound, no matter how great the damage. In truth, just as there were human doctors who specialized in specific medical fields, there were also elven. Human doctors had one distinct advantage over their non-human counterparts, though—their patients generally had the same physiology. That wasn't always the case with non-humans.

Of course, there *was* another difference—humans relied on surgery and drugs to repair. For an elf, it was basically a psychic talent—an ability to read the ebb and flow of the patient's life force to discover what was wrong with them. They then used their *own* life force to repair.

Which could drain them to the point of death if they went too far.

While I hadn't seen it happen, my best friend Darby had. She worked at the fae hospital and specialized in poisons, with a secondary specialization in wound repairs. She wouldn't be there tonight, though. Lugh, my brother, had recently given in to the sexual attraction that had burned between them for nigh on a decade, and the two had headed to Scotland for an extended four-day weekend break. I rather suspected Lugh intended to combine business with pleasure, however, as he'd casually mentioned before they'd left that he'd finally tracked down the dwarf who'd double-crossed us after our return from Ben Nevis's peak.

"Can you temporarily stop the bleeding?" I asked. "Because I need to do something before I go to the hospital."

He frowned. "I don't think that's advisable. The blood flow to that flap has been damaged, and it could die if left too long. No amount of elven healing will fix it if that happens."

"You can't give it a quick tweak or something?"

His frown deepened. "What is so important that you'd risk the prospect of a healed but craterous wound on your back?"

"I'm a pixie—"

"I'm well aware of that, young lady, but—"

"I caught and froze one of the men working with the elf responsible for the explosion," I cut in. "If he survived, I need to release him. Otherwise, he'll remain immobile, making it near impossible to treat him."

Not to mention question him. Which I *would* do before they forced me into that ambulance. It might be my only chance before the IIT got their hands on him.

He sighed. "Fine, I'll do what I can to repair and restore the vein, then I'll accompany you to find this felon."

"Good. Thanks." I wanted to add "please hurry" but resisted. Light elves could be ornery at the best of times and likely to do the opposite of what you wanted if you pushed too hard.

Of course, they'd do it with a pleasant smile. It was one reason humans—who too often judged others by surface beauty rather than actions and deeds—thought the divinely beautiful light elves were a far nicer race than their dark counterparts.

The medic asked me to shuffle forward on the trolley, then sat behind me and lightly pressed his fingers on either side of the wound. His energy rose, a warmth that cut through the throbbing ache in my shoulder and eased the chill running down my arm. My fingers twitched as he lightly repaired muscle and nerves, and a tingling sensation soon replaced the odd numbness in my fingers.

"Right," he said, with a heavy sigh, "I've gone as far as I dare. My patches are temporary and will not stand up to too much movement—as I said, I am no specialist and have no desire to make a wrong nerve or muscle connection. Where is this stranger?"

"He was close to the old oak that hangs over the wall just down the road, but I'm not sure where he is now. The blast would have thrown him back toward Stanley Place, though."

"Let's check then, so we can get you to the hospital."

He gripped my elbow to steady me as I slid off the trolley, then collected his bag and followed me out of the ambulance.

Cynwrig appeared around the corner of the ambulance. "Franklyn, what's going on? Why haven't you whisked Beth off to the hospital yet?"

"Because this young woman refuses to be whisked. Perhaps you can talk some sense into her?"

"Sorry, but that's generally a useless endeavor when she has her mind set on a particular course of action." His smoky gaze rested on mine, a warm mix of amusement and concern evident. "Dare I ask what that course of action might be here?"

"I captured one of the men who attacked me. If he's alive, we can question him."

"I do not believe questioning him was mentioned during *our* conversation." Franklyn glanced at me. "Is that not the task of the police or the IIT?"

"Well, yes, but—"

"Five people were likely killed in that blast," Cynwrig broke in quietly. "I can and will find those responsible, but Beth's captive might be our best chance to do so before anything else happens."

Franklyn raised an eyebrow. "Revenge is a dark path, Lord Lùtair, and one I thought you'd sworn never to tread again."

My eyebrows rose. Despite Franklyn's use of Cynwrig's official title, the two men obviously knew each other very well.

"This is different—"

"It is *always* different." Franklyn shrugged. "Your choice, your decision, my lord. Shall we proceed?"

Cynwrig nodded curtly and glanced at me. The warmth

I'd noticed earlier had fled, replaced by anger and dangerous ghosts from the past.

I wanted to ask him about those ghosts, because I'd seen them once before, but this was neither the time nor the place. I turned and walked down the road, Cynwrig on one side and Franklyn on the other. We hadn't gone very far when I spotted my prisoner lying along the base of the old wall on the opposite side of the road. He wasn't moving, but his expression said everything he verbally couldn't. He hadn't escaped the blast unharmed, though. His jacket was torn, there was a jagged bit of metal sticking out of his thigh, and his right boot was missing, although all his toes appeared intact.

"That's him, I take it?" Franklyn said.

I nodded, walked over, and lightly pressed a hand against his shoulder. "You will answer all our questions, obey whatever orders given to you by Franklyn, the paramedic, and you will not attempt to escape once I release you. Understood?"

He couldn't nod, but his expression spoke volumes.

I released him, and he pushed into a sitting position before Franklyn could say anything. If the metal in his leg was causing any distress, it wasn't obvious.

"They never told me there was a fucking pixie in the building. Might have asked for a higher payment if they had."

Not knowing a pixie was involved when accepting a contract had become a theme lately. Either felons these days were dumb, or the money was so good they just shut their mouths and took the job.

As Franklyn checked our captive's condition and began healing, Cynwrig said, "What is the name of the man who offered you the contract? How did he interact with you, and what exactly did the job involve?"

"His name is Keelakm. Don't know his surname, and the contact number I have is for a burner phone that will have been dumped by now. He hired us to run interference while his partner destroyed the building."

"Did he say why they wanted the building destroyed?"

"Only that a man inside killed people he cared about."

"Did he say who inside he might have been hunting?" I asked. "Or give you the names of the people he was avenging?"

It was unlikely, but better to ask than not.

"No, though he did say the target was an elf. Light elf, I gathered, not dark." He shrugged. "He referenced a lover at one point, and a father at another, but I didn't ask too many questions, did I, because it's generally better not to know the minutiae."

"Spoken like a true thug for hire," I muttered.

His gaze flashed to mine. "We can't all be playthings for rich lords, you know. Some of us have to work."

"Speak like that to her again," Cynwrig said, in a deceptively mild tone, "and you'll be paying a visit to the dentist to replace missing teeth."

The stranger didn't reply, but his face went decidedly paler. Not getting on the wrong side of a dark elf was generally a good motto to live by.

If you wanted to live for a good long time, anyway.

"Do you know anything about the stone Keelakm's partner was using?" I asked.

"I think it was a relic of some kind. Had this weird vibe."

"What kind of relic?"

He shrugged. "A ruby, from the look of it."

I stared at him for a long second and then swallowed

heavily. "This weird vibe it had—was it coming from a fire burning deep in the jewel's heart?"

"Yeah, it did."

I raised my gaze to Cynwrig's. "It's one of the rubies from the Shield of Hephaestus. It has to be."

And if that were true, then we were damn lucky to be alive.

Because the Shield of Hephaestus—which was part of the Éadrom Hoard, a cache of deadly relics stolen from under the noses of the Ljósálfar elves—belonged to the Greek god of smiths, fire, and volcanoes, and his rubies gave the user the ability to control the elements of fire and earth.

That red-haired elf might have had only one ruby, but he could have destroyed the whole damn town if he'd wanted to.

THREE

"THERE'S BEEN NO WHISPERS OF THE SHIELD OR ITS RUBIES ON THE black market," Cynwrig said. "If that's what we *are* dealing with, then our wielder must be linked to Gilda."

Gilda was the light elf my former lover—Mathi Dhār-Val—had been having an affair with while we'd still been an item. We'd discovered *after* we'd found her brutally dismembered that she had, in fact, been giving him Borrachero—a type of truth serum that put one into a twilight zone of consciousness—to pump him for information about the council's activities.

We'd also found one of the shield's three rubies hidden in Gilda's bedroom but had no idea how she'd acquired it. She'd obviously been working with someone, and just as obviously must have double-crossed them at some point given their brutal retaliation. We suspected the men responsible for her murder were the same people who'd kidnapped Mathi in an attempt to regain possession of Gilda's ruby, but we'd never know for sure now, given all four had been murdered while in IIT custody.

How that had happened despite the intense security that had surrounded the men, no one could say for sure. The last person to see them alive had been Carla Wilson, their lawyer, who'd since disappeared.

The general consensus was that she'd been murdered to stop any possibility of the IIT questioning her about her now-dead clients, but I doubted it. From what I'd seen in Eithne's Eye—the black seeing stone Mom had used to direct and amplify her second sight when relic hunting for the old gods, and which now formed part of a triune designed to provide we Aodhán with foresight, knowledge, and protection—Carla had not only been working with the organization that had stolen the Éadrom Hoard, but was high up the organization's ladder. Instinct said she was too damn important for them to kill off, especially when it was easy enough to buy a spell that could completely alter your features.

Hell, for all we knew, the Carla who'd visited in the cell wasn't the real one, but someone magically wearing her form in order to frame the real Carla.

Mathi was currently trying to get the IIT's security tapes but was having some difficulties despite having been given full access to the IIT's system by Ruadhán, his father, the man in charge of the daytime division.

But it was possible Sgott was thwarting his efforts. He might not be able to cut Mathi's access to the IIT's files, given he didn't run the entire division, but he could certainly make access far more difficult for Ruadhán's only son.

Sgott was also aware that my visions had pinned Carla as one of the people involved in Mom's death, but all he kept saying was, "Let me handle it." I loved and respected the man, and I totally understood his unwillingness to bend the law too much, even for family, but I would not idly stand by and do nothing.

Mom had been murdered by someone she trusted. Whether that meant she'd known Carla, or even the hereto-unknown man I'd heard Carla talking to in my visions, I couldn't say.

But I very much intended to find out, no matter how long it took.

"Do you know if the IIT has thought about hiring a spirit talker to attempt contact with Mathi's four kidnap-pers?" I asked. "If they *can* be contacted, they could provide some useful information about the ruby and how it came into Gilda's possession."

"Aside from the fact spirit talking is a legal minefield that requires the IIT to gain court approval *and* written permission from their nearest and dearest first, there's a time limitation for effectiveness."

I raised my eyebrows. "If that's true, why do so many bereaved people visit spirit talkers for years and years to commune with their loved ones?"

Cynwrig's answering smile held an edge of cynicism. "Many spirit readers are also good people readers, and repeat business is very profitable. Besides, those four men were probably nothing more than contractors rather than the brains behind the theft of the hoard."

"Maybe not the brains, but I'm pretty sure they were more than mere contractors."

"Possibly, but we may never know. The IIT are playing their cards very close to their chests regarding those men and their backgrounds."

I raised an eyebrow. "You haven't been conducting your own investigations?"

"Of course, but with little success. Those men, whoever they truly are, appear to have been new players."

"Is that usual in the black-market world?"

"Players come and go all the time, for all manner of reasons. It *is* unusual the gossip mills have no background information on them, however."

I glanced around at the sounds of approaching sirens. More ambulances, cops, and even several black IIT vehicles were arriving. I hoped the latter had thought to contact a witch, because no one was getting near that building until the ruby's unnatural flames were put out.

As two medical trolleys were hauled out of the ambulances and wheeled in our direction, Franklyn finished his ministrations on my captive, then sat back on his heels and sent a stern glance my way. "When those trolleys get here, I *will* take you and this young man to the hospital, and not even Lord Lùtair's presence will prevent that from happening."

The man in question held up his hands. "I have no intention of stopping you, trust me."

Franklyn sniffed, a disbelieving sound if ever I heard one. Obviously, Cynwrig *had* prevented someone from being transported in the past and that, once again, had all sorts of questions rising.

It was a shame Franklyn was an elf and therefore immune to my pixie wiles. I had a feeling he'd be able to answer most of them.

Cynwrig returned his attention to our captive. "How was the contract arranged? Did Keelakm contact you directly?"

The man snorted. "You should know better than that, my lord. Like all such things, they did it through a broker."

"Kaitlyn?" I asked.

"Yes."

No surprise there. She ran one of the UK's biggest brokerage services, and she didn't particularly care if said services fell within or without the boundaries of the law. She'd been responsible for organizing several contracts on me during our search for the Claws and had been warned off ever doing so again—a warning she would undoubtedly ignore if enough money was placed on the table. Kaitlyn wasn't a fool, but her agreement with Ruadhán—one that offered her protection against prosecution in exchange for information—had, from what I'd seen, given her a sense of invincibility.

That relationship wouldn't protect her from Cynwrig's wrath, however, and she was already walking a tightrope where he was concerned. I rather suspected she'd cooperate with both him and the IIT on this particular matter.

"When did the contract go out?" Cynwrig asked.

Our captive shrugged. "A week ago, if that."

From what I understood of the process, it took at least several weeks after the proposal's release for bids to be accepted and contracts finalized. Either this one had been hastily arranged or they'd placed a lot of money on the table to expedite proceedings.

"Was it just this one job you were meant to run interference on?" I asked.

"Oh no, it was an ongoing contract."

My stomach sank. A revenge-seeking nutter armed with a fiery relic running around an ancient city that was more wood than stone was not what we needed right now. Or ever, really. "Do you know who or what the other targets were?"

He snorted. "Would you hand complete strangers—

even if they were contractually sworn to silence—a list of potential targets, knowing full well that if things fucked up, said list would end up in the hands of authorities?"

I wouldn't, but there was no guarantee we were dealing with anyone sane. "Can you describe Keelakm?"

"About five-eleven, slim frame, dark skin and hair, blue eyes."

"Which is a pretty generic description of most dark elves."

"He had a scar here." Our captive touched his left cheek. "About an inch long."

Which meant he would stand out in any elven crowd as long as he wasn't using makeup or magic to disguise it. "Was he the only person you dealt with?"

"Until tonight, yes."

"Meaning this was the first time you'd seen or dealt with the witch using the stone?" Cynwrig asked.

"He was an elf, not a witch. Spoke all posh, like one of them highborns." His expression was disdainful, and I couldn't say I blamed him. Highborn light elves could be a pretty unlikeable bunch at the best of times. Mathi was a rarity in many respects, but even he had his moments.

"Thing is, I didn't actually see him," my captive continued. "He was covered by a shadow shield the entire time."

If our red-haired elf had hidden his features from his contractors, why hadn't he tried to conceal them from me when the streetlight had torn his shield away?

That really made no sense, especially given that millisecond of recognition that had flared between us.

As the medics arrived with their patient trolleys, I pressed my fingers to our captive's shoulder again.

"You will answer any questions the IIT asks, and you

will refuse any future contracts involving Cynwrig, his family, or their buildings." I hesitated. "You will also refuse any contract that involves me, my brother Lugh, or any premises or item we own."

We might not have been the targets of this particular contract, but who knew what would happen in the future, especially now that I was committed to doing the council's bidding for the next two years. It was a punishment that had arisen after I'd done a deep mind meld on my cousin Vincentia—the same cousin who'd been murdered by her employer in my loft. While using our command magic against other pixies in a minor way was generally overlooked, anything more went against the code.

My captive swore at me. Loudly and vehemently. No surprise, as I'd probably just curtailed a good chunk of his future earning potential.

Given the number of times I'd issued those exact same orders over the last few weeks, Deva might well experience a contractor shortage soon.

Franklyn rose, helped me to my feet, and guided me over to a trolley. Once secured, they swiftly wheeled me back to a waiting ambulance.

Cynwrig fell in step beside us. "Do you want me to ring Lugh and tell him you're off to the hospital?"

"Gods no. He doesn't take much time off, so let him enjoy a weekend."

Amusement touched Cynwrig's lovely lips. "He'll be pissed when he finds out you've been hurt."

"Yes, but I'll be healed by the time he does, so it won't matter. What are you going to do?"

I doubted he intended to come to the hospital with me, nor did I expect him to. He'd never allow the IIT to contact the relatives of those who'd probably died in the blast; it was a task he undertook personally, and *that* was one of the many non-physical attributes I admired.

"I'll liaise with Sgott's people when they get here—"

"His people?" I cut in, surprised. "Where is he? What else has happened?"

"He's on his way home from Scotland. Apparently, he took the weekend off to walk one of his granddaughters down the aisle."

"Oh yeah, forgot that was this weekend."

He'd mentioned some time ago that one of his granddaughters had decided to get married, which was an unusual step for brown bear shifters. Sgott never had; like their animal counterparts, males were serially monogamous. They lived with the same mate from several days to several weeks—generally until pregnancy was confirmed—then moved on in search of another. The more successful males often had two or three mates in a year. Sgott had five offspring he'd fully supported from birth and seven grandchildren. His youngest daughter, who'd been born just before he'd entered his relationship with Mom, was approaching breeding age—which, given bear shifters lived nearly six times longer than their animal counterparts, was around sixty years of age—and apparently already had several suitors.

"I also said it was pointless trying to ring you, as your phone had been destroyed in the blast," Cynwrig continued. "He said to tell you he hoped this wasn't the start of another wave of injuries unleashed on your person, because he wasn't sure he could handle the stress."

I grinned. It was easy enough to imagine him saying that—his Scottish brogue would be heavier than normal and filled with the weary acceptance of inevitability. It made me wish he was here, just so I could hug him.

"Well, that's certainly something I'm also hoping." As we neared the ambulance, I caught his shirt, dragged him down toward me, and kissed him. "Be careful tonight. Just because my captive said you weren't the target doesn't mean he'd been told the truth, and that elf is still out there."

"Yes, but unleashing that sort of force would have taken its toll, no matter how strong he might be magically. We should all be safe tonight, at the very least."

"*Should* be" and "*would* be" were often two very different things, especially where bad guys were concerned. "I'll call you when I get a new phone."

He gave me a nod and stepped back as they loaded me into the back of the ambulance. In no time at all, they whisked me across to the fae hospital, where they repaired the various injuries and kept me overnight for observation. Which was annoying, given I smelled of smoke and destruction and the hospital gown they handed me to change into revealed entirely too much of my butt.

They cleared me to leave the next morning. I shoved my feet into my boots, tugged on my coat to cover the butt's nakedness, then, after grabbing a transport voucher from reception because I had no money or credit cards on me, headed outside to catch a cab.

Home was a heritage-listed tavern in the historic heart of Deva's famous Rows area. Ye Old Pixie Boots—the name Mom had given it when she'd taken over from Gran—comprised of a street-level undercroft, one floor at "row" level, and our living quarters above that. Aside from a few layout changes upstairs and the necessary modernizations, it was basically the same building that had stood on this spot since it had undergone minor remodeling in the late 1400s.

My key to the front door was gods knew where in the remains of Cynwrig's building, right along with the rest of my belongings, so I entered via the rear door, which was key-coded.

The back of the tavern was a warren of rooms—a furniture store, fridges, stock stores, staff changing rooms, and toilets. Beyond the door dividing the rear section from the main tavern area lay the kitchen. The remaining space was unsurprisingly intimate, with the bar and four small tables on this side of the stairs and five larger tables in the front half. Bright pixie boots of various sizes hung from the exposed floor joists and beams, some of them real, some of them not, but all of them a nod to tourist expectations that a tavern bearing the name "Pixie Boots" would actually have said boots displayed.

I clattered up the stairs, my hand on the railing so I could feel the wood's warm pulse. It was a habit I'd gotten into after several break-in attempts—some successful, some not—in recent weeks. Thankfully, the only weight altering the timbre of that pulse was mine.

The next floor was larger, as there was no kitchen up here to take up space, and contained a mix of booths of varying sizes, a few tables, and the doors leading out onto the covered row area. The narrow stairs up to my living quarters were tucked away behind the bar. I'd recently had another key-coded lock installed alongside the alarm Sgott had fitted after one of the break-ins. Neither would stop a determined thief or thug for very long, of course, but the more difficult I made it for them, the better.

I deactivated the alarm, then opened the door and headed up the stairs worn down by centuries of foot traffic. As a pixie, I could have restored them, but their song was rich and warm, and I really didn't want to alter it. Mom and Gran had obviously agreed with me.

Even though the roof had been raised, it was still very confined up here. There was a combined kitchen-living area and two bedrooms—one had been Mom's and was now mine, while Lugh and I had shared the other as kids. It was now a spare. The bathroom was the second-biggest room in the flat and with good reason—it'd had to cope with four oversized pixies using it for decades. Gran had moved out of the tavern when she'd handed the reins over to Mom, but before then, she'd slept in the loft, which was only accessible through a hatch and a loft ladder—something that had never worried her, as she'd been remarkably spritely until the day she'd passed.

I stripped off, tossing the gown, the coat, and the bag holding my other clothes into the bin, then headed into the bathroom for a long, hot shower. Feeling—and smelling—a whole lot better, I made myself a big cup of tea. Then I headed down to the other end of the living room, released the loft ladder, and clambered up—all without spilling the tea, of course.

When Gran had moved out, Mom had converted this area into a chill-out zone so she could read her books in peace. There was little evidence here now of the destruction Vincentia's murderers had wrought in their efforts to find the Codex—the second relic within the triune and a book that supposedly contained all the knowledge of the gods— but traces of my cousin's blood still stained the old floorboards. I'd covered the area with a mix of baking soda and vinegar in the hope it would draw out the stains, but I hadn't yet checked if it had worked.

The badly crocheted rug I'd made to warm Mom's knees was once again covering the back of her chair, and her to-be-read pile was once again neatly stacked on the coffee table. Maybe it was stupid, but restoring everything to where it had been on that fateful night when she'd left to hunt relics and had never come home made me feel closer to her. Her soul might not be haunting this place, but the echoes of her presence nevertheless lingered. It helped me cope, if only a little.

I blinked back the threat of tears, placed my cup of tea on the small table beside the cushion-adorned sofa, then walked toward the wood heater at the back of the room.

Gran had created a small storage pocket in the back of the mesh that surrounded the flue by slicing it open and then bending it in to form a small shelf. She'd used it to hide her smaller valuables, but it had also been large enough to hold the Codex and the Eye. My knives—the third relic within the triune—were too big, but Cynwrig had solved that problem by replacing the entire length of decorative mesh for me. Not only had he widened the gap between the mesh and the flue to provide more storage space, he'd also made the inner "pocket" big enough to hold all three items. Then he'd added a door that, unless you knew it existed, wasn't visible.

I hooked a finger into the hole that served as a handle, opened the door, and reached down for the triune. My fingers brushed the Eye, and energy stirred, a sharp electricity that echoed deep within.

There were visions to be had.

I blew out a breath, not really sure I was up to a vision quest right now, especially when accessing the library would likely take a good chunk of physical strength. While both the Codex and the Eye were good resources of information about the relics I was now expected to find, there was never a "free" ride when it came to godly items. Using them always came at a cost. My knives differed, but they'd been designed to protect and seemed to have a life of their own rather than drawing on mine.

I collected all three items, then walked back to the old leather couch and sat down, tucking several cushions behind me to support my back. After placing the Codex and the knives on my lap, I held up the Eye by its chain and studied the stone now caged by metal. Lugh had designed it specifically to protect my skin against constant contact— and its continuous wash of energy—while allowing skin-to-stone contact via grip when necessary.

Though I wasn't currently touching it, purple lightning cut through the Eye's dark heart and, in the back of my mind, ghostly figures stirred.

I did my best to ignore them. Which probably wasn't a good move, but we needed information about the shield more right now.

I placed the Eye on top of my knives, then pressed them all against the Codex. When I'd first found it, it had been nothing more than a worn and very plain-looking leather notebook, but the blood-bonding ceremony had changed that, turning the old leather a glassy black. The light that rolled across its surface at my touch echoed that of the Eye but held none of its dangerous electricity. Which was an illusion, given the cost of stepping into the library's godly realm was strength; if you lingered too long, it could lead to death.

I took a deep breath that did nothing to ease the gathering tension, then said, "What can you tell me about the Shield of Hephaestus?"

For the briefest of seconds, nothing happened. Then light erupted from the triune, surrounding me in a dizzyingly bright whirlpool that swept me up and then swept me away. But it wasn't a physical departure so much as a mental—or perhaps even spiritual—one. I could still feel the old leather chair under my butt, could still hear the building's gentle song and, through it, the movement of staff on the floors below. But the song and the movement were little more than faint whispers against the sheer noise being generated from the colorful maelstrom I was now arrowing through.

I finally came to a halt in a bright, open space filled with a multitude of different shapes. Long and tall, thin, or thick, some round, but most square or rectangular.

Not shelves. Books.

Books that hovered in orderly rows in the nothingness of this place and glowed with an unearthly energy.

It is a pleasure to see you again, young Aodhán. What do you wish to know about Hephaestus's Shield?

The voice was neither male nor female and held no hostility or power. It exuded wisdom, knowledge, and an odd sense of welcome, but I had no doubt whatsoever that could change at the snap of a finger. Gods—and even those who looked after godly spaces such as this library—tended to smite first and ask questions later.

That's if all the family legends were to be believed, anyway. It wasn't as if I'd had all that much to do with them until recently.

Can you tell me where the shield might currently be located?

That is not within the purview of this library.

I didn't think it would be, given the library held ancient knowledge rather than modern, but I had nothing to lose by asking. *The shield gives the user the power of fire and volcanoes—does that mean they can actually raise volcanoes, or is it more a figure of speech?*

The glowing books whirled briefly, then one popped

out and floated toward me, hovering in the air while the pages flipped open.

There were no words to be seen, only images, and I suspected that was deliberate. Either the godly librarian feared I wouldn't understand the words—and to be honest, that was likely given I couldn't even read Latin, let alone a language as old as the gods themselves—or they simply didn't want to make things too easy. They might want me to find the missing relics, but that didn't mean they'd provide every scrap of pertinent information. Old gods— and perhaps even the new—had a long history of playing games with humanity.

The first image was of a man dressed in a white Roman-style tunic holding a bronze shield that very much reminded me of the Wandsworth Shield I'd once seen in the British Museum. The flange here held stylized flames rather than birds, and the boss held three red stones—the rubies —in a triangular formation rather than having a central ornamental stud.

The page flipped over. The next image showed ghostly green flames burning through a town surrounded by a lava flow.

I glanced up. *There's no volcano in this picture—does that mean the user can't actually raise them?*

The book snapped shut and zipped back to its place. *One does not need to raise volcanoes if one wields the means to make the earth run like fire, young Aodhán.*

But does one need the shield to do that, or can the rubies be used separately?

The room spun, and another book flew toward me. Pages flipped, this time revealing a set of three pictures. In the first, a glowing ruby presided over a ball of unnatural green flames—the same flames I'd seen last night. In the second, it was liquid, fiery earth oozing across a burning field. The third showed an anvil and hammer.

What does the third image represent?

They are the tools of a smith. What is made by one can be undone by one.

Can anyone—human or fae—wield the rubies? Or do you need to be a witch or a mage?

If Hephaestus's gifts are united within the shield, magical adeptness is not required. If they are singular, then perhaps.

Perhaps? You don't know?

This library contains all the knowledge of the known world. If the answers lay beyond the known, they cannot be retrieved.

Which sounded like a long-winded way of saying he had no idea.

How great a spread of destruction can a fully "armed" shield cause?

Pages flipped over. This time, the picture revealed a city being decimated by fire and earth, while whatever metal or iron was used in creating buildings and tools simply deformed and returned to their mineral form.

So, *not* world-destroying, but still pretty dramatic. Especially if our witch and his partner decided smaller targets were no longer working for them, and went larger. Like the whole of Deva. Or hell, even London. We had no idea just how far their revenge-seeking might spread, if indeed that was what truly lay behind these actions.

A wave of weakness washed through my non-existent body; it was a warning I could not ignore. I needed to finish this and get out of here—especially if I wanted any hope of having enough strength left to use the Eye.

I swallowed heavily and said, *Can the shield be destroyed?*

Another book spun to a halt in front of me, this time

revealing a mountain shrouded in fog and a ghostly, glowing arched gateway.

I didn't recognize the arch, but the mountain was Ben Nevis. Its peak stood at the junction of earth and sky, and it was a gateway to the gods themselves.

Meaning, obviously, that the shield had to be returned rather than destroyed in the godly furnace we'd discovered deep underground. Except for one point—the keeper of that gate had already told me no evil could ever enter, and the power within the rubies held a decided darkness. I had no doubt the shield would too.

The last thing I wanted was to be trekking up that goddamn mountain in the middle of winter, only to be turned away again.

Is that all, young Aodhán?

Yes. Thank you for your help.

It has been my pleasure. There was a slight pause. *It is good that the library is once again in use. Time passes too slowly in this place otherwise.*

How can you be bored when you have a library such as this at your fingertips?

A thin stream of amusement spun briefly around me. *A library such as this is not for the likes of me.*

I wanted to ask what he was if not a god, but I was pushed back through the maelstrom before I could, and my consciousness or spirit or whatever the hell went into that place returned to my body.

I gasped, dropped the triune into my lap, then hugged my body and rocked back and forth, trying to control the quivering ache that ran through my entire being. I'd been in the library far longer than it had seemed and I was now paying the price.

I forced myself to take deeper, slower breaths, but it still took a good five or so minutes before the desperate racing of heart and pulse eased.

I leaned sideways, and with still shaking fingers, picked up my mug of now lukewarm tea. And wished I'd thought to bring a block of chocolate up with me. Chocolate was my go-to cure-all for these sorts of situations, so maybe I need to keep a stash up here for emergencies such as this.

I slowly sipped my tea, but it took another ten minutes before I approached anything close to normality. I returned the empty cup to the side table and glanced down at the Eye.

It glimmered back at me almost impatiently.

I really, *really* didn't want to use it right now, but the ghosts were growing stronger.

I didn't know what would happen if I completely ignored them, but I couldn't remember Mom ever doing it, so it was probably best I followed her example.

I drew in another of those steadying breaths that didn't do a whole lot, then picked up the Eye by its chain and wrapped my fingers around the stone.

The minute it touched my skin, it came to full life, flooding my senses with power as it swept me away. This time it wasn't distant places that I saw or distant voices to be heard. This time, it showed me a place I loved—Deva itself. *Not my street but another, one lined with lovely old two-story red-brick terraces that were a mix of retail and residential properties. A white-painted betting shop dominated the corner opposite them, its doors open and a steady stream of customers going in and out. In the shadows of an old chimney onto which several antennae clung, air shimmered brightly. Red sparked within that turbulence, and tendrils of fire flickered. An explosion. A building destroyed and the terraces on either side alight with an unearthly green fire. A dark-skinned woman with sharp elven features buried beneath the remnants of the building, life-less eyes staring up in shock. Bodies strewn over all the street, one of them horribly, shockingly familiar. Then finally, a clock, counting down.*

And if that clock were to be believed, then I had little more than an hour to stop destruction.

CHAPTER
FOUR

THE VISIONS FADED. I RELEASED THE EYE, THEN CLOSED MY EYES and let my head drop against the back of the sofa.

As much as urgency pulsed through me, I simply didn't have the strength to move. Would using the Eye *ever* get any easier for me? Mom had never seemed to suffer these sorts of consequences, but maybe she'd been made of sterner stuff.

After wasting several precious minutes doing nothing but deep breathing to regain some sense of normality, I undid the Eye's chain and put it on. Then I picked up the Codex and my knives and carefully pushed upright. The loft spun briefly around me, and I had to lock my knees to remain upright.

What I needed was food and sleep, but that clock was ticking.

I walked a little unsteadily over to the woodfire, placed the Codex in its hidey hole, and then strapped on my knives. It felt ridiculously safer with their weight against my thighs, making me wonder just how badly things might go in the next hour.

By all rights, I should contact Sgott and tell him that Kaitlyn—the woman I'd seen so briefly in the vision—was about to be attacked, but the person I'd seen lying in the street, bloody and broken, had been him, and there was no fucking way I was ever going to risk that.

But I also wasn't about to go there alone.

I might be foolhardy, but I wasn't stupid.

Of course, Cynwrig would still be dealing with the aftermath of last night, and Lugh wasn't due home until tonight, so that left me with Mathi.

Which, to be honest, wasn't a bad thing. Not only was he a capable fighter, but also very determined to get to the bottom of the hoard's theft, though his reasons were more personal in nature. The bastards behind the theft had made the mistake of attacking him several times, and now his Ljósálfar soul wanted revenge.

Badly.

I headed down to my bedroom to grab a coat, picking one with a good-sized hood lined with thick fake fur that would go some way to hiding my features. If we were dealing with the elf I'd seen last night, he knew what I looked like. A concealment spell would have been better, but they took time and money, and I didn't have enough of the former right now.

I grabbed my spare credit card from its hidey hole—and made a mental note to cancel all the ones currently buried under Cynwrig's building when I had the chance—then clattered down to my office on the first floor to call Mathi from the landline.

"Bethany," he said, his cool tones holding the slightest hint of concern. "I heard there was an incident at Cynwrig's last night. Are you all right?"

"Yes, but I wouldn't call his entire building being blown apart and multiple people being killed a mere incident."

"I'm afraid that in the world of the Myrkálfar, it would be considered such. And it is, of course, the result of a major flaw in their makeup. Few of *our* enemies live long enough to blow anything apart."

I doubted those who double-crossed the Myrkálfar lived all that long, either. "This wasn't an attack against Cynwrig or his people, and most of those who died were light elves."

"I was not aware of that."

"It would have been all over the news."

"You know well enough that I dislike human news outlets. They are extremely unreliable."

I smiled. Just because he disliked them didn't mean he didn't watch them—like most elves, he monitored what the governments of the day were doing and saying in order to counter whatever effects their decisions might have on his family's business. Which just happened to be one of the largest forestry operations in the UK, and used the inherent ability of Ljósálfar elves to manipulate the living energy of flora to accelerate the growth of plantation forests. All their shiny marketing material went on and on about the protection this offered the remaining old-growth forests from logging, but the simple truth was there was big money to be made.

"Are you busy right now?" I asked.

"I am, rather extraordinarily, in the office working for a change, but there's nothing on my desk that can't be dropped if this is a booty call."

"You, me, and booty calls are no longer a thing, Mathi, and you know this."

"I do. That doesn't stop me living in hope."

"I thought the Ljósálfar dealt in realities rather than hope?"

"And the reality is we are good together."

"*Were* good together. Accept it and move on."

"I am not one to give up."

Indeed, he wasn't, and there was a part of me—an undoubtedly insane part—that enjoyed his chase, even if it would never end the way he wished.

"If you've a free hour or so, I need some help."

"As ever, you only have to ask. What's the problem?"

"The man who attacked Cynwrig's is about to go after Kaitlyn, and we need to stop it."

"Is that not a job better suited to the IIT?"

"Yes, and no."

"An answer that clarifies the situation perfectly."

I smiled. "The man who destroyed Cynwrig's place is an elf capable of magic, and he was using one of Hephaestus's rubies."

"Ah. Do you want me to pick you up or do you want to meet somewhere?"

I hesitated and glanced at the clock. If he was at the company office, it'd take too long for him to get through traffic to pick me up. "Meet. Shall we say twenty minutes at the side of the pub again?"

"Done. Should I come armed?"

It wasn't legal to carry weapons in the UK—hell, even police had to get special dispensation to do so—but Ruadhán bent the rules when and where it suited, and Mathi knew few would dare charge Ruadhán's only son.

I hesitated. "Our elf will be on the roof opposite Kaitlyn's place, and he'll be shielded from sight—"

"Such a concealment cannot stop a bullet."

"No, but you can't shoot what you can't see. However,

he had several thugs with him last night, so it certainly couldn't hurt."

"Excellent," he said, with the slightest hint of relish.

He really did have a bloodthirsty bent—something that hadn't been apparent in the ten years we'd been together. Of course, I hadn't gotten involved with cranky old goddesses or relic hunting during that time, either. His lust for fighting had only come to the fore after we'd all been dragged into the hunt for Agrona's Claws.

"I'll see you soon."

"I look forward to it."

I smiled again and hung up. After calling a cab, I had a quick chat with Ingrid—the short, fierce-looking pixie with curly green hair and deep brown eyes I'd recently promoted to full-time manager rather than just my relief—then headed out.

The driver dropped me off near the pub that stood at the intersection of Falkner and Charles Street about twenty-five minutes later. I climbed out of the cab, tugged the hood a little lower over my face, then walked over to the pub's side wall. The clouds were dark and heavy, promising snow rather than rain, and every breath came out frosted.

I huddled against the pub's side wall to steal what little warmth radiated from the old bricks and did my best to ignore the gathering sense of doom.

Where was Mathi?

It was unusual for him to be late, but maybe he'd simply been caught in traffic.

Of course, he wouldn't be driving here, and he certainly wouldn't be catching a regular old cab. Highborn elves generally preferred to be chauffeured about Deva's often narrow streets—hell, Cynwrig's chauffeur lived only a few doors away from him and was on standby twenty-four-seven. He was *extremely* well paid for the inconvenience, of course, and it wasn't like he worked more than a few hours every other day. Cynwrig did have a penchant for walking, though, and that suited me just fine. Unless, of course, the weather was absolutely horrendous. I might be the daughter of a minor weather god, but that didn't mean I enjoyed getting soaked to the skin.

Mathi appeared down the far end of Charles Street and strolled casually toward me. Like most light elves, he was lean and sinewy, his body powerful without holding the obvious muscular strength of the dark elves. His hair and skin were golden, his eyes the color of summer skies, and his face so perfect it could make angels weep.

I wasn't the type to weep at the mere sight of a beautiful man, but my hormones weren't beyond skipping a beat or two. But then, I'd been with him for nigh on ten years and was very familiar with the glorious satisfaction all that perfection could provide. I might not want us to be anything more than friends these days, but habit and proximity were sometimes difficult to ignore.

"Did you walk here?" I asked.

"Don't be ridiculous. I've been scouting the area."

He stopped so close that the scent of his aftershave—crisp and green, with hints of the oaks that dominated his homeland—filled my nostrils. Desire stirred lightly through me and echoed in his eyes.

The man was incorrigible.

I stepped back, but he caught my hand and pulled me against him. His body was warm and hard against mine, his lips so close I could almost taste them.

"Damn it, Mathi—"

"We have watchers," he murmured. "There're two of them—one near the terrace three doors down from Kaitlyn's, and another leaning against the wall of the building directly opposite the pub."

"Why didn't you take them out?"

His hand slid down and cupped my rear. The devilment dancing through his eyes dared me to object. "Because that would have alerted whoever stands on the betting shop's roof and perhaps forced him to react before we were ready."

"How do you suggest we play this, then?"

He raised a pale eyebrow, the devilment growing stronger. A heartbeat later, his lips brushed mine—a warm, familiar caress that promised heaven if I just gave in.

There was definitely a part of me that wanted to, but I already had two lovers. I didn't need the complication of a third.

"I suggest we move slowly," he said.

"Slowly is not an answer, and neither is standing here attempting to seduce me."

"No, but it is nevertheless delightful, is it not?"

I rolled my eyes. "Concentrate on the matter at hand, Mathi."

He chuckled softly and pressed me harder against his groin. The man was delightfully erect.

"Not *that* matter," I added dryly.

He sighed, an overly dramatic sound at odds with the amusement glowing in his eyes.

"If you insist—"

"And I do."

"Then we shall casually walk across the road to the side street, make our way to the lane that runs behind the betting shop, then head on up to the roof and take your head felon out."

I frowned. "Surely he'll have someone watching the back lane?"

"I couldn't see anyone, but if a watcher appears, we'll deal with them."

It wouldn't be that easy. It never was. And maybe we needed to prepare for that. "And the two watchers we *can* see?"

"The minute we take one man out, the other will react. It'd be better to cut off the hydra's head first, so to speak, then deal with the limbs. It's always possible said limbs will decide running would be the better option once we take their leader out."

"When have we ever gotten that lucky?" I said, voice dry.

"Almost never, but it also never hurts to hope."

"Hope is an emotion light elves disdain."

"That is a blatant lie." His blue eyes twinkled. "Take me, for instance. I live in the hope that you will come to your senses and warm my bed once more."

I rolled my eyes but didn't bother responding. There was little point. "In the eventuality that they *don't* run, or are there as a secondary means of taking out Kaitlyn should their boss fail, perhaps you should ring and warn her."

He raised an eyebrow. "It is your vision—would it not be more logical coming from you, especially given she is well aware of your talent?"

"It's because of my 'talent'—and the problems it has caused her—that she'll more than likely ignore my call. Besides, my phone lies somewhere in the mess that was Cynwrig's apartment."

"I really wish you'd come to your senses and stop seeing that man. He is not what he seems—"

"He's *exactly* what he seems," I countered. "A hot, sexy man who is outstanding in bed."

"You left me because I dared to have one other lover, but he—"

"No, I left you because you broke an agreement stating you would tell me when you took other lovers or started looking for a wife. Ring Kaitlyn before shit gets real."

He sighed, another of those overly dramatic sounds, then released me and made the call. It obviously went straight through to the answering machine because he hung up and sent a text message instead.

If we were lucky, she'd take notice and either leave or find a safe place.

If we weren't, well, on her head be it if things went ass up.

Mathi tucked his phone back into his pocket, then offered me his arm. I hooked mine through his and let him lead me forward. The man directly across the road was watching us with no little amount of suspicion.

"Keep walking and talking," Mathi murmured. "We're nothing more than lovers out for a morning stroll."

"Because the shitty nature of the weather doesn't make that suspicious at all."

He laughed softly. "You're the daughter of a weather god. You should be reveling in this crap."

We walked around the pub's corner and angled across Falkner Street, heading for the side street. Our watcher made no move to follow us, and his companion down the street seemed more interested in the car parked near his position. I hoped whatever was happening in that car continued to hold his interest.

Once in the side street, we walked down to the end of the betting shop. Two cars had parked on either side of the small lane that ran behind it. Mathi casually pulled some keys from his pocket, as if intending to open one car, and then studied the lane. I crossed my arms and did the same. It was small and narrow, with overflowing bins forming untidy lines down one side, while weeds lined the wooden fence on the other. A small external staircase ran up the betting shop's back wall to what looked to be a roof terrace atop the single-story back half of the building. There didn't appear to be any access onto the terrace from the first-floor portion of the building, but someone had propped an extension ladder in front of the solitary back window.

I studied the tiled roof but couldn't see anyone up there, nor was there any sign of the shimmering air I'd seen in the vision.

He was there, though.

I couldn't see him, but I could feel him.

Which was both weird and concerning, if only because if the connection went both ways, we might well be walking into a trap.

I frowned and rubbed my arms. Was the elf someone from my past? A lover or friend, perhaps? There'd certainly been a brief spark of recognition, but as of this moment, I couldn't place him.

"Have you any sense of him?" Mathi asked softly.

I dragged my gaze from the roof. "He's there."

"Then it's probably best if you take him out, given your knives will counter any spell he casts. I'll stay here and handle the watchers when they react."

I nodded and touched his arm. "Be careful. I've a bad feeling things could go very wrong."

A smile twitched his lips. "Is that pessimism or second sight speaking?"

"Former rather than the latter, but still worthy of taking notice."

"Notice taken. Go."

Movement drew my gaze back toward Falkner Street, but it was only a short woman in an overly large brown coat pushing a stroller across the intersection. I flexed my fingers and walked into the lane, making my way past the first lot of bins to the stairs at the end of the building. They were heavily rusted, covered in grime and rubbish, and looked ready to collapse at the slightest hint of weight. The whole thing wobbled alarmingly as I moved up them, but I made it onto the terrace without it collapsing.

I glanced around again. The terrace was empty, and the thick layer of moss covering the concrete suggested the area hadn't been used for a long time. There were no footprints evident in that moss, but elves did walk light.

On the street below, the brown-coated woman with the stroller was now in the side street and walking purposely toward Mathi's position. Maybe he was standing near her car... I frowned. There was something odd about her features... they looked weirdly unfinished. I couldn't see any indication of a shield or glamor, but trepidation never-theless stirred.

But it wasn't like I could warn Mathi that something was off with her—not without warning the man above that I was here, anyway—and besides, Mathi was more than capable of dealing with whatever problem she presented.

The window behind the ladder was cracked and held together by a multitude of yellowed tape. The various bits of furniture and old shelving units visible through the grimy glass suggested it might be a storeroom. Hopefully, it wasn't a store that was frequented often, because the last thing we needed right now was the regular police being pulled into the situation.

I stopped at the bottom of the ladder and glanced up. That weird sense of awareness hadn't wavered in intensity, and it told me that, just as I'd seen, the elf stood toward the front of the building and to the right, which placed him close to the old chimney. I had no sense of anyone else, and the knives weren't reacting, which hopefully meant there weren't any magical snares employed.

It should be safe to climb, but I couldn't escape the growing certainty that the shit was primed and ready to hit the fan.

I flexed my fingers, then gripped the sides of the ladder and went up.

I'd reached the halfway point when a softly accented voice said, "You never were very adept at climbing things quietly, dear Bethany."

I briefly froze. The faintest caress of magic accompanied the comment, and while my knives remained mute, my heart rate leapt.

I swallowed heavily and continued on. The wind stirred lightly around me, tempting me to gather her, despite the fact she'd proven useless against this elf's barrier last night.

"How do you know my name?"

My words died on the air almost immediately, captured and then whisked away by the faintest sliver of magic. He'd created some sort of magical sound bubble, and I couldn't help but wonder why when there was only him and me up here.

But perhaps he simply didn't want anyone in the rooms below catching our conversation and coming up to investigate.

"You don't remember me?" came the mocking reply. "I'm mortally wounded."

"Yeah, I can hear the pain etched into your voice." I paused when I reached the guttering and peered over to study the roof. As instinct had said earlier, it was empty, and yet my sense of danger leapt exponentially.

His soft chuckle scratched at distant memories, but gave me no answers.

"In truth, we were a good time, not a long time, thanks to your charming hulk of a brother. But you have obviously moved on to far greener pastures."

"You've been keeping an eye on me?"

I scrambled over the last rung in the ladder, then stood up and scanned the roof again. There was no immediate sign of a concealment shield, but maybe that was due more to the day's icy stillness. Air movement generally made magic easier to spot.

"I'm afraid last night was the first time I've seen you in over forty years."

Which meant I'd been in my late teens or early twenties when we'd been friends... and perhaps far more if his statement was to be believed.

"Which does not," he continued easily, "mean I was unaware of your presence—at least of late. It always pays to keep an eye on key players, especially the more dangerous ones."

I drew a knife and moved forward. "I hardly think I could be considered dangerous."

"Says the woman currently holding a knife as she stalks toward me."

Meaning he could see me through his shield even if I couldn't see him. "Why did you destroy the building last night?"

If I could keep him talking, I might not only be able to pinpoint his exact location, but perhaps even distract him enough to prevent destruction.

It was a long shot, but one worth taking.

"It was the easiest means to achieve my goal, but do not mourn for the dead, dear Bethany. While most of those within were not my direct targets, they were far from solid citizens, even by elven standards." He paused, and the sense of danger abruptly increased. "Do not move any closer, or you will pay the price."

His voice was coming from the area close to the chimney, though I was well aware his magic might be giving me the wrong impression.

"If you use that ruby to attack Kaitlyn's building, you will pay the price."

His soft laugh swam around me again. Memories tickled, blurry and indistinct. "You are not your mother. I have nothing to fear."

"Ah, but a lot can happen in forty years." I gripped the knife's hilt tighter. Light trickled down her fuller, a flutter that spoke of darker magic rising. It wasn't aimed at me. Not yet, anyway.

"Stop moving, Bethany, or else."

"Stop raising your magic, or else."

He sighed. It was a disappointed sound. "Then we do this the—"

I didn't wait for him to finish. I leapt forward, running full pace toward the ridge and the chimney.

I'd barely reached the latter when I was clubbed sideways by an invisible force and sent tumbling across the roof and over the edge.

CHAPTER

FIVE

I FLUNG OUT MY FREE HAND AND SOMEHOW CAUGHT HOLD OF THE guttering, bringing my fall to an abrupt halt and just about tearing my arm from its socket.

Pain ripped up my throat, but I clamped down hard on the scream and swung the air into action, sweeping it under my feet and thrusting myself back onto the roof. I stumbled forward several steps, fighting to catch my balance, and heard rather than saw the thunder of steps.

I looked up; the roof remained empty, but that was a lie because the elf was still here and so was whoever those footsteps belonged to.

And he was just about to barrel into me.

I threw myself sideways, rolled onto my knees, then lunged forward and stabbed at the empty-looking air. There was a brief second of resistance, then light sparked down the knife's fuller and the air shimmered and retracted, revealing a thickset man with shaggy hair and fists the size of clubs.

Clubs that were aimed straight at my face.

I swore and slashed the knife sideways. The blade sliced through skin and bone with the ease of butter, and several thick digits plopped harmlessly to the roof. Blood spurted across my face, and I gagged, but the hairy stranger was still coming at me, fists looming large. I dove sideways, then rolled away, and the blow that would have smashed my face hit the concrete instead. He didn't get a second chance. I caught the wind, wrapped it around him, and tossed him across the road to a rooftop several buildings away. If he decided to risk more missing digits, it would at least take him some time to get back here.

I scrambled upright and swiped an arm across my blood-splattered face. Then, with the knife gripped tightly in my right hand, ran back toward the chimney. The blade's pulsing light sharpened. The elf had begun to call on the ruby's powers.

I still wasn't seeing either him or his concealment shield, but the increasing intensity of magic told me he was no longer standing close to Falkner Street—a fact confirmed by the small fiery orb that now hovered several feet off the ground close to the building's edge on that side.

I swore, drew my second knife, and skidded down the roofline toward the orb but hit the concealment shield instead and came to an abrupt halt. A soft bark of laughter swam around me, and annoyance rose. He thought he had the upper hand... and maybe he did. But he was also relying on what he'd once known about me rather than what I now was.

I raised my knives and slashed them crossways through the shimmering air. There was a sharp retort, then the shield fell away, briefly revealing the elf's somewhat surprised features.

His eyes, I couldn't help but note, were a vivid green rather than the shadowed silver or rich brown of the Myrkálfar elves. Which, along with his red hair, suggested that while his accent was British, his origins weren't. As far as I was aware, none of the Myrkálfar elves here possessed that coloring.

Before I could say anything, before I could *do* anything, something smashed into me and sent me sprawling sideways. I hit the tiles hard on hands and knees, briefly skinning my knuckles before falling flat on my face. My teeth went through my bottom lip and the bitter taste of blood filled my mouth.

I swore and thrust upright. The rooftop briefly spun, and all I wanted to do was throw up, but the air was screaming, and it was a warning I couldn't ignore.

He was coming at me. Not the elf, the man mountain.

How in the hell had he gotten back here so fast? Was he a shifter? Some kind of monstrous bird?

I had no idea, and no time to contemplate it. I spun around. His expression was dark and furious, and he was trailing blood from the remnants of his right hand. But his left was clenched around a thick metal bar and there was murder in his eyes.

I flung the air between us. He hit the barrier hard and toppled like a tree. As a shudder went through the tiles, I grabbed another fistful of air and spun toward the elf.

Just as he lifted his hand, and his magic lifted *me*.

As he flung me away, I unleashed the air. Had a quick glimpse of him tumbling across several rooftops then dropping from sight before I smashed through a window on the opposite side of the street. I hit the floorboards hard and skidded several feet into the room, coming to a sudden halt against the front of a sofa, and immediately curled into a ball to protect my face and body from the brief rain of glass and wood that followed me in.

But even after that rain eased, I remained where I was, sucking in air and trying to avoid the deeper darkness that threatened to consume me. Everyone had their limits, and between last night's efforts and using the Codex this morning, I'd just about reached mine.

But this game was not over yet.

The soft song reverberating through the boards underneath me altered in timbre, indicating someone was moving up the stairs toward me.

It didn't feel like the elf, but I couldn't take any chances. I had to get up. Had to move.

With a soft groan, I rolled onto my hands and my knees, but couldn't go any further. I gripped my knives harder as the footsteps drew closer, tension rolling through my aching body even though there was no immediate sense of threat.

The echo of movement stopped, and a woman said sharply, "What the fuck is going on?"

"Sorry about your window." I pushed back onto my heels and then glanced at her. Her face was pale, but there was a glint in her eyes that suggested she could protect herself. "I need to get back down to the street—you got a door somewhere?"

Which had to be the stupidest question ever, but my brain didn't appear to be in full function mode right now.

The woman simply raised her eyebrow. "Of course I have, but you're not going anywhere until the cops—"

Meaning she'd already called them. Given there hadn't been all that much time between when I'd crashed through her window and her confronting me, maybe she'd seen us fighting on the other roof and had rung it in.

"Lady, we haven't got time to wait for the cops. There's a man on the roof opposite who's armed with a weapon that could destroy this entire block—"

"That's not possible."

"Tell that to the people who'd lived in the Watergate Street terrace that was destroyed last night." I climbed wearily to my feet, using the arm of a sofa as a brace, then swiped at the blood running down the side of my face.

I obviously looked as big a mess as I felt, because fear flickered briefly across her features, and she took a step back. Which was a totally sensible reaction in the circumstances, really.

"The door?" I prompted, trying to keep my voice as even and as non-scary as I could.

Her gaze swept me but after a moment, she said, "This way."

I followed her down, my hand on the banister, its soft song telling me there were three other people in the building, all huddled in what appeared to be a storeroom toward the rear.

When we reached the ground floor, the woman glanced over her shoulder and said, in a tight voice, "This way."

She led me away from the storeroom and her companions through a well-established nail salon to the front door. She opened it and then took several steps back. "Go."

"Thanks," I said, and hurried out.

She locked the door behind me. I sucked in a deeper breath that went some way to clearing the brain fog and then glanced up. I couldn't see the elf and I had no sense of the ruby's dangerous energy, but that didn't mean he wasn't there. I caught the wind and cast her toward the roof; she came back empty a few seconds later. The elf was gone, but his hairy friend remained. He'd obviously been knocked out cold when he'd toppled.

I turned and headed for the side street. Multiple sirens now filled the air, suggesting there was more than just one patrol car on the way. But all the emergency services would likely be on edge after last night's massacre, and the report of an elf, a pixie, and a hairy giant fighting on a rooftop would undoubtedly have spurred them all into immediate action.

I turned into the side street and discovered a battlefield.

Mathi stood in the middle of the road, surrounded by three men—one of them the stranger who'd watched us earlier. A fourth man lay at his feet, as did, rather weirdly, a pile of brown mud on top of which lay a coat the same color as the one the stroller-pushing woman had been wearing. She was nowhere to be seen, but the empty stroller lay on its side on the pavement to the right of the group. If it had contained a child or anything else, there was no evidence of it.

I reached for the air to help Mathi out, but pain exploded through my brain and my vision blurred. I swallowed heavily, drew a knife instead, and then ran, with what little speed I had left, straight at the nearest man.

He heard me at the last moment and turned, but I was already in the air. My feet thudded into his chest and sent him sprawling backward. The second man swung toward me as I fell back to the ground; I ducked under his blow, then slashed the knife across his calves, severing flesh and muscle with equal ease.

He howled and bent, clutching at his leg. I quickly

flipped a knife and smashed the hilt across his head. His eyes rolled back, and he crumpled to the ground.

Mathi took out the final man, then stepped forward and knocked out the one I'd sent flying.

I sucked in a quivering breath and said, "There's one more on the roof."

"The mage? Or someone else?"

"The mage has gone." Which surprised me a little. He hadn't seemed the type to be put off by a little toss across several rooftops. "But a hairy giant remains, and I don't have the strength to bind him with the wind."

He cupped a hand under my elbow to help me up, then guided me across to the nearest car. "You lean here. I'll go take care of the hairy giant."

"He's big and fast—"

"And I have a gun. Trust me, even hairy giants aren't fools." He scanned me, his expression concerned. "Will you be all right? You don't look in a fit enough state to deal with a troublesome gnat right now, let alone any of these bastards if they wake."

"I'm fine, Mathi."

He raised an eyebrow, looking unconvinced, but nevertheless turned and went. A few minutes later, there was an almighty crash. I turned around so quickly my head spun, and I had to grip the car's mirror to remain upright.

The stairs leading up to the roof terrace had collapsed, taking the giant with them. He lay unmoving on the ground, sandwiched between the stairs' metal remains. Mathi was standing on the edge of the roof terrace and, for several seconds, didn't move. Waiting, I suspected, to see if our giant was actually unconscious. When there was no sign of movement, he leapt lightly down, checked the big man's pulse, and then strolled toward me.

"He's knocked himself out and broken his leg, so he won't be going anywhere soon."

"He tried to break my head, so I'm not feeling any sympathy." I scrubbed a hand through my hair, feeling a lump but no obvious cut. "What happened to the woman? Why is her stroller over by that wall? Did you throw it?"

"I did indeed, but that was no woman. It was a golem."

Which explained the pile of dirt under the coat. Golems were animated, anthropomorphic, but incomplete creatures created out of mud or clay. They were also, if legends were to be believed, designed to be companions, messengers, and sometimes even a rescuer.

"Why on earth would the elf raise a golem? A correctly placed hit can easily destroy them, and that makes them ill-suited to thuggery."

"I don't think he *did* raise the golem, given it tossed my attackers aside to get at me."

I raised an eyebrow. "Why would anyone send a golem after you? It'd be far easier to send a pretty girl your way, wait for nature and your hormones to follow their natural course, and then take you out mid-coitus."

"That's been tried before, which is why I fully vet my lovers before they become so."

"You obviously don't vet deeply enough if Gilda is any indication."

"It was deep enough. Trust me on that."

"If that's true, then the key to this whole mess might lie in those files somewhere, because her murder is apparently the elf's motive. Do you still have access to them?"

"They're at my place. Feel free to come over and dissect them with me."

I gave him a long glance. "We can dissect on neutral ground."

"You are no fun anymore."

I rolled my eyes. "You never answered my question about the golem."

"Because it is patently obvious when you think about it."

"I have no brainpower left right now to think, so just tell me."

"It was no coincidence the golem was pushing a stroller. It was a reminder of dashed hopes and broken agreements."

I raised an eyebrow. "You think your ex-wife-to-be set the golem on you?"

"I'll find no proof, of course, but they do have a history of such stunts."

"To what point?"

"Pettiness? They dare not attack me or my family directly, but if I received an incapacitating wound to my manhood, they would consider it a just result of my severing our contract."

"The golem was going for your *balls?*"

"Indeed, she was. Her nails were surprisingly sharp."

My gaze dropped. There was, in fact, a tear in his jeans. "She got a little too close for comfort, it would seem."

"Had I not turned, the family jewels might not have remained in mint condition." He paused, devilment touching his eyes again. "Don't suppose you want to come back to my place and check everything remains in full working order?"

"No, and stop asking."

"No, because we both know you enjoy the attention, even if you won't admit it."

I couldn't actually argue with a truth like that. I glanced past him, watching several cop cars and an unmarked black vehicle pull up across the intersection. Even though it was impossible to see through the tinted windows of the latter, I knew it would be Sgott. The day shift might be Ruadhán's purview, but they often crossed into each other's operational territory if the case warranted it.

"You never did tell me why you reneged on the marriage arrangement," I said after a moment. "It had to be more than just the amount of compensation being asked. I mean, you let her redecorate your kitchen, so she had good reason to believe the deal was done."

Compensation—or a bride price, as it was more commonly known—was a payment the groom's family made to the wife's family and was a peculiarity of the highborn.

He hesitated for the briefest of seconds. "While it *is* true that highborn marriages are nothing more than a business dealing, the more I knew of Mariatta, the less I liked her. One does have to like the woman they are procreating with. Or, at least, I find I need to."

I grinned. "I've spoiled you for other women, haven't I?"

"That is quite possibly true, although I cannot confirm it as fact until I have experienced a greater range of women."

I laughed and glanced past him as the black car's driver door opened and Sgott climbed out. He looked around, issued a few orders, then made his way toward us. He did not look happy—a common occurrence when I got myself into a mess.

I held up a hand to forestall whatever he was about to say. "Most of the blood isn't mine and, aside from a few scrapes and a desperate need for food, I'm fine."

His gaze scanned me and came up a little less worried. Like most bear shifters, he was a big, thickset man with wiry brown hair, brown skin, and a fierce, untamable beard. "Is this mess related to the events from last night?"

"Indeed, it is—"

"Then why the fuck didn't you call me straight away? We might well have avoided this mess—"

"Or created a bigger one." I squinted wearily up at him. "Aside from the fact I didn't know if you were back from Scotland yet, I saw your people—and you—lying broken and bloodied on the road. There was no way known I was going to risk their lives, let alone yours."

"You risked mine," Mathi said dryly.

"You have as many lives as a cat and besides, you weren't in that vision."

"For which I am extremely grateful. As has been previously noted, there are too many women left in the world I have yet to seduce."

I nudged him hard with an elbow. He simply laughed.

Sgott muttered something under his breath and shook his head. "You really are your mother's child."

I smiled. "And if I was her equal, maybe we wouldn't be in this mess right now."

"She had centuries to learn her gifts, remember that. Now, you'd best give me your report, then get yourself home and grab some sleep. You look dead on your feet."

"I need to talk to Kaitlyn first—"

"How is she involved in all this, aside from being the broker?"

"She was the target this time."

"Do you know why?"

"Not really, but if my captive last night is to be believed, Gilda is somehow connected to the elf behind all this, and the attacks are revenge-based."

"Gilda didn't have any immediate family, that much I'm sure of," Mathi said.

I glanced at him. "The thug we interviewed never said she was related, but given how promiscuous Ljósálfar elves are, I guess he could be a half brother."

"Except your description of the man suggests that, aside from his red hair, he is of Myrkálfar stock."

"Ljósálfar and Myrkálfar elves are not mutually incompatible, you know, and there are light elves with green eyes *and* red hair."

"Strawberry blonde is hardly red."

"Let's not go off on a tangent that leads to nothing but conjecture," Sgott said heavily. "I will talk to Kaitlyn again once—"

"*I* need to talk to her, Sgott. I saw her *dead*. She might not believe it coming from you, but she's well aware I have my mother's skills and will believe me."

Which might not make her any more inclined to give me the information we needed, but it did give me a slight advantage.

He studied me for a moment. "Fine. But please go home and rest after that."

"I will, I promise."

He grunted, a disbelieving sound if I'd ever heard one. He got out his phone and recorded both our statements, a process that seemed to take forever rather than the ten minutes or so it actually did.

"And you've no idea where you've met this elf before?" he asked.

"None, but I was probably in my late teens from what he said, so that's not surprising."

"Might be worth talking to Lugh—he did chase off a couple of your so-called boyfriends."

Which echoed what our ruby-wielding elf had said earlier. "Do you know why?"

Sgott smiled. "It *is* the job of a big brother to weed out unsuitable suitors, and that's what this elf sounds like."

That would certainly explain the hasty departure of several boys I'd been keen on when much younger.

"I'll get this elf's description out immediately," Sgott continued. "You never know, we might catch him before things escalate any further."

"It'd be nice if things were that easy for a change." Even as I knew they wouldn't. "If Kaitlyn has anything of interest to say, I'll let you know."

"Do, and then go home and rest, or you'll end up in hospital again."

I smiled and rose on my toes to kiss his hairy cheek. "I'm sorry to be worrying you so much."

He raised an eyebrow. "No, you're not, not any more than your mother was. Now, be gone so I can clean up this mess."

I smiled and headed for Falkner Street, Mathi silently falling in step beside me.

Like most of the other buildings along this portion of the street, Kaitlyn's was a two-story red brick and, aside from the bright blue color of its wooden front door, rather unremarkable. A full-height window dominated the shop front to the right, although a privacy film had been placed over the lower portion of it. A small brass sign in the middle of the door said "Kaitlyn's Kurios", along with an intercom on the brick wall to the right. I tried the door handle and wasn't surprised to find it locked. I dare say most of the businesses along this street had locked their doors when the proverbial shit had hit the fan.

I pressed the buzzer with one hand and placed my other

against the door. I knew the building's layout well enough, having been here a few times now, but the altering song of the wood would tell me where exactly she was.

After a moment, I found her. She was in the basement, though there was an odd heaviness in the area that prevented me from pinpointing her exact location.

"She inside?" Mathi asked.

"In the basement." I kept my finger on the buzzer. It would eventually annoy her enough to answer.

"Probably a security bunker. Most of her ilk have one."

"A bunker wouldn't have protected her from a determined dark elf, let alone our elf. She should have heeded our warning and left."

"Except few dark elves can manipulate concrete, and those witches capable of magic powerful enough to destroy it wouldn't need her services. She wouldn't have known this was different."

"*We* told her it was different. That should have been enough."

The speaker crackled briefly, then a soft voice said, "If your sole aim is to annoy me, Bethany Aodhán, you have been successful. What do you wish?"

Her low, sultry tone had surprised me the first time I'd heard her speak, and it shouldn't have given she was of Myrkálfar stock. If rumors were to be believed, she'd used her inherited ability to charm and seduce her way to the top of the contractor tree.

"We need to talk."

"A brief warning of danger does not give you access privileges, my dear woman, and I believe I've talked to enough people for one day," Kaitlyn replied. "I have no desire to strain my vocal cords any further, especially by talking to you."

"Shame, because your place continues to be watched by the enemy, and I'm guessing the minute we step away, the elf mage will finish what he tried to start today."

"He will not succeed. I am well enough protected—"

"Not against this man," I cut in. "I saw you dead, Kaitlyn, buried under the debris of your concrete bunker. But hey, happy to walk away and let you chance the odds."

There was a long pause. "You saw this?"

"I did. It's the reason we came here rather than simply ring the cops or IIT. I saw them bloodied and broken. I saw *Sgott* dead."

And she was well aware of what Sgott meant to me. There'd be few in the underworld who didn't.

She didn't reply, but a buzzer sounded, and the door clicked open. It had, I noticed as I walked through, been recently reinforced by iron—no doubt to keep us troublesome pixies from breaking in.

The room beyond ran the width of the building and was filled with a multitude of glass cabinets that displayed a wide variety of antiquities. I'd learned enough from Lugh over the years to know many of the items displayed were rare and expensive, but I doubted any of them were illegally gained. Kaitlyn made no real secret of her underworld endeavors, but even she wouldn't be foolish enough to put stolen goods on display. Selling antiques such as these was her cover—a legit business that probably turned a nice enough profit to stop the tax man getting too suspicious.

The gentle song of the floorboards, though muted by all the concrete below and the reinforcing above, told me she was making her way up from the basement.

I walked over to the glass counter and leaned against it casually, though in truth, the weakness beginning to wash through me made it more of a necessity.

Mathi wandered through the aisles, studying the various pieces in what looked to be a disinterested manner, although anyone who thought he wasn't aware not only of where Kaitlyn was, but all the security measures she employed in this section of her building, was a fool. He'd spent his youth haunting IIT's offices and cells and had learned a trick or two from the less-than-auspicious inhabitants of the latter.

Kaitlyn finally appeared. She was a tall, elegant woman who, at first glance, appeared as ageless as any full-blood elf. Only her hands hinted at her true age, which, as far as anyone knew, was over a hundred. *How* far over was unknown. While half-bloods did live longer than humans, their lifespan was nowhere near the length of elves or even us pixies, and generally fell somewhere short of two hundred years.

She walked behind the counter, then leaned back against the rear shelving, briefly drawing my gaze to the variety of glittering rings and beautifully intricate necklaces on display there. One immediately caught my eye, as it reminded me of an Egyptian-style necklace Lugh had once given me for my birthday. He'd called it an expensive and rather exquisite piece; a sixteen-year-old me had thought it horribly old-fashioned and gaudy. I had no idea what had happened to it, as he'd rolled his eyes at my lack of taste and replaced it with something far more to my liking.

I pointed to the beautiful gold piece. "Is that Tausret's collar?"

She glanced around briefly. "I believe it is—why?"

"My brother once gave it to me as a gift."

"And you rejected it? More fool you." She crossed her arms. "Why on earth would the elf who destroyed the

Lùtair apartments last night now be after me? I did nothing more than arrange a protective detail for a contractor, and certainly cannot be held accountable for its failure. One cannot expect top-shelf muscle when a limited time frame is given."

"I doubt he cares about the men you provided. His need for revenge is more personal."

She raised an eyebrow. "Personal in what way?"

"What do you know of a woman called Gilda—" I realized I didn't actually know her surname and glanced at Mathi.

"Shannoni," he replied immediately.

"That is a servant class line, is it not?" She glanced at Mathi for confirmation, then continued, "Why would I have anything to do with such a person? They'd never be able to afford my services."

"Gilda was trading information and stolen goods," Mathi said. "That, I believe, brings her into your orbit."

"Perhaps, but it's not a name I recognize." She shrugged. "It would be unusual for someone of her ilk to arrange the distribution of such items. She would have had a handler. And I have already told your father all this, young elf."

Given Mathi was at least a hundred years older than Kaitlyn, her use of "young elf" was something of an insult.

Mathi raised his eyebrows, a dangerous light in his eyes —one Kaitlyn would be wise to heed. "My father would be very interested to know that you hold Ishita's torch in your collection here."

She stiffened. "Is that a threat?"

"No, just a reminder that however much sway you think you hold with my parent, it would come to naught if he realized you have stolen from—"

"I did *not* steal—"

"Perhaps not, but you nevertheless have the item on display here, and he would not view the situation kindly."

"Threatening me is not the best way to do business."

"And yet it is one of the many methods you employ to keep your business at the top, is it not? Or, at least, it is according to the files I've read." Mathi's smile was pleasant, everything his gaze was not. "Do *not* make the mistake of overestimating your worth to my father. He has dozens of informants and would not miss someone of your ilk. Trust me on that."

She stared at him for several seemingly long seconds and then sniffed. "I will search my records, but I cannot promise it will yield any results."

"What can you tell us about the man who wanted the protection detail?"

"I never saw him. I never do."

"No, but you always collect enough details to ensure you can find them if a payment fails to materialize," Mathi said dryly. "We want those details, Kaitlyn."

She sighed. "His name is Ka-hal Lewis."

Lewis certainly wasn't an elf surname. It also wasn't the name my captured contractor had given me, so did that mean we were dealing with two different men?

Maybe. And maybe he was just using a collection of false names.

"And his contact details?"

"I'll have to check."

"You haven't already?" Mathi said, in a clearly disbelieving tone. "I'd have thought it would have been the first thing you'd do after being interviewed by the IIT last night."

"Perhaps it was. Perhaps the details that man gave me are no longer accurate."

"But you were appropriately paid for your services first, I take it?" I asked.

Amusement touched her lips. "Of course. I also have a voice sample. If he contacts me using an alias, I will know, even if he is using a modulator."

"And will you tell us?"

"If it is required."

"It is," Mathi said.

She nodded but otherwise remained silent.

"What about the Shield of Hephaestus?" I asked.

She raised an eyebrow. "What about it?"

"Has any information about the shield or the rubies that lie within it crossed your desk?"

"The rubies? No, though I am aware of several parties—including your Myrkálfar lover, Bethany—currently seeking them."

"Who are the other parties?"

"For the most part, they are the usual black-market dealers of godly relics."

"For the most part?" I asked.

"There was a rumor of a dark mage seeking the Eyes of Hephaestus—which is the official name for your rubies, in case you weren't aware—but that fell silent a good seven or eight months ago."

Which was one or two months *before* the hoard had been stolen, and that made no sense given the shield was supposedly a part of said hoard. I glanced at Mathi, but he shrugged at my unspoken question.

"Do you know whether he was successful in finding them?"

"There were whispers suggesting he was, but I'm unable to confirm this."

If he had found all three, how had one of them come to be in Gilda's possession? Even if she was the lover he was avenging, she wasn't a witch of any kind, and it was doubtful she'd have been given anything as important as this to protect.

"Did you make any attempt to confirm these whispers?"

"Of course. There is always deep interest in *any* powerful relic that surfaces, be it on the open market or the closed."

By deep interest, she meant lots of money to be made. "Cynwrig never mentioned either rumor."

Kaitlyn smirked. "Well, he wouldn't, would he?"

"Why not?" Mathi asked before I could. "Are you implying—"

"I am implying *nothing*," she cut in. "However, it is a fact that there are those within the darker corners of the underworld who would never deal with the Myrkálfar. They would rather trust one such as me than risk death via an association with them. And before *you* get too smug, young elf, that can also be said of the Ljósálfar."

"Yes, but we make no claim to rule the black market."

"This has nothing to do with the broader market, because the Hephaestus Eyes would never reach it."

"What about the shield itself?"

Her gaze flicked back to mine. "I've not heard any whispers about it, either now or back then, but there *was* a gentleman in here the other day seeking information about it."

"Did you get his name?"

There was something close to amusement in her gaze, and I had a feeling I wouldn't like her answer.

"Indeed, I did." She paused, no doubt for dramatic effect. "In fact, he left a business card."

She reached under the counter, then handed me a small black card. Printed on it, in simple white cursive font, was a name:

Eljin Lavigne, Antiquarian, National Fae Museum.

The man who just happened to be my other lover.

CHAPTER

SIX

WHAT THE FUCK WAS HE DOING TALKING TO KAITLYN ABOUT THE shield? He was Lugh's assistant, having recently stepped into the position after Nialle—Lugh's coworker and long-time friend—had been murdered. Neither Lugh nor Nialle had been researching the shield as far as I was aware, so there was absolutely no legit reason for Eljin to be doing so.

There were plenty of *not* so legit reasons, however, including the possibility of him working for the other side. He *had* been vetted by Rogan, after all.

"Do we know the name?" Mathi asked.

"I do." I waved the card lightly. "Mind if I keep this?"

"Feel free. I am unlikely to ever deal with the museum or any of its employees, however tall, muscular, and threatening they are."

I raised my eyebrows. She obviously meant my brother, because there weren't any other tall, muscular men working the antiquarian department, and Eljin, for all his good looks, was a typical Tàileach pixie. And while Lugh certainly *could* be threatening if the occasion warranted it, I just couldn't imagine him doing so with someone like

Kaitlyn—not when there were other means to get what he wanted. This place might be filled with all manner of protections, but Lugh was a very experienced antiquarian, and his finds didn't always come from treasure hunts in remote places but the well-protected vaults of black-market collectors.

"If you come across *any* information about the shield or the rubies," I said, "call me. You have the number."

"I do, and I might even use it if I hear something."

"I suggest you make that 'might' a 'will,' or the next time someone attempts to kill you, I won't be in such a rush to save you."

She raised her eyebrows. "Does that not invoke the whole pixie blood curse thing?"

I gave her a sweet but totally insincere smile. "Only when we directly cause a death. It wouldn't apply if, say, my phone went dead, or I got stuck in traffic."

"For a curse, it seems to have quite a few 'get out of jail free' cards."

"Because the gods didn't hate us enough to be utter assholes." I tucked the business card into my pocket and pushed away from the counter. "If I were you, I'd be making yourself scarce for a few days. If Ka-hal is indeed the elf we're looking for, then the magic protecting this place won't withstand the ruby-gifted power he can bring to bear."

"*That* is a bit of information you should have mentioned first up, as it would have totally changed my responses."

"Meaning you suddenly remember Ka-hal's contact details?" Mathi asked coolly. "What a surprise."

"I spoke the truth in that. However, there are few within the black-market economy—the Lùtairs aside—with the

83

capacity to deal with such an item. I will contact them and request information."

"And pass it on?" Mathi said.

"A favor done is a favor owed," she said. Her gaze was on Mathi, but I had no doubt she was talking to me. "Perhaps one day you could help me out."

Perhaps one day hell would freeze over.

But I didn't reply and neither did Mathi. We turned and left.

It had begun to snow outside, the flakes a soft cloud of white stirred into a gentle dance by the wind. I shivered and hastily did up my coat. "Don't suppose you can call me an Uber?"

"I don't suppose I can. I will, however, call my driver and drop you safely at home."

"Actually, if you could drop me near Grosvenor Shopping Center, that would be good. I have to replace my phone and SIM, which remain buried under Cynwrig's building somewhere."

He nodded, made the call, and then hooked his arm through mine and led me forward. I didn't pull away, simply because I appreciated the help given my legs were not as steady as I was pretending.

Still, I didn't want him to think I was mellowing, either.

"We no longer have to misrepresent our relationship to a watcher, Mathi." My voice was dry, and he smiled.

"No, but aside from the fact it is pleasant to have you so close, you look ready to collapse. Now, tell me, whose business card was it?"

"Eljin Lavigne, my brother's new assistant."

Mathi frowned. "Why would he have been searching for the shield? Lugh has made no mention of seeking it... has he?"

"No, but I'll ask what's going on when he gets back."

After I'd questioned Eljin, of course. And he had better have a damn good answer or I'd be seriously pissed. At him, and at fate for throwing a perfectly eligible pixie my way, then making him a bad guy.

Mathi's car was already waiting for us by the time we returned to Charles Street. The driver climbed out to open the passenger doors; once we'd been ushered in, he smoothly drove away.

Mathi shifted slightly and studied me for a second. The devilish twinkle in his gaze had mine narrowing. "What?"

"Thought you might be interested to know I've been allocated as your liaison."

I blinked. "Since when?"

"Since yesterday's meeting."

"Cynwrig's my liaison, and that's a situation I'm quite happy with."

"Your relationship with him is the reason I'm now your handler."

I snorted. "And what of your personal interest in me?"

"I am a Ljósálfar elf, and keeping a clear division between personal life and business dealings is second nature to us. That is not always the case when it comes to the Myrkálfar."

"You did this deliberately, didn't you?"

"I will admit I find the decision delicious, if only because it is one Cynwrig will *not* be pleased with."

That would have to be the understatement of the century. When the position of liaison had first risen, he'd threatened bodily harm to anyone who tried to take it from him. I doubted he'd follow the threat through where Mathi was concerned, but it certainly wouldn't make the tension between the two any easier to deal with.

"But," Mathi continued, "I played no part in bringing the matter to the council's attention, nor did I have a vote, for the very reason you mentioned. I did, of course, put my name forward for the position, but I was in fact the only applicant. Your reputation, I'm afraid, has most of them wary."

"My reputation?" I spluttered. "What fucking reputation?"

"Let's just say it has not gone unnoticed that you have a similar disregard for rules, regulations, and personal safety as your brother."

"My brother gets things done—"

"Indeed, but we both know his methods have somewhat curtailed the upward momentum of his career."

I snorted softly. "The fae council are not above breaking a rule or two themselves."

He laughed. "No, they are not, but that is beside the point."

Because as far as most governing bodies were concerned, the rules only applied when it suited them. "When were they going to inform me—and more importantly, Cynwrig—of this decision?"

"I believe an official invitation to appear before the council tomorrow morning has been issued, which is when you would have received your first task as the council's deeded hunter." He paused. "Please do not forewarn him, as in truth, I should not have said anything."

"I won't."

"Promise?"

I rolled my eyes. "Yes. Now, tell me what my first hunting task is."

"They've arranged the list of missing relics in threat

level, and then alphabetized it for simplicity's sake. Borrhás's Horn is first up."

"There's no relic belonging to a god or goddess starting with *A*?"

"There's a number, but their relics are considered benign."

"I'm thinking no relic of power could ever be considered benign if it got into the wrong hands."

"I tend to agree, but the vote went against me." I could almost see him shrug. "They believe that, as it's likely the hoard has been broken up with the intent of selling them separately, this is a logical method."

"The hoard hasn't been broken up." Not if what I'd seen in the Eye so far was anything to go by.

"If the shield and its rubies are out there, other items will be."

I guess that was certainly true. I just had to hope they weren't in the hands of psychos.

It was well past the morning's peak, so it didn't take us all that long to get to the shopping center. As the driver hustled around to open the rear passenger door, Mathi said, "I shall pick you up tomorrow at nine."

I frowned. "Why?"

"Council meeting? Assignment of duties? That thing we were just talking about?"

"Ah, yeah, sorry." I paused. "Will Cynwrig be at the meeting?"

"That I don't know, but I certainly hope so. It will be a sight to behold."

I couldn't help grinning at the relish in his voice. "You are an evil man, Mathi Dhār-Val."

"When it comes to that man and your affections, very definitely."

"You had my affections. You rejected them."

"I did not. I merely explored their limits and went too far."

I rolled my eyes. "I'll see you tomorrow morning."

"You will. And make sure you get some sleep and some food before you do anything else."

I nodded and climbed out. As his car swept back into the traffic, I tugged up my coat's hood to keep the still-falling snow out of my hair, then shoved my hands into my pockets and headed across the road. The shopping center was surprisingly busy, but thankfully, the public restroom wasn't, so I managed to clean up the worst of the blood and grime before anyone came in to give me the side-eye. Then I headed out to get a new phone and replacement SIM.

It took forever, and by then, I was practically shaking with exhaustion and hunger. I tackled the latter first and headed for a favorite café for brunch, ordering a large coffee and breakfast pancakes with the lot—bacon, eggs, and maple syrup. And couldn't help grinning as I picked up my knife and fork and hoed in. Lugh would have been horrified that I'd "polluted" a decent breakfast option with pancakes.

The SIM had been activated by the time I got home, so I went online—a far easier option than trying to ring or even going in person and standing in line for hours—to arrange replacements for my lost bank cards and driver's license. Then connected to the cloud and began downloading all my stored data.

While *that* happened, I fell into bed and slept like the dead.

An insistent ringing woke me gods only knew how long later. I groped the bedside table for the phone, then opened an eye and glared somewhat blearily at the time. Seven o'clock. I'd slept for a solid six hours, but it felt like I'd only had two or three.

Then I realized it was Cynwrig calling and hit the answer button. "Hey," I said softly, "How's things going?"

"It's been a hell of a day, but I guess the worst bit is now over."

Meaning no doubt that all the relatives had been contacted. "What about the lady I pulled out of the rubble? How is she?"

"She's still alive. I believe she wishes to thank you for saving her life."

"There's no need—"

"It is a Ljósálfar custom, and it would cause a loss of face if you refused it."

Which just went to show how much I didn't know about the Ljósálfar, despite having been with Mathi for so long.

"Fine, I'll meet her when she's up and about. Did you managed to put the flames out?"

"It took the employment of a witch but yes, we did. The building is structurally and physically destroyed though. What remains will have to be pulled down."

"Shame, because it was a lovely old building." I hesitated. "The elf tried to hit Kaitlyn's place this morning."

"I take it you stopped him?"

"Yes." I quickly updated him and then added, "Who in your building would have had dealings with either Kaitlyn or perhaps even Gilda?"

"It's doubtful any of them had dealings with Gilda, unless they employed either her or her relatives." He made no attempt to hide the contempt in his voice. Cynwrig's family might have deep dealings with the black-market underworld but that didn't mean they held the servant class of elf in any higher regard than the Ljósálfar did. "That doesn't mean there wasn't some other connection, such as to those who killed her."

"Who we can't interview because they're dead, and their lawyer is currently missing."

"Indeed, but one of our tenants—Afran Eadevane—has in the past had some dealings with Carla Wilson. I've arranged to talk to his family this evening."

"Which is why you're ringing. You have to cancel our date."

"Sadly, yes."

"It's actually good timing, because I need to talk to Eljin about something Kaitlyn said today, anyway."

"Anything I need to know about?"

There was the slightest edge in his voice. The man did not like me so easily switching attention to the competition.

"Apparently he went there asking about the shield."

"And you'll use your pixie magic to ensure he's being truthful?"

"If it is necessary, yes."

"Then I'll see you tomorrow at the council meeting?"

"It's not like I actually have a choice of *not* being there."

He chuckled softly. "I guess not."

I was briefly tempted to warn him about the council switching him out as my handler but resisted. A promise was a promise, after all. And besides, as much as I enjoyed his company, as much as I wanted more than *just* a sexual relationship, I was also well aware that I couldn't allow myself to get too caught up in the glory that was him and me. *That* could only ever end in heartbreak.

Mathi, for all his flirting, was far safer for my heart to be around, and that allowed plenty of room for Eljin.

If he wasn't a bad guy, that was.

Gods, I hoped he wasn't a bad guy.

"Do you want me to pick you up?" he continued.

"Mathi has already volunteered."

He grunted. It was not a happy sound... and would become even more so in that meeting tomorrow.

I bid him goodnight, then hung up and climbed out of bed. I needed to ring Eljin, but I also needed a good pot of tea. And food. I padded out to the kitchenette, put on the kettle, then made myself a bacon butty as I waited.

Once suitably fortified, I grabbed my phone and made the call a good part of me was dreading.

"Bethany," Eljin said, his French origins accenting his warm tones just enough to be sexy. "This is an unexpected pleasure. What can I do for you?"

"I don't suppose you want to meet for a nightcap?"

"I am always ready for a nightcap—your place or mine?"

I smiled, despite the inner tension. "Middle ground. Say at the Golden Lion pub in half an hour?"

"Is there a problem?"

"No, but I do have a few questions."

"Ah well, let's hope I can answer them. I will see you soon."

He hung up, and I couldn't help sighing in relief. He didn't sound like a man who was hiding anything but then, he was also a man I didn't really know all that well— beyond the physical and from what Lugh had said about him, anyway.

I finished my tea, then pushed up and headed into my bedroom to get dressed. While it was bitterly cold outside —something I could feel in the wind's howl as it ran across the roof and rattled the loose slates—I knew from experience the Golden Lion was generally overly warm. It was run by an elderly human couple who'd come from warmer climes, and though they'd been here for a good twenty years now, hadn't yet gotten used to British winters. It was also Saturday night and likely to be packed, so after I'd pulled on jeans, boots, and a long-sleeved, lightweight crop top, I rang ahead and booked a table for two. Luckily for me, they had a corner one available.

I sent Eljin a text letting him know, then called an Uber and headed out. The wind was indeed bitter, but the sky was clear, and stars burned brightly overhead. I drew in a deeper breath that nigh on froze my lungs, but somehow felt better for it. Everything would be okay. More than okay. So said the night.

I really, *really* hoped that turned out to be true.

It only took ten minutes to get across to the Lion, and the noise and warmth hit me the minute I pushed through the lovely old wood-and-glass door. There was a three-piece band playing on the small stage to my right, and while I'd never heard of them before, they were obviously popular if the number of people singing along with them was anything to go by.

A dark-haired waitress appeared out of the throng, asked if I had a booking, and then led me over to a small booth in a shadowed corner that was well away from the stage and the hearth. Once she'd taken my order, she smiled, revealing dimples, and said, "I'll be back in five."

If she got through the crowd to the bar and back again in five, I'd strip naked and dance on the table.

And I hoped I hadn't just tempted fate. She did like a challenge.

I crossed my arms and leaned on the table, my foot tapping along with the catchy melody. The Lion had been a staple of my life as a younger pixie simply because it was one of the few venues that not only rocked live music every night, but also provided table service. From the demographics of the crowd tonight, they were still pulling in a younger crowd. Which, considering it was the middle of winter and tourists were few and far between, was brilliant to see.

The waitress appeared exactly five and a half minutes later and deposited my double whiskey and Eljin's French 75 cocktail—which was a rather potent mix of gin, champagne, and lemon juice—on the table. Once I'd paid for them both, she whisked back into the crowd to deliver the remaining drinks.

He appeared a few minutes later, looking decidedly delicious in black jeans that hugged his long legs and a leather jacket that sat nicely across his shoulders. Like most Tàileach pixies, he was golden skinned and on the leaner side, build wise, than us Aodhán. His face was perhaps a tad too sharp to be called handsome, but his eyes were the most delicious shade of old gold I'd ever seen, and his mouth was definitely made for kissing.

I knew *that* from experience.

He slid into the booth beside me and kissed my left cheek, his lips warm against my skin. "Thank you for the drink."

"Thank you for coming at such short notice."

"It is hardly a chore, my dear Bethany." He picked up his cocktail and took a sip. Appreciation flitted across his expression. "That is near perfect."

"There's a reason this place is always packed, and it's not just the excellent atmosphere."

"We shall have to come here more often, then. A decent 75 has to date been hard to find on this island of yours."

"You probably haven't been looking hard enough then."

He glanced at me, amusement twitching his lovely lips. "Well, between work and a certain luscious pixie, there hasn't been a whole lot of time left for exploration."

I laughed. "If you've time to sleep, there's time to explore. Or so Lugh would say."

"Yes, but he's a workaholic who apparently considers a couple of hours of sleep a night one hour too much."

That was a truth even *he* wouldn't deny.

I sipped my whiskey, then said, "I had to go see Kaitlyn, the broker who works out of Falkner Street, this morning. She mentioned you were in the shop the other day and left your card."

He frowned. "I did indeed, though I don't understand the suspicion I see in your eyes. It was an innocent enough task."

"That task being?"

His gaze flicked my length, then rose to meet mine. The deeper flecks of buttery brown in those golden depths gleamed in the pub's half-light, and they weren't happy. "I was going through a backlog of Nialle's old notes and found a mention of two relics with her name on them. He'd circled them in red, which made me think they were of importance. That is all."

"Why not ask Lugh about them?"

"Lugh wasn't around, and I needed to stretch my legs."

"Truly?"

He studied me for a second then held out a hand. "While I'm disappointed you trust my word so little, I'm quite willing to let you use your truth-telling magic on me."

I glanced at his hand then pressed my palm against his and twined our fingers. I didn't magic him, however. "I'm sorry, but after Rogan and everything else that is going on, I'm tending to be overly suspicious."

He squeezed my fingers. "If a brief bout of suspicion is the only problem you and I ever have, then I would consider us lucky."

So would I. "Tell me about the note."

He sighed but didn't remove his fingers from mine, and that was a relief. While he and I had a long way to go before we knew for sure something more permanent was on the cards, I didn't want a quick bout of suspicion jettisoning it all before it had really started.

"Nialle obviously wasn't a big cataloguer when it came to these sorts of things."

I raised my eyebrows. "He actually was—at least at home. I never saw his office there, but his basement was filled with neatly stacked and catalogued items."

"Well, let me assure you, that neatness did not carry over to his desk." He slated a somewhat wry glance my way. "You are perfectly welcome to come check if you want. I'm only halfway through the note piles at the moment."

"If I was so inclined to distrust, I could ask Lugh easily enough."

He nodded and seemed to relax a fraction. "Most of the notes related to his investigations of the Claws, which, after the business with Rogan, I presume is now a closed case?"

If you could call the Claws being taken into Annwfyn and therefore made inaccessible to anyone here, that was certainly true. But I wasn't sure how much Lugh had told Eljin, and it was doubtful the council would want the broader population to know what had happened, so I simply nodded and took another sip of whiskey.

"However, there were perhaps half a dozen scraps that mentioned various artifacts," he continued. "Most of them were unknown to me, but the two I recognized were the Shield of Hephaestus and Ninkil's Harpē."

"Ninkil being the rat god?"

I made it a question, although I was well aware who Ninkil was. Beira—who was not only the goddess of winter and storms, but a hag bound to Earth for past misdemeanors—had recently told me those who followed Ninkil —a minor god who reveled in destruction—had become a lot more active of late. She also believed they were behind the theft of the hoard, and the little I'd seen via my visions seemed to concur.

He nodded. "I had what could be a minor clash with his followers when I worked for the Louvre's fae artifacts department. We'd found a small cache of Ninkil artifacts on a dig, and they attempted a retrieval."

"Successful?"

"No." He grimaced. "They were captured but were subsequently killed in prison before they could be fully questioned."

Which was a rather grim echo of what had happened to Mathi's kidnappers. Were the same people behind both? It *was* a long bow to pull, given there didn't appear to be any real connection between either the shield, the harpē, or indeed their gods, but the fates did have a way of twisting these things.

"And the harpē? What is it exactly?"

"Traditionally, it's a sword with a sickle protrusion along one edge near the tip of the blade. From the little I managed to uncover, Ninkil's Harpē gives the user control over life and death."

"Not something we'd want out there in the general population, then."

"No, though the text did say only Ninkil's fiercest warriors can wield it."

Something I could check when I next visited the Codex's library. "Did Nialle's note mention why he wanted to talk to Kaitlyn about either?"

"No. And according to Kaitlyn, he did not ask her anything about them."

"She would say that. Aside from the fact she has no reason to trust you, she's as shady as fuck."

He smiled. "You forget I'm a man of hidden talents."

And one of those talents was the capacity to "read" people. It wasn't telepathy as such; he couldn't hear or see direct thoughts or memories, and the accuracy of any reading very much depended on who was being read and whether it was done casually during a conversation or via direct touch. It was simply a general insight—a glimpse into someone's past, their dreams, character, and their motivations.

His reading of me had certainly proven rather accurate.

I raised my eyebrows, a smile twitching my lips. "And did said talent reveal anything worthwhile?"

"That Kaitlyn hungers for what she will never achieve —to be an accepted part of elf society."

"She's half elf. She has to be aware that will never happen."

"Being aware and accepting it are two very different things." He shrugged and draped his arm around my shoulder, his fingers pressing lightly against the side of my right breast. My nipples instantly hardened, and desire surged, his and mine. It was a heady heat that warmed me deep inside. "But that is not all I saw."

"She knows where the harpē is?"

It came out slightly husky. His clever fingers were

causing all sorts of inner havoc, even though he wasn't doing all that much.

A knowing smile teased his lips. "No."

I took a hasty gulp of my whiskey, but it did nothing to ease the increasing ferocity of the inner fires. "When I was talking to her, she denied knowing the shield's location—does that mean she lied?"

I'd had no sense of it, but my inability to use my pixie wiles against her meant she could take me in as easy as anyone else.

"In that, she spoke the truth. However, she did sell an ancient text that mentioned it to one Loudon Fitzgerald." He paused. "I've arranged a meeting with him tomorrow evening and would like you to accompany me."

My heart began beating a whole lot faster. "Are you aware the council have made finding the shield their latest priority?"

"No, nor would I really expect to know. I work for the museum, not the council."

"Sadly, I *do* work for them."

His clever fingers briefly stilled. "Since when?"

"Since about a week ago. It's a long, rather involved story, but basically, I deep-magicked a cousin and my punishment is becoming the council's beck-and-call girl when it comes to anything relic related."

"This has to do with the missing hoard, I take it?"

"Lugh told you?"

"To explain Rogan's disappearance."

"Well, they want me to help them find it."

"With Lugh's assistance? Because that would certainly explain his absences of late."

"He's not an official employee, if that's what you're asking. In fact, there's probably some there who'd rather he *didn't* help." I couldn't help grinning. "He has ruffled a few high-profile feathers over the decades."

"Always a worthwhile pursuit, I find."

He resumed his breast caressing, and my pulse rate spiked again. We needed to get a room and soon.

"So where does Loudon Fitzgerald live? If it's in Deva, that hardly equates to a whole lot of time together." A smile twitched my lips. "Unless, of course, you plan to take advantage of my company and make an evening of it."

"Oh, I *definitely* plan to take advantage of the situation. Fitzgerald lives just outside Swansea, and I have booked an overnight stay in what is basically a treehouse surrounded by lovely old oak trees."

And Swansea just happened to be a place I needed to go to investigate a token we'd found under the bed of a dead man. The fates, it seemed, were falling in my favor for a change.

"A treehouse? I hope it has decent facilities, because I am not one for sleeping rough."

"You're a pixie," he said with a laugh. "All you should need is the song of the trees and a thick bed of leaves on which to lay."

"I'm a pixie born and bred in Deva. I love trees, I love forests, but I also have a deep and abiding love for a proper bed and bathroom facilities."

He shook his head sadly, though deep amusement glinted in his eyes. "I find this lack of adventure in a pixie troubling."

"My brother got all the adventure genes. I got all the ones needing basic comforts."

He laughed again. "Then you'll be pleased to know the treehouse comes with a basic kitchen and bathroom facilities."

"Basic I can cope with."

"Does that mean you'll accompany me?"

"Yes."

"Excellent."

I smiled at the satisfaction so evident in his voice. "I take you want me there not just for seduction purposes, but to enforce truthful replies?"

"No, because he's elf kind and immune."

"Fitzgerald isn't an elf name, though, so does that mean he's a half-breed?"

We *did* seem to be coming across a few of them at late, even though I'd been under the impression "accidents" rarely happened.

"As far as my understanding goes, he's full-blood. He apparently adopted the use of a more common name to make his dealings with humans easier. Distrust of elves does run high in some quarters."

And with good reason in many cases. "Unless he also changed his appearance, it wouldn't have helped all that much."

"I thought the same. But he is of Autissien stock, so I asked some friends who live near that compound if they could ask around. Apparently, he underwent plastic surgery after a fire in his youth left him disfigured. His family subsequently disavowed him."

Because light elves were, generally speaking, against any sort of plastic surgery. They considered themselves divinely beautiful—and they absolutely were—and believed therefore that their gods-given perfection should not be messed with.

"Then why am I accompanying you to see him if I can't magic him?"

He caught my chin with his free hand and lightly turned

my face toward him. Then his lips came down on mine, his kiss long and lingering.

"Aside from the fact I get to spend more time with you," he murmured eventually, "Loudon is something of a lecher, and you, my dear, are gloriously sexy. Wear something that suitably enhances your assets, and he will be too busy ogling to pay full attention to what I might be asking."

I laughed. "Well, if he follows the usual light elf creed, it shouldn't be too hard to distract him. But be warned—if he starts getting handsy, I'll smack him down."

"If he starts getting handsy, *I'll* smack him down." He kissed me again and then murmured, "Shall we take this elsewhere?"

"I think we should."

"Your place or mine?"

"Yours. Mine will be too rowdy, given it's Saturday night."

He finished his drink, then rose and offered me his hand. I pulled on my coat, then twined my fingers through his and let him help me up. We wound our way through the crowd, then waved down a cab and headed for his place, a penthouse apartment in a lovely old chapel conversion.

He ushered me out of the cab, and we made our way inside. The main room was a large, double height expanse, with lovely old oak trusses that had been painted white to give the room an even airier feeling. Their song, though muted, was rich and warm, a consequence of being one of the few churches that had undergone major renovations without major destruction. On the street side of the building there were two beautifully simple stained windows and, at the other end of the room, a compact but well-equipped kitchen. Beside this was a chrome-and-glass staircase that wound up to the loft bedroom.

After stripping off our coats, he led me up the stairs, then pulled me close. His body was hard and familiar, his scent—warm leather and exotic spices—intoxicating. I breathed deep, then quickly undid his shirt and pushed him back onto the bed. I slowly, teasingly stripped off my clothes, watching his face, his eyes, seeing his desire, wanting to taste it, taste him. When I was naked, I climbed on the bed and straddled him, claiming his lips, kissing him with all the passion that had been building inside. Then I worked my way down his magnificent length of his body, released his cock from the restraint of his jeans, and teased him, tasted him, with mouth and tongue.

When his desperate groan filled the air, I shifted position and let him slip slowly, oh so slowly, inside, and it was glorious. We moved, slowly at first but with increasing urgency, until all I could think about, all I wanted, was him coming hard. Then he did, just as my orgasm hit and thought became utterly impossible.

For the longest of time after, neither of us moved. When I could finally breathe again, I rolled to one side and tucked myself close.

He caught my hand and kissed my fingers. "Can you stay?"

"I have a meeting with the council at nine tomorrow."

"For a few hours then."

I smiled. "Is there food in the offing? I only had a bacon butty for dinner."

He tsked. "That is hardly what I'd call a sustaining meal."

I raised an eyebrow, amusement twitching my lips. "Depends on what I need to be sustained for, doesn't it?"

He laughed. "It does indeed. And given I intend to make

full use of my few hours with you, I had better ensure you are *very* well sustained."

And he certainly did—with both food *and* sex.

The fae council's headquarters was located next to the Deva City Council offices. Both buildings were utilitarian in design and totally uninspiring, which many thought was a perfect reflection on those who "ruled" over our lives on a daily basis. Of course, there *was* a reason for it—concrete couldn't be manipulated by elves or pixies. Some dark elves *could* manipulate steel, of course, which was why it was generally only used sparingly in most government buildings.

Mathi's driver deposited us in front of the glassed foyer, and one of the building's security people opened the door and waved us through into the foyer. We made our way up the bland but functional concrete stairs to the second floor, then down a long gray corridor, our footsteps echoing in unison. A second security guard stood down the far end near a sturdy-looking metal door. When we were close enough, he nodded and keyed us in. Magic swept the two of us when we walked through, which I knew from past experience was looking for physical weapons. No warning lights flashed this time, simply because I wasn't wearing my knives. The council weren't going to harm me—not when they'd so neatly arranged for me to do their relic-hunting bidding.

We walked down to the next set of doors, which opened automatically as we approached. The room beyond was a long, gray, boring expanse of concrete about the same size as a grand hall. There were no decorations, nothing in the way of wall hangings or crests, and the large oval table that dominated the center of the room was plastic rather than wood or metal. When a council consisted of people who could control many natural elements, plastic furniture was not only sensible but gave no one the edge when it came to possible weapons. There wasn't even the usual smattering of electronic equipment—no computers, no lights other than the spots high above, no stationery, and certainly no pens. They obviously recorded all meetings, but I had no idea how. Maybe there was a hidden, ultra-secure room somewhere nearby where a lone man or woman industriously recorded everything that was said and decided.

Of course, having no means of attack or defense *other* than physical strength would have given the shifters a serious advantage, and this was where the multiple layers of magic came into their own. They not only prevented spell attacks from within or without, but also prevented shifters stepping into their alternate shape—always a good thing when council meetings were not as harmonious as the general public believed, and often resulted in blood being shed.

Mathi had never mentioned anyone dying during physical altercations, but maybe he simply wasn't able to. The fae council wasn't above using blood oaths to restrict what information could be mentioned to outsiders such as myself. It was one of the reasons Mathi had never been able to talk to his father about the hoard's theft.

Most of the fae and shifter lines were represented here today—not always the case, apparently—which meant there were twenty-one people seated around the table in total. There were six representing the light elf lines and seven the dark elf, while the six shifter tribes were also fully represented. A lone dwarf and a Malloyei made up the remaining numbers. I wasn't entirely surprised by the low attendance numbers of the latter two. Dwarves tended to live in the Scottish Highlands and, according to the little Mathi had said about their attendance over the years, generally held little regard for the governance of city folk. When it came to pixie lines, the Malloyei had always been more politically inclined than the rest of us. Despite *our* council acquiescing to the fae council's request of ceding the use of my skills to them as a form of punishment, they tended to keep their noses well away from anything representing human or fae officialdom. It was a practice that had served us well during the war with humans, as we were the *only* fae who didn't lose lands or suffer huge numbers of deaths during that time.

There was also no one here from the ghuls, but again, that wasn't all that surprising. The only official meetings they attended were the night council ones, a small offshoot of the main council that dealt with—and made recommendations on—matters affecting all those who roamed or otherwise haunted the night.

Of course, few here would be comfortable in their presence anyway, even if they *had* been able to attend main meetings. The pale, insubstantial beings dined on the dead, but humanity for the most part seemed convinced their culinary tastes would one day switch to the living. It never could, of course, because their teeth simply weren't capable of dealing with the tougher flesh of a living being. I'd never met a ghul, but Mom had a number of times over the centuries. According to her, ghuls, despite their dining habits, held a deep fascination of the living and loved a good chat. It wasn't unknown for them to choose a "target" and follow them through the night, listening to their conversations and watching their movements. It made them the ultimate gossip gatherers, with eons of information behind them—something Mom had made use of more than once.

Maybe I needed to start doing the same rather than simply relying on the Codex. As good as it was, it was also written from a godly point of view.

My gaze skimmed the table until I found Cynwrig. He was wearing a black leather jacket with a dark teal shirt underneath that was partially undone, revealing tantalizing wisps of dark chest hair. My fingers immediately itched with the need to run through that tempting forest, and a slow, devilish smile touched his lips. He knew the inner havoc he was causing, damn him.

But that smile failed to reach his eyes, because his gaze shifted to the man walking beside me and hardened.

He'd been told, I realized, and he was *not* happy. Anger radiated from him in waves that damn near burned my senses, though the only physical evidence of his displeasure was the one clenched fist. The two men might have come to something of a truce during our relic-hunting adventures, but that might well have been shattered by the council's decision.

And yet, neither man was a fool, and they wouldn't jeopardize the task that lay ahead of us all over a woman—a pixie woman at that.

Mathi escorted me across to the vacant seat at the "head" of the oval table, then pulled out a plastic chair, seating me before moving around to the right to sit opposite the mousy-brown-haired man who held the gavel, which generally indicated who was running the show this evening. I had no idea who he was, but if his thin frame, sharp features, and beady black eyes were anything to go by, he was a rat shifter.

Not my favorite type.

At *all*.

I did my best to control the instinctive urge to edge farther away from him and said, "I gather you brought me here to assign my first relic hunt?"

"Indeed, although our plans have been somewhat sidelined by the other night's unfortunate event." The rat man's voice was like his face—sharp and unpleasant.

"That wasn't unfortunate, that was a deliberate, targeted attack, as you are well aware." Cynwrig's smokey and oh-so-sexy tone held a backbone of steel—one the wise would not ignore. It wouldn't take much to set him off.

"It was also *not* a solitary event," Mathi said. "The same man who destroyed Cynwrig's building attempted to do the same to Kaitlyn Avery's building."

A murmur rose, though the rat shifter and several others nodded. "The IIT promised a prelim report this morning, but as yet, have not furnished it. I gather you and Ms. Aodhán managed to prevent the destruction?"

"Yes, although the elf behind the attack unfortunately escaped," Mathi replied. "It is likely the men hired to provide protection know as little as those who were running interference during the attack on Cynwrig's building."

"And Kaitlyn herself?" a tall, thin light elf asked. Her green eyes said she was from the Gila-Ken line. "Did either of you interview her after the event?"

"We did," Mathi said. "She wasn't able to provide all that much information."

"And you believed her?" The big man sitting to Cynwrig's right snorted. "In that case, I have a bridge to sell you."

"Oh, she didn't lie. She didn't dare. Not to *me*."

Mathi didn't elaborate, but he obviously didn't need to. The big man—a bear shifter if his bushy hair and beard was anything to go by—simply studied him for a second and then nodded.

"She did, however," I said, "make one interesting comment. She said there'd been an elf seeking the shield and its ruby well before the hoard was stolen, and that those rumors fell silent about seven or eight months ago."

"Which is just before the hoard was stolen," the rat commented. "Perhaps our elven mage was involved in that theft."

"Except for one problem—the rumors are said to have gone silent because he found the rubies."

"But not the shield?" Cynwrig asked.

My gaze briefly got lost in the glory of his. "Not as far as she was aware."

"That makes no sense," the dwarf said, his voice deep and gravelly. "What use are the rubies without the shield?"

"You mean, aside from what a mage did with one of them the other night?" Cynwrig said, his mild tone countered by the anger in his eyes.

The dwarf waved a hand, perhaps in acknowledgement.

"From what I've been able to uncover about the rubies," I said, before things could get too antsy, "one holds the power of an unholy fire that can destroy all things, one can liquify earth, and the other has the power of the smith, which apparently enables the user to destroy anything created by a smith."

The bear shifter sniffed. "The latter doesn't seem too bad—"

"It would depend on the definition of a smith," Cynwrig commented, glancing at him. "A smelting works could technically be considered a modern-day smithy."

I nodded. "Combining all three within the shield will destroy land and building, but its scope is limited in size."

"So, city destroying rather than world," the rat shifter said. "I do not personally find that comforting."

"Given what the Claws were capable of, and what could have happened had Rogan targeted our world rather than Annwfyn, I tend to disagree," I said.

A gray-haired elf with heavily lined features grunted. He was what elves called an elder statesman, which basically meant he was well past breeding age and now in the twilight years of his long lifespan. "And now the Annwfyn have a relic with the capability of destroying *us*."

"Presuming, of course, they are capable of magic—"

"Oh, they are," Cynwrig commented.

The bear shifter glanced at him but continued, "—and whether they are even capable of touching let alone using something forged by the gods of *this* world."

"Let us hope that's something we never find out," the Malloyei pixie commented dourly. "Was not a stock-take done just before the hoard's theft? If the shield was already gone at that point, it would have been brought to our attention."

"Not necessarily," another light elf commented. He was the youngest-looking of the six in the room—younger even than Mathi. Although, given their timelessness, it was a perception that might not hold true. "Especially if the bibliothecary was working with those who stole the hoard. He was later found dead, was he not?"

"Yes," Mathi said. "His death remains under investigation."

"Is it true he was found in an old Myrkálfar tunnel?" another light elf asked, in a mild sort of tone.

His gaze remained on Mathi but there could be no doubt in anyone's mind who the comment was aimed at.

A chair scraped as a thickset dark elf whose energy held none of the magnetism of Cynwrig's rose. "If you're implying that *we*—"

"Bodhrán," Cynwrig cut in softly.

The other man glanced at him, annoyance evident, but he didn't finish his statement and sat back down. It was the first time I'd actually seen Cynwrig wield the power—however softly—that was his by right as co-heir to the dark elf throne.

"I'm *sure* Kytrain did not mean to imply anything by that question, Lord Lùtair," the rat shifter said with a dour look at the light elf.

I was damn sure he *did*, and the "blink and you'd miss it" smile that briefly adorned his pale lips said as much.

"Are we able to access the stock records?" my blue-haired counterpart asked. "Checks are done every six months, are they not? That would at least give some indication as to when—*if*—the shield disappeared earlier than the hoard."

The rat shifter glanced briefly at the ceiling. "Líadan, please submit an immediate request for the full records of the last stock take performed on the hoard."

"Submitting," a ghostly voice replied.

It didn't sound human, but it also didn't have a mechanical echo that was sometimes evident in the voices AI programs used.

The rat shifter returned his gaze to me. "It is the council decision that you should concentrate your current efforts on retrieving the shield and its rubies. Mathi Dhār-Val will act as council liaison—"

"A decision *I* was not involved in and do not agree with," Cynwrig growled.

"—and consult with Lord Lùtair as and when necessary," the rat shifter continued, with only the slightest twitch of his nose giving away his sudden nervousness.

"She is mine—"

"I belong to *no* one," I cut in, meeting his gaze steadily.

"—to *guard*," he continued, his eyes giving little away but that radiating energy speaking volumes. "Until the life owed is repaid."

That's not what he'd intended to say at *all*, and we both knew it. I just wasn't entirely sure what he *had* meant. It wasn't like we were—or ever would be—in a monogamous relationship.

"Be that as it may, we cannot afford our hunter to be distracted, given how imperative it has become to find the hoard—something well illustrated by the recent attacks," the elderly light elf said evenly. "The council decision on this matter holds, Cynwrig. Your presence and your vote would not have swayed the result in any manner."

"And *I*," Mathi said, with surprising earnestness, "did *not* raise the issue, in case that's what you were thinking."

Cynwrig stared at him for several seconds, then nodded imperceptibly. Explanation accepted and fury—at least as far as Mathi was concerned—diverted.

"Then who did?" I asked curiously. "What business is it of the council who I happen to be sleeping with?"

No one answered. No one appeared game, given the festering fury sitting at the other end of the table.

The rat shifter waved the gavel, drawing my attention. "That is not your concern—"

"It *is* if it continues," I cut in. "Let's get one thing

straight here—I may work for you, but I do so unwillingly, as a form of punishment. If you start sticking your fucking noses into my personal life, there will be consequences." I gave them a sweet smile that would have served as a dire warning of trouble arising to anyone who actually knew me. "After all, while the pixie council ceded you my assistance, they never guaranteed that assistance would be *fruitful*."

"Is that a threat?" the bear shifter growled.

"Sounded like it to me," Mathi said cheerfully. "And you would be well advised to heed it."

The gavel banged, briefly cutting through the rising tension. "I assure you, Ms. Aodhán, the council has no need and no desire to interfere in your personal life. It was merely our intention to separate the two. Mathi Dhār-Val was a logical choice given he is well aware of your... shall we call them foibles?... and no longer involved on a personal level."

In other words, Mathi was right. None of them had wanted to take Cynwrig's place, despite the fact most of them didn't know me and had never even interacted with me other than the one other time I'd appeared here.

My reputation—or perhaps that of my brother and maybe even Mom, given she'd worked for the council on numerous occasions—apparently *did* loom large. No matter the reason, though, I wasn't about to gripe about it. Not if it kept them from keeping too close an eye on what I was doing.

Which reminded me...

"There is *one* thing I'll need," I said, my pulse rate stepping up several notches. This the tricky bit—the bit on which all my plans to find Mom's killer basically hinged. "And that's full access to the council's records. I need to know what discussions might have been held on anything relating to the hoard or the items within it in order to understand what to look for and where."

An uneasy sort of murmur went around the room. Cynwrig merely raised an eyebrow, amusement briefly glimmering in his eyes. But then, both he and Mathi were well aware I had access to a godly library that contained all the information I could ever want—presuming I asked the right questions, of course.

"It would be impossible to grant such access without allowing access to all our records," the rat shifter said with a frown, "as it would take years to redact any non-relevant information and it is obvious we do not have that time."

"You want me to find the hoard? Then you give me access to the information. Hamstringing me from the start is not going to help the process."

The rat shifter glanced around the table, then returned his gaze to me. "We will discuss the matter privately and inform you of the decision. In the meantime, we can confirm that the ruby you and Mathi found in the murdered woman's apartment remains in our possession."

"It might be handy to know which one it is," I said. "Is there any way we can do that?"

"That could only be achieved via the input of a mage or, indeed, with the shield itself, as each stone has a specific location on its surface," the rat shifter said. "We haven't the shield and we certainly will not be hiring the former. To reveal the ruby's presence to anyone else in the current situation would be unwise. Even this council is not fully aware of its exact location."

Which was probably a good thing given what had happened to Mathi. And while all councilors were now undergoing daily blood tests to ensure they weren't similarly being drugged and then pumped for information, that didn't mean there weren't other means to use.

Like kidnapping and threats.

The latter were unlikely to work on light elves given how little they valued emotional ties and sometimes even family, but the rest of them were fair game, even the dark elves.

"Wherever you *do* have it, I'd be doubling the security measures," Mathi said. "While to date there's been no suggestion the elf mage is after the shield itself, we cannot take the risk."

"That has already been done," the woman who'd been adjudicator the last time I'd been here said. "Not even a ghost could approach its location without setting off multiple alarms and security measures."

Shame they hadn't employed said measures earlier; maybe we wouldn't now be looking for the entire hoard. Then I frowned. "Just how big is the hoard? No one's actually said."

The elderly elf said, "If my memory serves me correctly, there were fifty-seven artifacts and a dozen scrolls."

"Scrolls?" I said, surprised. "Are they not something the museum would be better suited to caretake?"

"The scrolls are said to be written by the hands of the gods themselves, and therefore dangerous to the mortal eye."

And *I* wasn't mortal. My heart began beating faster again. "Were the scrolls also taken?"

"No." His gaze swept me almost contemptuously. "And before you ask, young pixie, you will never be allowed to enter that room to examine them. *We* have never been able to do so. What guards them is... well, not of this world."

"How can you be sure they even exist if you can't get in there to verify?"

"I never said we can't see them. I just said we can't touch them."

Meaning I had to figure out a way of doing what they could not. No easy task when I had no idea where the scrolls were kept, and they were never likely to tell me. Presuming they knew, of course. Apparently, very few people had known the hoard's location, and yet it had still been stolen.

Maybe the Codex had information on them. It was certainly worth asking the next time I went there.

I nodded, then pushed upright. "Is that all?"

The rat shifter frowned. "We would like a regular update on progress."

"*If* there's any progress, then I'm sure Mathi will inform you." I hesitated. "Please let me know what your decision is regarding access to the records."

"We will, but do not place all your bets on full access being granted."

"Then don't place all your bets on the full hoard being recovered," I snapped back. "Look, I don't give a fuck what you lot might have decided in the past or even recent years. It's simply another avenue of research—those records could very well hold the clues as to how someone managed to access the inaccessible. And in case you weren't aware, examining ancient texts is how most relics are *actually* found."

Lots of scowls came my way. They really didn't appreciate being talked to in such a manner. I resisted the impulse to grin, gave them a polite nod instead, and headed out.

Two chairs scraped—suggesting that both Mathi and

Cynwrig intended to follow me—but the rat shifter said sharply, "Sit. We have other urgent matters to discuss."

I hoped one of them was my access to the records, but as the rat shifter had advised, I wasn't pinning any immediate hopes on it.

By the time I got to the ground floor, it was raining again. I pulled my coat hood up over my hair and then shoved my hands in my pockets and headed home. I'd never minded walking in the rain, but at least now I understood why. Having a minor storm god for a father made rain and storms feel like home.

I was halfway to my physical home when my phone rang, the tone telling me it was Lugh.

I hit the answer button and said, "Hey, brother mine, what's up?"

"Just thought I'd let you know we're on the way back."

I frowned. "I thought you were there until Monday?"

"We were, but Darby got a call from the hospital saying they were extremely short staffed and asking if she could fill a shift on Monday."

"She should have said no."

"I did," she said in the background. "They pleaded—and offered triple time."

"You need the sex more than you need the money," I commented.

"Oh, I've had plenty of sex over the last couple of days. My lady bits are extremely happy, let me tell you."

Lugh groaned. "Seriously, ladies, is there nothing you two consider sacred or off-limits?"

"That would be a big fat no," I said, with a laugh.

"And you knew this going into our relationship," Darby added.

"I just never expected..." He paused, and I had an image

of him waving a hand. "You know, the details being placed on the table."

"Oh, we've never discussed the nitty gritty," she replied, "but I'm sure we could—"

"No," he growled. "Just *no*."

She laughed, a warm sound I echoed. "How did the dwarf hunting go?"

There was a brief pause before he said, "How did you know I was dwarf hunting? Did you see it in the Eye?"

"No. It came from a deep understanding of how your mind works and the fact that you would never let such an opportunity pass you by, no matter how much great sex was in the offing."

"He does live and breathe relic hunting, doesn't he?" Darby observed dryly. "I swear the man works on problem solving in his sleep—what little sleep he actually gets, that is."

"Well, you've certainly not helped the situation when it comes to *that*," he mused. "Not that I'm complaining, mind."

"I should hope not, given how often you initiate—"

"I did manage to track Holgan down," he said over the top of her. "He was rather annoyed at me."

"He was annoyed at *you*?" I repeated, in disbelief. "Why?"

"Apparently us not leaving the sword in his car resulted in him not receiving the promised lucrative payment."

"Did you point out that he was basically double crossing us and didn't deserve to be paid?"

"Yes, but as *he* pointed out, he'd technically completed all contractual obligations to us the moment he'd led us safely from the summit of Ben Nevis."

Which was the absolute truth, I guess, but didn't make it morally right. "Who issued the contract? Kaitlyn?"

"No, surprisingly. It came through a small broker in Swansea."

I frowned. "Then why did the men we questioned say Gratham was responsible for hiring them to steal the sword?"

They actually couldn't have lied. Not when I was questioning them.

"This was a separate contract offered solely to Holgan on the off chance Gratham's people weren't successful."

Which they weren't. "Do you think that's why Gratham was killed?"

"Unlikely—the Eve token you found under his bed and the fact his office was ransacked suggest they were after something else."

And we had no idea what that something was, as last I heard, the IIT and local police were still sifting through his records to see what, if anything, had been taken.

"It's still a bit of a coincidence that both Holgan's contractor and the Eve coin came from the same area."

"I agree, which is why I think we need to take a drive over there tomorrow—"

"No need, as I'm heading down there this afternoon with Eljin." I paused. "Were you aware that Nialle had been researching relics from the missing hoard?"

"No, but it wouldn't surprise me. Researching one often uncovers mention of others. I take it this has something to do with your sudden decision to head to Swansea with Eljin?"

"I take it you haven't seen or heard the recent news?"

"Why—what's happened?" he said sharply.

"Another ruby showed up, this time in the hands of an elf mage—"

"I didn't think elves were capable of magic."

"The Myrkálfar are. It's how they lock the gates, remember."

"This one is Myrkálfar?"

"He has the dark skin, but red hair and green eyes, so either he's a half-blood or his lineage originated from overseas. He said we'd met before, but I can't for the life of me remember where. I thought maybe he might have worked for you."

"Not in my department, but it's possible he did work elsewhere in the museum. Why? What did he do?"

"He used the ruby to destroy Cynwrig's building and attempted to do the same to Kaitlyn's."

Lugh swore. "Many casualties?"

"Almost everyone who was in Cynwrig's building at the time."

He swore again. "I take it Eljin found mention of the rubies while he was sorting through the mountain of Nialle's notes?"

"Not rubies so much as the shield itself. The council has prioritized me finding both, though."

"Did you ask them for record access?"

"I did. They're contemplating their answer as we speak."

"Well, at least we have Mathi and Cynwrig on our side."

"Whether they can bring enough pressure to bear is another matter."

"Never discount the persuasiveness of a dark elf," Darby commented. "Not when there's something they truly want."

A comment that reminded me of what Cynwrig had

said, and begged the question—what did he truly want from me?

"I'll head into the office when I get home and see if Nialle recorded anything officially," Lugh was saying, "If not, I'll head down to the crypts. His workspace there remains untouched, so if he did find something on the shield, it's likely to be in one of the scrolls he retrieved from archiving. I take it you'll be asking around about the Eve token while you're in Swansea?"

"Might as well kill two birds, and all that."

"Just be careful. Remember, we have no idea why Gratham was killed or who was behind it, and the last thing we need right now is to set off another series of attacks against us."

"Will do. Take care."

He grunted and hung up. Thunder rumbled overhead, and the intensity of the rain increased. I swung into the lane and ran down to the tavern, reaching cover just as lightning split the sky.

Someone above was angry, and I had a bad suspicion I knew exactly who.

I stripped off my coat, hung it over the hook, then hurried toward the main bar.

"That weird woman is here again," Ingrid said from somewhere in the depths of the storeroom. "Put her upstairs this time—thought it better not to be scaring too many customers away given the scarcity of them on wintery days such as this."

"Thanks, Ingrid. Did you give her a drink?"

"I did not."

Hence the anger evident overhead. "Might be wise to do so next time. Puts her in a better mood."

"Will do." She sniffed. "It will not be the top shelf stuff though."

"Absolutely not," I agreed with a laugh.

I pushed through the door and then ran up the stairs to the next floor. The area was shadowed and quiet—or as quiet as any old building could be with the storm that raged above us.

She definitely *wasn't* happy, and its source was more than the lack of alcohol.

I stepped onto the landing and followed the building's song across the room. She was sitting at the corner table closest to the bar, and there was a part of me that was surprised she hadn't helped herself to a drink. But maybe even grouchy old goddesses drew the line at theft.

"Hey, Beira," I said. "Nice to see—"

"Don't you be sweet talking me," she growled with all the fury of the storm outside. "Not until you explain what the *fuck* you've done now."

CHAPTER
SEVEN

"It's impossible to answer that without knowing what it is, exactly, you think I've fucking done."

I walked straight past her, heading for the bar. While her temper could be as volatile as any storm, there was no way she'd unleash the dangerous energy that crackled all around her. Not when she and the rest of the hags wanted me to step into Mom's shoes and help them recover missing artifacts.

Which I was de facto doing now anyway.

I grabbed a bottle of Green Spot Single Pot Whiskey—one of six new ones we were currently trialing in the two bars—and a couple of glasses. It might not yet be midday, but I had a feeling I was going to need a drink to cope with whatever news she'd come here to impart. And whiskey really *did* put her in a better mood.

I sat opposite her, poured two glasses, then slid one and the bottle across the table. She accepted both with a scowl, though the glint in her eyes suggested her anger was mostly surface deep. She gulped the whiskey down, then poured another.

"Feeling better?" I asked, amused.

She sniffed, which in Beira terms meant yes. The bird nest that had sat so jauntily in her wiry hair the last time I'd seen her was missing today, though the odd twig and half torn leaf remained. Like all hags—although these days, there were only six, and four of those were considered minor goddesses with little power—she was short and slender, with sharp, unpleasant brown features. She appeared to have a hump today, but I doubted it was a new deformity given it was located close to her right shoulder and appeared to be twitching.

Maybe the bird that had been nesting in her hair had moved to warmer climes under the rags she called a coat.

"The wind tells me you're working for the goddamn fae council—is that true?"

"Unfortunately, yes, but it's not like I had a choice. Why? Why does it matter so much to you?"

"It matters because there's been a dangerous increase in Ninkil activity, and I fear the council may be at the heart of it."

I raised my eyebrows and repeated, "Why?"

She tapped her nose, making the overlarge wart sitting at its tip wobble alarmingly. "You're not the only one with a nose for trouble."

Amusement twitched my lips, and she scowled, raising a finger in warning. "Don't you be saying the comment I can see in your eyes. It's impolite."

My smile escaped, but I heeded the warning. "No one within the council has ever mentioned Ninkil or his artifacts to me."

"Well, they wouldn't, would they? Not so bluntly, at any rate. The Ninkilim are bright creatures with oh-so-sweet tongues and hearts filled with subterfuge. It's rare for them to show their true selves until they gain what they wish."

"And what is it you think they wish?"

Her scowl deepened. "You are well aware of what they want. Do not play dumb with me, young woman."

I took a drink to hide another smile. "What do you know of Ninkil's Harpē?"

She sucked in a breath, and overhead, thunder rumbled ominously. "The council have asked you to find that?"

"No, they've tasked me with finding the Shield of Hephaestus and its missing eyes."

"Then why ask about the harpē?"

"Because a note Nialle made about it just came to light, and his replacement at the museum mentioned it to me."

"And what do we know of this replacement?"

"Aside from the fact he's fantastic in bed?"

"You need to start thinking with your head rather than your loins, young woman."

"But my loins are having a damn good time." I held up a hand to stop the tirade that was undoubtedly about to hit. "He was fully vetted by Rogan—"

"Would this be the same Rogan who stole the Claws and damn near killed you?"

Her voice was dry, and I grimaced. "Yeah. But Lugh has seen his application and work history. There's nothing in his background that raises any sort of alarms."

"And you trust him?"

"He's given me no reason *not* to trust him."

She grunted, appearing mollified. "Just be wary of anyone new stepping into your life, especially if they appear too good to be true. The Ninkilim have a history of gently seductive coercion, and with your loins..."

She trailed off pointedly, and I laughed. "My loins are

not seeking or wanting a third lover. Besides, what would they want with me? They already have the hoard—"

"What makes you think that?" she said sharply.

"I did a scrying and heard a conversation between two of them. They said they were in the process of securing the hoard but hadn't done a full inventory yet, as they didn't want to risk any vibration along the psychic or magic lines."

And thinking about it now, it didn't really make sense that they were still securing the hoard months after it had been stolen. Had it been a past conversation I'd heard rather than a more recent one? It wasn't like they came with date stamps.

"Meaning we're not chasing fools. Shame." She poured herself another whiskey. "Did they specifically mention Ninkil?"

I nodded. "The man said their god was getting impatient, and the woman replied that he'd waited centuries for this moment, so a few more months would not hurt him."

"If they have not yet done an inventory, that plays to our advantage."

"Meaning the harpē wasn't part of the hoard?"

"It was, but your mother did have some worrying visions about it some eight or nine months ago, and it is a sad fact that the Ljósálfar protections in recent centuries have not been up to scratch. The wind sometimes whispers of its malice, and that should not be if it was fully and properly secured."

"The council does regular stock takes—"

She cackled, the sound harsh and unpleasant. "If you can call ticking off as present whatever chest or receptacle the relic might be stored in, then yes, they certainly do."

I frowned. "Surely *every* relic wouldn't be contained—"

"What, and leave them open for any numbskull human

or fae who fancies a little godly power boost to grab?" She snorted. "Not likely."

"Which means whoever stole the hoard might not be aware of what, exactly, they have or have not." And might not know yet if the harpē is there or not.

"If they *do* discover it's missing, your ability will put you in greater danger. There are few left in this world who can see and seek the unseeable."

It was that very ability that had killed Mom. She didn't say that, of course, but it was there in her dark eyes.

I took a long drink that didn't ease the inner ache, and then said, "I was told the harpē is a sword with a sickle protrusion along one edge near the tip of the blade, and that it gives the user control over life and death—is that true?"

She nodded. "What the records fail to say is the fact that it is the *only* means by which Ninkil can be recalled into *this* world."

"So, if we find the harpē first, we stop the Ninkilim's plans cold?"

"Basically, yes."

"Then I don't suppose you have any suggestions as to where we might start looking?"

"I don't suppose I do."

"Mom didn't say anything?"

"Her visions were undefined." She sniffed. "The wind still whispers, but she has little in the way of details."

"Well, that sucks."

Amusement glimmered briefly in her eyes. "It is the way of the gods."

"Never make it too easy on us poor mortals," I said, with a nod. "Got it."

"I'm a hag," she said. "This flesh suit is my punishment

and my prison. I cannot do or be what I once was."

"But you're still pretty damn powerful, and you can still talk to the gods, old and new, be they above, below, or even remain in this world."

"*If* they deign to talk to us hags or curmudgeons. Many don't." She sniffed, the sound contemptuous. "And many consider watching humanity's attempts to erase each other great sport."

Curmudgeons were the hags' male counterparts who, unlike the hags, could shapeshift away their unpleasant forms.

"Is Ninkil one of the ones who doesn't talk to you?" I asked curiously. "Is that why you're so worried about his rising?"

"I'm worried because I've seen the chaos his rising has caused in the past. Remember, I'm bound to this body and this world for eternity—or until the gods collectively decide the punishment has exceeded the crime. I'm not holding my breath for the latter, let me assure you."

"Hard to hold your breath and drink a fine whiskey," I mused.

She barked a laugh. "Never a truer word spoken."

"Is chewing me out for working with the council the only reason you came here? Or was there something else?"

"It was the major reason, yes, but I also wanted you to know that no matter what the Codex says, the shield cannot be returned to the confluence. It must be destroyed."

The confluence being the ghostly portal that sat atop Ben Nevis. I frowned. "Something I'd already suspected, but how do you know what the Codex—"

I stopped. She knew because I used the Eye in conjunction with the Codex, and my Eye was just one half of the pair once belonging to the goddess Eithne, one of the original hags who'd turned to stone. While the hags couldn't use the visionary power within their Eye, they could and had used it to communicate with Mom. I wasn't sure why they weren't using it to communicate with me, but maybe it was simply a matter of me using the Eye in a vastly different manner to Mom.

Mind you, Beira's liking of a good drop of whiskey might also play a part.

"Indeed," she was saying, "the echoes of whatever you see in the Eye come through to us."

"Then I had better not ask it anything too damn personal, had I?"

She cackled. "Not unless you want to scandalize the sensibilities of our more innocent goddesses."

I snorted. "I suspect there'd be little that could scandalize or shock the sensibilities of goddesses who have been earthbound for hundreds, if not thousands, of years."

"You might be surprised."

I certainly would be. "Why would the Codex say it must be returned if that's not the case? I thought it contained all the knowledge of the old gods?"

"The key there being 'old.' This world and its people is not the only one that has changed vastly since the Codex library was created."

"Meaning it's outdated?"

"No. What was written still applies. But the weight of time has altered opinions on the best method to deal with the relics of those gods who are, for whatever reason, no longer a part of this world or ours."

I frowned. "Then going forward, how the hell am I going to know whether to return or destroy? Via you?"

She shook her head. "For the most part, you will have to

discover the hard way, by seeking entry into the confluence and either being refused or accepted."

As had happened when I'd taken the Sword of Darkness up there. "Then what is different with the shield?"

"Sethlans reached out to me—"

"Sethlans being?"

"A god of fire, the forge, and metalworking who has been bound to Earth."

Meaning he was one of the three curmudgeons who remained in flesh form here on Earth. "I thought you said they hadn't been active for hundreds of years?"

"I did, and they weren't. But your father was active enough to ensure your existence, and now Sethlans has reached out. They're obviously keeping an eye on things even if they refuse to get involved in other ways."

"And he's the one who said the shield couldn't be taken into the confluence?"

"Yes. The shield is a destruction relic, and therefore would not be accepted."

"Aren't most godly relics destructive ones?"

"There are plenty that are not, but let's be honest here, the destructive ones are more fun. At least for those gods and goddesses who are not trapped in flesh form on this plane."

"I don't suppose he mentioned where it might be hidden?"

"He did not."

Of course not. "Could I use the Eye to seek its location?"

"If you had some point of reference, yes, but it does not work within emptiness."

I glanced at the time, then finished my drink and rose. "If that's all, I need to get moving. We have a possible lead on the shield we're following up."

She rose and swept up the bottle of whiskey with one slightly clawed hand—something else I hadn't noticed before. "Mind if I keep this?"

"Would you care if I said yes?"

She cackled in response, tucked the bottle under her arm, and headed back out into the storm—the ferocity of which immediately eased.

Note to self—always send her away with a nice bottle of whiskey, especially when there's a storm raging.

I headed upstairs to pack an overnight bag, then collected my knives and the Eve token. Like many magical tokens, this one was an air-dried clay coin about the same size as a penny. There were multiple tiny symbols etched onto its surface, and I had absolutely no idea what any of them represented, although the one that resembled a snake in a circle was, according to Lugh, the symbol that gave the token its name. Basically, they were designed to render the wearer irresistible to a particular person, but according to the witch I'd asked about it, this particular token also had what amounted to a sound bubble spell woven into it—one specifically designed to keep external sounds *out* rather than internal sounds in, as was usual.

After tucking the token and the knives safely into my purse—it was a *big* purse—I picked up my overnight bag and my coat and headed out to the back lane to wait for Eljin.

A rather compact-looking Mercedes SUV pulled up across the lane a few seconds later. Eljin climbed out and ran around to the passenger side to open the door for me.

His gaze swept me and came up amused. "As lovely as you look in jeans and a fluffy white jumper, it is not what I'd call as a sexy outfit."

"It's a nearly four-hour journey to Swansea," I replied

dryly. "I'm dressed for comfort. I can change once we get closer. This your new car? Or a hire?"

"Hire, but only because I'm contemplating buying one. Thought this would be the perfect opportunity to test it out."

"It's a small SUV—not what I'd call a chick magnet."

He laughed. "I'm a single male pixie in a city that has a dearth of them. I could drive a Reliant Robin and it wouldn't matter one jot."

"What the hell is a Reliant Robin?"

"A three-wheel plastic car made in the seventies that has a habit of tipping over when you turn a corner."

"And you know this because you actually had one?"

"No, but I've a friend whose dad was a miner in the north before they moved to France, and he had one. But only because they could drive it on a motorcycle license."

"Huh."

He took my bag, then ushered me into the vehicle. After storing the bag in the trunk, he jumped in, and we headed off.

The various traffic works along the way meant it took us just over four hours to get there. Conversation flowed easily though, and it was lovely to simply spend more time in his company, getting to know him better without the heady draw of sex getting in the way. As we neared Swansea, I shifted in my seat and said, "Once we've talked to Loudon Fitzgerald, do you mind if we detour back into Swansea? I need to talk to a witch who made a token I found."

He shrugged. "That's absolutely no problem. I gather the token has something to do with the shield quest?"

"It's more a leftover from the Claws quest."

He raised his eyebrows and glanced at me. "What sort

of token is it?"

"An Eve token. We found it under the bed of a dead man, and its presence still bothers me."

"Then find this witch we certainly will. I don't want you distracted when I've got a seduction evening planned."

An anticipatory smile teased my lips. "Do you now?"

He nodded solemnly. "It starts with a candlelit dinner, moves on to a deep spa bath—"

"I thought you said bathroom facilities were basic?"

"They are, spa aside. After that, we open the roof and make passionate love to the glorious song of the trees and the stars."

"And if there's no stars and it rains?"

"The gods wouldn't dare disrupt my carefully laid plans."

"The gods certainly would," I replied with a laugh. "Trust me on that."

He grinned. "Sounds like you're speaking from experience."

"More speaking from association."

He raised an eyebrow. "You've met them?"

I hesitated, suddenly wary though not entirely sure why. It was an innocent enough question and one I certainly would have asked had the roles been reversed. Still, given what Beira had said about her enemies being on the rise, it was probably better *not* to widely advertise her visits. One casual mention in the wrong place could lead to disaster.

"Mom did, not me." I shrugged. "Nothing much came of it."

Nothing aside from me and a long-lasting association with the hags, that is.

"Nothing much ever comes of meetings with the old

gods," he said. "Or rather, nothing much good. History tells us that."

"I guess."

I returned my attention to the road as we skirted around Swansea's center. A few miles later, we stopped at a pub for a drink but mainly so I could change into my so-called "sexier" outfit. *That* consisted of a black corset-style long-sleeved top that made the most of my assets without leaving me shivering, tighter-fitting jeans, and knee-high black boots that emphasized the length of my legs.

Eljin was texting someone when I reentered the dining room but glanced up as I neared the table.

His gaze briefly skimmed my length and came up heated. "Perhaps we should skip the questioning and get straight down to the seduction."

I laughed. "No, because there's no way I'm pouring myself into this outfit again tomorrow."

"Shame. You look amazing."

"I'd rather comfort over looks, thanks."

"The gentlemanly thing to say here is that I like both on you, but if I'm being honest…" He trailed off and, with a grin, hooked his arm through mine and escorted me out to the SUV. The evening had definitely become colder but the sky, at least for now, remained clear.

Fitzgerald's house was larger than I expected, given he was ostracized and unlikely to have any monetary input from the family's business. It was also a surprisingly modern, white rendered two-story building with a stepped-back wing on the left and a triple garage on the right. It sat on at least an acre that held little in the way of trees but did possess an awesome view over the ocean. While I appreciated the latter, it was an odd place for a light elf to settle.

Eljin parked the car, then climbed out and ran around to the passenger side to open the door. Then, with a hand to my spine, he guided me toward the steps that led up to the patio. It was stone rather than wood, which again was an odd choice for an elf. But perhaps he wasn't, as I'd been presuming, from a highborn line, but rather the merchant class. It would certainly fit his persona of a collector more.

Eljin stepped past me and rang the doorbell. Deep inside the house, chimes played, and a few seconds later, footsteps echoed lightly through the distant song of the floorboards.

That song seemed to hold a hint of... warning?

I frowned, stepped back, and looked up. To the left of the door was a security camera, and to the right, one of those small blue lights that went off when the alarm was triggered. There were also multiple, barely visible layers of protective magic, which, given the additional costs of hiding spell work, meant they were very expensive *and* very expansive. Far more expansive than anything I had protecting the tavern, anyway.

The door opened to reveal a tall, thin man with sharp blue eyes, pale silver hair, and tight-looking facial features that no longer resembled an elf's. A result of the plastic surgery he'd needed, presumably.

"Professor Eljin Lavigne, I presume? You are right on time, good sir. Please—" His gaze came to mine, and his eyes widened. "As I live and breathe—Meabh! What a great pleasure it is to see you again."

I simply stared at him, surprise holding me mute.

The very last thing I'd ever expected to find in a coastal city so far away from Deva was someone who'd known *Mom*.

CHAPTER
EIGHT

"No," Eljin said into the brief silence. "This is Bethany. I have no idea who Meabh is—"

"She was my mom," I said.

"She's left us?" Loudon shook his head, his tight features altering little but his eyes glinting in sadness. "That's a great loss indeed for the relic-hunting world. Please, come in. First door on your right."

He stepped to one side and waved us in. Eljin pressed his fingers against my spine again and guided me forward, the warmth of his touch battling the growing coldness deeper within. Why that existed, I couldn't say. Loudon obviously respected—had maybe even been friends with—Mom, so why was I suddenly fearful? I didn't know—and perhaps *that* was part of the problem. No matter how much I'd thought I'd known about my mother and her relic-hunting life, it was becoming increasingly clear that wasn't true. And running alongside that realization was the concern I'd eventually uncover something I didn't *like*.

I breathed deep and tried to control the irrational fear that swirled. I had no doubt that Mom had undertaken relic hunts that weren't exactly legal, just as I knew for *sure* not all of Lugh's retrievals were.

But she'd been my mom, and there was a part of me that just didn't want to look into the deeper, darker parts of her past.

The room we entered was what could only be described as a typical gentleman's study—rich woods, a vast antique desk, plush leather chairs, and bookshelves lining all four walls filled with beautiful volumes of gold-tooled leather-bound books. The floorboards were covered by rich carpets that did little to mute their music, and the odd note still ran through them. But its source seemed to be coming from a room close by and the woman who stood silently within.

"Please," Loudon said, appearing from behind us and motioning to the two green leather chairs sitting in front of his desk.

I sat and crossed both my arms and legs. It was a defensive action rather than a seductive one, mainly because the latter was now off the table. He'd known my mom. He wouldn't seduce her daughter. That much had been evident in the brief glimpse of sadness and respect I'd seen in his eyes.

"Can I ask how long you knew Mom?"

"Well over a hundred years, I suppose." His smile was filled with fondness. "She and I had a casual relationship for many years before she met Sgott."

Meaning he'd known her when she was much younger —and likely before my brother had been born. Pixies in general had a *very* long lifespan compared to humans, but both the Tàileach and Aodhán lines lived close to five hundred, supposedly due to the infusion of godly blood we'd received when we were appointed guardians of the gods' treasures. What *my* lifespan would be was anyone's guess, given the revelation that my father was an actual god, albeit a minor one.

As Loudon sat behind the desk, the iPhone sitting to his right pinged and the screen lit up. He read the message, his lips briefly tightening, then pressed the off button and returned his attention to us.

"Sorry, but some of my business partners have no boundaries when it comes to weekends or time off." It was said in an annoyed manner, but there was something else, something I couldn't place, lingering in his gaze. "Now, what were we discussing?"

"Mom," I said. "Did you keep in contact with her after your relationship ended?"

"Oh, on a professional level, most certainly. She occasionally came here seeking information about some relic or other, as she knew I have a considerable library and a love for ancient scrolls."

"When was the last time you saw her?"

He wrinkled his nose, though his skin was so tight the movement was only minute. "Perhaps eight or nine months ago."

Which was a few months before the hoard was stolen but around the same time she'd had visions of the harpē. Is that what she'd come here to ask about? "What was she seeking?"

"Nothing. It was a friendly visit. She was up this way and dropped in for a cup of tea." He shrugged, briefly dropping his gaze from mine, but not before I'd seen that odd flash again. He was lying, and he was uncomfortable about it. "Which reminds me, would you care for a drink? A tea or coffee, or something stronger perhaps?"

"A tea would be lovely," Eljin said.

I nodded in agreement, my gaze on Loudon and

wondering what was going on. There'd been genuine surprise and warmth when he'd first mistaken me for Mom, but something now felt off.

And it had happened *after* that text. Of course, that might have been coincidental and have nothing to do with Mom or our reason for being here, but something within feared the worst.

He picked up a small bell from the corner of his desk and rang it lightly. "Tea should be here shortly. In the meantime, what it is you wish to speak to me about this evening?"

"We were told you recently purchased a scroll that made mention of the Shield of Hephaestus," Eljin said.

Loudon frowned. "I've purchased several over the last month or so. You would need to be more specific."

"This scroll is one you purchased from Kaitlyn Avery."

"Ah yes, I remember now. It was one of the scrolls found in the attic of a dead collector. The museum claimed most of them, I believe, but this and a few others found their way onto the market."

Meaning they'd been taken before the museum had been notified of the collector's death and been able to get there to examine the artifacts. The black market was often far more profitable than officialdom, and some heirs had no respect for antiquities beyond what they could fetch. Or so Lugh said.

"Are we able to look at it?" Eljin said.

"I'm afraid not," Loudon replied. "It was in such a perilous state that I've sent it to a specialist restorer."

Another lie. Or, at least, a partial one, though I really couldn't say which part was lie and which truth.

The gentle song of the floorboards altered fractionally,

informing me an elf approached. It also told me that she was the person I'd sensed standing in the other room.

She wheeled a tea trolley in, her gaze lowered, appearing to concentrate on where she was going rather than meeting anyone's eyes. The faint dusting of gold across her skin suggested she was of Moelyn stock—one of the servant class light elf lines—though her hair was brown rather than their usual dark gold. After placing the tray on the table, she turned, her gaze briefly meeting mine. Her brown eyes—which were, like her cheeks, flecked with gold—held a warning. Of what, I couldn't say, nor did the music elaborate. Then her gaze dropped, and she stepped past me, quickly leaving the room.

But the floorboards' song of her steps halted not all that far up the hallway, and then it altered, rippling lightly as a finger ran across its surface. It was a message written into the music—a warning not to drink the tea, and a request to meet her, with a time and place given. There was a pause in the music before she added, *Do not share. We will only meet you.*

Then her finger lifted from the floor, and she moved on.

Leaving me wondering why she didn't want Eljin to accompany me and how I was going to get away from him and his seduction plans in a few hours' time.

"Please, help yourself," Loudon said.

I jumped fractionally. Eljin raised his eyebrows questioningly, but Loudon was watching us, so I simply picked up the teapot and began to pour. There were two cups on the tray, not three.

"You're not having one?" I asked Loudon.

"No, it's too late in the day for me to be drinking any sort of caffeine."

While I could hear no lie in the response, the maid's

139

warning loomed large. I handed Eljin a cup, briefly meeting his gaze in an effort to impart a silent warning, then poured milk into mine and picked it up. I didn't take a sip, however, just nursed it instead.

"Do you read the scrolls when you buy them?" I asked.

He half shrugged. "Sometimes, depending on their state. I did not risk doing so with this one."

"You've nothing else in your archives about the shield or its rubies?" I asked.

"I don't believe so, but let me check." He pressed a button on the side of his desk; a portion of the top slid aside and a computer rose. He tapped the keyboard for several seconds then shook his head. "Nothing on file, I'm afraid."

"What about Ninkil's Harpē?" I asked impulsively.

Something flared in his gaze. Something close to fear. It never touched his frozen features though, and certainly didn't color his reply. "Ninkil? The Rat God? Not a favorite among many collectors, including me, I'm afraid."

"Can you check?"

He shrugged and did so. "Again, nothing on file, I'm afraid."

Again, I just didn't believe him, but straight out calling him a liar would only get us marched straight out the door. Better to keep him onside, at least for the moment.

"Ah, well, it was worth a try," Eljin said, his tone philosophical. "When the scroll is returned, would it be possible to view it then?"

"Of course." His gaze came to mine, and there was something more than mere curiosity there. There was an intentness that didn't mesh with his earlier easygoing manner. "May I ask, why are you so interested in the Eyes of Hephaestus or even the harpē? I couldn't imagine the museum would want the latter on display, given how dangerous it is purported to be."

"We were just following up on some notes I found in my predecessor's desk." Eljin shrugged. "We were coming down this way anyway, so I thought it worth dropping by."

"Then you're not following in your mother's footsteps and becoming a hunter?" Loudon asked, with an oddly intent gaze my way.

I smiled, although the unease increased. "Sadly, I don't have her skills or her knack for finding things."

"Ah, that is a shame."

"Not really, given relic hunting is what led to her murder."

Shock ran through his expression. It was very quickly controlled, but it nevertheless made me relax a little. Whatever was happening here, it didn't involve Mom or her murder. Maybe I needed to come back here and talk to him alone.

"I didn't know," he murmured.

"That's hardly surprising, given you weren't even aware she was dead," I said. "The IIT are dealing with it."

"Sgott is not a man I'd want to be on the wrong side of, that's for sure." He pushed to his feet. "If there's nothing else, I'm afraid the irritating business partner I mentioned earlier wishes to meet with me."

I placed my untouched tea back on the tray, then accepted Eljin's still full cup and placed it beside mine. Either he'd caught my warning or his ability to "read" people had him suspecting Loudon's tea-offering motives.

We both rose and followed Loudon out of the room. The elf maid, I noted, was nowhere to be seen, and her presence no longer echoed through the wood song. Loudon bid us both a pleasant goodbye, then closed and locked the door before we were even off the patio.

"What do you make of all that?" Eljin said as he started the SUV and headed down the driveway.

"That text he received changed his whole manner. I'd love to know what it said."

"It was some kind of warning, though I couldn't see enough of the screen to know exactly what it said. But he was definitely warier after it came in."

I shifted in the seat to look at him. "Was he lying about the scroll?"

"As far as I could tell, no, although I'm not certain whether that applies to its state or it being at the restorers." He grimaced. "There are times I seriously wish my talent was a direct form of telepathy rather than a means of reading emotions, dreams, and the past."

"What about when he was speaking about Mom? Did you pick up anything there?"

"He genuinely cared for her, but he wasn't telling the truth about her reason for last seeing him."

"I thought the same."

He glanced at me. "Was your mom really murdered?"

I nodded. "Lugh didn't tell you?"

"No, although I was aware she'd died." He paused. "Was she truly murdered on a hunt?"

I raised my eyebrows. "You couldn't read the truth?"

"My ability to read you is often sketchy and requires concentration. Loudon was watching us too closely by the end, and I dared not risk tasting the truth of your statement."

"What do you think he was hiding?"

"That I don't know, but I suspect we need to find out."

"How? There's no way we could break into that place—

there's multiple layers of magical and physical protections."

"I agree, but let's keep it simple first off and follow him to wherever his appointment is."

"He knows what our car looks like."

"He knows we drive a small silver SUV, but they're a dime a dozen on the roads these days. If we keep far enough back, he likely won't even notice us."

"Maybe."

My doubt shone through my reply, and he placed a hand on my knee, squeezing lightly. "If he does see us, well, nothing lost. We can just go find your witch or better yet, start seduction proceedings."

But not as soon as you would like... I wrinkled my nose, tempted to tell him about the maid's message. I had no idea why she didn't want him with me, but if she had information about Mom and why she'd gone to Loudon's, then I had no choice but to obey her wishes.

"You have a one-track mind." The amusement in my reply sounded slightly forced, but thankfully, he didn't seem to notice.

"I'm a man—it comes with the territory when there's a sexy woman in close proximity."

I laughed again and, as we came out onto the street, pointed to an empty parking space between two cars several properties down. "If we stop there, we can see which way he goes and then discreetly pull out."

"Discreetly pulling out is not a favorite thing of mine," he murmured.

I rolled my eyes in response. He laughed and added, "Okay, no more sexual innuendo for the time being."

"Good, because it's not like we can deal with rising passion right now."

"Oh, my dear woman, that comment points to a surprising lack of imagination."

"Need I remind you of my earlier comment about preferring comfort? It applies to more than just clothes."

And also depended on the man I was with. I seriously liked Eljin, but when it came down to it, I wouldn't risk arrest for lewd behavior in a public place with him.

Cynwrig, on the other hand...

As if merely thinking about the man conjured his presence, my phone rang. I hit the answer button and held it to my ear in an effort to prevent Eljin hearing both sides of the conversation.

"Hey," I said. "How did the council meeting go?"

"It was a long and extreme waste of time. Would you like to go out to dinner tonight?"

"Can't. I'm out with the competition."

A comment that instantly had the attention of the man sitting beside me. I glanced at him, and he raised an eyebrow, amusement lurking. He was well aware that I was seeing someone else—both of them were, in fact—because the last thing I'd wanted was to get involved in *any* sort of relationship, casual or not, based on a lie.

There was a long pause. "You never mentioned that the other night."

"It was a last-minute thing, and a bit of business mixed with pleasure. I'll tell you about it when I get back home."

"Where are you now?"

"Swansea."

"Following up on the token, I take it?"

"That and a lead on the shield."

"Call me when you get back, then."

"I will, but it'll be late tomorrow."

"I'll be here and waiting."

All sorts of unwise comments pressed against my tongue, aching to be unleashed, but I held them back and said a simple goodbye.

Fun time, not a long time, I reminded myself fiercely.

I hung up and put the phone away.

"From the little I could gather, the competition was not pleased."

"He's a dark elf. They like a harem, but they don't like members of said harem having one of their own."

"A little competition never hurt anyone," he said sagely. "It makes a man up his game."

"Ah, this little seduction plan of yours now makes more sense. You do realize, however, that you could be setting up long-term expectations that are going to be hard to keep."

"Let's get to long-term first and worry about it then." He nodded to the road up ahead. "Our quarry departs."

I glanced up the road and watched the sleek red Sportback Audi pull out and head toward Swansea. Eljin waited a beat then started the SUV and slipped out behind a small white Ford.

As we followed Loudon through Swansea's outskirts, I changed into more comfortable boots. I loved high heels, but they weren't easy to run in and did tend to be a little dangerous to the health of my ankles on uneven or cobblestoned footpaths.

Loudon eventually turned into a small side street and parked down the far end. He glanced our way briefly but didn't seem to notice us; he simply locked his car and hurried across the road.

"Stop and let me out," I said, once we were safely past him. "Otherwise, we might lose him."

Eljin immediately stopped. I grabbed my puffer jacket and purse, and then clambered out. The car behind us

145

blasted his horn and gave me a hurry up motion when I glanced at him. I slammed the door shut, and Eljin took off, turning left at the corner.

I shoved my arms through my jacket's sleeves, then hastily tugged my hood over my head just in case Loudon decided to look back. He didn't. He simply strode down the street, every step seeming to vibrate with annoyance. He obviously wasn't happy with whoever had sent him here or perhaps what he was here to do.

He disappeared into a small, single-story building that sat between a bubble tea store and red-painted coffee shop. I glanced up at the sign propped on the building's roofline and my stomach twisted.

Enchantments by Einar.

It couldn't be, I thought. The witch I'd seen in Gloucester had told me the Eve token had the resonance of a man from the Einar line, and that he'd come from Swansea rather than Cambridge, which was where most of them lived these days.

Granted, she'd also said the Einar line had originated from this area, so there was likely to be more than one Einar in the area, but still...

I pulled the token out of my purse, then gripped it in my hand, said, "Take me home," as the witch had directed, then placed the token on the hood of the nearby car. For several heartbeats nothing happened, then energy stirred, and the token vibrated lightly. The snake that sat at its center came to life and shifted into an arrow-like position.

It was pointing straight at that little building.

"Where'd he go?" Eljin said from behind me.

I jumped and half turned. "Damn it, you scared the hell out of me."

"Why?" He glanced past me and saw the token sitting on the hood. "What were you doing with that?"

"The token has a location tracker on it. It was made inside that shop, the very same shop that Loudon went into."

"Could be a coincidence." His expression suggested he no more believed that than I did. "How do you want to play this?"

I glanced across at the lane that ran between the bubble tea place and Einar's. There was one of those metal bins on wheels sitting across most of it, barring entry, but there looked to be enough space remaining between it and the wall to slip past without having to move the thing and risk drawing attention.

"I'll head down the lane and see if there's a rear entry. Luck might be with us and let me hear what they're discussing. It might be innocent."

"I think we hold the same opinion on *that* possibility." He pursed his lips for a moment. "It could be dangerous, though. Maybe I should—"

"I'll be fine. Besides, I've got my knives—"

"You're carrying *knives*? Why?"

I grinned. "They're special knives. I never travel anywhere dangerous without them."

"We weren't exactly going anywhere dangerous today."

"Let's just say that visiting a witch's place of business has proven rather dangerous in the past."

"And what do these special knives actually do?"

"They counter magic."

"Handy, though I was more worried about a *physical* attack than magical." He held up a hand to counter the argument I was about to make. "I know, I know, you can handle yourself. But just remember, few women, no matter how strong or skilled they are, can counter the sheer strength of one equally skilled man, let alone two."

Loudon hadn't struck me as a man who was in any way skilled at fighting, but that didn't make Eljin's comment any less relevant. I might have fought off multiple attackers in past escapades, but the truth was, that probably had been more luck than skill.

"If they attack in unison, I'll run."

"Is that a promise?"

I half smiled. "Maybe. Probably."

He looked decidedly unhappy but after a moment, growled, "Fine, but please, promise me you'll remain in the lane. Anything else could be dangerous. I'll keep watch from out here and send a text if he comes out."

"If he comes out, follow him."

He frowned. "And abandon you?"

"I'll be fine. I'll find somewhere to have a cup of tea and wait."

He nodded toward the building directly opposite. "Bubble tea?"

"Gods no," I said with a shudder.

He hesitated and then nodded. "Be careful."

I nodded, put the token back into my purse then, after waiting for a car to pass, headed across the road. The gap between the bin and the wall was tighter than I'd thought, and grime smeared across my jacket where my breasts squashed across its metal surface.

The curving cobblestone lane beyond was filled with old take-out containers, cups, and sad-looking weeds. Down the far end was the grimy rear wall of another building with a metal door that had been wedged open. The luscious scents drifting out of it suggested it was a curry kitchen, and my stomach rumbled a reminder that it hadn't been fed in a while.

I walked down, keeping to the side of the lane blocked by the bin so that no one on the main street could see me. Einar's building ended about three quarters of the way down the lane, but a six-foot-tall concrete wall continued on, blocking any access or vision into the rear of the building. I couldn't hear any conversation suggesting my targets were close, but I nevertheless swirled the wind into the rear courtyard, just to be certain. She came back empty of activity or sound.

I looked toward the street to double-check I couldn't be seen. I'd vaguely agreed to remain in the lane and keep safe, but that wasn't going to get me answers. I leapt up, grabbed the top of the wall, then slung one leg over and hung there for a second or two while I waited to see if anyone spotted me. There was no reaction, so I dropped down, my fingers briefly sweeping the gritty ground as I caught my balance. The courtyard was small—probably no more than ten by ten—with two rather grubby-looking plastic chairs sitting close to the junction of the building and the wall. The ground around them was littered with cigarette butts.

There were no windows along the back of the building, and the wooden door had seen better days. I padded across and pressed my hand against the wood. Its song was barely audible through the layers of paint and neglect. I deepened the connection, pushing past the surface music until the building's interconnected network of power and song appeared in my mind's eye. I slipped along the golden arteries that bound the building together, using the highway as a means to understand the building's layout and, more importantly, uncover where my two targets were. After a moment, I found them both in the front half of the building. There was no one else present, but that didn't mean the back half was unguarded. It was a witch's place of business, after all.

I pulled my knives from my purse and strapped them on. While there was every chance I wouldn't need them, the last thing I wanted to do if I came under attack was fish around in my purse for a weapon.

I drew one blade and lightly touched its tip to the doorhandle. There was no reaction, which meant there wasn't even a minor entry warning spell attached. Surprising, although given the amount of cigarette butts lying about, maybe he only activated his protections out of hours. It'd be far easier than having to weave in multiple exceptions, I supposed.

I resheathed the knife, then carefully opened the door and peered inside. The long hallway beyond was shadowed and, as the wood song had said, had three doors running off it. There was a fourth down the far end which led into the main room. I looked up, scanning the ceiling, but couldn't see anything obvious in the way of physical security, and there was no hint of magic.

Maybe he did his main business elsewhere and saw no reason to protect this place. If his window display was anything to go by, this shop catered to tourists more than anything more magically serious.

I slipped inside, keeping my fingertips against the door to stop it from slamming. The air was warm and filled with the rich, bittersweet scent of wormwood. There were no trees nearby, so Einar obviously used it in his spell work.

I crept forward, keeping close to the wall where the floorboards were less creaky. The closer I got to the end door, the more the harsh sound of an argument intruded on the silence—Loudon's more urbane tones juxtaposed against a stridently female one. Not the witch who had made my token, then.

As I drew closer to the closed door, my knives sparked in warning. I stopped and, after a moment, spotted the faint glimmer of spell work. While my knives could undoubtedly take care of it, doing so might give those in the other room warning and time to escape. Right now, knowing what they were discussing was far more important than confronting either of them—especially when I couldn't force the truth from Loudon and had no idea who the woman was, or indeed, whether she too was an elf.

After a brief hesitation, I knelt and pressed my fingers against the floorboards. The voices sounded very close, and the wood song confirmed they were standing a few feet to my right—the woman behind what felt like a counter of some kind while Loudon paced on the other side. There was no one else in the shop, but the front door was now closed, so perhaps they'd wanted to ensure they weren't interrupted.

"This is unacceptable," Loudon was saying. "I was told to come here and retrieve the item. I was told you would have it ready for me. So where *is* it?"

The woman didn't ask the obvious question—what item was he talking about?—which meant she already knew.

"I told you; I don't know. Gannon received a call about an hour ago and left soon after."

Meaning Gannon had received his call around the same time as Loudon had received his text. And yeah, it could have been a coincidence but there were too many of them starting to stack up.

"He left nothing for me?" Loudon growled.

"No. He simply said he would be back soon and to tell you to wait."

"Aside from the fact I'm a busy man, it is dangerous for me to be seen here."

"I *am* aware—"

"No, I don't think you are." His pacing increased, his footsteps echoing angrily across the floorboards. "I got a visit from Meabh's daughter today, and she was searching for information on the shield."

The woman sucked in a breath. "What did you tell her?"

"That the scroll was currently under repair."

"Which is the truth."

"Yes, but—"

"Loudon," the woman cut in harshly, "none of us currently know where the shield is. That's the honest truth, and not even Meabh's daughter could sense a lie where there is none. Now, as to the other matter, I have your number and will call you when he—"

She stopped abruptly and silence fell. Neither of them moved or spoke, not for several seconds. Then I felt it. More importantly, the *knives* felt it. Power surged through the blades and light pulsed from their fullers, seeping out from the top of the sheaths and spinning through the shadows.

They weren't reacting to the usual sort of dark magic that came from a spell or even a blood ceremony, and the source of the foulness wasn't anywhere within this building.

But it was a force I'd felt twice now in as many days.

The elf with the ruby was here, and he was about to destroy this building.

"Oh, fuck," the woman said. "Run."

"What—" Loudon said, confusion evident.

"Go or fucking die," the woman growled.

Loudon immediately turned and ran, a bell chiming wildly into the tension-filled air as he flung the door open. As his weight disappeared from the song of the floorboards, the woman ran for the door I stood behind. With no chance to retreat or hide, I simply pressed back against the wall as she flung the door open, stretching but not snapping the spell threads surrounding it. She took a step, saw me, and stopped, her eyes widening.

"There's no time to explain who I am or why I'm here." I grabbed her wrist. "We need to get the fuck out of here before the madman armed with that ruby unleashes its power."

I turned and ran, dragging her for several steps before she obviously decided the threat behind her was greater than the threat gripping her arm. The dangerous energy coming from the ruby increased, and my knives burned against my thighs. I was tempted to reach for one but knew I'd risk the woman balking and that could mean death for us both.

I reached the external door and punched it open with enough force to smash back against the rendered wall, sending bits of concrete and pale dust flying.

We were three steps into the courtyard when the ruby's power was unleashed. With a huge *whoomph*, the building at our back exploded and sent us both flying.

CHAPTER
NINE

I SLAMMED INTO THE BRICK WALL ON THE FAR SIDE OF THE courtyard so hard, it knocked the air from my lungs and made my head reel.

I fell in a heap to the ground and weakly flung my arms over my head, battling to breathe, to think, as a rain of concrete, metal, and wood debris fell all around us.

It was all I could hear, all I could feel, for too many minutes.

Then, as the rain eased, I smelled the smoke—a thick, acidic, and unnatural scent. Multiple alarms were sounding, many of them from cars, and screams of pain and confusion rang on the air.

I pried open an eye. There was nothing left of the little building. Nothing except uneven piles of stone, broken fingers of wood that reached for the sky, and green flames that burned unnaturally between the two. The woman who'd worked in the shop lay several yards away to my left. Like me, she'd huddled close to protect herself, so I couldn't see if she had any injuries, but she was at least breathing.

I returned my gaze to what was left of the building. I

hadn't thought to look for the red-haired elf here in Swansea, and I guess *that* was a stupid mistake, given it was blatantly obvious now that this wasn't *just* about revenge. They were getting rid of anyone they'd had dealings with or who had information about the rubies or the shield.

Why else would he have targeted Kaitlyn and now Loudon?

Fuck, Loudon...

I pushed into a sitting position. A multitude of aches immediately sprang to life, and I bit back a groan. Splinters of concrete, wood, and slate fell from my clothes and hair, but there was no blood amongst that rain, and that was always a bonus—though I'd undoubtedly have a wild array of bruises down my spine tomorrow if I didn't get to a fae medic today.

I dug out my phone from my battered purse and quickly sent a text to Eljin, letting him know what had happened, that I was okay, but he needed to grab Loudon ASAP and get him somewhere safe because there was now a very large target on his back.

As I hit the send button, the other woman sat up and swore profusely. I shoved my phone away and scooted over to her. She looked as grimy as I felt, but her face was pale and sweaty, her eyes slits of pain, and she was nursing a wrist that looked broken.

"What's your name?" I stripped off my jacket, which had been torn in multiple spots, providing solid evidence of just how close I'd come to being hurt, then unsheathed a knife and hacked off a long strip of material.

"Margaret. Margaret Falconer," she hissed as I carefully slid her arm into my makeshift sling. "I'm guessing you'll be Meabh's daughter."

"Yes. How did you know her?"

"Had some dealings with her over the years. She paid good money for advice." She squinted up at me. Despite the pain, avarice glinted in her murky brown eyes. "I expect nothing less from the daughter."

"The rate of pay depends on what you have to say."

She laughed, though it ended in a serious, hacking cough that suggested she might be the one responsible for all the butts.

"I'm thinking, given what Loudon was saying in there, that what I have to say is something you very much want to hear."

I was briefly tempted to enforce compliance, but if Mom had worked with her on any sort of semi-regular basis, then maybe she was a resource I needed to keep onside.

"Did your boss ever work with her?"

"Gannon?" She laughed, then coughed again. "He avoided her like the plague. Had too many secrets he feared she might wheedle out of him. Spent years developing a spell to protect him from her pixie wiles."

"Did it work?"

"Doubt it, given he'd be selling it at huge margins if it did."

The sharpening sound of sirens had me glancing toward the broken building again. Though there was no sign as yet of anyone trying to enter it—no doubt because of the green flames—it surely wouldn't be too long before someone thought to come around the back. I needed to be gone before then.

"What sort of payment rate are we talking about?"

"Usually a grand a pop, but in this case, because some bastard tried to kill me, I'll halve it."

I couldn't help smiling. "Quarter it, and I'll give you the name of the person who tried to kill you."

"You'd be telling me something I already know. I've felt that sort of energy once before, when we sold the ruby to that elf."

My pulse rate picked up. "Are we talking about the shield's ruby?"

"Of course."

"And is the elf's name Ka-hal Lewis?"

"No, Keelakm Montraie."

The name scratched at memories that refused to provide any information. "So, he also has a ruby?"

She frowned. "What do you mean, also? We only had the one."

"Then you've never dealt with Lewis?"

"No."

There were official sounding voices out on the street now, though the ferocity of the flames consuming the building's remains continued to keep everyone at bay. I had minutes left, if that, to get my answers and leave.

"Is Keelakm slim with pale hair and blue eyes?"

"Yes, although I'm sure you're aware that's a description fitting the majority of elves out there."

I touched my cheek. "He has a horseshoe-shaped scar here."

"He certainly does."

I smiled, swung my purse around, and pulled out the token. "Is this one of yours?"

She barely even glanced at it. "One of Gannon's, yes."

"I don't suppose you can remember who had it made, and why?"

A smile touched her lips. "Are we in agreement on payment terms?"

I sighed. "Yes."

"Then it was made for Loudon so he could distract a collector up Ben Nevis way."

My pulse rate leapt again. "Biran Gratham?"

"That's the man. We'd discovered he'd gotten hold of a ruby with almost the same energy signature as the one we'd sold."

"*Almost* the same?"

She nodded. "Ours felt... heavier, if that makes sense. Like it was weighted with steel and iron rather than the fierier touch I felt today."

Suggesting it might be the stone that gave the power of the smith rather than the one that turned the earth liquid. Whether that was a good thing or not very much depended on what Keelakm intended to do with it.

That they hadn't yet called it into action was rather ominous, however.

"According to my sources," I said, "none of the shield's rubies have ever hit the black market—"

She smiled. "I never said we purchased it, and it certainly never hit the market, black or regular. In fact, I doubt the collector is even aware the ruby he so proudly displays is nothing more than a synth."

Meaning they'd somehow magicked the real one out, which would have taken time, effort, and some serious spell work, as most collections—private or public—usually had a thick weave of spells in place to counter any prospect of magical theft.

"I take it Loudon's efforts to distract Gratham and steal the second ruby were unsuccessful?"

She nodded. "Loudon found some records that said the ruby had been purchased three days before he got there."

Meaning he'd likely been responsible for the utter mess we'd found Gratham's office in. "I don't suppose either he or Gannon mentioned who purchased it? Or perhaps even their contact details? Loudon obviously wouldn't have left that information there."

"He didn't, but neither he nor Gannon gave me the records to trace."

"And they never spoke about it?"

She grinned, revealing stained teeth. "Not within my hearing. Not as far as they were aware, anyway."

I raised an eyebrow. "Meaning they did speak about it?"

"Yes, in truth, they never mentioned the name, only a location—Deva."

I guess *that* wasn't so surprising, given Deva seemed to be ground zero when it came to their revenge plans. "I don't suppose you overheard an address?"

She hesitated. "No, but he did say something about it not being far from the Fae Museum, so he might pop in and see what he could find out about the shield."

"It wouldn't have been much, I can assure you of that."

"Not much would have given us more than we currently have."

A metallic squeal rent the air. I glanced around and lightly spun the wind toward it. She came back filled with whispers of voices and movement coming from the top end of the laneway. A number of people were attempting to move the metal bin and gain access. I had to hurry things up if I wanted to avoid another round of tedious police questioning.

I glanced back to Margaret. "What was the package Loudon was sent here to retrieve?"

"Gannon never said anything about a package, though we *are* waiting on the arrival of a scroll. He just said to keep Loudon here as long as I could." She sniffed. "That bastard set me up to die, didn't he?"

"Seems like he might have." I paused briefly as another metallic squeal echoed. "Look, I need to go, but—"

"You're not going anywhere without me, young lady. You ain't the only one wanting to avoid chatting to the cops."

I motioned to her arm. "You're not going to get over the wall with that."

"Don't need to, do I? You think a man like Gannon hasn't got an escape route built into all his premises?" She made a "come here" motion with her good hand. "Help me up."

I grabbed my jacket and pushed to my feet, doing my best to ignore the various aches that instantly sprang to life, then caught Margaret's good hand and helped her upright.

"This way," she said, and kept a fierce hold of my fingers as she limped toward the spike-topped wall dividing this courtyard from the next.

She didn't stop in front of it. She simply walked straight into it. It was an illusion. A solid, very real-looking illusion.

Its magic briefly pressed against me, but the knives remained inert, and, after a beat, we stepped into a narrow cobblestoned lane that ran along the rear of the remaining buildings. I glanced behind me. The wall looked as solid and as real on this side as it had the other. I cautiously reached out and touched it. It even felt like concrete.

"The magic is programmed to respond only to me or Gannon," she said, releasing me and moving on. "That's why I had to hold your hand as we went through. You wouldn't have gotten over it—those spikes are programed to be deadly, let me assure you of that."

I glanced up. The metal tips glinted ominously in the sullen glow of the green fire. I returned my gaze to hers. "We need to get you to a fae hosp—"

"No need. My wife can fix me up just fine. She's a healer, you see."

"She's an elf?"

I couldn't help the surprise in my voice, and her smile held a touch of bitterness. "Half elf, and unwelcome in their circles, even if she has the healing gift."

"Sorry," I said, even though there was a long history of that sort of discrimination. Elves might be randy bastards, but for the most part, they didn't welcome half-breeds into their communities or their lives. Or, at least, the highborn didn't. The foresters and servant class were bit more open to the prospect. Certainly, Darby's family wouldn't have any objections to her marrying Lugh, especially now that her older brother had provided an heir to carry on the family name.

Of course, they'd also had years upon years of her being very clear about her intentions when it came to my brother. I just hoped that now their relationship had eventuated it would work out for them both.

"No need for you to be sorry," Margaret was saying. "It is what it is."

I dumped the jacket in one of the half-filled bins we passed, then asked, "Why isn't she fixing that cough of yours?"

"Because," she said, her testy tone suggesting it was a bone of contention between them, "I refuse to give up smoking like she wants, so she leaves me suffering the consequences."

"I'm gathering said consequences would not be allowed to precede too far."

She sniffed. "*That* is something neither of us have discussed. But elves, even if half-breeds, can be bloody-minded sometimes."

They certainly could be. Even Darby, who was one of the loveliest people I knew and who I adored like a sister, could be rather single-minded when she decided on a particular course of action. Even Lugh had eventually succumbed to the force of her determination—though I didn't for a second think he had any regrets about finally accepting the inevitable.

Once we'd reached the end of the lane, Margaret pulled a set of keys from her pocket and handed them to me.

"My car is the old Toyota across the road. We only live ten minutes away, and we can talk more there."

I did my best to ignore the inner voice suggesting I might possibly be stepping into a trap. I'd sensed no lie in what she'd said about Mom, or anything else for that matter. That in itself wasn't a guarantee of safety, of course, but it was very doubtful she—or Gannon, or anyone they might be working with—would go to this extent to entrap me. Especially when they couldn't have known we'd follow Loudon to that shop.

I opened the passenger door, helped her in, and then ran around to the driver's side. My phone pinged as I was about to climb in, and I hesitated, grabbing it from my purse to check the screen.

Eljin had Loudon "in hand" and was taking him somewhere safe. I sent back a quick "be careful," then tucked the phone away and climbed in.

"Where to?" I said, starting the engine.

She gave me the address, and my heart rate did another of those zooms. It was the same address that Loudon's maid had messaged me through the song.

It seemed Fate was having a grand old time weaving her threads into my life today.

I waited for a car to pass then pulled out. "Does your wife work for Loudon?"

"Yes." Margaret glanced at me, amusement briefly breaking the pain haunting her expression. "He and Gannon might be partners, but Gannon doesn't trust him, and he pays Jaikyl well to be his spy. Why?"

"I saw her today. She said she wanted to speak to me."

"Jaikyl doesn't speak. She's mute."

"She signed a message through the song of the wood." I briefly glanced at her. "I don't suppose you know what it might be about?"

Margaret shrugged. "I daresay we'll both find out when we get home."

I guessed we would.

Despite the traffic, we quickly left the city center behind us. I couldn't see anyone obviously following us, but with the heaviness of the traffic it was hard to be sure. Still, there was no one behind us when we turned into Margaret's street, and no cars had cruised past by the time we'd parked outside Margaret's small two-up, two-down. A curtain covering the downstairs window moved briefly, then, a heartbeat later, the green-painted front door opened and the woman I'd seen at Loudon's appeared.

The air of downtrodden meekness that had surrounded her there had completely disappeared here.

She ran toward us, her fingers flying. I had no idea what she was saying, but Margaret laughed. "I'm fine, really I am. Just a broken—" She stopped, watching Jaikyl's still flying fingers. "Yes, there was an explosion at the shop, and no, it was no accident."

Jaikyl glanced at me rather pointedly.

I held up my hands. "I wasn't responsible for the explosion; it was courtesy of the man who has caused two similar explosions in Deva. But we need to move this conversation inside, because it might not be safe out here."

If we *had* been followed, it likely wouldn't be safe inside, either, but I didn't bother adding that.

Jaikyl hesitated then wrapped an arm around her partner's waist and helped her inside. I followed them in, then closed and locked the door behind us. It wouldn't stop a ruby-wielding elf intent on destruction, but it would at least give anyone else pause, even if only for the few minutes it took them to break in.

Those few minutes would give us time to escape.

I followed them down the short hall and then into a living dining area. The kitchen lay to the left, positioned behind the hallway stairs. Jaikyl pulled out a kitchen chair, placed Margaret down, then carefully eased her broken wrist from the sling. Her gaze narrowed and energy rose, a warm caress of healing power that was far softer than the energy Darby raised.

It obviously healed just the same, however, because after a few minutes, color returned to Margaret's cheeks, and she sighed in relief. "Thank you, dear heart."

Jaikyl nodded and glanced at me, one eyebrow raised in question.

I waved her concern away. "I'm fine."

She snorted, moved around the table, and pressed her fingers against my spine. Pain slithered through me, and she snorted again. Her healing energy rose, and the pain faded away.

"Thank you," I said, when she stepped away.

She nodded and moved back around the table, once again speaking with her hands. Margaret watched then glanced at me. "You should go have a quick shower while we boil the kettle and make a pot of tea—or coffee, if that's your poison of choice. Jaikyl also wants to assure you that *this* time your drink won't contain a truth potion."

"Tea would be good." I pushed to my feet. While I didn't have a change of clothes here, it'd certainly be good to wash the worst of the grime away. I doubted they intended me any harm, but on the off chance I was wrong, well, I still had my knives. "But why would Loudon instruct you to give us a truth potion? And *how* did he instruct you, given all he did was ring that bell?"

"The bell is the key," Jaikyl said through Margaret. "He only rings it when he wishes to pry information from his guests."

"It's why he's such a successful collector, and why Gannon is a well-regarded reseller," Margaret added. "People come to Loudon for advice and information, and he instead bleeds them dry."

"Surely people would realize—"

"No," Jaikyl said through Margaret. "By the time they leave his house, all memory of the episode is gone. They just remember whatever it is Loudon wished them to remember."

"That's one hell of a truth elixir."

"He can afford to pay for the best." Margaret motioned in the general direction of the stairs. "There's clean face flannels and towels in the linen closet, and the bathroom is the first door on the left at the top."

I thanked them and headed up. The first-floor landing was small, with a bedroom to the right, the bathroom to the left, and, directly in front, a sliding door fronting the small linen closet.

I grabbed a flannel and towel, found a fresh cake of soap in the bathroom, and then stripped off, shoving my knives back into my purse but keeping it within easy reach. Once

I'd shaken out the worst of the dust and remaining debris from my clothes in the shower cubicle, I switched on the water and had a quick shower. Ten minutes later, feeling fresher and cleaner despite my worse-for-wear clothing, I headed back downstairs.

Jaikyl placed a large pot of tea—which was covered with a cheery-looking knitted cozy—and three mugs on the table, then sat down. Margaret followed with a jug of milk and an opened packet of Jaffa Cakes and sat beside her wife. She slid the packet across to me, then poured the tea.

I plucked a Jaffa Cake free. "What did you want to see me about, Jaikyl?"

"It was about your mom," she signed. "Loudon lied about her reason for being there."

"I gathered that." I bit into the orangy chocolate goodness, and my stomach rumbled in appreciation. Almost getting blown up really *didn't* affect my appetite. But then, few things could. "Did Loudon drug her?"

Jaikyl smiled and through Margaret said, "He tried. She, like you, did not drink."

I wondered if the wood song had warned her something was wrong, or if she'd simply sensed the oddness in his behavior. She'd always been far better at reading people than me, and she'd had the extra advantage of knowing him. "Was she there about the shield and its rubies?"

"No," Jaikyl said. "Something called Ninkil's Harpē."

I just about choked, and hastily took a sip of tea. "Are you sure?"

Jaikyl gave me a look that suggested even *asking* that question was offensive. I held up a hand. "Sorry, it's just that I hadn't even heard of the harpē until yesterday, and now it seems to be everywhere. Did Loudon know anything?"

She wavered a hand, then signed. I glanced at Margaret, who said, "He told her he didn't, but he lied. He rang someone almost as soon as she left, letting them know."

"You don't know who?"

She shook her head again. Frustration stirred, so thick that the bitter taste of bile briefly rose. It was always one step forward, two steps back when it came to finding any information about what had led to Mom's murder. "And was this eight or nine months ago, as Loudon has said?"

"Yes," Margaret said, watching her wife sign. "After the call, he went into his vault and destroyed several oldish minute books. I don't know what they contained, as I don't have access to the vault. But it was broken into several days later."

My heart skipped several beats again. It was definitely getting a good workout today. "Do you know by who?"

"No. But the power was cut, the backup generator failed to cut in, and the protection spells were sliced apart."

Sliced apart... by knives capable of countering any sort of magic, perhaps? The same knives I still wore?

"Was anything stolen? Did Loudon report either the break-in or the theft?"

"To the police? No. But he did ring someone. He was, in fact, rather frantic. Apparently the scrolls taken contained information regarding Ninkil, whoever he might be."

Mom. It had to be. It was too much of a coincidence, given what Beira had said about her having unsettling visions about the rat god. She'd come to Loudon for advice and had known he was lying, even without using her pixie magic.

"Did he mention the harpē?"

"Only to assure whoever was on the other end that there was no mention of it in the scrolls taken. It would be reasonable to assume *that* information was contained in the ones he destroyed."

There couldn't have been too much information in them, given Beira's belief Ninkil's people continued to search for the harpē. But maybe that *wasn't* what had been destroyed. Maybe, given what Jaikyl had said about them being minute books, they were far more recent records—perhaps ones that contained the details of all those who belonged to the rat god club. It *would* make sense to destroy them if they'd been worried about Mom getting too close, especially given they hadn't stolen the hoard at that point.

So, if Mom *did* steal the scrolls, where were they? I hadn't seen any lying about at the tavern, so maybe she'd checked them and then handed them on to either the council or perhaps even the museum. I'd better ask Lugh about them when I saw him again—he'd at least know if the latter had happened.

"How did you manage to overhear any of this?" I asked curiously. "I'd have thought someone in Loudon's line of work wouldn't allow any of his employees anywhere near secure areas."

"He doesn't," Jaikyl said. "But one of the benefits of being a mute is the fact most people tend to think it extends to hearing and sight. I also know most of his access codes. I can't get into the vault, of course, because he uses an eye scanner, but I can get close enough when he's inside to hear his side of any conversation. He rarely locks the door, you see. Got caught in there once and had to hire a locksmith and coder to break him out."

I couldn't help smiling. He didn't sound like the sharpest knife in the drawer, but I guessed even the most intelligent man could get caught by circumstances occasionally. "Was Gannon aware of Loudon's destruction?"

"He never mentioned it to me," Margaret said. "It's possible, though, given they've been working together for a very long time."

It was also possible that Gannon had no idea Loudon was a rat god devotee. I mean, why else would he have been keeping the minute records?

Which meant, of course, that Loudon and I needed to have a serious conversation. Eljin's seductions plans for the night were becoming less and less likely to happen.

"Did Mom happen to stop by Gannon's shop any time around her visit to Loudon, either before or after?"

"Not that I'm aware of, and I work there most days."

"What do you actually do?" I asked curiously. "You're obviously more than a mere storekeep selling trinkets to tourists."

"I'm their researcher. I have a gift for talking to those who once were."

I raised my eyebrows. "You're a medium?"

"I am far more than a *mere* medium," she retorted. "Mediums are limited by time. I am not."

"Meaning you've spoken to the man who wrote Loudon's scroll?"

"I don't speak to them as such. I use them more as a..." She hesitated. "A speaker, I guess you could say. Or perhaps an amplifier. I can see the wisps of their spirits and, through that, their memories. But it is their resonance—the timbre of their being, which I hear in much the same manner you pixies can hear the music of wood and trees— that enables me to trace particular items or relics. A maker's resonance always sticks to their creations, and it is a song I trace if still exists in this world."

That was one hell of a talent. No wonder Mom had been willing to pay her fees. In fact, a grand was probably cheap considering the possibilities. "Wouldn't the resonance fade over time? Wood song does."

"Only if its nature has been severely compromised, is that not true?"

"Yes, but—" I stopped. I guessed if an old building could hold its song after centuries of human use and alterations, then a scroll created by human hands could certainly hold a resonance, however faint it might be. "I take it this talent only applies to things created by humans, not gods?"

She nodded. "But man—human or fae—has a long history of writing things down. Even the elves, who have guarded the relics for eons, made long lists that can be tracked all these centuries later."

"I take it that's how you found the ruby in France?"

She nodded again. "I tuned in to a bibliothecary once responsible for recording artifacts. He had a love of precious stones and often handled the ruby Keelakm commissioned us to find."

"Only that one?"

"Unfortunately, yes. I had no sense of the others, so I do not know whether he simply didn't risk handling the others or if they were already missing by then."

"I take it you have been searching for someone who might have handled either the other rubies or even the shield?"

"Yes, but it's a bit like spitting into the wind. You never know exactly where it's going to land."

"It" being her talent, obviously.

So where had Gratham found the ruby he'd presumably sold to Ka-hal? And where the hell had Gilda's come from?

"When did Keelakm commission Gannon and Loudon to find the ruby?"

She wrinkled her nose. "Three or four months ago."

Before Gilda had been murdered, then. "What about the other two? He never mentioned them?"

"No." She paused. "When he arrived to pick up the ruby, there was a man—an elf—with him. I remember him because he had red hair, which is unusual in an elf."

It certainly was. It also meant my guess that Keelakm and Ka-hal were partners in crime had been spot on. "Did he touch the ruby? You mentioned hearing its song once before."

She nodded. "It didn't respond to him, though, only to Keelakm."

Which suggested the rubies were capable of picking their wielders—but was that any surprise? We were talking about items made by a god who delighted in destruction—he'd surely ensure only a mind with similar aspirations could wield his weapons.

"Is Keelakm someone you've dealt with before?"

"No, but clients such as him come recommended via a vetting source we trust."

"I take it you have Keelakm's contact details but said details are now as destroyed as that building."

She smiled. "Yes, but I can give you the contact details of our vetter."

I raised my eyebrows. "Why would you do that? What happened to protecting your sources and all that?"

"May I remind you that someone just tried to blow me up? Cherry did the background checks on him, so any loyalty I have to her is now null and void. And it's not like I'm feeling very charitable toward Gannon right now, either, given he basically hung me out to dry along with his partner."

To be fair to Cherry, elves could be mighty persuasive

when they wanted to be and could certainly work any human system of checks and balances to their favor. Gannon, however, was another matter. Although it had to be asked, why would he waste a talent like Margaret? As far as I knew, her tracing skills were rare, and it had obviously made both him and Loudon a good chunk of change over the years.

"I don't suppose you know who made that call to Gannon, do you?"

"No."

"What about the scroll Loudon purchased from Kaitlyn? He said it was being restored, but is that true?"

"Also no."

"Then it *is* at his place?"

She snorted. "Not when he and Gannon went halves in its purchase. Once something disappears into Loudon's vaults, it rarely comes out. There was too much money on the table for Gannon to risk that happening with this scroll."

"Then where is it? Not in the shop, I hope."

"I can't tell you where it is. Gannon never said, and they never got around to asking me to do a spirit seeking on it." She sniffed. "And it's not like I'm going to help them now."

"Then what will you do?"

She grinned. "There's plenty of brokers wanting a woman of my particular talents. Hell, Kaitlyn herself made an offer only a few months ago. Might take her up on it now, even if it does mean a move to Deva."

I hoped she did. Asking her for help and information would be far easier if she were living close to home.

"Can I get Cherry's details? And Gannon's? I need to speak to him."

"Can I have my payment? I'm apparently unemployed right now, and I need the cash."

Jaikyl signed something, and Margaret replied, her fingers moving so fast they were almost a blur. Jaikyl sniffed, suggesting she didn't agree, but then shrugged. Margaret returned her gaze to me and said, "Five hundred, as agreed?"

I reached for my phone, then entered her bank details and made the transfer. After viewing the receipt, Margaret retrieved a bit of paper and a pen from the sideboard, wrote down two addresses, then slid it across the table to me. Unsurprisingly, Gannon lived in Swansea, but Cherry was stationed much closer to home.

"Liverpool is a long way from Swansea," I said in surprise.

"In the age of the internet, distance no longer presents a problem, and Liverpool *is* considered a center of arts and culture."

All true, but for some of us, face-to-face would always be better. It was far easier to judge truth from lie in person.

"Just a word of warning on Gannon's new place," she said. "The area is undergoing serious development and refurbishment, and it'll probably be something of a ghost town at this hour."

I nodded, finished my tea, and then rose. "Thanks for the help, ladies."

Jaikyl signed through her partner, "Welcome, good luck with your hunt, and be careful."

"Given the man behind the attack today seems intent on killing anyone with knowledge of the rubies, I'm not the one who needs to be careful. In fact, it'd be best if you both disappeared for the next week or so."

"Loudon will expect—"

"Loudon is being escorted to a safe place as we speak, so he likely won't be needing Jaikyl's services for a while, anyway." I picked up my purse and moved toward the hallway. "Oh, while I remember—what does Gannon look like?"

"He's a stocky bald man with a ginger beard and a penchant for colorful cravats."

"Hard to pick out in a crowd, then," I said, amused.

"Indeed," Margaret said with a laugh. She plucked a coat from the hall stand and handed it to me. "Here, you'll probably need this more than we will. You can return it next time you see us."

"That's presuming there will be a next time."

"Your mom once said the same thing, but we ended up seeing her at least three or four times a year. I suspect you'll be no different if you're now stepping into her relic-hunting shoes."

"I'd like to say you're wrong, because relic hunting isn't really a calling of mine, but—" I shrugged. "Thanks for the coat."

She nodded and opened the door. I bid them both goodbye and headed out. The wind was sharp and cold, and the skies heavy with the threat of rain. I shivered my way into the coat, then, after retrieving my phone, slung my purse over my shoulder. A quick check on Google Maps told me Gannon's place was too far to walk, so I called an Uber. Eight minutes, came the message back. I stepped into a nearby bus shelter to get out of the wind and then called Eljin. It rang for a very long time before he answered.

"Sorry, Bethany," he said, his voice almost inaudible over the thumping background noise. "Left the phone in my coat and didn't hear it until it was almost too late."

"Where are you?" I asked curiously. "There's a hell of a racket happening behind you."

"I'm in an old auto repair shop. Or rather, above it. The noise is a backup generator that kicked in a few minutes ago. The damn power is out in the area, apparently."

"Why the hell are you at an auto repair shop? Did you have an accident?"

"It's owned by one of Loudon's friends, and he uses it to store some of his larger collections in."

"In an auto *repair* shop? Surely a place like that wouldn't do much to keep his precious relics in good condition."

"The run-down state of the building is merely a front. Trust me, it's humidity and temperature controlled and chock-full of all sorts of security measures."

"I take it this is his safe place?"

"Yeah. It's not under his name, and he swears few people knows he even uses it."

"You'd better ask him if Gannon does, because it's likely that bastard set him up."

"How do you know? Was Gannon in the shop?"

"No, he'd well and truly gone by the time I crept in."

"I seem to remember you promising to stay in the lane." His voice was dry, and I grinned.

"I didn't actually say yes. I said maybe."

He snorted. "Then why do you think Gannon set Loudon up? They're very successful business partners, if what Loudon has been saying is anything to go by."

"He's been talking?" I asked in surprise.

"Well, not about anything we'd find interesting."

"You haven't tried to read him?"

"Hard to read someone who is constantly pacing. He's

also frightened and on edge, and that never helps. And you didn't answer the question."

"What quest— Oh, yeah. Sorry, I heard some of the conversation Loudon had with the woman running the store before the ruby's energy rose and I got the hell out of there."

"Ah, that makes sense." He paused. "Did anyone get hurt?"

"I don't know, because I didn't stick around long enough to find out. But there wasn't much left of the shop."

"And the woman who worked there?"

"Again, I just don't know." I felt bad about lying, but the fewer people who knew she survived, the better.

He grunted. "Where are you now?"

"Waiting for an Uber so I can head over to Gannon's place."

"How'd you get his address?" There was surprise, and maybe, just maybe, a hint of suspicion in his voice. Or was I reading too much into it again?

"Googled it," I said with a somewhat forced laugh. "It might not be our Gannon, of course, but still worth checking out. How long are you going to be?"

"Don't know—maybe another twenty minutes or so? Loudon wants me to check his security systems—"

"Why? You're an antiquarian, not a security systems specialist."

"Yes, but one by necessity leads to some expertise in the other." His voice was dry. "If I can't get through it, then he should be fairly safe. If I can, then he's agreed to move."

"And, in the process of checking, he will calm down and you might finally get a reading on him."

"That's the hope."

A white Nissan came around the corner, its number

plate matching that of my Uber. "Listen, my ride is here. Where do you want to meet?"

"Are you hungry?"

"Always."

"I meant for food."

"Oh, so did I," I said, with just enough huskiness to belie my words.

"So, Chinese served on a big soft bed?"

"Sounds perfect. Just remember to send me the address so I can meet you there."

"Will do." He paused. "Be careful if the address does belong to our Gannon. He might also be a marked man."

"I know, and I will. See you soon."

"Looking forward to it," he replied, and hung up.

I hopped into the Nissan, gave the driver Gannon's address, and then sent Sgott a text, giving him the information about Cherry. Given she might well do a runner once she heard of events here, it would be easier and quicker if he sent his people over.

By the time we'd gotten through the traffic, night had settled in. I climbed out, slung my bag across my shoulder, and studied the building in front of me. It wasn't, as I'd been expecting, a house, but rather a five-story apartment block built right next to the concrete breakwater wall. The buildings on either side were surrounded by scaffolding, and the houses behind me were in various stages of completion. Lights burned brightly at either end of the curving street, but there was nothing but darkness in the middle. None of the other buildings in the immediate area were lit, and even Gannon's was mostly dark. Margaret hadn't been kidding when she'd said it'd be something of a ghost town at this hour.

Just as well the damn Annwfyn hadn't been active lately.

I dug out the note and checked if she'd written down the apartment number. She hadn't, so maybe she didn't know. I frowned and headed toward the glass front door. It was locked, so I studied the intercom on the left. There were nine buttons in all, meaning there were two apartments on each floor except for the top one, which was a large penthouse. There were only two names listed on the buzzer, however—a K and R Richardson, who lived on the ground floor, and Gannon, who'd claimed the penthouse.

I pressed the buzzer, waited for several seconds for a response, then pressed it again.

I frowned, moved back to the middle of the road, and looked up. The light situation hadn't changed in the few minutes since I'd last looked up, so either he wasn't there, or the sheer size of the apartment meant I wouldn't see any light leakage coming from any of the rooms on the other side of the building.

Several cyclists zoomed toward me, their flashing bike lights bright in the shadows otherwise clinging to the street. I quickly stepped off the road and walked around to the sea-facing side of the building. The wind hit ferociously, and my steps briefly faltered before I caught my balance. The heavy scent of rain filled my nostrils and, overhead, thunder rumbled ominously. There was no hint of Beira in that rumble, but I nevertheless felt her frustration.

Or maybe the storm was simply echoing mine. It wasn't as if things had gone exactly to plan so far today.

I pulled out my phone and glanced at the time. Close to twenty minutes had slipped by, so maybe I should just give up and head for the treehouse Eljin had booked for the night. Maybe hot food and hotter sex would not only clear my mind but clarify what my next step should be.

I returned to the front of the building. As I neared the street, a cab pulled up on the opposite side of the road, and a big man with a ginger beard climbed out.

Gannon.

It was fucking Gannon.

I quickly stepped into the shadows, and not a moment too soon. His gaze swept the street, his expression cautious, wary. With good reason, really. I had no idea who'd given him a warning to leave, but I doubted it was Ka-hal. It made absolutely no sense to kill one partner and leave the other free to talk to the police and IIT.

If these explosions *were* about Ka-hal erasing everyone who knew anything about his recent history, that is.

The cab driver must have said something, because Gannon ducked down to reply before slamming the cab's door closed and stepping back. As the cab left, he scanned the area again, then moved onto the road.

Just as a white van screamed around the left corner and accelerated toward him.

Gannon threw up a hand against the glare of headlights, but barely had time to do anything else. The van hit him with bone-destroying force and sent him flying up and over its roof.

The vehicle didn't brake, didn't stop. It simply swept toward me, its windscreen shattered, and blood and gods only knew what else smeared over what remained.

Then, for one second, time seemed to slow, and the driver's gaze met mine.

Ka-hal.

It was fucking Ka-hal.

The bastard had obviously followed Gannon... or had

he? He'd said on that rooftop near Kaitlyn's that it always paid to keep track of all players, especially the more dangerous ones. What if he hadn't meant Cynwrig, as I'd presumed?

What if he'd meant *me*?

Him tracking me wouldn't really explain his appearance at Kaitlyn's, given he was there before us, but it could certainly explain his random appearance here. Maybe he was simply getting rid of anyone I talked to about the rubies before they could speak to someone more official.

But if he was tracking me, how was he doing it? Granted, white vans were a dime a dozen in this country, but surely I'd have noticed if there'd been one constantly tucked behind us. I'd been checking fairly regularly.

Then another memory rose—a needle, punching into my skin a heartbeat before teeth had ripped through my shoulder.

Fuck, had that needle injected a bio-tracker? They were a type of miniaturized internal medical scanner adapted to use the body's natural electromagnetic field to fuel a constant, low-level but unique signal that could be tracked. While Cynwrig had said they were expensive to purchase and not often found on the open market, neither Ka-hal nor his light elf partner seemed strapped for cash *or* contacts.

If I *had* been bio-tagged, then I couldn't afford to meet Eljin or anyone else before I got the thing removed.

Time snapped back into place, and the van accelerated toward the next corner. I dragged out my phone and managed to photograph its rear end before it disappeared completely. The image would undoubtedly be blurry, but hopefully Sgott or whoever his IIT counterpart down here was would be able to clean it up enough to get the number plate.

Although given Ka-hal had made no attempt to conceal his presence—and why was that? —I daresay the van was not only stolen but would be dumped within minutes. Still, if luck decided to play nice, they might be able to lift a careless fingerprint or two.

I shoved my phone away and ran down to Gannon. He was a crumpled mess. One arm was twisted unnaturally behind his back, and the lower part of his left leg pointed off at a weird angle to his knee. His face was so severely scraped, a chunk of beard was missing, and blood oozed from a thick cut just behind his ear.

But he was alive and breathing, and that was a miracle given the speed at which he'd been hit.

The babble of approaching voices had me glancing around. An older couple were coming out of Gannon's apartment building.

"Call an ambulance," I said. "He needs help fast."

"How bad is it?" the woman asked as the man hobbled back inside.

I knelt and touched Gannon's neck; his pulse was thin and thready, and his breathing labored but rapid. He might be conscious, but death was closing in. Her darkness swirled on the wind.

"Very bad, I'm afraid," I replied absently. Gannon's eyes were fluttering, and he appeared to be mumbling something. I leaned closer and still couldn't quite catch it.

"Do you need help?" the woman said. "Are you a medic?"

I glanced up somewhat impatiently but bit back my angry retort when I saw how pale and frightened she looked. "I'm not a doctor, but even if I were, I don't believe it would help. I think all anyone can do right now is comfort him in his dying moments."

"Oh," she said in a small voice, and wrapped her shawl tighter around her shoulders.

"Go back inside where it's warmer," I said gently. "There's nothing you can do here."

But her presence somewhat hampered what *I* could do.

She hesitated. "Do you need anything. A blanket, perhaps, to keep him warm, while he... you know?"

I did know. "I guess it couldn't hurt."

Once she'd moved back inside, I lightly pressed my fingers against Gannon's neck. His pulse rate was weaker and becoming more erratic. He was running out of time. *I* was running out of time.

I had to do this, even if it was all sorts of wrong to force a dying man to talk.

"Gannon," I said, gently infusing my words with pixie magic, "where is the scroll you and Loudon purchased?"

His mouth moved for several seconds before he was able to say, "Pink... Unit fifteen... Newport."

I had no idea how far Newport was from Swansea, but I knew it wasn't close. "Have you got the keys?"

"Pin," came the whispery response. "Phone."

"You don't know the number?"

He reeled off three numbers before his voice faded, leaving me wondering if that was it or he simply couldn't remember the rest. I mean, he was dying, and there I was forcing him to remember things. Bad things, irrelevant things, at least where life and death was concerned.

I glanced up again, saw that the woman hurrying back with a dark blanket. I rose and met her on the pavement.

"You don't want to come too close. It's... well, he's a mess."

"Oh," she said, in that same small voice. Then she touched my hand lightly. "Are you okay, dear?"

"I'm fine." I let my magic rise again, threading it through the fingers still on my hand. "Go back inside and keep warm."

She nodded, released me, and went in. I quickly returned to Gannon and lightly placed the blanket over his broken body. Then, with my back to the woman's building so they couldn't see what I was doing from any of the windows, I quickly rifled through his pockets until I found his phone. I shoved it into my coat pocket and tried to ignore the wash of guilt. Robbing a dying man wasn't an action to be proud of, but it was nevertheless necessary if we were to bring down his killer.

His breathing had become more labored, and wings of death were now so loud they almost drowned out the howling wail of an approaching siren. I pressed my fingers against his neck again. His pulse was whispery. *May death be kind to his soul...*

I swallowed and said, "Why was Loudon targeted, Gannon?"

"Knew names."

"What names?"

But I knew, even before he replied.

"Ninkilim."

"Were you a devotee?"

"Yes, but not... same extent."

"Who called you and told you to get out of the shop?"

"Tyr..."

His voice faded, and his eyes fluttered open. Just for an instant, recognition sparked.

"Meabh," he whispered. "I'm sorry. So very sorry..."

And with that, death claimed him.

CHAPTER

TEN

Shock held me immobile for too many seconds.

He'd known Mom. More importantly, he'd known what had happened to her. Why else would he have apologized?

I hadn't even thought to question him about her.

Which was stupid. Absolutely *stupid*. For fuck's sake, I'd known Loudon had been friends with her, so why hadn't I taken the next logical step and presumed Gannon would have been too? Margaret might have said he avoided her, but maybe that hadn't always been the case. And maybe he kept attempting to find a spell to counter pixie magic for a damn good reason.

I sat back on my heels and tiredly rubbed my eyes, smearing moisture across my skin. But I wouldn't let those tears fall. I couldn't. Not until her killer was found.

Once I started crying, I might not be able to stop.

I took a deep, quivering breath, and pushed away the regret and inner anger. Short of asking a clairvoyant to contact his soul, any answers he might have given were now out of reach. Better to concentrate on the shield search and the answers we *did* have. Although in truth, half a name didn't really help us all that much. But whoever he was, he held enough power to order a hit on the man who'd been the organization's trusted bookkeeper for a very long time.

Hell, this Tyr might even be the man I'd heard in my visions a few times.

But if he *had* ordered Loudon's death, why hadn't he done so *after* Mom's visit? Why do it now, after mine? From what Jaikyl had said, he'd already destroyed the relevant files, so even if I *had* been able to wrangle a way into his vault, I wouldn't have found much.

Jaikyl... *fuck.*

If Ka-hal *had* followed me here rather than Gannon, then he very likely knew I'd been to Margaret's.

I reclaimed his phone from my pocket, unobtrusively pressed his finger against the scanner, then went through his contacts list until I found Margaret's number.

The call rang out. I left a message, then doubled up, copying her number onto my phone to send a text message.

I shivered, hoping for the best but fearing the worst.

I went back into Gannon's phone and reset the pin and fingerprint scanner, then returned it to my pocket as the sharp sound of sirens drew closer.

They were too late to save Gannon.

Maybe even too late for Margaret and Jaikyl.

I hoped not. Hoped that the traffic remained bad, and that Ka-hal hadn't gotten there yet.

An ambulance pulled to a sharp stop several yards from us, its red and blue lights washing eerily through the darkness. As the crew climbed out, I grabbed my purse and pushed back to sit on the pavement, hugging my knees and watching as they ran over and did their best to revive Gannon.

A cop car pulled up a few seconds later. A small, stout woman with short blonde hair walked toward me while her partner began putting up tape and cones.

"I take it you saw the accident?" the woman asked.

"It wasn't an accident. It was deliberate."

She raised her eyebrow and took out her phone. "What makes you believe that?"

I waited until she'd begun recording. "The fact the driver sped around the corner and accelerated toward Gannon. He didn't try to stop, he didn't try to swerve, he didn't even blast his horn."

"I take it you knew the victim?"

"I knew his first name and his address. I came here to talk to him."

"About what?"

"A scroll he and his partner purchased a few days ago." I squinted up at her. "I took a pic of the van as it drove past. I daresay it's blurry, but you should be able to clean it up enough to get the plate number."

She nodded. "And the driver? Did you see him?"

I nodded and gave her a description. I didn't mention his name. I didn't want to get bogged down with a multitude of questions about how I knew *that* and what my relationship was with him.

"Did anyone else witness the event?"

"There's an old couple in the building behind me who came out when the hit-and-run happened—the gentleman placed the call—but I don't know how much they saw."

She took my name and contact details and asked me to send her the photo. When I had, she added they'd be in contact if they needed further information and that I could go. I pushed wearily to my feet and walked away. Once I was out of earshot, I called Sgott.

"Darling girl," he said effusively, "how are you this fine evening?"

"My, aren't you sounding altogether *so* happy this evening, given your shift has barely even started—what's happened?"

"We finally caught the man whose been on the top of our most wanted persons list for over a year. It was an operation months in the planning, and it went off without a hitch."

"Congrats then."

"Well, it's certainly a relief to have him off the streets. I received your text, by the way, and have already sent a team out to talk to her. But I take it this isn't a follow-up call? Or hell, even a personal call?"

There was a hint of censure in his voice, and guilt stirred. "I *do* make personal calls, you know, but yeah, this isn't one of them."

"What's happened?"

"Too much to go into detail over the phone, but I think I might have another bio-tracker embedded—"

"How the fuck did that happen?"

"During the fight we had with the men who hit Cynwrig's apartment."

"When your shoulder was shredded, you mean? Don't think I don't hear about these things."

"The shoulder is fine—"

"Yes, but one day it won't be. One day, you'll be too far away from any help, and it'll be all too late."

The echoes of grief in his voice said he was talking about Mom, even if he didn't mention her by name.

"I can't control fate any more than she could," I said softly, "but I'm doing my best not to head into dangerous situations alone."

"Good," he said gruffly. "Now, where are you? I can get someone out to remove it immediately."

"I'm in Swansea—"

"What the fuck are you doing there?"

"Combining passions, you might say."

"With which man?"

I grinned. "Eljin. Cynwrig and Mathi were both caught up in a council meeting, and the latter is out when it comes to passions."

He grunted. "Well, I've a good man down that way who should be able to remove it easily enough. I'll send you the address after I give him a heads-up."

"Thanks." I paused. "I don't suppose you've turned up any information about the elf who hit Cynwrig's and Kaitlyn's?"

"No, which suggests either he hasn't a record or his name is a false one."

"Have you tried searching birth or passport records? There can't be too many British-born Myrkálfar elves with red hair around."

"I've placed a request with passport control and Cynwrig has his people going through their records now."

But would he share the information if he found anything? Part of me suspected not, given the Myrkálfar did have a serious proclivity for revenge.

"Also, what do you know about Loudon Fitzgerald?"

"Nothing more than he'd been your mother's lover before I came onto the scene, and that she used to call on him for relic information. Why?"

"I suspect he might know more about what Mom was searching for before she died than what he's saying, and I can't use my pixie wiles on him."

"Then I shall issue a warrant immed—"

"There's a complication."

He sighed. "There always is. What is it this time?"

"Ka-hal went after him, but missed."

"Ah," he said, "This would be the explosion in Swansea, then. I take it you were on the scene? Because, really, where else would you be when something dangerous is happening."

I grinned. "I was there, and I survived unscratched."

"Long may it continue," he muttered. "Where is he now?"

"Eljin's taken him to what Loudon believes will be a safe place. Once I get the address, I'll let you know."

"Thanks. That it?"

"For now."

"Enjoy the rest of your evening then."

"You, too."

I hung up then glanced down as the phone pinged. It was Eljin sending me the treehouse's address. I sent back a number of emojis that included a bottle of bubbly and an eggplant, and got back a bread roll, a honeypot, and flames. I laughed, pocketed my phone, and then headed for the main street. Sgott sent me the address of his expert a few seconds later, so I hailed a passing cab and headed over.

The man who opened the door barely looked twenty. I glanced down at the message to ensure I had the right address, then said doubtfully, "Officer Downy?"

"Please, call me Harry." He stepped back and waved me inside. "Sgott tells me you've a bug needing urgent removal."

There were voices coming from the kitchen—a woman's and a couple of children—so unless he'd started procreating very young, he had to be at least in his late twenties. "Yes indeed."

"Second door on the right," he said. "How long has it been in there?"

I entered the room, which appeared to be a cross between a study and a medical examining room. A vast range of books filled the shelves, and there were medical bits and pieces everywhere. "A couple of days. Why?"

"The longer they're in, the harder they are to find and remove. This should be easy enough though. Where is it?"

"Back of my neck."

He motioned me to sit on the chair next to the table and then moved behind me. His fingers brushed my neck and shoulders, quick and impersonal.

"Are you a cop?" I asked curiously.

"No, a medical examiner who specialized in electronic and magical causes of death. I've worked with the IIT for years now—and yeah, I know, I don't look old enough."

I grinned. "How long have you known Sgott?"

"About ten years." He stepped away and retrieved what looked like a small scanner with a cone and syringe attached. "You'll either have to remove your top or I can cut the back open. Your choice." He paused. "I can call my wife in if you'd like."

"That's not necessary."

Once I'd stripped off, he placed the small cone to the right of my neck, closer to my right shoulder than my spine. There was a soft click, followed by a soft humming. My skin was sucked up by the device, then pain flared as a short, sharp needle stabbed into the risen flesh.

A second later, he grunted in satisfaction and stepped back. I pulled my top back on and then turned around. He was holding a small tube with what looked like a metallic dot no bigger than a freckle inside.

"That's the bio-tracer, I take it?"

He nodded and offered it to me. I took it somewhat gingerly, though I wasn't sure why—it wasn't like it could escape the tube and jump back into my skin.

"Despite its meager size," he said, "it'll hold enough charge to send a signal for another fifteen or twenty minutes. I suggest you place it on a bus or something similar to lead your followers astray while you escape unnoticed."

I glanced at him sharply. "Would my coming here have put you and your family in danger?"

He smiled and patted my shoulder. "No, this place is chock full of all sorts of electronic redirects. Whoever placed this will know you're in the area but not exactly where. There's a bus stop down the end—may I suggest you start your escape there?"

I grabbed my purse and jacket and then rose. "Thank you for the help."

He smiled. "I owe Sgott more than a few favors, so it's the least I can do. Say hello to the big man for me when you see him."

"I will." I'd also be asking him about Harry, because I suspected there'd be a good story behind their friendship.

He opened the front door, then plucked my jacket from me and handed me a bulky, rather garish-looking blue one instead.

"More conspicuous is definitely less so in a case like this," he said with a smile. "They'll be looking for your black coat, not this."

"You've done this before, from the sound of it."

"Always be prepared is a necessary motto when you work with the IIT. You never know what they might throw at you."

I laughed, thanked him again, and headed out. The

night was cold, and the threat of rain so sharp that I could almost taste it. I was alone on the street, and there was no traffic, though I could hear it in the distance.

I shivered my way into the coat, then shoved my hands into its pockets and hurried down the street. A bus came along just as the rain started. I had no idea where it was headed, but it didn't really matter. I tucked the tube deep into the gap between my seat and the next, waited for several stops, and then tugged my hood over my head and got out.

The bus drove on. I hunched over in an effort to downplay my height, and casually walked into the nearby side street. I was barely a dozen steps in when the back of my neck tingled. I resisted the urge to turn around and crossed the road instead, risking a sneaky glance back. A brown sedan was briefly spotlighted by the streetlight on the corner. In the passenger seat was a red-haired, dark-skinned man.

Not only had they been following me, but they'd picked the signal up *really* quickly.

I had ten minutes, if that, before the signal died and they realized they'd been played. I had to get the hell out of the area before that happened.

I pulled out my phone, checked Google Maps to see where exactly I was, then ordered an Uber to meet me outside a pizza place two streets away. It arrived the same time as I did, so I jumped in and headed for the address Eljin had sent. Thankfully, it was outside Swansea's main business center and well away from my current position.

The rain's ferocity had increased by the time I reached my destination, the droplets dancing off the road surface as sharply as hail. I tugged my hood over my hair and walked toward the path leading deeper into the woods. The old trees lining either side of the well-lit path filled the air with a joyous rain song, and it washed through my being, momentarily sweeping away everything else—all my worries, all my concerns, all my tiredness.

I breathed it deep and simply enjoyed.

Our accommodation was a small cabin that had been built around the trunk of an ancient oak so carefully there was no interference to the old tree's song. And it wasn't alone—there were at least six other treehouses farther down the path.

External lights flickered on as I stepped onto the ramp that wound up the outside of the structure, and a few seconds later, the door opened and Eljin stepped out.

"I was starting to worry."

"Had a few problems." I wrapped my arms around his neck and kissed him hungrily. "Gannon was killed, and I was bio bugged."

Shock ran through him, so thick I could taste it. "Why on earth would someone put a tracker on you?"

"They're searching for the same thing I am—the shield —so why not use me to make their task easier?"

"How did you remove it then? They're in-skin things and hard to trace, from what I've read."

"They are, but thankfully, Sgott knew someone in the area who specializes in that sort of thing."

"Which is where you got that rather garish coat, I take it? Because that's not the one you were wearing when I last saw you, and it doesn't look like something you'd willingly purchase—unless my admittedly meager knowledge of your tastes is way off."

I grinned. "There is nothing meager about you, my dear man, including your tastes."

He laughed and ushered me into a room that comprised

a kitchenette, a bed large enough to party in, and a multitude of windows that looked out into the canopy. The walls were lined with untreated wood that sang in gentle accompaniment to the oak, and there was a big old bath sitting in front of double-width glass doors that opened onto a small balcony. The bathroom was the only separate room in the cabin.

"This is lovely," I said. "Shame we're here only for the night."

"Perhaps we should consider it a precursor for an extended holiday at some point in the near future. Drink?"

"Please." I stripped off my coat, hung it over the hook to dry, and then followed him into the room. "How's Loudon?"

"He was safe in his hidey hole when I left him. Whether he remains there is another matter—he was very jumpy."

No surprise, given he was almost blown apart. "I thought he was certain he'd be safe there?"

"He was initially. I think he was having second thoughts when he realized I wasn't staying to protect him."

"Have you got the address? I need it to send to Sgott."

"Considering I drove the man there, I do indeed."

His tone was dry, and a smile tugged my lips. I typed the address into a message and pinged it off to Sgott. "Do you need to head straight home tomorrow?"

He shook his head and handed me a glass of wine. "Why? You intending to question Loudon yourself?"

I hesitated. Optimally, I would have loved to, but while we'd removed Ka-hal's bug, it was no guarantee they didn't have a secondary means of tracking me. Right now, Loudon was too big a source of possible information to risk. Better to leave him to Sgott and his people.

"Before Gannon died," I said eventually, "I managed to

get the location of the scroll Loudon had. We need to get over there and retrieve it before our foes beat us to it again."

"With Gannon dead and Loudon in safe keeping, that shouldn't be a problem."

"If there's one thing I've learned over recent weeks, it's never to underestimate your foe." I took a sip of wine and rolled it lightly around my tongue. It was crisp and fresh, with notes of peach and nectarine and just the right amount of acidity. Perfect for summer but pretty damn good in winter, too. "This is lovely—who's the maker?"

"It's Cat Amongst The Pigeons—an Australian wine I had shipped back during my extended trip over there."

I raised my eyebrows. "I didn't know you'd spent time in Australia."

"I had a commission down there a while ago," He shrugged and motioned toward the tubs of food sitting on various trays. "Shall we make ourselves comfortable and eat? Otherwise, the food will get cold."

"I suspect the food might be the only thing that *does* over the next few hours."

"Only a few hours?" A wicked smile tugged at his lips. "My dear woman, I intend to keep us warm the entire damn night."

If there was one thing I learned over the course of that glorious evening, it was Eljin was a man who kept his word.

Sleep came late—very late—into the night.

But with it came the dreams.

Dark dreams filled with betrayal and death.

Dreams I couldn't remember after they'd woken me up, the Eye burning on my chest and my heart racing uncomfortably.

Dreams that kept me awake as dawn's light slipped across the night and Eljin slept beside me.

A quick Google search gave us the address of Gannon's storage unit, and the code he'd stored on his phone also worked on the gate. His shipping container was at the very end of a long pink row of them.

We climbed out of the car, and I walked across to the electronic lock to punch in the code. Once it had released, Eljin grabbed the door lever and hauled open one side of the container's double set. Inside, it was cool and clean, but basically empty except for a couple of boxes that had some sort of laminate coating across the outside surface.

"Not the best environment to be storing old scrolls in," Eljin said. "But at least he's used proper archival document boxes."

I squatted beside the first one and carefully pried the lid off. "Maybe this was never meant to be a permanent storage option. Maybe he just wanted to keep the scroll temporarily away from Loudon."

Eljin squatted in front of the other one. "Why would he want that? From what Loudon said in the car, they were longtime partners."

The musty, earthy scent of old paper rising from the box made my nose twitch. "Yeah, but Loudon has a fetish for old scrolls, so Gannon always kept hold of the ones they'd been commissioned to find. Apparently, if they disappeared into Loudon's vault, they never came out."

Inside the box were a half dozen or so yellowed and rather fragile-looking scrolls, along with at least five manuscripts of varying sizes. I didn't pick any of them up. I knew from various things Lugh had said over the years how damaging the oils from skin could be to fragile documents.

"There's a random collection of scrolls and manuscripts

in this one, some vellum, some parchment," Eljin said. "How did you uncover that about Loudon?"

My stomach briefly clenched. Damn it, I'd forgotten I hadn't exactly been truthful when it came to the events around the explosion. I should just fess up and be done with it—if only to save further awkward moments like this —but instinct was saying *don't*. I had to trust her, even if I had no idea why.

"I gathered it from that conversation I overheard," I replied as casually as I could. "They were arguing about the scroll."

He studied me for a moment, then returned his gaze to the box. I had a suspicion he didn't believe me and no idea why that worried me. Was it simply a matter of knowing lies, no matter how small, always caused problems further down the track?

Or was guilt making me read things into his expression that weren't there?

Probably. It wasn't like I lied all that often or was very good at it.

"We should get these back to the museum where they can be stored in optimal conditions and make it easier to study them," he said.

"In an ideal world, yes we should, but the museum will want them catalogued and preserved before it lets anyone near them, and right now, we can't afford to waste any time. We've two madmen out there desperate to find the shield, so the sooner we can find and destroy it, the safer everyone will be."

"One does not necessarily lead to the other when those same two elves are armed with the rubies."

"Yes, but without the shield, their power cannot be amplified." I placed the lid back on the box, then picked it up and rose. It was heavier than it looked. "We'll take them to Lugh's. His workshop is kept cool by ultra-thick walls, so they should be okay there for a little while."

He lifted the second box and followed me out of the container. "If Lugh has no objections, I'll help the two of you sort through the scrolls."

"I'm sure he won't." After all, it was part of his "revenge" plan to see me married off—or at least, happily settled—with Eljin. That's why he'd handballed me the assignment of picking him up at the airport when he'd first arrived. He'd been hoping we'd click. And we had. Whether it would go the full distance was anyone's guess at this point.

Though it would definitely help if I stopped the lies, however minor they might be.

We dumped the two boxes into the trunk of his car and then made the long trek home. Once we were near Deva, I called Lugh.

"Hey," he said, by way of hello. "Sgott tells me you ran into trouble up in Swansea."

"Just a wee bit, as he would say. Got the information we needed, though."

"Meaning you found the witch who made the Eve token?"

"I did. Unfortunately, he was the victim of a hit-and-run."

"That was no accident, I'm gathering."

"No." I gave him a quick update on everything we'd discovered without going into too much detail or mentioning the Ninkilim, wary of confirming Eljin's suspicions about my lies.

"Well, at least the mystery of the token has been solved, even if it has led to further questions."

"Which we may well find answers to in Kaitlyn's scroll, which we found this morning."

"Actually," Eljin said, "we found a good dozen of them."

"And you need them translated ASAP, I'm guessing," Lugh said.

"Yes indeed. We're heading for your place as we speak."

He grunted. "I'm at the museum right now, but I should be able to finish up and get there within the hour."

"Eljin's going to help us translate."

"You might want to call in Mathi and Cynwrig too, given speed is of the essence."

"Cynwrig is still dealing with the fallout from the building collapse, but I'll ring Mathi. I need to update him anyway so he can make a report to the council."

Even if Cynwrig hadn't been busy, putting him in the same room as the competition was *not* a good idea. The tension alone would be fierce enough to ignite a forest, at least on Cynwrig's part. Hell, he bristled at the mere mention of the man.

"Coward," Lugh said, obviously not buying my excuse. "Cynwrig is civilized. He'd behave himself."

He undoubtedly would, but right now I preferred to keep the two men in my life separated. They knew *of* each other, and that was the important thing. There was no real reason for them to meet, given they had very little in common other than me.

"It's not something I'm ready to deal with right now, Lugh."

And in truth, probably never would be. As much as I enjoyed being with both men, I knew it couldn't go on forever. I wasn't a player, not at heart. And for Eljin and me to move forward and give our relationship any chance, I would have to let Cynwrig go.

But what I *should* do and what I actually *would* do were entirely two different things. At least for the moment, anyway.

"Coward," Lugh repeated.

"No, sensible," I retorted. "Stop shit-stirring, brother mine."

He laughed. "After all the years you spent teasing me about my love life, consider this minor revenge. See you soon."

He hung up before I could reply.

"And Mathi is?" Eljin asked. "Not the competition, I take it?"

"He's a former lover, now a good friend, and the go-between between me and the council."

"Your handler, in other words." He glanced at me. "Why are you working for the council when you have your own business to run?"

I grimaced. "It's a punishment for deep controlling a cousin."

"I take it there was a good reason?"

"A life-or-death sort of reason."

"The best kind."

"Sounds like you've some experience in that field."

A smile teased the corners of his lovely lips. "I'm not the powerhouse relic hunter that your brother is, and my relic-hunting field work is limited by comparison. The closest I've ever come to life and death is when the head of a dig took a shine to me, and it was *not* reciprocated."

I raised an eyebrow. "I take it she didn't take rejection kindly?"

"*He* definitely did not. But that was more a 'you'll never work in this field again' situation than a life-endangering one."

Hence his field work being limited, from the sound of it. I leaned over and patted his leg. "Stick with me, laddie, and you'll definitely be introduced to more than a few life-and-death situations."

He laughed softly. "Not sure about the latter, but definitely up for the former."

"You were certainly up last night. I'm not entirely sure how you're still awake."

"The competition is a dark elf," he said wryly. "My game needs to be on point if I'm to win the fair maiden."

I laughed and called Mathi. It immediately switched over to voice mail, so I asked if he could come around to Lugh's later that evening to help translate some scrolls we'd found. A text arrived a few seconds later confirming he would, so he was obviously in a meeting and unable to talk. I sent back a request for pizza and hoped he didn't just roll his eyes and ignore me, as he wasn't overly fond of what I considered the sixth essential food group. Chocolate was, of course, on the main list.

Lugh lived in a decommissioned power substation that was one of the ugliest buildings I'd ever seen. Its brown bricks were blackened by grime decades in the placing, and the black wooden door—situated in the middle of the long, single-story building—still had the rusty old electrical warning signs screwed into it. But it had the one thing vital to a man of Lugh's size that no other house in the area did —high ceilings and tons of storage space.

Eljin found parking a few houses down, then handed me the lighter of the two boxes and took the other. I punched in the code once we reached the front door and then nudged it open with an elbow. Unlike the outside of the building, the interior was bright and surprisingly modern. The foyer was large and airy with two doors leading off it—the left into the main living area and two bedrooms, the right into his office and storage area.

I headed right and dumped my box on one of the desks. Eljin placed his beside mine and then looked around. It was a large room with tons of shelving storage and several desks, the latter stacked high with paper and the remnants of broken pottery and small figurines.

"Nice setup. Bit messy though."

"His office and storage area were raided a few weeks ago, and he's obviously still in the process of cleaning up. Coffee?"

He nodded and followed me across to the living area, perching on one of the stools in front of the counter as I made us both a drink. After sliding his cup across to him, I raided the pantry—which was fully stocked with fresh, in-date rather than out-of-date food now that Darby stayed here a good portion of the week—for a packet of biscuits and then sat down beside him. Lugh came in a few minutes later and nodded a greeting to Eljin. He was a six-foot-six giant of a man with short but unruly red hair and frost-green eyes who'd always made me feel small by comparison, even though I could hardly be described as short when I was five-eight.

He was also extremely wet.

"Raining, hey?" I rose to make him a coffee as he headed into his bedroom.

"Pelting down."

He came out in fresh clothing and rubbing his hair dry with a towel. I handed him the coffee, then moved around to sit down beside Eljin again. "I don't suppose you remember me dating a Myrkálfar elf with red hair when I was a teenager?"

He raised his eyebrows. "Why the hell would you be asking me that? You dated them, not me."

"And obviously they weren't very good dates if you have no memory of them," Eljin said.

I nudged him with my shoulder, and Eljin laughed. "Well, a good date is never forgotten, is that not true?"

"Don't ask me," Lugh said, "According to my sister, I rarely had dates let alone good ones back then."

I rolled my eyes. "This particular date suggested you'd run him off."

Lugh's gaze sharpened. "You're talking about our ruby-wielding terrorist, aren't you?"

I nodded. "I spoke to him briefly when we were at Kaitlyn's."

"How did he escape if you were close enough to talk?" Eljin asked.

"He wasn't alone, he had layers of magic protecting him, and I never got close enough to use my knives on anything more than his protecting shield." I shrugged. "We did manage to stop his destruction, though, and that was the main thing."

Lugh scratched his stubbly chin, his expression thoughtful. "You did go through a period where you dated anything Myrkálfar—"

"Really?" So why had none of them made a lasting impression? Hell, I wasn't ever likely to forget Cynwrig, no matter how senile I got. "How old was I?"

"Nineteen? Twenty? Something around there."

"Were any of them red haired and green eyed?"

"I think there was one who had green eyes, but can't remember his hair color. There'd always been something not quite right about him."

"So you did run him off?"

"Yes, because you came home one night in tears and having obviously been beaten. I tracked the bastard down and bluntly told him if he ever touched you again—if he ever even *saw* you again—there would be no place on this earth he would be safe."

Warmth tugged at my heart. "Love you too, brother mine."

And I would do exactly the same—threaten the same—if anyone hurt him. In fact, him being injected with a deadly truth serum was the sole reason I'd gotten involved in the hunt for Agrona's Claws.

But the truth of the matter was, I couldn't remember the incident, and that was confusing, especially if I'd been beaten so badly.

"You didn't report him? Sgott didn't charge him?"

"You refused to press charges, so Sgott's hands were legally tied. He did, however, use every resource possible into finding the bastard and passing that information on."

My confusion deepened. "Why wouldn't I press charges? That really doesn't sound like me."

"No, but you were damnably adamant about it and made me swear not to go after him."

I scrubbed a hand across my eyes. "I don't remember any of this."

"It's well known that victims of trauma can suffer a shutdown of episodic memory," Eljin said softly. "It's not unusual for the memories—or even just fragments of them —to resurface years, or even decades later."

"That's the trouble—they're not resurfacing." I blew out a frustrated breath and took a drink. And couldn't help wishing it was something much, much stronger. "Don't suppose you can remember his name?"

"After all this time? Not likely."

"Does Ka-hal ring any bells?"

"Not a one." He paused, frowning. "Ka-hal doesn't sound very elvish—could it be an anagram of his actual name?"

I wrinkled my nose. "Lahak? Hakla? Halak?"

He snapped his fingers. "Halak. That's the one. Came from the Cloondeash area from memory, but was here for work."

"Where the hell is Cloondeash?"

"Ireland," Eljin said, then added when I glanced at him in surprise, "I was talking to an elf from that area in the pub the other night."

"And were you alone at this pub?" I asked mildly.

"Sadly, yes." His expression was woebegone, but laughter danced in his eyes. "My one true love was out dancing with another man."

"Yeah, because a very single, very eligible pixie has no other choices waiting in the wings." My voice was dry, and he raised his eyebrows.

"Perhaps he prefers to wait for the *right* choice."

"And perhaps it is too early in *any* relationship to tell whether a choice is right or not."

"Very true, but perhaps he is also a man of patience."

Our gazes held for several very long seconds, and something within me shifted. A weight, perhaps, or maybe even simple trepidation.

He was serious.

I just had to decide if I was.

Which I was... and yet, an odd reluctance remained. Or maybe that was simply the lure of forbidden fruit. A hankering for what I could never have on a permanent basis.

I tore my gaze away and gulped down some coffee. "Do

you remember where he was working? Was it with Cynwrig or somewhere else?"

Lugh shrugged. "I wouldn't have thought the Myrkál-fars here in Deva would be importing talent, given they're one of the largest encampments in the UK. But rather than us theorizing, just ask Cynwrig. As his father's heir, he has full access to the records."

"Cynwrig *Lùtair*?" Eljin said. "*He's* the competition?"

"You didn't know?" Lugh said.

"I knew there was competition. I just didn't realize how high caliber it was."

"Well, if one is going to do a dark elf," I said with a grin, "one might as well go for the top-shelf kind."

"Indeed," he said. "It'll definitely force me to keep my game above par."

"Which I cannot be sad about." I leaned sideways and dropped a kiss on his cheek. "Especially after last night."

"No man can keep up that pace forever."

"Cynwrig can."

"Hmmm" was all he said to that.

I grinned and returned the conversation to safer topics. "If Ka-hal is an anagram of Halak, maybe his partner's name is one, too."

"Possible." Lugh wrinkled his nose. "Leekkam? Mkkeela? Makkeel?"

I laughed. "Talk about very unelvish-sounding names."

"The older elf generations did love their strange-sounding names and spellings," Eljin noted dryly.

Maybe, but none of them twitched my instincts, so if Keelakm *was* an anagram, Lugh's guesses weren't close. I took another drink and then said, "Lugh, did you get a chance to head down to the crypts and check if Nialle left any more notes there?"

He nodded. "I did a quick search of his desk but not the stuff he kept on hand in several of the museum's old display cabinets. I couldn't find mention of the shield, the rubies, or anything else for that matter. There were a few brief notes about some Nordic ice horn he thought the museum might be interested in acquiring, but that's it."

"Borrhás's Horn?" I asked in surprise.

"That's the one—how do you know about it? The council?"

I nodded. "Before the shield shit hit the fan, it was meant to be my first finding task."

"I'll gather the notes for you, then, and see if I can find anything else. Might as well get a good head start if we can."

I smiled at his use of "we." While I might be the official hunter for the council, Lugh had no intention of letting me do it alone—and not only because of what had happened to Mom. He simply wasn't ready to settle down into a more normal life—which was probably why he'd refuse Rogan's position if the museum ever offered it to him. He didn't want the responsibility, the paperwork, or—more importantly—the necessary need to curry favor from politicians and sponsors to ensure a continuation of funding. Of course, the museum's powers-that-be were well aware of his propensity for straight talk rather than sweet, which was why they were never likely to offer him the position.

"That would be brill. Thanks."

He leaned forward and plucked several Jammy Dodgers from the packet. "How bad a condition are the scrolls in?"

"They looked all right, but we didn't touch them so can't be sure," Eljin replied. "It'd still be best if we examined them within a climate-controlled room—"

"Which I have here," Lugh said.

"It's finally finished?" I asked, surprised. "Because you've been digging out that thing forever."

"I employed dwarves to work on it rather than digging it out myself but yes, the cellar is now humidity and climate-controlled and fully operational." Amusement danced through his expression but there was a serious glint in his green eyes. "And just in time to provide a bolt hole in tough times."

Which, given recent events, might just come in handy. "As long as those behind the tough times don't employ said dwarves to dig their way in." Which had happened before, although it hadn't been his friends, and they'd gone into his storeroom via an old sewer tunnel that ran under the building. They'd also been after information rather than artifacts and had ransacked his office and tried to burn it down. Only our timely arrival had stopped complete disaster.

"That won't be a problem—the room is strengthened by heavy steel, which they can't break through." Lugh paused. "Well, not without serious effort, anyway."

I grabbed another biscuit and took a bite. "I wonder why Nialle would make a note about the Shield of Hephaestus or even Ninkil's Harpē but not mention any sort of reference material? He's usually not that economical with words or notes."

"No," Lugh agreed, "but I guess it would depend on when and where he uncovered information about them. If he was in the midst of the Claws hunt, then it's possible he just wrote enough to jog his memory when he had time."

I glanced at Eljin. "Did he tag any of the books or scrolls on his desk that might provide us with some clue?"

Eljin shook his head. "Although in truth, I haven't been through every single book and manuscript. There are a lot of them."

"Might have to make that a priority when you get back to work again tomorrow," Lugh said.

"What about his workstation within the vault?" Eljin asked. "It's surely more likely we'll find something relevant down there."

Lugh grimaced. "Aside from the fact you're still on probation, I haven't the clearance to give you access."

Eljin shrugged, a casual movement that belied the frustration that briefly crossed his expression. "Just a thought."

Lugh nodded. "We can broach the subject of early access with Rogan's replacement, when and if they decide on one, that is."

"If?" I raised my eyebrows. "Why on earth wouldn't they replace him? The department was already struggling to keep up with only two active antiquarians and a few researchers."

"They're debating as to whether the department is actually necessary. They're considering merging us with modern antiquities."

"Which makes total sense, because regular archeologists have spent absolute *decades* studying the ancient ways of magic, relics, and the old gods." My voice was dry, and he smiled.

"Sadly, human interest in said old gods has waned rather drastically over recent years."

"And that's probably why the remaining old gods are now stirring humanity's pot, so to speak," I said. "There's no better way to reawaken interest than to rattle some figurative cages and prove you still exist."

Lugh wrinkled his nose. "Not sure something like that would work—humanity in general isn't as gullible as it once was."

Eljin snorted. "I'm not so sure about that—just look at some of the so-called politicians they keep voting in."

"A major truth right there," I said, lightly tapping my coffee mug against his.

Lugh shoved another biscuit into his mouth. "How many scrolls we got to examine?"

"Probably a dozen or so," I said.

"Meaning we're in for an all-nighter." He paused and glanced at Eljin. "Well, you're not. You need to keep impressing the powers-that-be while you're still on probation. Good men are hard to find these days."

Eljin smiled. "Thanks for the compliment."

"Thank my sister. She's the one who says you're good."

Eljin glanced at me, eyes twinkling merrily. "I suspect you and she might be talking about two very different types of good."

I laughed and lightly slapped his arm. "Good is such a mediocre term and one I would never use in reference to you."

"I'm so glad to hear it."

"Thoughts on the task ahead, not bedroom delights, people," Lugh said, the twinkle in his eyes belying the severity of his tone.

I grinned, saluted him with my coffee cup, then downed the rest of my drink and slid off my stool. "Shall we get to it?"

"You read old Latin?" Eljin said in obvious surprise.

"Not a word, but Lugh will write down what phrases I need to look out for." I shrugged. "At worst, I can be the tea and biscuit lady."

"There will be no tea and certainly no biscuits down there," Lugh commented. "The last thing we need is crumbs or—gods forbid—coffee spilt all over the place."

"Then you're stuck giving me a quick lesson in old Latin."

He nodded and led us into his study—where Eljin and I picked up the boxes and he grabbed a notepad and pen—then moved on through to his storeroom. It hadn't really changed all that much from last time I'd been here; four long gray shelving units still ran the full length of the room, and filing cabinets lined the rear wall. This time, though, there was a massive five-door walnut armoire where industrial shelving had once lined the right wall.

"That looks rather incongruous in a place like this," I said dryly. "And if it's hiding the entrance into your cellar, it's a little too obvious."

"Sometimes the obvious is the best defense," he said, in an odd echo of Harry's comment. "Trust me, no one short of Hercules himself would be able to move that thing now that it's filled with all my bits and pieces."

"Which suggests access into the cellar is through the armoire itself," Eljin said.

"If it is," I commented before Lugh could reply, "then it's going to be a tight fit for a certain overly large pixie."

"Please note the double doors in the middle, sister dearest. I am not that silly."

I grinned and watched as he opened said doors, pushed the two laden shelves aside, and then pressed a hand against the middle at the back. Light flickered around his fingertips for several seconds, then the back panel slid to one side and pale light flicked on, revealing wide concrete stairs going down.

"Cunning," I said.

"Clever," he corrected. He took the box from me and headed in.

Eljin and I followed. Despite his assurances, it was a bit

of a squeeze, even for me, but the stairs themselves were wide and easy to move down, and the room at the base— although not large—was fresh and surprisingly bright considering the soft lighting. It didn't hold much in the way of furniture—just an empty shelving unit, five well-used chairs, and a long wooden table with drawers along one side.

Lugh placed the box and notepad on the table, then retrieved cotton gloves from one of the drawers and handed a set to each of us. After prying the lid off the first box, he removed a scroll and cautiously unrolled it. The vellum was in surprisingly good condition and the lettering crisp and clear.

"It talks about the god Cronus," Lugh said, after a few minutes.

"Who was the king of the Titans and the god of time," Eljin said to me, "and not to be confused with the god Khronos, although the two are often depicted as one and the same."

"And who might Khronos be when he's home?" I asked when he didn't go on.

"An incorporeal god who is apparently serpentine in form but possessing of three heads—that of a man, a bull, and a lion. He and his consort"—he paused and glanced down at the scroll—"Ananke emerged with a primordial world-egg in their coils and split it apart to form the ordered universe of earth, sea, and sky."

"Fascinating," I said.

He smiled. "It actually is, you know."

"Which is why you and Lugh studied this stuff, and I did not. Does it mention any other gods in relation to old father time?"

"Some." Lugh grimaced. "But if Kaitlyn said Loudon's

scroll only contained a *mention* of the shield, it means we'll have to read every single one of them. Unless, of course, we get lucky early on."

And when had that ever happened? "Then, as I said, write down the words I need to look for. If I find anything that matches, I'll hand them over."

He nodded, pulled the notepad closer, and began writing. Eljin continued reading the scroll.

"No mention of Hephaestus, his shield, the rubies, or even the harpē." He carefully rolled the scroll back up. "I was hoping the one on top would be the last scroll Gannon had purchased. It would have made our task so much easier."

"Our luck never runs that way," I said.

He smiled. "It's possible my natural good fortune will counter your streak of ill-fortune."

"You'd have to use up a lifetime's supply before that ever happened." I carefully plucked another scroll from the box. "There's not going to be enough room on this table for all of us to fully unroll one of these things—"

"No," Lugh said, "but it's not necessary to completely unroll. Just examine them in smaller sections, rolling and unrolling as you go."

"This really *is* going to take all night," I muttered.

"Welcome to the long and often tedious life of an antiquarian," Lugh said, and slid the note my way. "Have at it, sister mine."

I sighed in mock-heaviness, then turned the note around so I could see the words I needed to look for and got down to work.

There was little conversation for the next few hours. Although we didn't take a break—other than the occasional pit stop to the bathroom—we'd still only gotten through three scrolls when a chime echoed in the room above.

"That's the doorbell," Lugh said, and glanced at the time. "Good grief, it's close to seven."

"No wonder I'm starving." I pushed upright and stretched my back muscles. "Let's hope it's Mathi, and that he arrives with pizza."

Lugh waved a hand toward the stairs. "If the man bears pizza, you had best get up there before said pizza gets sodden and inedible."

"I don't suppose there's a good red to be had in this establishment?" Eljin rubbed the back of his neck wearily, but his gaze found mine, and devilment danced. "It'd certainly go a long way to lubricating mind and body for the next round. Although a good shoulder massage wouldn't go astray either."

I grinned. "If it's a mutual massage, and we're both naked, that might be a possibility."

"There will be no nakedness in the basement either," Lugh said, tone dry.

I snorted and raced upstairs to rescue our pizza.

"About time," Mathi grumbled when I opened the door. "The food isn't the only damn thing getting wet out here. Lugh needs to put up a veranda or something if he's not going to answer the door in a timely manner."

"Bad day at the office, I take it?"

I retrieved the sodden pizza boxes, then stepped aside as he picked up two plastic bags—one filled with take-out containers and the other with a couple bottles of wine.

"Indeed. We lost a contract to a competitor whose products and production capabilities are not the quality of ours. Questions were asked as to why."

"They blamed you?"

"Tried to. But then, my dear cousins would try anything to take the directorship of the company from me."

"I thought Ljósálfar royal lines didn't allow women to run companies?" I kicked the door closed and followed him into the living room. "You do realize there's enough here to feed a small army."

"They don't, but that has never stopped a daughter from trying." He sniffed, a disparaging, haughty sound. "As to the amount of food, I've crossed paths with Lugh's appetite in the past and was actually debating whether I had enough."

"Four extra-large pizzas is plenty," Lugh said, as he and Eljin walked in. "That still leaves two pizzas for everyone else to share plus whatever you have in those take-out containers."

"I kept with the theme and ordered ravioli with ricotta, red peppers, and almonds, a baked pasta with meatballs, aubergine, and smoked cheese, and several tubs of parmesan chips."

"You can keep the first two, but the third option is an inspired choice," Lugh said. "Goes with pizza perfectly."

Mathi shook his head and pulled the various tubs out of the plastic bags. "I am so glad Bethany never shared your heathen tastes. I daresay our relationship would not have lasted as long as it did."

"I'm an equal opportunity eater," I said with a grin. "I'll eat greasy shit just as happily as upmarket."

Mathi harrumphed and then glanced rather pointedly at Eljin. "And who might this be?"

"This, my friend, is the competition."

Mathi looked him up and down, a wide grin splitting his features. "And worthy competition, if I'm any judge."

"And you're really not," I murmured. "Although in *this* instance, you're also not wrong."

Eljin flashed me an appreciative smile, then held out his hand. "Eljin Lavigne, newly installed antiquarian at the Fae Museum. I take it you're Mathi Dhār-Val?"

He nodded, his expression thoughtful. "Have we met? Your name sounds familiar."

"Not as far as I'm aware," Eljin replied easily. "Perhaps you saw mention of my appointment in the museum's e-newsletter."

"Perhaps." Mathi shrugged, though I knew him well enough to understand he'd not let it go until he remembered. He could be dogged like that.

Lugh placed four glasses on the counter, then opened the two bottles of red. "Enough chit-chat. We need to eat and then get back to reading the scrolls."

"What scrolls are we talking about?" Mathi asked. "The one Kaitlyn sold Loudon?"

I nodded, grabbed plates and cutlery out of the drawers, and placed them on the counter beside the pizzas and tubs of food. "Unfortunately, it's one of twelve, so we'll have to go through each one to find his."

Mathi picked up the ravioli and scooped some onto a plate. "I'm surprised Cynwrig's not here, then. He has a deeper understanding of Latin and the older languages than me."

I gave him *the* look. The one that said, "Don't be daft."

Bedevilment danced through his eyes. "It's good to know the fishing remains excellent around you."

I rolled my eyes and piled a mix of chips, pizza, and baked pasta onto my plate, much to Mathi's obvious horror. You'd have thought that after having ten years to get used to my eating habits, that would not be the case, but elves were nothing if not determined when it came to achieving goals. It didn't matter if said goals were minor—such as educating my palate or stopping my penchant for swearing —or major—such as getting me back in his bed—he would keep reaching for that win.

We took our time eating and drinking, the conversation flowing easily between the four of us. I couldn't help but notice how nicely Eljin slid into the group. Cynwrig had as well, of course, but it was far more important—at least for future possibilities—that Eljin got along with the two most important men in my life. Mathi would never share my bed again, but he remained a close friend, and I never wanted that to change.

As we got up to head back downstairs, my phone rang, the tone telling me it was Cynwrig. The man definitely had a knack for knowing when I was thinking about him. I tugged it out of my purse, said, "I need to take this," then headed into the spare bedroom and closed the door behind me.

"Cynwrig, how goes things?" I flopped back onto the bed and stared up at the ceiling. And couldn't help wishing I was staring into smokey silver eyes instead.

"As well as can be expected, given recent events."

He sounded tired, and my heart twisted for him. "You need to get some sleep."

"What I need is to find the bastard behind all this."

"I take it you've had no luck linking anyone in the building to our murderous elf?"

"Not our murderous elf so much as a link to Gilda."

"Mathi's Gilda?" I asked in surprise.

"We're still checking, but I believe so. The description fits."

"What sort of connection was there?"

"She worked for Afran Eadevane."

Eadevane being the only dark elf line that had pale skin and were often mistaken for light elves despite their build and abilities with stone. "In what capacity?"

"Maid and bed companion, from what has been said. She was fired under suspicion of theft, but nothing was ever proven, and no charges ever laid."

Which is probably why Mathi's people had never found anything when he'd ordered a background check on her. "Firing someone surely wouldn't be justification enough to destroy an entire building, though."

"That often depends on state of mind and the statement the destruction is meant to make," he said. "I've asked Sgott to check whether a violence report was placed against Afran. Apparently he had a history of abuse."

"I doubt she would have. Ljósálfar royalty often treats the servant class as less-than-human." It would, however, explain the revenge-seeking destruction.

"I know, but it pays to follow every lead, however unlikely it is to result in a satisfactory conclusion."

"Was Afran one of the casualties in the building's collapse?"

"No, although if he *was* our elf's target—and at this point, he's definitely a candidate—then for all intents and purposes, they would have believed him to be home."

I raised my eyebrows. "Why?"

"His chauffeur drove the car into the underground parking—"

"The building had underground parking?" I cut in. "Where?"

"Underground."

Amusement ran through his tone, and I rolled my eyes. "Clever."

He laughed. "We installed a car lift behind the building, accessible via the lane. You wouldn't notice it if you didn't know it was there."

And I obviously hadn't. "Who was in the car if not Afran?"

"A friend he'd rented the apartment to for the next two weeks. Afran is currently staying in the penthouse suite located next to his office in London." He paused. "How did the trip to Swansea go?"

His tone was neutral—very carefully so, I suspected. "It was a mix of results. We retrieved the scroll Loudon purchased from Kaitlyn, but it was amongst a dozen others, so we're currently going through them all."

"We?"

"The usual suspects," I said evenly. "But I think I know why you're having no luck finding our red-haired elf. Lugh remembered kicking a green-eyed Myrkálfar elf out of my life when I was around twenty, and his name happened to be Halak, which is an anagram of Ka-hal. He couldn't remember Halak having red hair, but it's possible the color is an illusion to throw us off track. He came here from the Cloondeash area looking for work, apparently."

"I'll instigate a search. Halak is an unusual enough name, so if he worked for us, it should yield some results."

"Hopefully." I hesitated. "I'm likely to be at Lugh's most of the night reading these damn scrolls, but would you like to catch up for breakfast tomorrow?"

"Café, your place, or mine?"

"Your place is wrecked, and mine isn't practical."

"We've worked with impractical before," he replied, with a hint of a smile in his voice. "And I've other apartments, remember."

"Liverpool is too far to drive for breakfast."

"Liverpool is a family-owned building, not mine. I've several investments scattered around Deva, both within and without the old city, and there's currently two with vacancies, thanks to it being off season."

Meaning they were lets rather than permanent rentals. "Then I'll meet you in one of them—although I should warn you, I might possibly fall asleep in my pancakes."

He laughed, a soft, warm sound that had desire skittering through me. "You might not be the only one."

"I also don't know what time I'll get there. It just depends how long it takes to find the right scroll."

"Text me when you're leaving, then."

"I will. See you tomorrow.

"I'll wait with bated breath."

"I'd rather you wait with pancakes at the ready. Certain appetites need to be filled first before others can be satisfied."

He laughed again and hung up. A few seconds later, an address pinged onto my message app. The apartment was in Nuns Road, which, from memory, was near the racecourse and not all that far from where he'd been living.

I pushed off the bed and headed back down to the cellar to continue working. By the time Eljin left at eleven, we'd gone through seven scrolls and still hadn't hit the right one. I walked him to the front door and kissed him goodbye, long and lingering.

"Ring me tomorrow night," he said softly. "We'll do dinner or something."

I suspected the "or something" was the higher priority in his estimation, and I couldn't say that I disagreed. The sexual drought I'd suffered after Mathi and I had broken up might have been altogether too long, but I was certainly making up for it now.

"I will."

His gaze dropped briefly to my lips, and heat stirred through his eyes. But he neither reacted nor reached for me again. He simply nodded and left. I locked the door and briefly rested my forehead against the old wood, listening to its comforting if distant song as I wondered who would win this battle—head or heart. *Not* that the latter had any stakes in said battle. Not yet, at any rate.

I ignored the tiny voice suggesting I was kidding myself and headed downstairs. The night slipped by slowly, and I eventually catnapped on a couple of chairs.

"Bingo," Mathi said, who knew how many hours later. "Found it."

I started awake, then scrubbed a hand across weary eyes and got up, walking around the table to stand beside him. The scroll in front of him wasn't written in Latin like the others, but rather a language that appeared far older. The scroll itself was in a poor state and had obviously suffered water damage multiple times over the years—maybe even decades—rendering much of it unreadable.

Mathi lightly pressed a finger above the faded text. "Given the dangerousness of Hephaestus's weapon, it was decided separation..." He paused, frowning. "Not sure what the next bit says—"

"Damn mold has never helped *that* situation," Lugh muttered. "Wonder where it was stored that it got so badly damaged?"

"Not amongst the council's records, that's for sure," Mathi replied, "though it *is* purported to be a record of council proceedings. Can't read the year, unfortunately."

"Deva's council?" I asked.

"Uncertain but unlikely, given we've never had scrolls go missing."

"You never had the hoard going missing until recently, either, so that's no guarantee of anything."

"Our council was not responsible for the hoard." Mathi's frown deepened as he moved his finger down several lines. "It says here the shield was hidden in the dark heart of Gruama."

"Where the hell is that?" I asked.

"Don't know," Mathi said. "It's not a name I recognize."

"Me neither." Lugh pointed to a bit of text further down. "That looks like Cluain Déise, which I believe is where the English form of Cloondeash came from."

"Oh, wouldn't it be the mother of all ironies if the shield is stored in the very encampment our red-haired elf was born in?" I said.

"Cloondeash was never called the Gruama encampment as far as I'm aware, but I'm sure Cynwrig will be able to tell you." Mathi glanced at me somewhat speculatively. "You are seeing him this morning, aren't you?"

"Yes."

He sniffed, a disparaging sound if I ever heard one. "You should concentrate on the possible rather than the impossible. I'd hate to see you hurt."

"Like you hurt me?" I said mildly.

He waved a hand. "We were different."

He wasn't really wrong there, given I'd never been in any danger of falling in love with him. I'd enjoyed his company, and I'd certainly enjoyed the sex, but I'd known from the outset he wasn't the one. That he could *never* be the one.

Of course, I'd known all that going into the relationship with Cynwrig, too. And yet, somehow, it felt totally and utterly different. Possibilities sang brightly between us, but they were dark promises that could never be fulfilled.

"Does it say anything else?" I asked in an effort to redirect the conversation back to a safer subject.

"No," Mathi said after a few moments. "It does say 'beware of that which protects' or something along those lines, but the rest is illegible."

"I'll hand it over to restorations and tell them we need it restored ASAP," Lugh said, "but I'm not sure they'll be able to salvage much."

"Even with an urgency order, it could take months if not years, given the poor state it's in. We haven't that much time." Mathi pushed upright and stretched his back. "We might as well check the rest of them while we're here. There's only a couple more to go."

I glanced at my phone and saw it was close to five thirty. No wonder I'd fallen asleep on the damn chair, "You do that, and I'll follow up our lead with Cynwrig."

"If he does happen to know where Gruama is," Lugh said. "Don't head there without us."

"Cynwrig is more than capable—"

"But he's not impervious. The more of us there are, the greater our chances of success."

I hesitated and then nodded. "I'll let you know what he says."

"Make sure that you do, or I won't be happy."

I smiled, kissed his cheek, then headed upstairs to grab my purse and call an Uber. Ten minutes, it said. I sent a text to Cynwrig to check if he was there and received a simple "yes" a few seconds later.

The Uber arrived right on time, but I directed it over to the tavern first so I could grab a quick shower and the essential toiletries, plus enough clothes to last three or four days, just in case Cynwrig knew where our mysterious location was and we had to head straight out.

It didn't take long to reach the address Cynwrig had sent. I climbed out of the car and studied the building as I made my way up the long steps. Overall, it was circular in shape, but wide paths divided the four separate and curving sections. A grassed courtyard lay in the middle of these sections and contained seating and a fountain, while another concrete path ringed the inner perimeter of the buildings and linked all four. There were six stories in each, with the top floor being penthouses—at least, that's what the security unit on Cynwrig's building said. I typed in the code he'd sent, then made my way across the simple but elegant foyer and called down the elevator. It arrived within seconds and, once I'd punched in the code, headed back up.

It came to a rather unnerving bouncy stop before the doors swished open, revealing a wide expanse of curving glass that revealed sweeping views over the racecourse. The room itself was a kitchen and living space combined, with four rooms leading off it. On the left, at the end of the kitchen, was what looked to be a pantry and laundry. Farther along that wall was another door that led into a massive-looking bedroom. On the other side was a second bedroom and a bathroom. It was a simple but effective layout, and perfect for short-term holiday stays.

Cynwrig wasn't in the kitchen, but the warm smell of cinnamon rode the air, and the dining table had been set with a mix of strawberries, caramelized bananas, and maple syrup. I stripped off my jacket, placed my bag down, and then walked over and snared a piece of banana.

"Keep doing that and there won't be enough for the pancakes," Cynwrig noted, as he came out of the main bedroom. His short dark hair was damp, and he was wearing loose jeans and a baggy sweater that did abso-

224

lutely nothing to enhance his physique. Just as well my imagination was up to the task of imagining the gloriousness of the flesh underneath.

"You've cooked them?"

"They're in the warmer." He caught my hand and pulled me close. His kiss was soft and passionate, demanding and yet not.

A somewhat regretful sigh left my lips when he finally pulled away, and he chuckled softly. "Says the woman who demanded food before other pleasures."

"Perhaps I'm rethinking that demand."

"To which I'd reply, I have not slaved over a hot cooktop for you to change your mind. Sit, woman."

I laughed and sat, watching as he made us both coffee and brought them and a large platter of pancakes over to the table.

"You're going to make someone a mighty fine husband one day," I said as he sat down.

"I aim to please, though I hope it's a task my wife will share."

I plucked a couple of pancakes from the platter, then scooped on bananas, strawberries, and maple syrup before dolloping clotted cream on top. "If you feed her like this every day, I'm sure she'll find an excuse *not* to cook. Besides, haven't you got personal chefs at the palace?"

"I don't, not when it comes to everyday meals, at least." He took the platter from me and filled his plate. "My father has, but that's necessary because of his medical needs, and my sister does because she hates cooking and burns water."

I laughed. He raised an eyebrow, amusement dancing in his eyes. "You think I jest?"

"I think you and your twin are equally capable at all

manner of tasks. I can't imagine a Lùtair heir being otherwise."

"She's a far better diplomat than me. I tend to speak when it would be better to hold my council."

"In that, you're like Lugh. Unlike him, of course, your free-speaking nature won't cost you the job."

"No, although there are times I wish it would." He grimaced. "Enough of that. How did the scroll-reading go last night?"

"It was long, boring, and smelly."

"Hmmm," he said, "I was wondering what that slightly odorous scent was."

I plucked a strawberry from my plate and tossed it at him. "I don't smell."

He caught the strawberry with a laugh and ate it. "Even if you did, I wouldn't care, simply because it means a shower might be in order, and I could help soap your back."

Having had my back soaped by him before, my hormones were immediately on board with that suggestion. My stomach, however, rumbled a loud reminder it had priority.

"We did find Loudon's scroll, but it was in a really poor state. To be honest, I'm surprised Kaitlyn didn't have it restored first—she could have commanded a much higher price."

"But that would have eaten into her profit margin, and if Loudon was willing to buy as is, why would she go to that trouble?"

I picked up my knife and fork and started eating. It was absolutely delicious, especially with the caramel bananas and clotted cream. "It did make translating it that much more difficult, though."

"With at least two if not three men there well versed in

Latin and the old languages, that should not have been a problem."

I smiled at his blatant attempt to uncover who else had been at Lugh's. "It is when there's water and mold damage making the writing illegible."

"Then you weren't able to pull any worthwhile information from it?"

"We did." I sipped on my coffee. "It was an old council record of events—"

"Our council? Because that would explain why they've been unable to find much information about it."

"Mathi didn't think so. It said the shield was hidden in the dark heart of Gruama—"

"Gruama?" he cut in sharply. "Are you sure?"

I frowned at him. "Yes—why?"

"Because," he said bluntly, "at a time when the old gods still roamed the world freely, Gruama was an ancient Myrkálfar settlement that existed within Hibernia."

"Which is?"

"Ireland."

"What happened to it?"

"According to our spoken history, a god armed with the shield made the earth run like water and totally erased all that was." His gaze met mine, his expression grim. "The shield can't be hidden in Gruama, because Gruama no longer exists."

ELEVEN

"Why would the scroll specifically mention it then?"

He shrugged. "Perhaps they wish to throw hunters off the track. Did they mention any other location?"

"Cloondeash, but only as a reference point, from what I could gather."

"The Cloondeash encampment was established by those who survived the Gruama destruction."

I scooped up a bit of pancake slathered with clotted cream. "Then it's possible they'll have records of what, if anything, remains of the original encampment."

"Perhaps." He picked up his coffee and leaned back in his chair. "I'll contact them—"

"Why can't we just go out there?"

"There is no we—Cloondeash is a Myrkálfar encampment—you would not be allowed entry."

I raised an eyebrow. "Even if I accompanied the heir to the throne?"

He smiled. "Being heir isn't an open key that provides entry into all encampments."

"Well, what good is being king then?"

"I'm not, but it is a question I often ponder."

The odd seriousness in his tone had me frowning. "You've said before that your sister is currently running the day-to-day operations, but what does that actually involve?"

He shrugged. "Our monarchy is little different to the human one—"

"The human one is a constitutional monarchy, and the queen no longer has a political or executive role even if she still has constitutional and representative ones. While the Myrkálfar throne no longer officially exists, her king still presides over the rules and regulations of your people."

"That doesn't give us the right to enter other encampments at will. Said rules and regulations need to be followed, even for those of us destined to rule."

I ate the last piece of pancake and leaned back in my chair. "And what of Gruama? Would it be considered out of bounds to me? Because you can't go there alone, Cynwrig."

"I'm *not* the one prone to such foolishness."

I half smiled. "I *am* getting better in that respect. Take the recent trip to Swansea as an example."

"Hmm" was all he said to that.

My smile grew. "You didn't answer my actual question."

"No, Gruama would not be under such a restriction, because it is no longer considered an active encampment but rather a graveyard."

"Active or inactive?"

"Active."

"Cloondeash use it to bury their dead?"

"It's considered sacred ground to this day."

"How can the dead be buried if the place no longer exists?"

"It no longer exists as a settlement, but the running

earth did not destroy the entire encampment. Pieces remain."

"Does anything live there at all?"

"Not that I'm aware of." He eyed me for a second. "Why?"

"Because the scroll said to be wary of that which guards."

"As I said, the area is sacred and few venture there for anything more than funeral rites. There've been no reports of any godly or supernatural events as far as I'm aware, but Cloondeash would have a record of it if there was." He drained his coffee and pushed to his feet. "I'll start making some calls."

"Now?" I said. "When we've that big old bed to explore?"

He laughed. "You look ready to fall asleep, and that's never a momentous start for lovemaking."

"Maybe lovemaking will revitalize me."

"But sleep definitely *will*. Get some rest. We can party in that big old bed once the arrangements have been made."

I sighed in mock disappointment, then blew him a kiss and headed into the bedroom. After finding the remote and closing the blinds, I stripped off and climbed under the heavy comforter. I was asleep in minutes and slept solidly and undisturbed.

It was the delicious smell of bacon that finally dragged me back to the land of the living. I yawned and stretched, then glanced at the other side of the bed. The dent in the pillow beside mine suggested that at some point, Cynwrig had slept, even if he was now out in the kitchen cooking.

I flung off the covers, shivered my way into one of the dressing gowns hanging on the back of the door, then padded into the main area. He glanced up, his gaze sweeping me and coming up amused. "That thing does absolutely nothing for your luscious curves."

"But it's warm, and that's all that matters. Hasn't this place got any heating?"

"It does, but it's obviously not much good. I'll have to get it fixed before the tourist season begins."

I perched on one of the stools near the counter and snagged a bit of bacon before he could object. The clock on the kitchen stove said it was just after twelve, meaning I'd been asleep for about five hours. Which was nowhere near enough, but better than nothing.

"How'd you go with Cloondeash?"

"Better than expected. We're heading for the airport at two to fly across."

"We? As in, you and me? I thought you said that wouldn't happen?"

"When it comes to the Cloondeash encampment, that remains an undisputable fact. However, I did get directions to Gruama's remaining accessible areas."

"What about our red-haired elf?"

"There're seven Halaks listed in the database—five of those are dead, one is an elderly statesman, and the other is his grandson, and barely in his teens."

"That suggests Halak might be a family name and that our red-haired elf is far older than he looks."

Although that wasn't actually unusual—both Cynwrig and Mathi were centuries older than me, even if in lifespan terms we were around the same biological age.

He nodded. "I've asked for him to be interviewed and for the written records to be checked as a matter of urgency."

"Written records?"

He nodded. "Compulsory registration of births didn't

start happening in the UK until the mid-1800s, remember, and Cloondeash was one of the last settlements to welcome computerization. The records room there is huge and, if the old man doesn't come through with any leads, it could take them days for them to find the information we need."

And we didn't have days. We barely had a day.

I shivered but didn't chase that sliver of intuition any further. I wasn't ready for more bad news just yet.

He flipped a couple of poached eggs onto two plates, handed me one, and then pushed a platter of toast and bacon my way. I helped myself to both.

"Did you ask if there was anything we needed to be careful of when we enter Gruama?"

He sat on the stool next to me, his jean-clad leg brushing mine. The heat that skittered through me echoed in his eyes. The man had seduction on his mind, and I couldn't wait.

But there was bacon on my plate, and that could not be ignored.

"Only that most of the old tunnels are impassible. They sent a photo of a map listing the layout and location of the remaining viable ones."

I frowned. "Dark elves control earth and stone, so why hasn't anyone gone into Gruama and restored it?"

"Because what a god destroyed mere mortals cannot restore."

"Meaning it was tried?"

"Only once. The attempt to undo resulted in the destruction of all those involved."

"If godly magic still lingers there, will you be able to manipulate earth or stone if we come across a blockage or something?"

He nodded. "As I said, Gruama is a place of the dead,

which means it needs to be regularly checked and repaired."

"I'm guessing they had no information suggesting where the shield might have been placed?"

"No."

Meaning I'd probably have to call on the Eye for help if we didn't want to be wandering through dark, dank tunnels for days, if not weeks.

I sighed and got down to the serious business of eating. Once we'd finished, Cynwrig turned my stool to face him, then caught the sash end and undid it. He slid his fingers between the gown and my skin, not touching me but nevertheless causing all sorts of inner havoc as he slid the gown from my shoulders and down my arms. It pooled around the bottom of the stool and left me naked, but despite the lack of heat in the room, I was far from cold. The heat in his gaze ensured that as it did a slow journey down my length.

"Glorious," he murmured.

"Unfair," I said. "I'm naked and you're not."

He laughed, scooped me up in his arms, and carried me to the bedroom.

And then lightly tossed me onto the bed.

I laughed as I bounced several times, then scrambled under the blankets and watched as he stripped off. He was gloriously erect, and I wanted nothing more than to feel every inch of him on every inch of me.

Over the course of the next hour, I certainly achieved that aim.

We took a private plane across to Ireland and then collected the keys of the SUV Cynwrig had hired. Once we'd tossed in our bags and Lugh's caving gear, we drove down to our accommodation for the night—a lovely old traditional hotel in Westport. Lugh and Mathi had their own rooms, while Cynwrig and I shared a twin. Us sharing a solitary double would have been cozy, but also ultimately uncomfortable given his tendency to spread out even in a boat-sized bed. Besides, I did need to sleep at some point.

"I might grab a shower before I head down for dinner." I dumped my bag onto a bed and glanced around. The room was small, but it had the important stuff—an ensuite bathroom and tea-making facilities. "I also need to read the Eye and see what it has to say about the shield."

He nodded and drew me in for a kiss. "You want me to order you a whiskey?"

"You want to have sex later?"

He laughed and released me. "I'll order you a double, then."

Once he'd gone, I had a quick shower, then sat cross-legged on the bed. After placing the Codex and my knives on my lap, I tugged the Eye from around my neck, but didn't immediately reach for the power that pulsed within it. Instead, I fixed the image of the shield in my mind, then layered the images a Google search had revealed of the bleak, stark mountains that had once housed Gruama over the top of it.

Only then did I press the Eye's cage into my palm. When stone and flesh met, the Eye pulsed in response. Jagged lightning cut through its heart, sending bright beams of purple shooting past my clenched fingers. They always reminded me of a lighthouse beam—one that was seeking rather than warning.

Then the room disappeared, and I was spun into another place—one that was dark, damp, and narrow. A tunnel, I realized after a moment. And, really, where else would it be? The old gods seemed to have a propensity for using lakes in underground caves as hiding places for their more dangerous relics.

In *this* one, water dripped from blackened walls and, in the distance, spirits wailed, a soft song of sorrow and anger. The image skidded forward, flowing through the tunnel's twisting path so fast, it felt like I was on a roller coaster. Eventually, we reached a vast lake. Its waters were shallow and still, but deep in its heart, silver gleamed.

The vision snapped forward over the water.

It was the shield.

But someone—something?—gripped it. Those fingers were long, black, and sinewy, and they held the shield so tightly they'd dented the metal.

I couldn't see the creature itself. The water might be crystal clear even in this darkness, but the creature was not. Only his hands were visible.

Those hands were *huge*.

Were we dealing with some sort of giant? There were plenty of folktales of the giants who'd once roamed the ancient lands, but I couldn't ever imagine one being leashed underground, let alone underwater.

Of course, it was unlikely we were dealing with a flesh and blood type of giant here, but rather a supernatural—or perhaps even demonic—one.

At least I now knew it was there, and that gave us a chance to plan how we were going to deal with it. I shifted slightly, and then imagined the atrium Cynwrig had briefly described. His map had highlighted the three useable exit points from that area, but we simply didn't have the time to waste roaming willy-nilly through miles of tunnels.

The vision shifted abruptly, spiraling back up the darkly

claustrophobic tunnel until we reached the atrium. It was basically a massive rock cavern with multiple sun tubes dotted across its ceiling. In daylight, they probably bathed the area in golden light, and at night, would draw in the silvery light the moon. Right now, neither daylight nor starlight was visible, which, given it was dusk, suggested I was seeing this in real time.

A good portion of the area was inaccessible, thanks to an impregnatable wall of shiny black stone. But the intricate carvings and bright splashes of color that remained on the other walls despite the passage of time suggested this place had once been beautiful to behold.

The Eye spun around a forest of stalactites growing in the center of the plaza, in the remains of what had once been a fountain, and then turned to face the tunnel we'd come out of. It had a couple of wavy horizontal lines carved in the stone above the door. Simple but effective signage.

The image faded, but the Eye was not finished with me yet. A new vision rose, one filled with tension and fury. While darkness also dominated this place, it was more the result of the vision being sound only. It had happened before, though I had no idea why some were full of sensory details, and others were not.

But the voices echoing through that darkness were familiar. I'd heard them multiple times now, first discussing my mother's murder, and then the men who'd been involved in Mathi's kidnap. It was through one such vision I'd learned that not only had they been sent to question Gilda about the ruby she'd held, but to also seek the other two. I had no idea if they were in any way connected to our mad elves, but I wouldn't have thought so, given the horrible way she'd died.

How goes the hunt? the man asked, his voice cold and oddly tinny-sounding this time.

Which suggested he was using some sort of voice modulator, and possibly had been all along. And if he was disguising his voice, then he might also be disguising his appearance, even from Carla Wilson, the other partner in this conversation and the woman who appeared to be not only his lieutenant but his day-to-day operations manager.

If true, then whoever this man was, he was someone so important he dare not reveal his identity to even those he trusted most.

Which made it all the more frustrating that I wasn't getting visuals. Even if the man was hidden or disguised by magic, the background might have given me some clues as to where they were.

The hunt continues at a snail's pace. Carla's voice was dry. *The council have created a list, but the harpē is not a high priority.*

The man swore. *And the pixie witch?*

Meaning me, of course.

Has not yet taken the bait. It restricts what can and can't be done.

What damn bait were they talking about? That was definitely something I needed to discover as a matter of urgency.

Loudon?

Remains alive.

That will have to be dealt with. There was pause. *I'm aware Gannon is dead, but what of his amplifier?*

Unknown, but she is no threat to us.

She might not be, but her mute elf partner could become so. I'd wager she saw and heard far more than Loudon knew.

In that, he was definitely right.

The mad elves seek the amplifier and may yet do the job for us. There was a brief pause. *We should have gotten rid of those two when we had the chance.*

Fuck, these people not only knew Halak, but whoever Keelakm was. And had, from the sound of things, worked with them. Which made it even more urgent I found Halak before anyone else and somehow made him talk.

They were too useful.

Right until the moment they got what they wanted. This destruction lies at our feet.

We are not responsible for their—or Gilda's—acquisition of the rubies.

Someone on the council is. The four men gave us that much.

Neither she nor they gave us a name, so it is for the moment a dead end.

Neither she nor they? Did that mean these two had questioned Gilda before she'd been murdered? Or were they the ones who killed her?

The thought had my nose wrinkling. Carla obviously had no qualms about killing, but her penchant seemed to be poison rather than tearing someone limb from limb.

The council is your purview, the man continued. *It's for you to investigate this matter, not me. But at least this destruction does have one benefit—it keeps Lùtair's mind on revenge rather than the witch.*

Why wouldn't they want Cynwrig concentrating on me? Surely the opposite should be true, given they wanted him *out* of the Hoard hunt. Unless, of course, they simply didn't want *me* distracted by his hotness.

Halak is now beyond our leash, and I fear the consequences if the witch catches him.

He does not know who I am.

He is aware of where you work. She is quite capable of putting two and two together, given enough information.

Then ensure she never gets that information.

Carla muttered something this audio-only vision didn't quite catch. *You need to remember that Ninkil is not the only power playing in this pool. Our opposition does too.*

Our opposition are as restricted in what they can do as Ninkil—

Ninkil does not as yet hold flesh. They do, and should not be discounted.

Obviously they were talking about the hags—and to a lesser extent, the curmudgeons—as they were the only gods left in this world who held human form. I'd better send Beira a warning, even though she was well aware the Ninkilim were active.

I discount no one. Do what you can to make the harpē's retrieval a priority.

We need to move slowly. The witch remains cautious, and we cannot risk her becoming aware of us. She is far more dangerous than her mother ever was.

By all accounts, she has not reached her full power—and may never.

That does not mean you should underestimate her.

Oh, I found myself thinking, *please do.*

I did so once, the man was saying, *it will not happen again, I assure you.*

His reply suggested he and I might have crossed paths before, in real time. But when? And how? It was damnably frustrating to get all these bits and pieces without the means of gluing them all together.

And if she becomes a problem more than an asset?

An asset? How the fuck was I an asset to them? They were obviously keeping an eye on me, but how... The thought trailed off. The council. They'd already said they had eyes and ears in the council, though up until now, it was something we'd merely suspected.

Then we get rid of her, the man said. *In the meantime, use your influence and get the harpē pushed up that list.*

I will do what I can, but security has been tightened, and I cannot risk my identity there to force the issue. We lost my Carla persona. We cannot afford to lose any others.

Meaning this woman—whoever she truly was—had more than one identity, and that at least one of them was deeply connected to the council. But how? Was she a sitting member? Or was she, perhaps, the lover of one—or even several—of them?

Multiple identities would also explain how she'd managed to disappear so completely—she'd simply discarded her Carla persona.

But it was one thing to hold multiple identities and quite another to use them at will. The building in which Deva's council met, like all governmental buildings, had magical inhibitors layered into their fabric as a matter of course. Her Carla ID was a prominent lawyer, which meant she simply couldn't be using an identity-disguising spell. Besides, not even the most powerful of them could maintain an ID flip for hours—or days—on end.

Which left one other possibility—that she was a face shifter. Unlike their animal counterparts, face shifters could take on the form of any same-sex human they desired as long as they'd had skin-on-skin contact with that person.

Of course, they were also extremely rare, and the few that existed were legally required to be registered. But if she'd come in from elsewhere? Or the registration process had somehow been avoided? It would certainly explain how she was moving around with impunity. She just shifted into whatever form she needed to get her task done.

Keep me updated, the man was saying.

When I hear, you'll hear, but do not expect miracles.

I do not. Ninkil is another matter.

His rise has been centuries in the making. We dare not risk our progress by rushing our final steps.

The man grunted, and the vision fragmented, leaving me battling for breath and trembling with exhaustion.

I released the Eye, shifted my legs, and flopped back onto the bed, spending the next few minutes breathing slow and deep in an effort to control my erratic heart rate.

Using the Eye—or indeed, the Codex—never seemed to get any easier. But then, they were godly artifacts, and the old gods always demanded some form of payment in return for borrowed power.

Which made me wonder, what was the cost of using the rubies? The closeness of the two attacks suggested it wasn't a physical cost, but there *had* to be some sort of price paid.

Maybe I needed to go back into the Codex and ask... but not right now. I needed those promised whiskeys and a good helping of hot chips to restock the energy well.

I sighed, slung the Eye over my neck, and then put the Codex and knives back in my bag. After sending Sgott a text telling him everything I'd seen in the Eye—including the possibility Carla was a face shifter—I headed downstairs.

The hotel had two bars—a larger one for guests, and a smaller one for locals. The former had a sign up saying it was closed during off-peak periods, so I headed into the other, finding Cynwrig, Lugh, and Mathi sitting around a table looking up at the TV on the wall. Silence held the room, and after a moment, I realized why.

Images of destruction filled the screen.

Not just any destruction, but *melted* destruction.

Keelakm had finally unleashed the ruby capable of undoing what smiths had made. In this case, it was a building of metal and glass. The concrete walls had not been touched, but with the steel supports gone, they'd simply concertinaed.

The buildings on either side were covered in dust and pitted with holes that must have come from concrete fragments being ricocheted away during the collapse of the building's floors, but most of the damage appeared minor.

I sat down hard on the empty chair next to Cynwrig. "Where is this? It doesn't look like Deva."

We didn't have any buildings that tall, for a start.

"It isn't." Cynwrig's voice was carefully controlled, but I could almost taste the fury that vibrated underneath it. "It's London."

London. Fuck. For some damn reason, I hadn't expected their revenge to be so wide-ranging. But revenge is rarely restricted by time or place—how many times had I heard Sgott say that?

"What happened? Who—what—did he attack?"

A waiter appeared, not only placing a double whiskey down, but also a bowl of hot chips and several tomato sauce sachets. Cynwrig—or perhaps Lugh, given he knew well enough of my love for chips smothered in tomato sauce—had anticipated my needs.

I nodded my thanks, picked the drink up, and downed a good half of it. The fiery liquid burned away some of the tiredness, but not the sick certainty that this was just the beginning of our elves' destructive plans.

"It's the Eadevane Holdings building," Cynwrig was saying.

I glanced at him sharply. "As in, Afran Eadevane?"

He nodded. I swore again. "Many hurt?"

"Unknown at this stage," Lugh said. "There're reports that a warning was issued five minutes before the building started melting, but that remains unconfirmed, as does the number of people who might have been inside at the time."

"Eadevane Holdings allows work from home," Cynwrig said. "The reports are saying many took advantage it."

I picked up the sauce sachets and squeezed them over the chips. "And Afran? Was he in the building this time?"

"Some witnesses are saying he was."

"They're also saying the top floor—where his offices were located—had been locked off by forces unknown before the call came in and the building evacuated," Mathi said. "The building melted before the fire brigade could even attempt a rescue."

I couldn't help but wonder if Halak had phoned Afran first to confirm he was there—and then kept him on the line while Keelakm melted his building around him. It was an action that would make sense after he'd escaped the destruction at Cynwrig's. "What does Eadevane Holdings do?"

"They're basically a mining exploration and development company," Cynwrig said. "And that building is its organizational heart."

My eyebrows rose. "I wasn't aware the Myrkálfar were into mining."

Mathi raised his eyebrows, amusement evident. "They control earth and stone—what else did you think they'd do?"

I waved a hand to the man at my side. "Run the black markets."

"That's what the Lùtair line does, not the other six,"

Mathi said. "When it comes to brutal reputations, however, the Eadevane have it all over the Lùtair."

"Meaning what?" I said. "They're a mining company—they'd have to play within certain rules, wouldn't they? Bribery and corruption will surely only get you so far in this day and age."

"In this day and age, the means of bribery and corruption might be less obvious," Mathi said, "but trust me when I say there remain plenty of authorities with their snouts in the trough."

I raised my eyebrows, amusement rising. "That sounds an awful lot like the voice of experience talking."

Mathi smiled and didn't bother denying it.

I returned my gaze to the destruction. "The captive we interviewed outside Cynwrig's building said this was all about revenge. I guess the next question has to be, what did Afran Eadevane—and his company—do to our elves? This is about more than revenge for Gilda's treatment at Afran's hands."

"Gilda worked for Afran?" Mathi said sharply. "When?"

"Quite a few years ago," Cynwrig said. "Gilda never reported Afran's violence, and he has the power and money to silence anyone else who might have been inclined to do so."

"How did you—" Mathi stopped. "The building collapse loosened tongues."

Cynwrig nodded, though the glint in his eyes suggested it was more likely his utter fury that loosened those tongues.

"Which means," I said, "that Halak, and whoever Keelakm truly is, are connected not only by Gilda, but whatever tragedy resulted from Eadevane's actions."

Cynwrig nodded again. "I've already contacted my

people and ordered an urgent search through the archives. Given our suspicions Halak is from the Cloondeash encampment, I've requested the search concentrate on any developments Eadevane might have had in that area."

"Except that Halak, at the very least, came to Deva for work when he was young."

"Young by our terms," Lugh said. "Possibly not young by his."

Which was true enough. I'd never been overly concerned about *actual* ages when it came to elven partners because of the differences in lifespans. "Do we think their destruction ends with Afran? Or will they go after the whole damn family?"

"You're obviously not aware of the Myrkálfar motto," Mathi said dryly. "Kill one of ours, and we'll take all yours."

"Isn't that the Ljósálfar motto?"

"Their motto," Cynwrig said blandly, "is fuck with our businesses, and we'll fuck with you."

I just about choked on my chip. As mottos went, both summed up the different outlook of the two groups damnably well. "Has Afran got brothers and sisters?"

"One of each. They were all advised after the destruction of my building to be on guard." Cynwrig shrugged and motioned for another round of drinks. "I doubt they took much notice."

"Maybe now," I said, waving a hand toward the TV, "they will."

"Or they'll simply use the opportunity to claim Afran's position as sole company director," Cynwrig said. "None of the siblings liked each other, and the only thing uniting the younger two was their hatred for Afran."

"He wasn't well-liked by anyone," Mathi said. "But the company was too powerful for most to go up against."

I scooped up more chips. "Meaning your company has clashed swords with him a few times?"

"Only the once."

"Who won?"

"He won the battle; we won the war."

"Afran's oldest sibling did not heed the Ljósálfar motto," Cynwrig said. "Which is why Afran's oldest sibling no longer exists."

"I'll have you know it was an extremely unfortunate accident that took Rankin's life," Mathi said blandly.

"I'm sure the official reports listed it as such."

"Oh, come on," I said, when neither man elaborated. "You can't just leave a statement like that hanging out there and not give details."

"I assure you, we most certainly can. There are some things in this world better left unsaid and unknown."

I was sure there was, but that would never stop curiosity. Or, at least, it would never stop mine. But the finality of Cynwrig's tone meant I'd be questioning Mathi later rather than him.

"To bring this back to the matter at hand," Lugh said. "Why was the third ruby found at Gilda's? Even if she *is* connected to our nutcase elves, she didn't have the power or nous to use it."

"Maybe she was doing nothing more than keeping it hidden until they found the shield," I said. "Remember, they need the three rubies to unleash the full force of the shield, and there's not many who would have uncovered her hiding spot."

It was lucky *I* had.

"She was servant class," Mathi said. "She could not have moved about with the impunity needed to steal the stone."

"And there lies the arrogance of the elves," I said. "The so-called servant class hears and sees more than any of you could ever guess. They are all but invisible to high-borns unless they want to fuck or in some other way use them."

"Afran did accuse her of stealing," Cynwrig said before Mathi could reply. "I never discovered what, exactly, she'd taken, but it's more than possible she and our two elves had a long history of stealing goods and information."

"And she *was* drugging you for information, if I remember correctly," Lugh said mildly,

Mathi gave him a rather dark look. "That's different."

"Not really," I said. "But there's something else—something that *does* tie all this conjecture together. According to what I just heard in a vision, Halak, Gilda, and Keelakm were definitely working with someone on the council to steal information and goods."

"Everyone on the council has been vetted," Mathi said. "As have their immediate connections."

"Vetting didn't catch Gilda." I hesitated. "That same vision told me Carla had dealt with both Gilda and our elves, and that she has multiple identities, including one as a standing council member."

"Carla *Wilson*? The lawyer?" Mathi said, disbelief evident.

I nodded. "According to what I overheard via the Eye, they weren't behind Gilda's acquisition of the ruby, but someone on the council *did* give them information that led to it."

"They?" Lugh said. "Who are 'they'?"

My gaze met his. "Carla and the man I'm hearing but not seeing. They are Ninkil followers and were responsible for Mom's death."

Lugh swore and scrubbed a hand across his eyes. "And you've no clue as to who the man might be?"

"None, although I believe the reason I'm not seeing visuals is because he's using a shield and some kind of voice modulator." I shrugged. "I just don't know enough about the Eye to be sure. I'm sorry."

He reached across the table and squeezed my hand. "Don't be. You're doing an amazing job under trying circumstances, dearest sister. Don't ever doubt that—or yourself."

Tears prickled my eyes, and I hastily blinked them back. When the gods had been handing out big brothers, they'd certainly given me one of the best.

"If Carla had gotten the contact's identity from those four men, my father surely would have," Mathi said. "He did interview them extensively before she arrived."

Extensively being code for using non-approved methods. I finished my whiskey as another arrived. "Thing is, even though she used Dahbree, she never got a name. Your father would likely have had the same result—and even *he* wouldn't go up against the council without reason."

Mathi pursed his lips. "On that I agree."

"What about Gilda's background check?" Lugh asked. "Did that reveal any other elven—or non-elven —contacts?"

"It didn't even reveal Afran's presence," Mathi said, "so obviously it was not as thorough as it should have been."

I took a drink. "Who did the check? Is it worth doing a background on them?"

"It went through the usual channels, but I'll request the file and the name of the researcher." Mathi frowned. "There *have* been instances of reports being altered if enough of a financial incentive was offered, but it *is* rare."

No doubt because of the Ljósálfar motto. Just because it was generally applied to businesses didn't mean they wouldn't also bring the hammer down on double crosses of a personal nature.

"Any idea of Carla's new identity?" he added.

I shook my head. "But given the heavy layering of spells around the council's halls to prevent any kind of magic, is it possible she's a face shifter? If so, she could be anyone."

"Face shifters are rare, so it gives us a possible lead," Mathi said. "I'll see if my father can pull some strings and get a list of all those currently listed within the UK."

"She might not be registered with us, though."

"Carla has been a practicing lawyer here in the UK for a very long time," Cynwrig said. "If she was a registered face shifter, she would have been disbarred."

"Still worth checking," Mathi said.

Cynwrig didn't disagree. "In the meantime, I'll start an underground investigation to see which, if any, of the currently serving councilors have black market contacts."

"Here's hoping," I said grimly, "we get enough of a lead from one of these searches to stop these bastards."

"Amen to that." Cynwrig paused as the waiter appeared to take our dinner orders. Once he'd done so, he added, "Did you see anything else in the Eye?"

I told them what I'd seen of Gruama then added, "No giant can live underwater for so long—not the giants folklore speaks about, anyway—so I'm not sure what we might be dealing with."

"Something suitably dangerous, godly, and hard to kill," Mathi said.

"Oh, that's a certainty," I muttered.

Lugh snared a chip. "Given everything we know to date about the shield—"

"Which isn't a whole lot."

"I'm thinking," he continued, giving me a disapproving glare for interrupting. Which, of course, only amused the hell out of me. "...that it won't be an actual giant. It's more likely to be either a supernatural entity or even a partial god."

"A godling?" Cynwrig said. "Present company aside, there's not many of them around these days."

"But the shield wasn't hidden in these days, was it?" Lugh countered. "So, the possibility very definitely remains."

"Why would the scroll warn of 'that which roams' when the thing in that lake has no means to roam?" I said. "It's a pair of hands without a body attached."

"Hey," Mathi said. "There're plenty of legends surrounding murderous autonomous hands to imply they might once have been a thing."

"Let's hope not," I said. "I saw *Evil Dead II* as a kid. I'm still scarred by it."

Lugh laughed. "That was one hell of a fun movie."

I rolled my eyes but didn't disagree with him, even if, at the time, I'd been traumatized by the whole chainsaw scene. "If there is a godling—or even just murderous hands —down there, how are we going to deal with them?"

"Anything made with cold iron or silver will take care of most supernatural entities," Lugh said. "And lucky for you, I do have two such items in my kit."

He was referring to the hefty-looking foot-long metal stakes that he'd, rather incongruously, named Jack and Jill. Jack was cold iron while Jill was silver with an iron core, and, according to Lugh, they'd come in handy multiple times against a wide range of hellish ghouls often hanging around relic sites.

He was also of the belief that I should name my knives. According to him, names had power, and all godly items of power should bear them. He'd claimed that neither Mom nor Gran had done so because they weren't theirs to name.

I thought the whole thing ridiculous.

The knives had been in our family for eons, so if naming them had been crucial to their usage, it would have been done well before now.

But if we *were* dealing with a godling, then using them would certainly sort out another family legend—that, thanks to the fact they'd been blessed by multiple goddesses, they could not only take out magic, but also certain gods. *Not* goddesses. Which did make sense— they'd hardly bless a weapon that could take *them* out.

We just had to hope that if the long black hands *did* belong to a godling, it was male not female.

Our meals came and we moved on to other subjects. The news reports continued to show scenes of destruction, but it did seem the five-minute warning had resulted in most people getting out in time.

Maybe our mad elves had a limit as to how many innocent lives they'd take.

While there was a part of me absolutely doubted that would be true, another part—the same one that steadfastly refused to remember my relationship with Ka-hal or Halak or whatever the hell his real name was—couldn't believe I'd get involved with someone so inherently evil.

And yet, I obviously *had,* given what Lugh had said about him hitting me.

So, what the hell was going on? Why couldn't I remember either the event or him? Had I been so traumatized that I'd simply pushed any memory of it away?

Maybe.

And maybe something else was going on. I'd always had a fairly good radar when it came to that sort of thing, and while I had over the years gotten involved with a few shady characters who at first had seemed perfect—too perfect, as it had turned out—I still remembered their faces, if not all their names. And they'd never been evil in the way these two were. Revenge was one thing but this— this was another plane entirely.

We made plans to meet at six the next morning, which would get us to Gruama just before the sun rose. I had no desire to be roaming through tunnels in darkness, but at least if we headed out early, it'd be more obvious if someone followed us. Given what I'd heard in the vision, it was pretty obvious they'd found some means of keeping an eye on my movements.

Cynwrig and I spent an hour or two partying in one of the too-small beds before he moved into the other and almost instantly fell asleep.

I, however, stayed awake for entirely too long, haunted by feelings of betrayal and uncertainty. Not only had Mom been double-crossed by someone she'd known, but it was also very possible the very same thing was happening to me.

But by who?

No one in my small circle of close friends—and even smaller circle of lovers—would do something like that. I was utterly certain of that, if nothing else.

But what if I was wrong?

I scrubbed a hand across my eyes. Fear, doubt, and uncertainty were probably natural in this sort of situation, but I couldn't let them overtake me. Besides, when I'd found Egeria's coin—a token dedicated to the goddess of wisdom and good fortune, and one that had been in my family for generations—abandoned at the entrance to the tunnel in which Mom had been killed, I'd gotten no sense that her betrayer had been someone truly close to her. She'd definitely trusted him—or her—and had some sort of working relationship with them, but that was it.

Nothing in that recent vision had suggested they had a spy within my circle even if they did have one within the council. As for the bait—that could be anything. Hell, for all we knew, they had someone working at the museum, and the bait they were talking about was the notes Eljin had found amongst the papers on Nialle's desk.

That was a *far* more likely scenario than anyone on this quest betraying me.

Still, the unsettling knowledge that there were under-currents in my life that I couldn't yet see but would eventu-ally cause turmoil would not be ignored, and it was well after midnight before I finally found some sleep.

Cynwrig pulled off the narrow road and stopped the SUV. On the opposite side was the long strip of rough land that separated Doo Lough from its smaller partner. A mean-dering gravel path followed the edges of the lough and then moved off toward a mountain Google informed me was part of the Mweelrea Range. The peak directly ahead of us resembled a conical volcano that had lost a good portion of one side. But that peak hadn't been a volcano, and that lost section wasn't the result of some sort of lateral explosion. Not of lava, anyway. It was the result of a furious god melting away the rock and stone.

This was Gruama.

Or rather, what remained of it.

The land between the road and Gruama was wild-looking, the ground covered in rubble and grasses that were green and high. It was going to be a long, unpleasant hike. Thankfully, Lugh had dropped by the tavern to collect my hiking boots before we'd all gotten onto the plane, so at least I wouldn't be crossing the terrain in less-than-suitable gear.

After we'd donned our coats and backpacks, Cynwrig locked the SUV, tucked the keys out of sight under the front wheel arch, then led the way across the fields and up the mountain.

It was every bit as tiresome and tedious as I'd feared. By the time we'd reached the breach in the bowl-like top of the mountain, I'd stripped off both my coat and sweater—something I'd no doubt regret once we got inside.

I shrugged off my pack, took a drink, and then tore open one of the trail bars Lugh had packed for us, munching on it contemplatively as I studied the wide bowl. Though it was now strewn with boulders and solidified rivers of black stone, it wasn't without vegetation. Aside from the grasses and compact shrubs, the straggly remnants of once beautiful trees sang wistfully of a time filled with plentiful growth. This place had once been a well-tended and very large garden.

Cynwrig stopped beside me. "Are you doing okay?"

"Considering how unfit I am, yes."

A wicked smile tugged at his lips. "There are varying types of fitness, and yours definitely lies in other areas."

I snorted and nudged him lightly. "Where was the entrance before the shield took out this part of the mountain?"

He nodded to the right, where a wall of black rock reared up a good hundred feet. From where we stood, it actually looked like a frozen waterfall. "There was a long, well-guarded tunnel leading into this forecourt area."

"Which, if the remaining trees are anything to go by, was a gorgeous, well-loved parkland."

"More a well-tended wildland, but yes. The new entrance lies to your left, behind the boulder."

I glanced over, but the boulder blocked all sight of the entrance. "I take it that stone was strategically and deliberately placed?"

He nodded. "This is now a burial site, remember. None but the invited are welcome into it."

"That sounds like there's magic here."

"There is."

I wasn't sensing it, and more importantly, perhaps, neither were my knives. But given the magic's intent was more protection and repelling, that wasn't really surprising.

I finished my trail bar, tucked the wrapper back into the pack's side pocket, and then put my sweater and coat back on. I was still overly hot from the walk up here, but that would change soon enough once we got inside. Besides, the additional layers would come in handy in the tighter tunnel spots. It was always better to scrape clothes than skin.

Mathi walked up and stood beside us. "How deep are we likely to be going?"

"Quite a ways." I looked at him in amusement. "You can return to the car, you know."

"I know, but you have no idea what grips that shield, and my gun might just come in handy."

"Bullets won't kill a godling."

"Perhaps not, but silver bullets will certainly take care of anything supernatural. I know this for a fact."

"You do?" I asked, eyebrows rising. "Since when have you ever had to deal with the supernatural?"

"I am not just a pretty face—"

"There are some who would argue with that," Cynwrig murmured.

Mathi studiously ignored him. "And I do run an international business. There have been times when we've had to deal with... shall we say entities?... less than pleased about our takeover of their lands."

"You never said anything to me about it."

"You weren't around at the time."

"Ah yeah," I said. "I keep forgetting you're a much older man."

"As is Cynwrig."

"By comparison, no," Cynwrig replied mildly. "In elf terms, you're a good century older."

"Seventy-two does not a century make," Mathi said dryly.

Cynwrig smiled but didn't reply as his phone beeped. As he pulled it free from his pocket, Lugh approached and handed us each a headlamp.

"We should get going," he said. "We have no idea how long it'll take us to reach the lake—"

"I can tell you that once we get inside," Cynwrig said. "I can also search for whatever other problems we might encounter."

He meant physical blockages rather than any sort of metaphysical ones.

Lugh nodded. "I'd still rather avoid stumbling down this mountainside at night. Too easy for others to set a trap."

My gaze jumped to his. "You think we were followed?"

"No, but doesn't mean we weren't."

"Which is why," Cynwrig said, "I've arranged for us to take the emergency tunnel out. We'll be met by the Cloondeash historian, who will drive us back to the hotel so we can collect our bags before we head to the airport. He'll also hopefully have an update on Halak."

"And the SUV we just left?" I asked.

"Will be picked up once we have safely exited the other side." He cast me an amused glance. "I'm not so trusting that I'd leave car keys in such an obvious hiding spot if it were not necessary."

"I did wonder." And had thought that, given this was a dark elf area, few would actually risk theft.

Cynwrig smiled and moved forward. I slung my pack over my back and followed. The song of the trees grew fainter the closer we moved to the entrance, no doubt due to the solidity of the stone covering this area. Not even the hardiest of them would be able to survive in a ground that now resembled black diamonds.

The entrance itself was just wide enough to carry a casket through. Though in truth, I had no idea what Myrkálfar funeral rites were, or even if they used caskets.

Magic pressed at us as we walked the arch—a soft caress of power that somehow felt judgmental. We were allowed to pass, but I couldn't help but wonder what would happen if we'd tried this without Cynwrig or another dark elf accompanying us.

The long, wide tunnel that lay beyond the entrance's deep arch sloped gently down. In the distance, light twinkled, a golden glimmer that danced across the solidified black stone lapping at the tunnel's exit.

Our bootsteps echoed, but nothing else stirred in this place. Nothing alive, at any rate. The ghosts I'd heard in the vision were a low-range, distant hum. Although they didn't haunt the cavern up ahead, I couldn't help hoping they weren't in the tunnel we needed to go down. I really didn't want to walk through their shrouds and misery.

We reached the atrium, and it was every bit as beautiful as it had looked in the vision, despite all the centuries that now lay between it and its heyday. The ceiling arched high overhead, and the long streaks of blue still evident through the growing forest of stalactites suggested it had once all been that glorious color. The remnants of what must have been vast murals depicting various landscapes, both foreign and domestic, colored the walls, and in some places still looked real enough that it appeared you could just step into them.

"Is your encampment this beautiful, Cynwrig?" I asked.

"Better," he said softly. "Maybe one day..."

My gaze shot to his, but he didn't finish the sentence. Maybe because he knew "one day" was never a real possibility for us. Gran might have boasted about being snuck into the Myrkálfar encampment by her lover, but mine was a king in waiting, and he would not similarly bend the rules. Not for me.

"This way," he continued, and moved forward once again.

I moved around the stalactite-covered fountain that glittered in the golden light coming in from the remaining sun tubes and followed him. A large portion of the floor in this section was slabs of polished quartz stone unmarred by time, melting stone, or stalactites, and in the warm glow of the sun coming through, the tubes appeared shot with veins of gold.

The magic that protected this place was obviously stronger than I'd presumed if it *were* gold.

"It's one thing to hear about the tragedy of this place, quite another to actually see it." Lugh's gaze was on the waterfall-like barrier that sliced the length of the atrium in half. "I take it not even the Myrkálfar can manipulate stone that has become diamond sharp?"

"We can manipulate all manner of stone, no matter the sharpness, but as I said earlier, we cannot undo what a god has done."

"Is that why Gruama has never been reoccupied?" I asked.

"It's never been reoccupied because few want to live amongst the ghosts of tragedy that haunt this place."

Couldn't say I blamed them. I certainly wouldn't want to. And while there were known methods of clearing houses or buildings of spirits and other entities, I wasn't sure they'd work on this sort of scale.

The tunnel we needed lay directly ahead, Cynwrig paused to read the lay of the ground within the deeper confines of the tunnel, his energy briefly washing across my senses. Which should not really be happening, given it was more an innate talent than a spell. I guessed it was just one more instance of our deepening connection... and I absolutely *wasn't* bitter at the gods for showing me the possibility of relationship perfection all the while knowing it could never be.

Not bitter at *all*.

The wave of his power died, and he glanced around. "I'm not sensing any rockfalls and other traps, but the tunnel does narrow significantly as it nears the lake."

"How significant are we talking about?" Lugh asked. "I'm the tallest and widest here—will I get through?"

Cynwrig nodded. "You might lose some skin on those shoulders, though."

"Would be the first time," Lugh said and motioned Cynwrig to lead once more.

The rivers of solidified stone that ran around the entrance were testament to just how close it had come to destruction. The tunnel itself was smooth, wide, and easy to traverse, which was a nice change as far as these things went, even if it didn't last. Our lights danced across the shiny black walls, creating hundreds of tiny stars that made it look like we were walking through a bright night sky.

But the deeper we went, the fainter those stars became as the melted black stone gave way to regular rock. Cynwrig periodically trailed his fingers against the wall, but if he sensed anything untoward up ahead, he didn't mention it.

The water I'd seen in the vision began to trickle down the walls, and moss soon slicked the ground, making every step that much more dangerous. A damp mustiness touched the air, and the tunnel drew ever closer to our shoulders. Anxiety—or something close to it—pressed against my spine, but this time, it wasn't mine but rather Mathi's. Ljósálfar elves had an inborn fear of deep underground places like this, and it said a lot about his determination and courage that he'd come in here willingly.

We finally reached the "roller coaster" portion of the tunnel. After pausing for a drink, we continued on, our pace necessarily slower. The peaks and troughs in the ground were often so sharp we had to help each other up the incline before moving on. It was just as well we weren't coming back this way, because if trouble struck, getting out in any sort of hurry would be nigh on impossible.

Things didn't really improve all that much when the jagged rises in the ground gave way to a steady downhill slant. The air became thicker, staler, and an odd sense of weightiness now came from up ahead.

The thing in the water was awake and aware.

I shivered. While there was no immediate sense of

threat, I knew well enough that could change in a heartbeat.

It certainly had in the past.

"We're close to the lake," Cynwrig said. "I can feel its weight on the stone."

"Is there any other sort of weight, though?" Mathi asked. There was no sign of discomfort in his voice, let alone fear. Anyone who didn't know him would think this was little more than a walk in the park for him. "Anything that might indicate what Beth saw in her vision?"

Cynwrig once again brushed his fingers against the wall. "No, but that doesn't mean there's nothing there. If it's supernatural or even some sort of godling, it might not have weight to press against stone."

"What about magic?" Lugh asked. "Beth, you sensing anything?"

"No," I said, "and the knives aren't reacting."

But then, would they if we were indeed dealing with another godling?

We continued on, our pace slowing as the tunnel grew ever tighter, forcing me to press my hands against my boobs and squash them flatter in several places in order to get through a bit easier. Which, of course, resulted in my hands getting scratched and my coat torn.

Lugh had it far worse, though—in one section, he was forced to slither through snake-like on his left side, because there was no way a man of his height would have gotten through the narrow, almost diamond-shaped section otherwise.

Just as the tunnel began to widen again, the darkness swamped us, swallowing the light of the headlamps and leaving us in utter blackness.

"This," Lugh said heavily, "reminds me an awful lot of

the impregnable darkness we encountered just before we found the forge."

"It can hardly be called impregnable, given you did get through it and found the forge," Mathi said somewhat blandly.

"Well, impregnable to anyone not armed with Beth's magic knives."

"And let's just hope," I said, "that its exit counterpart doesn't transfer us to an undisclosed, out of the way, and totally inconvenient location like that one did."

Cynwrig glanced at me, though I couldn't see his expression thanks to the headlamp's light being little more than a pale-yellow puddle that didn't illuminate any part of his face.

"If there'd been any magical transfer events," he said, "I would have been told of them."

"Unless, of course," Lugh said, "they're transported somewhere inhospitable to life, and are simply listed as missing."

"You can always rely on my brother to come up with the most cheerful possibilities," I said wryly.

"Hey, I'm the only experienced relic hunter in this outfit, so trust me, it's always better to believe the worse than hope for the best."

"I guess I can't argue with that." Though there was part of me that definitely wanted to—no doubt the same part that was desperately trying to ignore the growing sense of danger.

"It might be best if we're roped together," Cynwrig said. "This darkness might not be designed to stop us, but it's possible it could separate us."

Lugh immediately got one of the ropes out of his pack

and, within minutes, we were all lashed on. Only then did we cautiously move forward.

Not being able to see anything made for slow, almost torturous progress forward. The darkness seemed relentless, and the deeper we stepped into it, the more the grief of the dead—who'd been strangely silent up until this point —began to wrap around us, until it became a shroud so fierce and cloying it made breathing difficult.

The sense of danger sharpened abruptly.

"Cynwrig, stop, there's something happening ahead."

He immediately halted, something I knew by the sudden lack of tension in the rope. "I'm not sensing anything through the stone."

I raised a hand until my fingers brushed his body, then stopped and drew a knife. Light flickered down her blade, and both the song of the dead and the utter blackness faded. Not by much, but enough to at least see what lay ahead, and that meant this darkness was being enhanced by magic.

And what lay ahead was a jagged crack in the ground not three feet away.

If I hadn't called for a halt, he would have fallen into it, and possibly dragged me in before Mathi or Lugh could react.

Cynwrig glanced at me, his silvery eyes glimmering in the knife's flickering light. "The earth makes no mention of that chasm. I didn't even sense the magic concealing it."

"Neither did I," I admitted. "I just felt the wrongness."

"Well, thank gods for instinct." He took a cautious step forward and peered over the edge. "Impossible to see how far it drops, but it feels a long way down."

"A final trap before we reached the shield?" Mathi said. "Or merely the first?"

"I'm hoping for the former, but betting on the latter." I raised the knife higher. Its light brightened, a beacon that washed the darkness from the chasm's other edge. "It appears an easy enough jump now that we know it's there."

"Indeed," Cynwrig agreed. "But perhaps you should take the lead once we're on the other side, just to be safe."

I nodded, and one by one, we leapt over the void. The voices of the dead sharpened after each successful jump, as if in disappointment that no new souls would be joining them in darkness today.

We rearranged the rope and continued on with me in the lead. Thankfully, the blanket of darkness soon faded, and the headlamps once again shone brightly. A dozen steps later, we came out on a wide stone platform that overlooked the dark, still lake I'd seen in my vision.

In the heart of the lake, a fiery light gleamed.

I shivered. There was no reason for that gleam. No reason other than godly luminance, perhaps.

Once we'd undone the rope tying us all together, Cynwrig bent and pressed a hand against the stone. "The lake doesn't weigh heavily, so it's not that deep. I'm still getting no sense of what else lies in that water, though."

"There's usually only one way to uncover that," Lugh said, "and that's to spring whatever trap the gods have left."

I swung my pack off. "And seeing I'm the one with the magic knives, I'd better be the one doing the springing."

"Does the exit tunnel lie off this cavern?" Mathi asked. "Because we should probably secure that as a matter of priority."

"Agreed," Cynwrig said. "It's at the far end of the lake. I'll head left, you head right."

"And in the meantime," I said. "Lugh and I will head

into the middle of the lake and see what awaits."

Mathi unzipped his coat, then undid the retention clip on his gun holster. "Give us a few minutes to ensure the area is secure."

"Is that thing really loaded with silver bullets?" I asked.

He raised an eyebrow, his expression somewhat amused. "You've known me for how long? When, in all that time, have I ever joked about something like that?"

"Well, never, but you've also never revealed the fact that you owned and used guns until recently, and certainly never mentioned the fact you possessed silver bullets for them."

"Mathi works on a need-to-know basis," Lugh said. "You didn't need to know about the gun, just as you didn't need to know about the other lovers."

"I've admitted it was wrong to conceal the latter." It was mildly said, but his annoyance was nevertheless clear. "And this sort of discussion gets us no closer to our goal."

With that, he turned and walked down the slope to the right shoreline.

If a backbone could glower, his definitely did. He really *didn't* like being called to task for past actions, however lightly.

Cynwrig picked up my pack, motioned for Lugh's, and then said, "If anything attacks, I'll try to fence it within stone, but given we have no idea what lies underneath the water, that may or may not be successful. Just... be careful."

I nodded. He slung the packs over his shoulders and strode down the left ramp. I returned my gaze to the water. Despite the fact it was as black as hell, I could see the stones dotting its bottom. Could see the remnants of wooden beams lying in crisscrossed bits and pieces, suggesting structures of some kind had once dotted this lake. No wood song rose from those beams; it would have been drowned under the weight of the water long ago. The lake was mirror-still; despite the stalactites that dotted the cavern's roof, nothing dripped to disturb its surface.

Perhaps it feared to wake whatever lay in wait.

I shivered and rubbed my arms.

"How we going to play this?" I asked. "And don't say carefully, or I *will* smack you."

Lugh chuckled softly. "We approached armed and ready for a fight. Other than that, we'll have to play it by ear."

I nodded and raised my gaze, following the progress of the two men via the bobbing light of their headlamps. I had no idea how big this cavern really was, but if what I'd seen in the vision was anything to go by, they were probably halfway around.

I shifted from one foot to the other, trying to ignore the sudden urge to get this over with. Rushing in where fools feared to tread never went well for anyone; I knew that from the multiple stories Lugh had regaled me with over the years.

"What happens once we get the shield and get out of here?" I asked. "Are we going to head straight across to the forge?"

"Well, it's either that or you spin it up into the sky and let it hang out in some storm system somewhere over the North Sea."

I glanced at him. "You know what? That actually might be our best option, especially given our mad elves seem to have a knack for showing up wherever I am."

"Well, they're mages. They're obviously using some kind of tracker spell."

"Except tracker spells need something belonging to the target to work this reliably."

"Maybe he has something from your time with him."

"I'm not in the habit of gifting boyfriends with personal items," I said wryly.

Lugh shrugged. "Maybe he took it without you knowing. Hair from a brush or something."

"Would hair from a brush still hold any sort of resonance after such a long time?"

"I wouldn't have thought the resonance was important, but rather the DNA."

That *did* make more sense. I wrinkled my nose. "Why would he be holding on to something like that after all this time, though?"

He cast me an amused sideways glance. "Perhaps he was unable to get past his desire for you and was hoping to use it at some point to lure you back into his arms."

I snorted. "Given you're the one that apparently got rid of him, not me, I think it more likely he'd be keeping something of yours to exact revenge."

Lugh raised an eyebrow. "You still can't remember him?"

"No, and it's damn frustrating."

"Your memory isn't usually that bad—and it's not like you've had a ton of lovers you need to sift through." He paused thoughtfully. "Wonder if he employed some sort of memory smudging spell?"

"I would have sensed magic being used." I'd always been sensitive to its presence, even before I'd inherited the knives.

"If you were awake, yes. But magic is just as easily applied to those who sleep."

"But why would he bother?"

Lugh shrugged. "As I said, he wasn't a nice man, and he had some pretty nasty contacts. Perhaps he feared you'd seen or heard something that could give him away to Sgott or the IIT."

"If Sgott thought he was a problem, he would have chased him off well before you did." At the very least, he would have done a background search. He might be a stickler for rules but every now and then he did bend them just a little.

"Except," Lugh was saying, "Sgott tended to step back and let you make your mistakes."

That was true enough. I'd made a couple of less-than-bright choices when I was younger, but he'd never done anything or stepped in to help me unless I asked him to. As stepdads went, he was the absolute best.

The gently bobbing lights drew closer together, then briefly disappeared. Checking the viability of the exit tunnel, no doubt.

"If he did use a spell to fudge my memories, is there any way we can undo it and get those memories back?"

"It might be worth trying a memory regression mage. There is one in Deva, I think."

"I might need to make seeing him or her a priority. If Halak did smudge my memories, we need to find out why."

Down the far end of the cavern, a familiar power surged. A heartbeat later, a shudder rolled through the stone underneath us. Given nothing happened within the cavern itself, Cynwrig was obviously clearing a pathway or a blockage in the exit tunnel.

I gathered the still air, sent it swirling lazily around each of us, then glanced up at Lugh. "Ready?"

He raised Jack and Jill. "And raring."

I smiled, drew my other knife, and then walked down the left ramp. The two lights reemerged from the darkness at the far end and stopped. I warily stepped into the water.

Small waves rippled out from our entry point but didn't spread far across the lake's mirror surface. And yet, deep in the center of the lake, something stirred.

Waited.

I shivered and forced my feet on, walking warily toward the warm glimmer of metal. Each step was a little harder than it should be, simply because it felt like we were wading through thick goop rather than water. Perhaps there *was* magic here, though I had no sense of it and the knives weren't reacting to anything.

The awareness coming from the center of the lake sharpened, and with it came a tremor of expectation.

Of hunger.

For a fight. For a meal.

"Am I the only one getting a very bad feeling about whatever is gripping the shield?" Lugh said. "I'm talking about a 'we're about to be lunch' sort of feeling."

"No, and there's no need to sound so cheerful about it, brother."

He chuckled softly and flexed his fingers against the two stakes. "It's been a while since Jack and Jill had a decent outing. It'll do them good to bite into flesh again."

"You're really quite mad, aren't you?"

"I think it runs in the family."

I think it did. After all, despite every bit of me wanting to do nothing more than to run, here I was, striding forward beside him, knives gripped fiercely and the air continuing to stir lightly around us.

That air might not be capable of totally stopping whatever lay ahead, but it was at least an additional barrier between us. I fed it a little more speed, just in case, though it wasn't enough to slow our progress in any way.

The closer we drew to the center of the lake, the more

the shield seemed to glow. The hands that gripped it were thin streaks of darkness against its luminescent surface, but there were blobs of white within the black skin now.

Knuckles, glowing with the force of their grip on the shield.

I stopped three feet away from it while Lugh moved around to the other side. The shield's metal was untarnished by water or time, and the stylized flames that ringed the flange flickered and danced with a fierce golden light under the black water, a testament to the deeper danger that lay within its bronze heart.

"Those hands don't look big enough to belong to a giant," I said.

"What they appear to be and what they are might be two entirely different things."

"That's always a cheerful thought."

"But a rule to live by as a relic hunter." His gaze swept the shield thoughtfully. "I'm thinking neither of us will have the strength to pry it free from them."

"Agree." I studied the ground, looking for anything that might indicate exactly who or what those hands belonged to. But the lake's bed here was no different to what we'd walked across. "I think we should stab them instead. Jointly, I mean."

"Sounds like a plan." He hefted Jack and gave a fierce grin. "Ready?"

I gripped the hilt of the knife in my right hand tightly. "And raring."

He chuckled softly. "On three, then."

I nodded. He began the short countdown and then, as one, we plunged our weapons into the black hands.

And unleashed a fucking nightmare.

CHAPTER

TWELVE

I<small>T ERUPTED OUT OF THE WATER SO FAST</small>, I <small>GOT LITTLE MORE THAN</small> a glimpse of a tree-like structure before I was sent flying. I tumbled through the air for several yards, then dropped face-first into the water, mashing my nose against the stony bottom and scraping my forehead on something long and sharp. I instinctively gasped, regretting it the instant water rushed into my lungs rather than air, and hurriedly pushed up onto my hands and knees, coughing and spluttering and trying to breathe.

The distant tremor of Cynwrig's power ran through the ground, but it never reached beyond the stony ledge surrounding the lake, let alone to where the creature stood. Cynwrig might be able to manipulate the cavern's walls, but there was definitely magic here even if I couldn't feel it, and it was preventing him from controlling the lake's rocky base. He wouldn't be able to cage the creature. Not unless it left the lake's shallows.

A gunshot echoed, followed by an ungodly scream, the noise piercing and furious. Dust fell like rain all around me, and I glanced up sharply. The headlamp's light wasn't strong enough to fully illuminate the roofline, but I could still see cracks forming as the stalactites shuddered. If the creature kept screaming, he'd bring the roof down on top of us.

Maybe *that* was his intention. It was certainly one way of stopping any threat to the shield it clung to.

I pushed upright and swung around, my knives raised and blood oozing from skinned knuckles. As each drop hit the water, an odd sort of chime sounded, and the creature —a spindly thing with multiple branch-like limbs connected to its trunk—grew fractionally taller, looked fractionally stronger.

It wasn't only a goddamn living, moving tree that had no song, it was *feeding* on my blood.

Lugh stood on the other side of the nightmare, deftly using Jack and Jill to swat away the multiple branches attacking him. Every hit had splinters spinning into the air, but the creature seemed unharmed by the loss. Worse still, perhaps, was the fact that those splinters *didn't* fall; they just hovered several feet away from Lugh's body, as if waiting for the right opportunity to attack.

It was then I realized the air I'd spun around us both was not only intact but protecting *him* from those splinters.

At least that was something.

I plowed through the water toward them, but it was thick and gloopy and made any sort of speed impossible.

Another gunshot reverberated. The bullet hit the creature's head and lodged deep into wooden flesh, sheering away a big chunk of its featureless face. The creature howled and clawed at its head with fine, fingerlike branches, and it took me a second to realize why—flames now flickered where silver met wood.

The keening grew in volume, and the whole cavern

trembled. Chunks of stone and stalactites fell from the roof, hitting the water hard enough to send thick sprays into the air.

What *didn't* fall were the splintered remains of the creature's face. They simply spun and arrowed into the darkness, heading toward the exit and the two men standing there.

I sent the air chasing after the deadly counterattack, pushing hard to ensure it had enough speed to reach Cynwrig and Mathi before those splinters did.

Something in my head twinged, but I ignored it. From the edges of my vision, I spotted silver drop into the water. The bullet... Then the air howled a warning, and I glanced up to see a thick limb sweeping toward me so fast, its outer branches were little more than a blur. I ducked, twisted around, and slashed at the limb as it flew over my head. My knives sheered through the wood as easily as butter, and multiple branches fell. But this time, instead of hovering or attacking, they dropped lifeless to the water's surface and swiftly sank.

The knives might not be sensing the magic giving this thing life, but they *could* kill it.

More branches swept toward me, coming in from the left and the right, this time skimming the water's surface to prevent me from ducking again. I swore and did the only thing I could—reached for the wind, leapt up, and then thrust the gathered air under my feet to push me even higher.

One branch snagged my boot and sliced down its side, cutting leather and drawing blood. Pain slithered through me, but I pushed it to one side and, with every ounce of strength I had, threw a knife at what remained of the creature's head. It must have sensed the movement at the last moment, even if it had no idea what was coming, because it half turned, revealing a broken face that held no eye or nose.

The knife pierced the center of its forehead rather than the side of its head, thudding hilt deep into wooden brain.

This time, it didn't simply roar but rather, opened its mouth and emitted a high-pitched keening. It echoed so sharply, so violently, that the cavern's walls shuddered, and thicker chunks of roof started coming down.

The air under my feet gave way, and I hit the turbulent water hard. I swore, but gathered my balance and ran toward the creature. It was flailing wildly, its movements erratic and seemingly uncontrolled. The knife remained lodged in its forehead, but a black wave of deadness was now spreading out from the point of its entry, sweeping down onto the creature's trunk and then across its various limbs. As that wave hit each portion of its body, it froze.

Lugh stepped through the forest of deadness and plunged Jack and Jill deep into its wooden heart. There was heavy *thunk* not unlike that of an axe cutting into a tree, then the creature toppled backward, into the water, into the ground.

Through the ground.

And it was taking my knife with it.

I swore, lunged forward, and pulled the blade from its forehead. Almost instantly, the deadness began to retreat.

The knife hadn't killed it, as it had the outer branches. It had merely immobilized it.

I turned and slashed at the wrists holding the shield, severing them away from the creature's body. The fingers didn't move or react, but they also didn't release it.

It didn't matter. I sheathed my knives, grabbed the shield, and tossed it toward Lugh. He grabbed it with one hand, then reached out with the other, helping me over the creature's body. As its limbs began to twitch, we raced for the shore, stone and stalactites spearing the ground all around us. I pushed more force into the air, felt a sharper stab of pain in my head, and knew I was reaching the limits of my capabilities. It didn't matter. Nothing did except getting out of here in one piece.

We climbed out of the water, onto the ledge, and then ran on.

But the creature was keening again, and the cavern's gyrations grew more violent. A huge chunk of rock splintered off the wall yards ahead of us, but before it could fall, power surged and a sling of stone caught it, pinning it in place, allowing us to get past.

The keening sharpened.

Wood rose from the lake in response, thick chunks of ancient beams that threw themselves at us. I thrust out a hand, shielding us with air, and the pain in my head became needle sharp. I gasped and stumbled, but Lugh caught me, supported me, as we ran on.

The assault of wood and stone increased, making it harder and harder to see where we were going. The ledge's stone shuddered under our feet, then violently rose upward, creating an arched tunnel for us to run under.

Up ahead, through the thick swirl of dust, I spotted Mathi gripping what looked to be a thick slab of black rock, standing over Cynwrig—who had both hands pressed against the cavern's floor and his eyes closed in concentration—in the center of the exit tunnel, grimly battering away the bits of rock and wood that threatened them.

Cynwrig rose when we were close to the tunnel, his face gaunt and skin gray. I wasn't the only one who'd pushed their limits here today.

Mathi caught the shield Lugh tossed him, sharply told us to follow him, then ran into the tunnel, his footsteps barely audible on the glassy rock floor.

I risked a look over my shoulder, saw Cynwrig with one hand pressed against the exit's wall while he used the shield to batter away the worst of the wooden weapons aimed at him.

Stone shivered and moved. A heartbeat later, rock enclosed the entrance, and silence fell.

Mathi stopped and swung around, his headlamp so bright I had to throw up a hand to shield my eyes. "You're hurt—"

"I'm fine—"

"There's a three-inch cut on your forehead, and your foot is bleeding like a stuck pig," he said, almost angrily. "So, no, you're not."

I waved his concern away. "In the scheme of things right now, neither is a priority. Getting out of here before that thing comes after us is."

"I've blocked the entrance," Cynwrig said as he approached. "It will take at least some time for it to pull it down."

"If it keens too loud or too long, it could bring the whole damn mountain down on top of us."

And finish off what the old god had started eons ago.

I didn't say that out loud. I didn't need to, because everyone was obviously thinking it.

"You still need those wounds tended," Lugh said and held up a hand before I could protest. "That thing fed on blood. You don't want to be leaving it any more than necessary to rebuild its strength."

That was certainly a good point. Mathi swung off his pack and retrieved a first aid kit.

I sat down on a nearby rock and raised my eyebrows. "You're the last person in this outfit I thought would be allocated first aid duties."

"It's company policy that all employees have a first aid certificate, and the CEO is not exempt."

"Have you ever used it before today though?"

He glanced up, cold amusement briefly gleaming. "Probably not in the way it was meant to be used."

He didn't elaborate, and something within me suggested it was better not to ask. He quickly and efficiently tended to the more serious wounds on my forehead and foot, using butterfly bandages to close the wounds, then sticking a wound pad over the former and a waterproof bandage over the latter. My fingers got an array of colorful plasters.

From behind us came a low-grade boom, and the whole tunnel shuddered. I loosened the laces on my left boot and forced my foot back in, then quickly rose. It hurt like hell to put any sort of weight on it, but that was the lesser of evils right now.

"Time to go," Cynwrig said, and motioned Mathi to take the lead again.

Lugh fell behind him, the shield now attached to the back of his pack. The creature's fingers remained on the shield, and I had a bad feeling we should have taken the time to pry them away even if they still looked withered and unresponsive. But the booming behind us was getting louder, and thick cracks in the floor were now harrying our steps. We might not be able to hear the creature's keening, but those cracks were warning enough that we needed to get out of here, and fast.

We reached what looked to be an old rockfall area, which momentarily slowed our pace as we scrambled through the gap Cynwrig had obviously cleared earlier. A few seconds later, we hit a T-intersection.

This tunnel was wider, the footing smoother. Mathi went right and increased his pace. We'd barely taken a dozen steps when the goddamn fingers came to life, scuttling up the shield's fiery surface and clamping around Lugh's neck.

He made a gargling sound and reached up, trying to pry the wooden fingers away. Mathi spun and reached for one wrist, but new fingers erupted from the top of the creature's hand, swiping at him with knife-like precision.

I swore, drew my knives, and flipped one to Cynwrig. "Stab the knife through the remains of its wrist. It's the only way to stop it."

He nodded and as one, we stepped forward, and thrust the blades at angle through the wooden wrists, aiming the blades away from Lugh's neck.

The fingers stiffened in shock but didn't release. Lugh dropped to his knees, his face red, his lips turning blue. I swore, reached past the knife, and gripped several fingers, trying to pry them away. Knife like-splinters erupted from still living bits of wood, slashing desperately at my hand. A gun hilt appeared between them and my fingers, taking the brunt of the blows. I continued to tug uselessly at the creature's fingers as new shoots of wood erupted and desperately swiped at me. But the deadness now flowed across the back of the creature's hand, over its knuckles, and down into its fingers, stopping the growths. I snapped one finger free, then the next. Mathi removed the others, then pried the hand away from Lugh's shoulder. He threw it on the ground, drew his gun, and shot it. A heartbeat later, a second hand joined it. As Mathi shot it as well, flames flickered around the edges of the first hand's wound. Both hands were being held lifeless by the blades, so neither could create new fingers to remove the bullets as their trunk had.

As the flames intensified, I dropped to my knees beside my brother and wrapped an arm around his shoulders, comforting him as he sucked in great gulping gasps of air that shook his entire body.

The hands burst into flame and were consumed. Cynwrig gathered the broken bits of fingers and tossed them on top of the small fire. In very little time, there was nothing left but ash. I raised a breeze and scattered it to the four winds.

From behind us came a distant roar, and the ground underneath shook.

"We need to go." Cynwrig's voice was grim. Strained. "I can't hold it back for much longer. Lugh?"

"I'm fine," he said, sounding anything but. "Let's go."

He pushed to his feet, and I rose with him, keeping close in case he needed a hand. He didn't, but he didn't look great, either. There was deep bruising around his neck, and several bloody puncture wounds where the fingers had burrowed into his flesh. They were bleeding but not profusely, and his sweater and jacket were doing a good job of soaking up the blood.

We ran on through the wide old tunnel as the creature raged behind us. Up and up, we went, past offshoot tunnels in which ghosts lingered and keened, their sad song jarring against the fury chasing us. These ghosts hadn't been killed in the god's destruction but rather the aftermath. They'd tried to save the unsavable and had lost their lives in the process.

Even elves with the power to move a mountain could do too much. Push too far.

I glanced back sharply at Cynwrig. He caught the movement and smiled. "I'm fine."

"That seems to be a common response in this outfit right now, and I no more believe you than I did Lugh."

"We're close to the surface exit. That creature will not follow us outside."

"You can't be sure of that."

"It lives in darkness, draws strength from blood, and is burned by silver. What other creature does that remind you of?"

"No myth I recall ever mentioned anything about vampiric *trees*."

"That does not mean—" He stopped abruptly. "Fuck, here it comes. Run. Run hard."

I wasn't sure any of us other than Mathi had the capacity to increase our pace, but we nevertheless did our best, speeding through the tunnel and moving ever upward. The voices of the dead got louder and louder, as if in warning of the danger that now dogged our heels.

Then those voices were drowned out by a sharp keening, and the entire tunnel began to fracture. As thick chunks of stone slammed all around us, I thrust up a hand and created a swirling umbrella of air to protect us. But every chunk of roof hitting my barrier felt like a physical blow, and it was sapping my strength fast.

I couldn't last. Wouldn't last.

Then, from up ahead, came a glimmer of light.

Mathi and Lugh somehow found new strength and began to pull away, but I had nothing left in the tank. Lugh must have sensed it, because he paused, reached out, and caught my elbow. Cynwrig grabbed the other, and the two of them lifted me and ran on.

The light grew stronger, even as the keening grew louder.

It was close, so damn close.

I glanced over my shoulder. Saw, through the dust and falling stone, the thick fingers of wood reaching toward us.

Then we were out of the tunnel, into the air, into the rain.

Thunder rumbled overhead, and its power echoed through me. It was tempting, so tempting, to reach for that power, to let it burn through me and unleash it against the ungodly thing that still followed us. But I dare not call to the lightning. I'd almost died the last two times that I had.

But I could do something about the reason it followed us.

"Wait," I said. "I need to cast the shield into the air. It's following us for that."

The two men immediately stopped and released me. Mathi returned, reloaded his gun, and then pointed it at the rain-shrouded tunnel exit.

Lugh unlashed the shield from his pack and handed it to me. I sucked in a deep, quivering breath, then called on the air, wrapping it around the shield, mirroring the violence that rumbled above us and making it self-perpetuating, just as Beira had taught me. Then I cast the shield aloft, deep into the heart of the storm. The storm would move on, over the land and out to sea, and would eventually fade, but my echo would not. Not for at least a month.

That, surely, would give us the time to not only catch the elf bastards but to recover enough to deal with the shield's destruction.

A thick howl echoed from the depths of the tunnel then the creature erupted, all limbs and fury. It saw us, paused, then turned and scrambled up the remains of the mountain top, trying to reach what was now out of its grasp.

Mathi emptied his gun into it.

The creature howled with every hit, but it kept on climbing, reaching with ever lengthening fingers of wood for the storm-clad shield high above.

Flames flickered to life and spread unhindered across the creature's trunk, until it was completely alight. It continued to keen, and the mountain answered in kind, shuddering and shaking.

Then the keening stopped, and the creature became ash that the wind caught and blew away.

We were safe.

I dropped onto my knees and cradled my head in my hands. It hurt. *Everything* hurt. But we'd secured the shield and ensured the bastards with the rubies could not get the power boost they were desperate for.

It was at least a step in the right direction.

Cynwrig bent, gently picked me up, and cradled me close. He didn't say anything. He just turned and led the way down the rocky slope. The rain continued to pelt down, making it difficult to see where we were going, and to be honest, I didn't really care anyway.

Unconsciousness called, and this time, I didn't resist.

I woke to the realization things had obviously changed for the better. I was naked in a bed that felt like a cloud, and covered by a comforter that was thick and warm. The air smelled faintly of honey and toast, and while the storm still raged outside, it was definitely easing in ferocity.

I lightly probed for the storm pocket concealing the

shield. It was not only there but was indeed self-perpetuating. While I *had* designed it that way, I hadn't been in the greatest condition, and it was totally possible for me to have missed a step or two. That I hadn't, even when I'd been all but unconscious, was something of a relief.

I glanced at the pillows next to mine. They hadn't been used, so Cynwrig either hadn't slept, or he'd done so elsewhere. I spotted my phone—attached to its charger—on the bedside table and reached across to check the time and date. It was six in the evening—the same evening, not the next—which meant I'd been asleep for a little under five hours. That would definitely explain the lingering weariness.

I stretched the kinks from my body, then threw off the covers and padded into the nearby bathroom. The shower was big enough to party in, and both the tiles and the tapware looked to be made of diamonds, though it was more likely to be some sort of non-slip crystal. Wherever the hell we were, it wasn't an everyday sort of hotel or B&B. I caught a glimpse of my face in the mirror and noticed the wound had been healed. A quick look down at my foot revealed the same. Either a fae healer had been called in to patch me up while I'd been unconscious, or my healing abilities had gone into overdrive.

I switched on the taps and, when the water was hot enough, stepped under. For several minutes, I did nothing more than simply enjoy the stinging dance of heat across my skin, then, using the supplied L'Occitane soap and shampoo, got down to the business of getting clean.

The towels were thick and fluffy, and big enough to wrap around my body several times. I padded back out to the bedroom and spotted my clothes—freshly laundered and also patched, by the look of it—sitting on a chair. My backpack was on the nearby table. I was still wearing the Eye but quickly checked my knives and the Codex were inside, then got dressed and walked back over to the bed to retrieve my phone and its charger. A quick Google search revealed the name of the memory regression mage in Deva, and she had several vacancies for tomorrow morning. I booked one, just in case. We might not get back there in time, but if we did...

A soft knock had me looking around. The room had a number of doors, and the knocking came from the one on the other side of the bed. I walked over, opened it, and discovered Lugh manning a waiter's trolley stacked with covered plates. Beyond him was not a kitchen but another bedroom.

"Heard the shower going and thought you might like something to eat."

"Always." I stepped back and motioned him in. "Where are we?"

"In the visitors' suites at the Cloondeash encampment."

I blinked. "I thought Cynwrig said we'd never get permission to enter the encampment?"

"We didn't. He's in the encampment; we're on its outskirts and on top rather than underground." He stopped the trolley near the table and began pulling off the various lids. "It's accommodation designed for and used by those human or fae dignitaries needing to deal with the Cloondeash Myrkálfar."

I picked up a plate and began helping myself to the scrambled eggs, bacon, and toast. "Is Mathi here or was he allowed into the inner sanctum?"

"He was in the room on the other side of me, but he headed out a half hour ago."

I frowned. It was unlike him to leave without the rest of us. "Was there a reason? Has something happened?"

"Yeah, he had to go meet the man who ran the background. Apparently he called with some information on Gilda."

"Why didn't the fellow just tell him over the phone?"

"Because he said someone had broken into his house and attempted to kill him, and he wanted a guarantee of safety before he said anything."

Alarm slithered through me. "That sounds a little too much like a trap to me."

"Mathi said the same thing."

"But he still went?"

Lugh nodded. "He ensured the meeting point was a fully concreted structure."

"From what I understand, most concrete structures have reinforced steel."

"I said that. He said that had been considered." Lugh picked up a slice of toast, slathered butter on it, and then swirled it through his baked beans. "The entire area will be closed off and patrolled several hours beforehand, and given it appears using the ruby requires proximity—"

"Halak's might," I cut in, "but we don't know if the one Keelakm's using does."

"But we do. He was spotted on security cams outside the Eadevane Holdings building, and there was a red crystal in his hand."

I just about choked on my bacon. "We have a picture of him?"

Lugh nodded, dragged out his phone, and pulled up a photo. It showed a tall, slim man with pale hair, sharp cheekbones, and a horseshoe-shaped scar on his cheek.

A memory twitched. I *knew* that scar. Knew the man

behind it. We'd been lovers, once. A threesome. Me, Halak, and him.

It was just so frustrating that I couldn't remember *more*.

"What?" Lugh immediately said.

"I did that," I said, motioning to Keelakm's face.

"You did?" He turned the phone around and studied the image. "I can't remember you dating anyone like this."

"Neither did I until just a second ago."

He swore softly. "We need to get you to that memory regression mage ASAP."

"I've already made an appointment."

"When for?"

"Tomorrow morning." I hesitated. "Presuming, of course, we'll be out of here by then."

"We will," Cynwrig said as he came through the door. "We leave in an hour, in fact."

Lugh offered him a plate, but Cynwrig shook his head and helped himself to the coffee instead.

"Did you get anything useful from the historian?" Lugh asked.

Cynwrig perched on the arm of my chair, his big body washing warmth across my senses. But there was tension there, too, and an odd sort of distance. I couldn't help but wonder if it had anything to do with the fact we were within—even if on the outskirts of—a Myrkálfar encampment. He *had* slept elsewhere, after all.

"The man going by the name of Ka-hal Lewis was indeed born here, and his first name is indeed Halak. His father worked in a mine owned by Eadevane not far from here, but died when he was forced to do a double shift that drained too much of his life force. Apparently, it was a common issue back then."

"Health and safety did not exist back then, obviously," I commented.

"Nor unions, though I'm not sure if Eadevane takes much notice of either even today," Cynwrig said. "Halak's mother moved the family to Peckforton not long after. From what I've been able to gather, he had a falling out with their sponsors—"

"Sponsors?" I asked, eyebrow raised.

He glanced at me. "We're a very large encampment, and room has been at a premium for some time. To limit growth, we've restricted new arrivals to those who have family within the encampment willing to sponsor their arrival and guarantee their ability to make a valuable contribution."

"Huh." I knew Mathi's people were having similar problems—land was a finite resource these days, thanks to the ever-increasing number of humans also needing space—but I hadn't figured the dark elves would be facing a similar situation. In theory, at least, underground possibilities for expansion were endless.

"Do we know what the falling out was about?" I picked up a bit of toast and spread marmalade across it. It wasn't my favorite jam but there was nothing else on offer.

"Neither his sponsor nor his mother were willing to say on the phone, but she did admit she'd been in contact with her son recently and that she could possibly help us find him."

"Which doesn't sound a bit too convenient at all," Lugh said, voice dry.

Cynwrig smiled, something I felt deep within rather than saw. "We're meeting in Peckforton. Neither she nor her family would dare make trouble there."

Because they might just find themselves buried deeper in the ground than they could ever wish.

"Doesn't mean the information they provide won't be a trap," I said.

He leaned into me briefly, a caress that wasn't, and one that sent warmth spinning through me. "I'm well aware of that."

"In other words, don't be attempting to teach the teacher his job," Lugh said with a grin.

"Indeed." Cynwrig rose. "I have to make a few final arrangements, so I'll meet you in the foyer. It's through that door"—he pointed to the one he'd come through—"and left down the corridor."

We nodded and he left, coffee in hand. I frowned after him for several seconds and then returned my attention to Lugh. "Have you contacted Darby to let her know we're okay? She'd be getting worried by now."

He nodded. "She's picking us up at the airport."

I raised an eyebrow. "Cynwrig hasn't arranged cars?"

"He said he would, but Darby wanted to pick us up." He shrugged. "He's not even taking the same plane as us—he's flying direct to an airstrip closer to the encampment."

"I guess that's no surprise, given how badly he wants to catch Halak." And yet, disappointment stirred. Which was totally, utterly illogical.

My phone rang, and I picked it up to see who it was. Eljin. A silly smile touched my lips as I glanced back to Lugh. "Sorry, have to take this."

"Meaning it's the other boyfriend and romantic tomfoolery will no doubt ensue." He rose. "I shall leave immediately and let you get on with it."

He placed the tea and the last bits of toast on the table, then wheeled the cart out of the room. I hit the answer button and said, "Eljin, lovely to hear from you again so soon."

"Not really. Not given you were supposed to ring me tonight for dinner."

"I was?"

"Yeah. We spoke about it when I left Lugh's—"

"Ah fuck, yes. Sorry, it's been a hell of a day, and it totally slipped my mind."

"You're forgiven." He paused. "I'm happy to come pick you up if you still need dinner."

Dinner being a code word for sex, I suspected.

"I do, but I need sleep more." It was a statement that horrified at least a good portion of my hormones. "I've spent the day underground relic hunting—"

"Meaning you found the shield's location?"

"We did."

"And?"

"It's now well beyond anyone's reach."

"Good. At least that's one less thing for you to worry about." He paused again. "Where are you now?"

"Ireland, but we're heading for the airport in a couple of minutes."

"Do you need a ride home?"

I hesitated. While there was a part of me that wanted to do nothing more than to go home and contemplate Cynwrig's sudden distancing, in truth it didn't really matter. Besides, Eljin and I definitely needed to spend more time together if we wanted to discover if this attraction had any sort of legs. We couldn't do that if I kept making excuses.

"I promise to take you straight home," he continued into the silence, "no passing go, no detours for hot sex—"

I laughed. "Fine, you can pick me up and take me home—"

"My home, or yours? Because I promise on the soul of my sainted mother to do nothing more than feed you and let you sleep."

I laughed again. "I need fresh clothes for an appointment I have in the morning, so it's probably better if you come back to mine for a change. I have to warn you though, my bed's proportions are far smaller than yours."

"All the easier to cuddle you close, my dear."

Cuddling would eventually lead to other things, and we both knew it. I told him where to meet us, and we chatted for a while longer before I reluctantly bid him goodbye and got ready to leave.

Cynwrig met us in the foyer and led us out into a covered area where two cars waited. A chauffeur waited beside the rear door of the first, but we were led across to the second. Lugh jumped into the front seat as Cynwrig opened the rear door for me. He appeared very distracted and even more distant than before. He didn't kiss me or even bid me goodbye. He simply gave me a nod, closed the door, and walked over to the other car.

While I wondered if something had happened in the brief time I'd been unconscious, it did go some way to hardening my resolve to concentrate more on my relationship with Eljin even if I wasn't yet ready to give Cynwrig up.

But that time would come, and probably sooner than I might have guessed only days ago.

When we finally arrived back at Deva's small airport, Darby and Eljin were standing side by side chatting. She was a typical light elf in look—tall and slender, with long pale gold hair platted into a thick rope that ran down her back and eyes the color of summer skies. Her features were sharp but ethereally beautiful, and every movement was lightness and grace. She and I had been friends since school, and I couldn't imagine life without her in it. Having her as a sister-in-law would be the icing on the cake, as far as I was concerned.

"I see you've introduced yourselves," I said with a grin.

"Indeed," she said, eyes twinkling mischievously, "and I highly endorse your latest selection of lover."

"Are they always so open on these matters?" Eljin said to Lugh in a bemused sort of way.

"Oh, it gets far worse," my brother said. "Every detail, no matter how intimate, is fair game in their discussion books. You get used to it."

I grinned and hooked my arm through Eljin's. "It just means you have to bring your A game. No slacking off, or it will be discussed."

"To reiterate, that's not an idle threat." Lugh's gaze met mine, amusement and love gleaming. "Do you want me along for support tomorrow morning?"

"No, I'll be fine. Besides, you'd better make an appearance at the museum before they think you've hightailed it and stop paying you."

"Unlikely, given they will not easily get another antiquarian with my sort of experience." He cocked an eyebrow at Eljin. "No offense meant."

"None taken. I'll willingly admit I'm not half the field hunter you are, nor do I ever want to be. I prefer my comforts."

Lugh grinned and patted his shoulder. "A few hunts with me, and you'll see the light, lad, I promise you that."

"Says the old man to the much younger one," I said dryly. "I mean, there's all of, what, five years between you?"

"Seven," Eljin said. "And it'll take longer than that to

convince me into any more wretched tunnels or boring old digs."

"Was Rogan aware of this field reluctance when he hired you?" I asked curiously. "Because a fair chunk of Nialle's work involved physical hunts."

"He was," Eljin said. "But I think he was desperate to fill the position and, like Lugh, was convinced my mind could be changed. I assure you, it cannot."

"I suspect there's a good story behind that statement," Darby said. "Perhaps you can explain it one evening over dinner."

"Dinner would be lovely," Eljin said. "I might even be convinced to tell a tale or two."

"Excellent. I'll be in contact."

She gave me a look I knew meant she and I would not only be having a long discussion about the man on my arm but also, I suspected, my reluctance to commit more fully to the chase, then bid us both goodbye and led Lugh across to her car—a new SUV she'd purchased because his height and her beloved old mini just weren't compatible. She still had it; she just didn't drive it when he was a likely passenger.

Eljin guided me across to his hired Merc, opened the door, and ushered me in. It didn't take us all that long to get home, and he was as good as his word, making me dinner and cuddling me to sleep.

The morning, however, was a different matter entirely, involving several hours of slow and very, *very* thorough lovemaking. To say I was a satisfied woman by the time we finally climbed out of bed to make breakfast would be the understatement of the year—in a year that had been full of them.

Dr. Catherine James was a small, dark-haired woman who radiated power and friendliness. The former probably wouldn't be evident to anyone not sensitive to magic, and the latter was undoubtedly designed to put her clients at ease.

It was definitely putting me at ease.

She steepled her fingers against her chest and leaned back in her chair. "What can I do for you this fine morning?"

I hesitated. "I believe someone might have smudged my memories of a particular event and person, and it's very important I retrieve what I lost."

She raised an eyebrow. "I take it, given the fact you are here rather than at a regression therapist, you think they've been magically smudged?"

I nodded. "It would have happened a good forty years ago, though—is retrieval possible after such a long time?"

"Anything is possible, it just depends on the memories and the skill of the mage behind the smudging." She studied me for a moment. "I sense magic on you, but not the smudging kind. Are you carrying a charm or some other protective magic?"

"Not a charm. Knives that are goddess blessed."

"May I see them?"

I hesitated, then picked up my bag from the floor and took them out. She didn't reach for them. "Draw one."

I did. Blue flickered briefly down the fuller then fizzled out. A reaction to the magic protecting this place and an acknowledgement that it was no threat.

"The goddesses do not gift such weapons lightly."

"No, but gifts like these always come at a cost."

She smiled. "Indeed, but it is interesting how few realize that. What do you know of mage-directed memory regression?"

I sheathed the knife and tucked it back in my bag. "Nothing."

"Well, it's generally agreed that there are three levels of being. They are the conscious mind, the subconscious mind, and the superconscious mind, which is what the spirit, soul, or higher element of a person is considered to be. Mage memory regression works along the same lines as regression therapy, in that I will put you in a light trance—which eases your mind's natural resistance—and guide you into your subconscious mind. That's usually where these smudging events take place, as that's where thoughts, feelings, and memories are usually stored for easy retrieval. Tell me, have you had any minor memory triggers of the events you're trying to recall?"

"Only a few."

"A few is good. It means the memories were indeed smeared, not erased."

"Magic can erase memories?"

She hesitated. "Not really, but it can smudge access to certain memories, and it can certainly ensure pain hits when you make any attempt to remember."

Who knew magic could be put to such a devious use?

"What happens once I'm in a light trance and guided into my subconsciousness?"

"If there is any smudging—or indeed, something deeper magically—I'll pull up its threads and allow the memories to come through."

"Will you see those memories?"

She smiled. "A common question, easily answered. No."

"And the magical wall?"

"Given the length of time it has been in place, it is probably better not to interfere. It can disrupt whatever processes the mind has put in place to deal with the event or indeed the lack of remembering." A smile touched her lips. "Which, in plain terms, means some memories are best left behind walls on the off chance a deeper trauma lies behind them. There have been cases—few and far between, granted—where the sanity of the subject has been... altered... by the flood of remembrances."

That did make sense, and I mentally crossed all things that I wasn't hit by any sort of residue trauma once—*if*—my memories were restored.

She pushed a number of papers across to me. One was the pricing—and holy hell, it wasn't cheap—the other a form stating that I was undergoing the regression at my own free will, and she was not responsible for any trauma raising the memories might cause, blah, blah, blah. I signed it and pushed it back.

She filed it, then rose. "Follow me, please."

She led me through into a connected small room that held little more than a comfy-looking chair and a height-adjustable, well-padded, reclining therapy bed.

What most people wouldn't see were the layers of magical protections that ringed the room. I suspected they'd protect her from magical and physical assaults, and it said a lot about her confidence in them that she'd allowed me to bring my knives in with me.

"Please," she said, motioning toward the bed. "Sit and make yourself comfortable."

I did so. It was every bit as comfortable as the cloud I'd woken up in yesterday.

"Before we begin, you do consent to being lightly

hypnotized in order for us to reach your subconscious state?"

"I do."

She nodded and asked me to close my eyes. Barely audible relaxation music began to play then she spoke—softly, calmly, slowly. Phrases like "you are now slipping deeper and deeper into this beautifully soothing relaxation state" and "every sound you hear causes you to go deeper into calmness" flowed over me, until I'd reached a state that was sleep and yet not. Aware and yet not.

Her magic flowed over me, through me, a gentle touch that was warm and non-threatening. She kept speaking, kept guiding, drawing me ever closer to the memories that would not be remembered.

Eventually, we reached the block—it was a small blot of darkly entwined threads against the brighter lights of accessible memory. The pulse of her magic sharpened, and its fingers plucked at the darkly balled threads, moving them, pulling them apart piece by piece, until enough had been lifted that I could slip past and remember. Not full memories, but rather bits and pieces. It reminded me a little of a picture wheel, with each image coming briefly into focus before being spun away by a new one. Perhaps too much time—and too much damage—had been done for anything more.

I saw a man. No, two. Brothers and yet not. Lovers who did not enjoy each other sexually, instead finding satisfaction through an intermediatory. Me, in bed, with those brothers. A flash of another woman, another lover, briefly glimpsed and never seen again. *Gilda.* The reel's speed surged, showing flashes of a street, a restaurant, a hidden door that led into a deeper darkness. A place protected by magic and unseen by the public who unknowingly passed it every single day. Then a knife. A game that went wrong and ended in blood. Fury, violence. Not Halak. Mkalkee, the man we'd been calling Keelakm. A raised hand, hitting hard, once, twice, before Halak grabbed his hand and stopped him. Magic. Then nothing. Nothing until I was back home at the tavern and Lugh was demanding who the fuck had split my lip...

The memories slithered away as the barrier fell back into place. Words flowed over me again, calming my racing pulse, drawing me back to full consciousness while ensuring the memories remained on a conscious level.

I sucked in a deep breath and opened my eyes. Catherine James looked pale, gaunt, but the smile remained in her eyes.

"Were we successful?"

"Yes, indeed."

Because I not only remembered what we'd been to each other and who his partner was, I now knew where to find them.

Better yet, I still had the key to get into their "special" place.

THIRTEEN

THE FIRST THING I DID ONCE I'D PAID HER FEE AND LEFT HER building was ring Cynwrig. The call went straight to voice-mail, so I quickly outlined what I'd discovered and asked him to call me back when he had the time, sent a text just to be double sure he got the message, then hung up and rang Mathi.

He answered immediately.

"Well, you're obviously still alive," I said, "so it wasn't a trap, then."

"To the disappointment of some, no doubt." His voice was dry. "We got access to the security vids placed around Renaldo's building. It wasn't our elves going after him—it was another dissatisfied customer."

"And he used your need for information to get a safe house?"

"Well, not so much a safe house as a secure building, but yes. We decided a jaunt through Europe to see some relatives was in his best interests, and he was safely boarded onto a plane this morning."

And I doubted he had any choice in the matter. Given the circumstances, he was lucky he hadn't been planted under a tree somewhere. "Did he give you any useful information about Gilda?"

"Only that he was indeed paid a handsome amount to favorably enhance her background. The 'who by' was unsurprising."

"Was she related to them? A cousin or something?"

I didn't think she was, given what I'd just seen, but fucking or even marrying first cousins wasn't actually illegal here in the UK. Frowned upon, perhaps, but not illegal.

"No. But he gave me the full report he did before he was given a hefty bribe to alter the information." I could hear the annoyance in his tone. "As suspected, she and her partners had a long history of milking information from her carefully selected 'lovers.'"

"Who was her lover before you? Afran?"

"Yes."

I wondered if he was where she'd gotten the information about the shield and the rubies from. The timeline made it seem likely, especially given he'd accused her of stealing from him.

It also made me wonder if Afran had been behind Gilda's bloody death. Mkalkee's comments to the contractor we'd interviewed would seem to confirm it, as did what I'd glimpsed in that memory sideshow. The three of them had been working together for a very long time.

"I was given a list of her past residences," he continued, "and we're in the process of investigating them now."

"We?"

"Well, the IIT. I'm just tagging along."

I smiled. "How would you like to untag yourself and meet me at the tavern?"

"Is untag an actual word?"

"Don't know, don't care."

He laughed. "I can be there in twenty. I take it we have a lead?"

"We do. Tell you about it when you arrive."

I hung up, called an Uber, and then rang Sgott. It also rang out, so I left another message, telling him what I'd discovered and what I needed, and then went down the street to meet my Uber.

The tavern hadn't opened to the public yet, but I could hear the chef and kitchen hands preparing for the day. I dropped into the office to check if Ingrid needed me to do or sign anything, then ran lightly up the stairs to my living area.

I chucked my bag onto the sofa and strode across to the spare bedroom. Lugh had moved out years before I'd met Halak and Mkalkee, and I'd taken to hiding my teenage "treasures"—dumb things like notes from boys I'd fancied, or jewelry and other tokens they'd given me—underneath a loose floorboard. Mom and Gran undoubtedly knew of its existence—however little my treasures might weigh, they still altered the timbre of the song in that area—but had let me keep the pretense of it being my "secret" place.

I'd eventually moved on from such silliness and forgotten about the stash. Its memory hadn't been part of the smudged section, but the memory session had nevertheless forced it back into conscious thought.

I knelt beside the bed, pushed it sideways a couple of inches—the bedroom was tiny, so there actually wasn't much room to maneuver with all the other furniture in here—then felt for the indentation in the board. My fingers were bigger now than they had been then, and it took a few minutes to find it.

As the cover popped open, the gentle whisper of music told me Mathi had arrived upstairs.

"Hey," I said, as I dropped onto my stomach and peered into the small box I'd carefully melded onto the joists.

He leant, arms crossed, against one side of the doorframe—an image that came through the gentle song rather than me physically seeing it. He might never have stayed here overnight during the course of our relationship, but he'd certainly been here often enough that the fabric of the building had built up a "musical" impression of him.

"Can I ask why you haven't just moved the bed totally out of the way?"

"Because that would involve moving the bedside table, and I can't be bothered."

I carefully pushed the bits of yellowed paper and oddments of jewelry, stones, and chains aside until I found what I was looking for—a small clay token with a heart etched into its front and a multitude of symbols on the back.

This was the key. Mkalkee had given it to me just after we'd met when I was eighteen so I could slip through the multiple barriers of magic that protected their safe place. It existed in the heart of old Deva, close to the Northgate, underneath what was now a tapas bar—one that I'd unknowingly gone to multiple times over the years since.

I wondered why Halak hadn't taken it off me before they'd taken me home, but maybe he'd simply forgotten about it.

I resealed the box, pulled the bed back over it, and then rose.

Mathi stepped aside to let me pass. "And just what are we doing with that?"

"We are going to unlock an invisible door." I placed the token on the bench, flicked on the kettle, and then shoved a couple of slices of bread into the toaster. I might have had a good breakfast—in more ways than one—but the regression session had left me hungry.

He reached out for the token, but I snatched it away with a quick "Don't."

His eyebrows rose. "Why?"

"Because it remains active, and it's primed to send an alert if anyone but me uses it."

Thankfully, it had never reacted to *my* touch, nor had it ever sent either man a warning of my approach.

But then, they'd always liked being surprised.

I hoped they still did.

Hoped like fuck they still used the place, so I could watch the shock spread through their smug expressions as I took their asses down.

"And this invisible door will lead us to our elves?"

"Hopefully, if they're still using the place, and I can't see why they wouldn't be. Only four of us knew about the place —at least when I knew them—and Gilda's dead."

"Meaning you've remembered your relationship with Halak?"

"And Keelakm—or Mkalkee, as he's actually known— though it took the help of a memory regression mage," I quickly updated him. "This token won't let you or anyone else in, but I can do an initial scout and see if the place remains in use."

"And if he's there? Or has set alarms that your token can't get past?"

"I'll have my knives, and you and Sgott will be close by."

"Sgott? Why not my father? He's the day commander—"

"And Sgott is basically my stepdad. Do you honestly think he'd let anyone else be in charge of an operation involving me?"

"Well, no but—"

"There's also the point that your father doesn't do street operations anymore and I'm not the most trusting soul when it comes to operatives I don't know."

Especially right now, when it was becoming ever more obvious that the people behind the hoard theft *and* Mom's murder had contacts within the IIT.

The toast popped, and I quickly spread butter and peanut butter all over it. "You want a piece?"

"Always. But not of toast."

I snorted. "You're incorrigible."

"I've been called worse."

And sometimes by me.

"I do think there's a couple of problems with your plan," he added.

"Only a couple?" I leaned against the bench and bit into my toast. "Things are definitely on the up."

He shook his head, his expression slightly annoyed. "I *am* being serious—"

"Oh, so was I."

He rolled his eyes. I grinned and motioned him to continue.

"The biggest of those," he said, "is the fact that, if they are there, there's nothing stopping either of them using their rubies to bring down the entire building on top of you."

"They're not suicidal, Mathi."

"And yet Halak revealed his presence to you several times—"

"Because we were once lovers, and he was testing whether the magical smudging he did on my memories still held."

"And Mkalkee? He could have used a sunshield to prevent being seen at Afran's building collapse and didn't."

The building's music altered, telling me Sgott and three others were headed up the stairs. "They've always gotten off on the thrill of danger, but I'd still bet he had some sort of magic protecting him, even if it wasn't visible."

"I don't think you should be going into their place alone. They will have escape holes—rats always do. If they overwhelm you and run, there won't be much any of us can do."

"Which is why she asked me to bring along a bio-tracker and a bug, and why we'll have our own rat in the area," Sgott said as he and the others entered the room.

I raised the kettle in silent question, and he nodded. The three people with him—the rat shifter and the blonde woman I'd met once before, and a tall, ethereal-looking woman who trailed magical energy behind her like a comet —all shook their heads.

"They're likely to have preventative measures installed against both," Mathi stated. "It's common practice in most workplaces these days."

"Maybe in the places you work," Sgott said dryly. "But they couldn't risk the identifiable footprint those preventative measures emit. The regulars do run random monthly checks for such things."

"Regulars" being human cops.

"Would it not be better if we simply lay a trap for them?

I'm not onboard with Beth going into an unknown situation—"

"And you think I am?" Sgott raised his eyebrows. "Laddie, how long have you known me? How long have you known *her*? It isn't like either of us could persuade her to do the sensible thing. She is her mother's daughter."

I handed them both a coffee. "I'm glad this fact has finally been accepted—although I will point out we have little real choice this particular time. I'm the only one the key will respond to, and if we go in all guns—and magic—blazing, we might just destroy any chance we have a capturing them."

"The latter I concur with," Sgott said. "Astrid is here simply as magic backup, should it be needed. Although she is very good at the 'all magical guns blazing' approach."

Astrid grinned. A woman who enjoyed her work, obviously.

Sgott motioned to the blonde, and I put my cup down, turned around, and tugged up my sweater. She pressed the bio bug under my hairline at the base of my neck, then injected the bio-tracker into the skin just below my left shoulder blade. Then she stepped back and studied her phone.

After a moment, she said, "Signal on both clear and strong."

"Good." He drained his mug and handed it back to me. "Once you finish that drink, we'll head out. I already have people discreetly covering the old wall and the nearby streets."

I dumped his cup into the sink and then emptied mine out beside it. Aside from the fact I couldn't drink hot fluids as fast as he did, I just wanted to get this whole thing out of the way.

Before my two former lovers could cause us any more problems.

We headed out, Mathi and me in Sgott's unmarked car and the others in the car behind us. It didn't take long to get across to Northgate, and we parked in a small street that ran between the old Roman wall and the canal.

As we all climbed out, a short, chubby man I didn't recognize stepped out of a nearby single-story brick building with red-painted window frames. "Everyone is in place, boss. Lord Cynwrig has sent Ryka along, too, just in case we require earth removal."

Meaning he had gotten my message even if he hadn't responded, which naturally led into the next question—why? What had happened? Something must have given how intent he'd been in tracking down these two.

"Ryka is a dark elf we've worked with on a number of occasions," Sgott said, with a glance at me before motioning us inside. The rat shifter slipped away, crossing the street and disappearing under the arched gate.

The room was small and cluttered with desks and chairs. From the bits and pieces of information up on the walls, it appeared to be some sort of office dealing with homeless folk. Sgott's people had set up various monitoring stations on the desks, with camera views at differing angles along the wall in both directions, as well as Water Tower Street, which ended in a dead end just after the hidden access point into Halak's underground bunker. Ryka was tall and shapely, with long, platted dark hair and a calm rather than overtly sexual demeanor. Which was no doubt why she'd been chosen to work with the IIT—the last thing anyone would want in a siege or hostage situation was a Myrkálfar's natural "charms" distracting anyone.

"We've run a scan of the area," a woman at one of the

desks was saying. "No shielding, no alarms, no magic that we're aware of."

Sgott glanced at me. "The equipment is sensitive enough to pick up the faintest caress of magic—it may be that they no longer use this bolt hole."

"Maybe, but they are Myrkálfar, and it's possible you'd not sense their magic anyway."

Scott frowned. "Where's the entrance?"

"Between the chimney breast and the wine bar's entrance."

"Checked it," came a reply. "Didn't find anything."

"I'm sensitive to magic, and I've never been able to spot it, either."

I'd once asked Halak why, and he'd explained that the magic was based more on a Myrkálfar's natural ability to manipulate stone, with simple redirection and concealment spells woven in between. The presence of the former made the latter undetectable.

I strapped on my knives, then tugged the Eye from my neck and tucked it safely at the bottom of a knife sheath. Neither Halak nor Mkalkee might know what it was, but they'd always liked shiny things, and I wasn't about to risk them taking it. Of course, they'd undoubtedly take my knives if they did somehow overwhelm me, but it was unlikely they'd be looking for anything else hidden in the sheaths. Externally, at least, there didn't appear to be enough room in the sheaths for anything else.

I slipped their charm over my neck and let it sit against my chest. It felt familiar. Felt foul.

The foulness was new.

It meant their magic had changed. Darkened. Perhaps it was due to their use of the rubies, or perhaps it was always destined to darken simply because they were, in essence, beings of violence and darker needs. It also meant this charm might no longer work, even if its magic remained active.

My knives didn't react to the presence of the charm, but maybe that was because it was designed as a key rather than a threat. If that changed—if, on entering their bunker, they somehow restructured the magic already inhabiting the charm—all bets would be off where the knives were concerned. Their energy echoed through the distant reaches of my mind, an intangible but dangerous force ready and waiting to be unleashed.

That was a new development, though it was possibly due to the knife tip pressing against the Eye. Direct contact between the individual items of the triune did seem to enhance the strength of all of them in general.

"Final signal check?" Sgott asked, glancing around at the blonde.

"Still strong and clear."

Sgott nodded and touched my shoulder lightly. "Ready?"

"As I'll ever be."

"Be careful. And yes, I know, you always are."

A smile ghosted my lips. That had been Mom's standard reply on the few rare occasions he'd said something to her.

"If I say his last name—which is Montraie, by the way —come a-running, all guns blazing."

He nodded. I flexed my fingers in a vague effort to ease the gathering tension, then turned and headed back out.

The day felt colder than it had only a few minutes ago. Fear, rather than an actual drop in temperature, I knew. I gathered the air around my fingers and felt oddly safer for its presence. There wasn't a storm on the horizon—the one I'd hidden the shield in had already moved out to sea—but even still air could be used as a weapon if I gathered enough of it.

And I seriously hoped that *wasn't* a forewarning.

I walked under Northgate's arch. The lane on the left wasn't particularly long, and it was dominated by the stone steps that ran up the side of the old wall to the top walkway. Down the far end was a small wine bar, its window frames and door painted a bright yellow, no doubt to draw attention to its existence. Six wooden tables with bench seating lined the steps on the right and, on the left was a blue-painted double-glass door and a chimney breast. The hidden door lay to the left of this, in the three-foot gap between it and the wine bar's bright entrance.

The end building had been empty over the three years I'd used the secret entrance, but I doubted it becoming a wine bar would have worried them. In fact, they undoubtedly enjoyed the extra layer of risk it offered.

I flexed my fingers again, resisted the urge to draw a knife, and then strolled down to the end of the lane. I didn't immediately approach the entrance, instead leaning back against a table and pretending to study my phone while I surreptitiously looked for any hint of magic. New magic, not old.

Nothing.

No surprise, given Sgott's people hadn't found anything, either.

I shoved my phone into my jeans' pocket and, after a quick glance around to ensure no passersby were paying me any attention, stepped toward the wall. The token came to life, its touch burning my chest with its foulness. I resisted the urge to rip it off and took comfort in the fact that the knives remained inactive, though not inert. Their pulse in the back of my mind had sharpened.

I was a foot away from the wall and contemplating stopping before I smacked into it when there was a subtle shimmer across the bricks. Then they faded away, revealing a narrow set of stone stairs that plunged into deeper darkness.

A darkness that smelled faintly of patchouli.

Mkalkee's scent. They were still using this place.

A weird mix of anger, trepidation, and perhaps even anticipation swept through me. I wasn't entirely sure the latter was due to my need to get back at these bastards for all the damage they'd done recently. The "unsmudging" of my memories had given me a brief, tantalizing glimpse of the good times we'd all had here. They might be extremely dangerous people, but they had been, even back then. And there was definitely a part of me that had enjoyed the danger. Had enjoyed the darkness.

At least until it all went to hell on a broomstick. Or knifepoint, as the case had been.

A flicker of movement caught my attention. I glanced around and spotted the rat sitting in the shadows of one of the tables. I gave him a nod—and hoped even as I did that it was Sgott's man and not some random rodent—and then carefully stepped onto the top stair.

The door behind me closed, taking with it what little light there'd been to illuminate the stairs. I got out my phone but didn't immediately turn on its flashlight, listening instead to the silence and trying to get some sense of whether either man was here.

Nothing.

Of course, they might well have a sound screen activated. I guess the only way to find out was to head on down.

I drew in a deeper breath, then hit the flashlight button. Light swept the darkness away, so bright it made me blink.

The stairwell's stone was clean and dry, and there was no sign of cobwebs. The latter might be unusual, given cellar spiders were generally found in most basements these days here in the UK, but Mkalkee had always hated them, no matter how small. He obviously still had his deterrents in place.

I carefully edged down the steps, keeping my back to the wall as much as practical, wary of any traps that might be waiting. There hadn't been any the last time I'd come down, but lots of things had changed in the forty-odd years since then. They'd grown darker; I'd grown wiser.

Or at least, I hoped I had.

I neared the bottom of the steps and paused again. A wall of darkness rose a few feet away from the last step, reflecting the light back at me and preventing me from seeing what lay beyond. It wasn't new, but I'd always hated going through it. The pair of them would often have some sort of magical "trap" waiting for me. Generally, they'd been simple spells, designed to discomfort rather than physically hurt—like ensuring my clothes were torn away the minute I stepped into the room, leaving me naked and with nothing to return home in unless I begged them for clothes—but the specter of those past humiliations nevertheless rose.

Why the fuck had I put up with the pair of them for so damn long? Had they been so damn good in the sack I'd been willing to ignore their shit?

Or was, I thought suddenly, it more of an addiction? I'd always fancied dark elves, before them and after. Dark elf magnetism was an undeniable force, and it could some-times make you do things sexually that you might not otherwise consider. There'd certainly been instances of women—and men—becoming so hooked on the sensation that they basically became groupies. And there were plenty of dark elves who saw no problem in supplying the drug of choice. They did like their harems, after all. Cynwrig was a case in point.

And yet, while it would be so easy to place all the blame on their magnetism and my own lack of age and maturity, it would be a lie. There'd been something within me—a darkness that resided deep, deep down inside me—that had responded to the darkness within them.

I drew a knife. I had no idea if they would work against the sort of magic that might await, but I still felt better gripping the hilt.

With another of those useless breaths to shore up my courage, I moved down the final few steps and through that curtain of darkness.

Nothing happened. No magical traps fell around me.

Relief rose, but I quickly squashed it. Just because there wasn't a trap here didn't mean there wouldn't be others elsewhere.

The chamber—a combined living and kitchen area—wasn't dark, as there were several small sensor lights scattered about the room, and the one close to this entrance had activated when I'd entered. There were other chambers within the underground complex—bedrooms, bathrooms, and a "play" room—but they'd all been excavated beyond the footprint of the building above.

My gaze swept across the familiar room. The TV was new, as were the paintings on the wall. The sofa and kitchen were not. Memories surged and a frisson of... fear? excitement?... ran through me. We'd had plenty of good times in this room.

I gripped the knife a little tighter and walked over to the kitchen. The light near the entrance winked out when the one sitting on the nearby counter went on. There were dishes sitting on the sink's drainer, but they were all bone dry. I moved over to the kettle and lightly touched its side. It was warm. At least one of them had been here very recently.

I flexed my fingers around the knife hilt, then moved around the counter and headed for the doorway leading into the other chambers.

The air stirred in gentle warning, and I froze.

Someone was coming.

Someone who smelled of earth, sweet wood, and muskiness.

Mkalkee.

I stepped back, but as I moved, magic surged. The knives came to bright, fierce life, a warning I didn't really need. The spell coming at me, whatever the hell it was, felt foul.

I drew the second blade and braced myself, the knife spitting fiery sparks to the solid earthen floor. As the spell erupted from the darkness, I raised the knives and sliced them crossways through it. Bits of shattered magic fell like confetti to the floor.

"Well, well, well," came a smooth, darkly familiar voice. "It looks like our little pixie has gained a stinger or two since we last saw her."

"It's been at least forty years since you last saw me, Mkalkee. Lots of things of changed since then." I eyed the dark hallway warily. There'd once been sensor lights down there, so either the batteries were dead or he'd turned them off.

He didn't reply to my comment, and the silence crawled

across my nerves. Which was no doubt his intention. He'd always liked delaying the moment to drive up tension and expectation.

I flexed my fingers against the knife hilts. "Why are you and Halak intent on destroying Eadevane Holdings? What did they do to you?"

Again, the silence stretched. I wanted to retreat, to step back and even run, but held firm. He couldn't hurt me magically. I believed that if nothing else.

"Where did you first learn of the rubies, Mkalkee? Did Gilda steal the information from Afran? Or did she steal the ruby she'd hidden in her home from him?" A deepening sense of danger itched at my skin. I wasn't sure if it was a result of his continuing silence or intuition trying to warn me. "Did he kill her in revenge for that theft?"

Still no reply.

Was he waiting for me to step closer? To go into the confined space of the hall, where he'd gain an even bigger advantage than his size and reach already gave him?

Or was he simply waiting for Halak? The pair of them had always liked playing in unison... I shivered and did my best to ignore the fragmented bits of memory that rose.

"Why destroy Eadevane's headquarters, then? The people working there had nothing to do with your father's death," I tried. "You were always a cruel man, Mkalkee, but you had certain lines you would not cross, and taking innocent lives—"

I cut the rest off as the knives flared to life again. A heartbeat later, the ground under my feet shifted ever so slightly. He wasn't spelling—he was using the Myrkálfar ability to manipulate earth and create gods knows what.

I swore, bent, and drove one knife deep into the hard ground. The blade burned brighter, and the shifting stopped. The knives might not be able to sense Myrkálfar magic but they sure as hell could stop it—at least when it was being manipulated with intent against me.

That was good to know.

Mkalkee cursed softly. Angrily.

Anger was good, if dangerous. An angry Mkalkee would react instinctively rather than think and plot.

"Your magic no longer affects me, so come out and face me like a man."

The silence stretched on once more, ramping up my tension and the distant ghosts of old fear.

I couldn't play his games. If I couldn't drag him out of the shadows, then I either had to risk going in or give Sgott the go-ahead. The "all guns blazing" approach might not capture him but for all I knew, he was already in retreat. Neither he nor Halak was stupid, and he'd surely suspect I wouldn't have come here alone.

I drew in another of those deeper breaths. Time to play the most dangerous card of all...

In a mocking tone, I said, "It would appear you're afraid to face a lone, armed woman. But then, you always were a coward who preferred tormenting the vulnerable over anyone who could actually—"

He erupted out of the darkness, a force of rage moving so fast he was almost a blur. I stepped back and slashed with the knife, slicing through his leather jacket and down into flesh. He didn't care. He didn't stop. He just hit me full force and sent me flying backwards. I crashed onto the earthen floor hard enough to wind and slid backward several more yards until I hit a coffee table. Wood splintered, and glass fell around me, slicing skin and drawing blood.

The air stirred in warning. I looked up, saw him in the

air, arrowing feet first toward me. Saw the magic flowing around him. I wasn't sure if it was a shield or some sort of enhancer, because the speed he was moving made it impossible—

Move, idiot, my subconscious screamed, and I rolled desperately out of the way. His feet thudded where my face had been only seconds before, and I slashed wildly with the knife. The blade skimmed across the shield surrounding him and again its magic fell like rain. He lunged at me and, before I could react, grabbed my hand and pinned it to the floor—a movement that brought his pretty face far too close to mine. I clenched my free hand and punched with all the force I could muster. The blow hit his cheek and the side of his nose; blood and snot sprayed, splattering across the arm and hand he'd pinned. He laughed, raised a foot, and stomped down on my forearm.

Pain ripped through me, and my grip on the knife suddenly felt tenuous. Broken bone, I thought with a surprising degree of clarity.

"Let go of the knife, Bethany."

"Go fuck yourself, Mkalkee Montraie."

And hoped, with all my might, that Sgott and his people were paying attention. This could go very badly indeed if they weren't.

"Your determination and courage is admirable. It's certainly what made you my favorite toy."

"I've grown some brains since then."

He raised an eyebrow, his lush but bloody lips stretching into a smile that was warm and seductive. But if he was using the natural magnetism of the dark elf alongside that smile, then it sure as hell wasn't working.

"Perhaps we should test whether those brains have made any difference to your hungers—"

He paused to avoid my fist and then ground his foot onto my arm. A hiss of pain escaped, and the flare of desire sparked in his eyes.

"Perhaps," he continued, "we should have a little warm-up session while we wait for Halak. Of course, he is currently on his way over to Peckforton to cause some havoc, so it could be—"

I jackknifed before he could finish, kicking the back of his legs hard enough to unbalance him. As he staggered backward, I scrambled upright, flicking the knife from my right hand to my left hand as I backed away.

Magic surged, fierce and bright. Not his. Astrid's.

They'd heard. They were coming.

"Well, well, aren't you full of surprises," Mkalkee drawled. "Shame their assault on our defenses will amount to nothing."

He flicked his hand and magic rose, a bright whip that lashed toward me. I slashed wildly at it, but it didn't come anywhere near me. A distraction, I thought.

Only to realize far too late that it wasn't.

Something solid smacked across the side of my head and I went down hard onto my knees, battling the wave of unconsciousness as warmth spilled past my ear and down my neck.

"Be a dear, Bethany, and do not move for the next few minutes. I need to deal with the rats outside before you and I can ignite old passions."

Like fuck...

But the words didn't make it past my lips. The darkness in my mind was increasing, and the chamber was now moving in and out of focus. Or was that the walls? I blinked past the blood. They *were* moving.

He was creating a secondary barrier of earth and stone.

If he succeeded—if Astrid couldn't break his shadowy magical wall to give Ryka the chance to destroy his earth one—then I was dead. But he wouldn't immediately kill me. First, he would play...

Nausea rolled through me. I swallowed heavily and somehow pushed upright.

He tsked. "Bethany, Bethany, will you never learn?"

He moved one hand from the wall he was extending over the dark sheet of his magic and flicked another magical rope my way. I spun and dropped to my knees. The thick bit of wood swinging toward my good arm sailed over my head instead. I slashed at the magic controlling it, watched the threads disintegrate, and wearily pushed to my feet again.

To see Mkalkee grinning and his wall complete.

I was out of time.

I dropped my bad arm to my side and splayed my fingers, silently calling to the other knife. Light flicked around its hilt as the blade slowly pulled free from the ground, but Mkalkee didn't notice. He just strode toward me, anticipation shining from his blue eyes.

"Give up, Mkalkee," I said, voice hoarse and without strength. "Or I *will* kill you."

He stopped ten feet away but directly in front of me and flung his arms out wide.

"Try it. I dare you."

I flung the knife in my hand and then called to the other.

My throw was bad. Deliberately so.

The call was not.

He laughed as the knife clattered to the floor a foot away from his feet, then stopped, his eyes going wide and the smug superiority melting from his expression and eyes.

Blood seeped from a small wound at the front of his neck, a wound from which a sharp point of silver gleamed.

The knife had sliced through his spinal cord at the back of his neck.

"Eat dirt and die, Mkalkee."

He did.

Eventually.

CHAPTER
FOURTEEN

"You need to go to the hospital," the medic was saying. "I've repaired the break but there could be muscle and nerve damage I'm not skilled enough to see or fix. Plus, you need a head scan because—"

"I haven't got time for a head scan right now," I said. "But I promise to get one as soon as I can."

"The delay could cause permanent damage."

"Some would say that might be an improvement."

He scowled. "I'm being serious."

So was I. "Look, I will get one, but right now, aside from a headache, I feel fine. But our dead man's partner is out there, and he's armed with a relic that can bring down buildings. Stopping him is more important now, I'm afraid."

The medic glanced around as Sgott approached. "Chief Inspector, can you please talk some sense into her? She's refusing—"

"I know, and no, I can't."

The medic sighed and packed up his kit. "Fine, then. On your head be it, young lady."

I didn't say anything. I just watched him leave.

Sgott sat beside me, wrapped an arm around my shoulders, and pulled me closer. I allowed myself to relax into his big body, feeling some of the tension if not the guilt melt away.

"How are you?" he said gently. "Really, I mean?"

I was silent for a long minute. Then softly, brokenly, said. "I just killed him—"

"In self-defense."

Yes, and it wasn't the first time I'd done that. But this was somehow different. All the other times they'd been strangers, people I didn't care about. This time, it had been someone I'd known. Someone the stupid teenager I'd once been had fancied herself in love with. *That* had been an illusion, of course, one enforced by Myrkálfar magnetism and perhaps even by the hereto-acknowledged darkness within me—the very same darkness that had rejoiced at his death. Had wanted it. *Needed* it.

I shivered and did my best to ignore the whispers suggesting that now that darkness had tasted freedom, it would not be put back into its box.

"I could have aimed that knife anywhere, Sgott. I could have maimed him, but I wanted him to pay. I wanted him to suffer. And now he's dead, and he can't help us."

"He's dead because he raised both a magical and an earthen wall to stop us entering, and it succeeded for far too long. You severed his spinal cord, Bethany, but that isn't always a death sentence. Had we been able to reach him in time, he might still be alive. That lies on him, not you."

I knew all that. It didn't help. Wouldn't help, not when the demons of guilt in the long nights ahead rose and forced me to remember the last moments of his life. Made me see the impotent fury gleaming in his eyes as he silently raised multiple spells only to have the knife protruding from his neck slice each and every one of them apart. But he never gave up. Not once. Not until his very last breath.

The darkness might have rejoiced in all of that, but I did not.

I'd one-handedly patted him down once he was dead, battling nausea and guilt with every movement, but had eventually found the blacksmithing ruby in the pocket of the coat he'd slung over the hooks down the hallway. I'd been right—there were multiple exits in and out of this place.

Mathi had taken possession of that ruby and was now transporting it back to the council. He'd promised to personally ensure the damn thing was stored correctly this time.

I hoped they did, because I sure as hell didn't want all this to have been for nothing.

I pulled away from the warmth and security of Sgott's embrace, though it was damn tempting to stay right there for as long as possible. But as I'd said to the medic, Halak was out there, on his way toward Peckforton, intent on doing gods knew what. "Have you been able to contact Cynwrig?"

I'd tried a couple of times while I was waiting for Sgott and his team to break through, but hadn't been able to get a signal underground.

"No," Scott said. "But if anything catastrophic had happened at the encampment, we would have heard about it. Now, let's get you home."

He caught my hand and pulled me up. But as we were going up the stairs, my phone rang. Hoped flared briefly, then died. It was an unknown number.

My gaze met Sgott's. "We taking bets on who this is?"

He shook his head, his expression grim. "Answer it. The bug is still on and recording, so if it *is* him, we'll at least have something tangible to work with when it goes to trial."

If it went to trial. Halak's mentality had always been that it was better to die fighting than to live and face a future of incarceration.

I would *not* give him that. Someone had to pay for all the deaths, and he was the only one left.

I hit the answer button. "Bethany speaking—who is this?"

"I'm sure you've already guessed who it is, dear Bethany, so please don't attempt to drag this conversation out so Sgott can pin my location."

"How did you get this number? It's not listed."

"I applied a little charm to a relation of yours. It's amazing what you can get if you just ask nicely. Or unnicely, as the case may be."

Fear and fury hit in equal amounts, and my grip on my phone tightened so much my knuckles went white. "If you've hurt him—"

"My magic doesn't hurt, Bethany—not unless I wish it to, as you are well aware, given the games we have played in the past." His laugh was softly mocking. "Of course, I might have delivered a punch or three after he was bound, but he's awake and alert. You can even speak to him."

There was a brief pause, then, "Bethany?"

I closed my eyes against the rage that swamped me, overrunning even the fear. I had to stay calm. It was the only way either of us would survive.

But that inner darkness was awake, and it wanted to hurt.

Badly.

"Bethany," Lugh said again. "Don't give—"

There was a grunt and a curse, then Halak said, "If you follow your dear brother's advice and don't give, he will die. Painfully. And you know how good I am at the whole pain thing, don't you, sweet cheeks?"

Outside, thunder rumbled, a deep sound that echoed my inner fury. There might not have been a storm on the horizon earlier, but there sure as hell was one now.

"What do you want, Halak?"

"I want you at Observation Point in the Bulkeley Woods, with the shield, in thirty minutes, or the ruby will consume your brother's flesh as easily as it did your boyfriend's home."

I wanted to swear, wanted to curse, but did neither. An emotional response was what he wanted—what he always wanted.

But overhead, thunder cracked with such force, even the basement shook.

As Sgott stepped away to make the necessary arrangements, I said, "Thirty minutes doesn't give me much time."

"I know. But you'll nevertheless get here on time, or I'll start burning bits of your brother away. Oh, and leave your knives behind. I see them—or cops—he dies."

He hung up. I swore and rubbed a hand across my face, sending dried flakes of blood flying. The wound on my head had been repaired, but I hadn't yet had the chance to clean up. And maybe that was for the best. Seeing me in this bloody state might just rattle him—especially when I told him whose blood it was.

I looked up as Sgott returned and handed me an energy drink. "We're ready to leave. I've ordered our shifters into the area, and they'll keep to their alternate forms so that Halak won't suspect—"

"If there's a dozen different birds suddenly flying over the woods, he's going to suspect."

He gave me a somewhat disparaging look. "Give my people a little more credit than that, please."

I waved a hand in apology and popped the drink open. I'd never been a fan of energy drinks, but right now, I needed all the damn energy I could get.

"Astrid and I will wait at the Coppermine Lane entry point. He won't be able to see us from there, and even if he does, he's unlikely to consider one unmarked car dangerous. Especially when he knows your relationship with me and would be well aware the only way you could get there in time is via a police escort."

I nodded and finished the drink. "We should go."

"Our car awaits," he said, and motioned me ahead of him.

Thunder rumbled as I stepped into the lane, the clouds thick and ominous, heavy with power ready to be unleashed. I drew a deep breath and felt the storm's energy sweep through me, as sharp as the lightning that waited deeper within the stormfront's heart.

Beira had warned me not to call down that power unless I had a means of dissipating the force of it from my body. I now did—my knives—but it remained a dangerous process. One I'd chance in a heartbeat if it meant saving my brother.

Halak had no idea of the fury he'd unleashed by kidnapping him.

No idea that in threatening Lugh, he'd released the last restraints on that inner darkness.

I understood the need for revenge, more than he could ever know, but up until now it had remained unacknowledged. Controlled. But if he killed Lugh, no pixie curse and no amount of time would stop me tracking him down.

And I *would* watch him die, as I had watched Mkalkee die.

We climbed into the car and sped out of Deva, the silence stretching as the siren wailed. It began to rain as we turned off the A41, and by the time we reached the Copperhill Lane entrance to the woodlands, it was absolutely pelting down.

I didn't mind. The wind and the rain were my friends, not his.

"Use the same code word to call us in," Sgott said, as we both climbed out of the car. "Do not take risks, Beth, and do not pull your punches."

"I can't do anything until I know if Lugh is okay and somehow get him out of there."

"If he's okay, he won't want to 'get.' He'll want to play a part in Halak's capture."

I knew that. I also knew that while he remained, I'd be hamstrung.

Rain seeped past the collar of my jacket, but I didn't bother zipping it or pulling on the hood. Halak would want proof that I wasn't carrying my knives before I entered that clearing, so I'd likely end up stripping off and getting wet anyway.

And it wasn't like I was in any way cold. The rain pelting my skin might be icy, but the storm's rage infused every inch of my body, and it warmed me in a way no number of clothing layers could.

I pulled my knives free, tugged the Eye out of the sheaths and put it on, then threw the sheaths back into the car. The knives I'd drop closer to the meeting point. There probably wouldn't be many walkers out in this weather, and I could still call the knives to me even if someone did pick them up. But the less distance they had to travel, the better.

"He'll no doubt raise some sort of shield once I enter that clearing," I said. "So tell your people to keep clear unless I say the code word."

He smiled again, but there was a seriousness in his eyes that belied the amusement. "If I so much as *suspect* he's getting the better of you or Lugh, we will breach that clearing and take that bastard out, magic or not, code word or not. Understood?"

I echoed his smile. "Understood."

"Good. Go then, but do try not to break anything this time. I'll end up with a full head of gray hair at this rate."

I laughed, kissed his cheek, and headed down a dirt path that was becoming muddier by the moment. As I went through the old wooden gateway that signaled the wood's entrance, the song of the trees rose, a fierce, joyous harmony that filled my soul with hope and courage. I'd initially been a little surprised by Halak choosing a meeting place in the middle of a wood, but a quick search on Google Maps showed the clearing was fairly sparsely treed. Besides, he knew I wouldn't in any way hurt a living tree, let alone rip it free from its soil in an effort to stop him.

I followed the path around to the left and then up a rock-crusted slope. As I neared the top, magic touched the air. My gaze swept the ground ahead of me, and after a moment, I caught the slightest shimmer of a spell. The knives sparked faintly, suggesting the magic was aimed at me but not an immediate threat.

I studied the nearby old chestnut trees whose forms had been twisted by the periodic coppicing in times past, and singled out one several yards off the path. Its song held an underlying thread of emptiness and loss, the source of which was a cavity caused by a branch being broken off in a storm long ago.

I walked over. The trunk's hole wasn't large, but it lay on the opposite side to the main track and provided the perfect hiding spot for the knives. I placed them inside, then pressed a hand against the trunk to reassure her the blades would cause her no harm before continuing on.

A dozen steps from the top of the hill, his magic flared both behind and in front of me, creating a barrier that ran off to the left and right. I had no doubt it would ring the entire clearing, and I mentally crossed all things that it wasn't domed.

Thunder rumbled, and the storm's power sharpened within. Just for an instant, firefly specks of incandescent light danced all around me.

Mine to release, whenever I wanted.

And gods, I wanted. Badly. But I had to find where Lugh was first.

"I'm here as you asked, Halak. Where's my brother?"

"First I must ensure you don't have those magic-busting knives of yours aboard."

His voice came from the right of the clearing, in the area where the rocky outcrop that formed the viewing platform was. But a foul caress of energy lay to the left, and my gut twisted. I had a bad feeling he was using the ruby's flames to cage Lugh, and if that cage had a top, I was in trouble. No matter how mighty my storm, it wouldn't affect the ruby's unearthly flames.

Hell, I wasn't even certain the knives could. They might theoretically be able to kill certain gods, but did that mean they could also counter the powers raised by the deadly weapons of the gods?

Dare I risk destroying the knives in godly fire to find out?

If it meant saving Lugh's life, fuck yeah.

"Has using the ruby's power addled your senses?" My voice sounded remarkably calm given the turmoil that raged within. "Because if I had the fucking knives on board, I'd be busting through these shields of yours and attacking your ass right now."

He laughed. "Had you attempted that, your brother's life would have been forfeit."

"It'll be forfeit anyway, and we both know it. You can't afford to let either of us out of this clearing, can you now?"

"A truth few would have realized so quickly. Strip down to your undergarments, Bethany. I want to be sure you're not carrying anything you shouldn't be."

He wasn't talking about weapons. He was talking about wires.

I quickly stripped everything off, even my underwear. I might have been addicted to the touch of a dark elf as a teen—and undoubtedly still was as an adult—but Halak's appetite for sex was legendary. Even back then, he was nigh on insatiable. Nakedness would distract him. It always had.

I shoved my boots back on and then said, "I've done as you asked. Now let me see my brother."

"Once I've done my check, I most certainly will."

A brief break in the front wall of magic appeared. I stepped through, my gaze sweeping the clearing. I'd guessed right—Halak was standing on the stone outcrop, and his shield did encircle the entire clearing—but didn't, I was relieved to see, arch over us.

I looked left, and sick fear twisted through me. Lugh was caged by a cylindrical tube of fire. I was too short to see if the fire enclosed the top, and the flames were too fierce to see if he stood within or not.

"Well, this is a delightful surprise," Halak said. "And may I say, the skinny teenager has certainly filled out magnificently. Lift your hair, sweet Bethany, and turn slowly around."

He was wearing a long coat that fell past his knees and a rather sad-looking woolen cap that should have shadowed his features but somehow didn't. His face was angular, holding none of the perfection of Cynwrig's or even Mkalkee's, but his eyes were as entrancing as they'd ever been, shining with an almost otherworldly light.

I clenched my fists against the urge to cast him off that goddamn ledge and smash him to the ground below, and lifted my hair. But my fury reached upwards, and lightning speared the sky. It briefly illuminated the clearing and revealed the shadow standing within the flames.

Lugh. It had to be. There were few other men in Deva as big as him.

Relief hit so hard, my knees threatened to buckle. But the flash had also revealed something else. Not only were his hands and feet tied, but there was a rope wrapped around his neck, and it was leashed to the rope binding his arms. There could only be one reason for that—it was a noose, one that would tighten with any attempt to escape.

I slowly rotated as Halak had asked, and silently directed a sliver of wind toward my brother; it rolled over the ungodly flames and then bled down the cylinder's inside. The cylinder wasn't capped, and I could get Lugh out, as long as my reactions were faster than Halak's.

Once the wind had skimmed Lugh's body, it returned, thick with the scents of fury and blood. He was hurt but not badly.

I turned the rest of the way until I was facing Halak again. "Satisfied?"

"For the moment." His gaze slowly toured down my length, and while the spark of anticipation lit his gaze, all I felt was revulsion. "Where is the shield, Bethany?"

His gaze was on my breasts rather than my face, and I clasped my hands behind my back, a move that not only emphasized their fullness but also hid the movement of my hands. Slowly, carefully, I reached for the wind again.

"It's close by. Release my brother from his cage, and I'll fetch it; not before."

"That's not how this works. I say, you do. Or your brother will be punished."

He took a hand from his pocket, revealing the ruby. Just for a moment, light flared deep in its bloody heart, and the intensity of flames behind me increased. Lugh hissed, a sound that shot through my heart.

"Stop," I said, and did two things.

Unleashed the wind, and called for the knives.

As the hilts thudded into my waiting hands, Lugh was ripped from his cage and snatched high into the air. I directed him across to Sgott, depositing him softly on the ground without releasing him. The minute I did, he'd come running straight back.

"Well, that was unexpect—"

"There's one thing you don't know about me," I cut in. "Actually, there's two, but the most important one is the fact I'm not *just* the daughter of a pixie."

His expression was surprised but not yet fearful. I'd wait for the fear. Savor it, as he had so often in the past.

My inner bitch had definitely risen to the surface.

"I don't care what you are, Bethany, beyond what you can do for me." His gaze raked me. "Produce the shield, or I will unleash the fire and melt little pieces off you until you do as I wish."

"Hard to do when you don't hold the ruby," I said, and flung the full force of the wind at him.

He tumbled backward over the edge, but I didn't let him fall. I caught him, raised him, and then ripped the ruby from his hand and tossed it toward Sgott.

Halak's face was a picture, and gods, did it feel good.

I released the wind's hold on Lugh and then tugged Halak closer. Lightning danced around him, an echo of my fury though not of my doing.

His fear filled the air, but he nevertheless raised and cast a spell. I had no idea what it was, but it felt foul, ominous, and deadly. I shredded it with the knives, watched the threads fall, even as he cast another. It met with the same fate.

"I can do this longer than you can, Halak."

He stopped mid-spell and glared at me. Despite the bravado in his expression, fear now glimmered in his lovely eyes. "What are you?"

"I'm the daughter of a storm god, and you chose a hell of a day to kidnap my brother."

"And the second thing?"

"I killed Mkalkee tonight."

Rage and grief flooded his expression, but I gave him no time to retaliate or speak. I simply flicked him into the nearest tree hard enough to break a bone or two and knock him out.

It was tempting, so damn tempting, to kill the bastard, but I wasn't about to give him an easy way out.

Not when Lugh was alive.

But Halak would pay for the deaths he and Mkalkee had caused, both now and in the past.

I released the wind's hold on him but kept it close in case he revived before the cavalry got here.

Tree song reached out to me, telling me they were close. Lugh reached me first, his steps slowing as he entered the clearing. His lip was split, and he had the beginnings of an impressive black eye, but other than the serious-looking rope burns around his neck and wrists, didn't appear to be badly hurt. His gaze swept from me to Halak and back again, then he stripped off his jacket and held it open for me. I shoved my arms in, then turned around so he could zip it up for me. It was so damn long it covered my knees.

"How did Halak capture you?"

"He was waiting for me when I left the museum. Leashed me with magic and shoved me into the back of a van. He's obviously done that sort of thing before, given how fast and efficient the whole process was."

He hadn't been into kidnapping when I'd known him, but that was a long time ago.

Sgott and his people appeared. He motioned them over to Halak, then continued on to us and handed me my clothes. "No blood and nothing broken this time. The gray hairs are in retreat, at least until the next event."

I smiled and hurriedly dressed. "Hopefully, the next hunt won't be anywhere near as stressful or involve madmen intent on revenge."

"From your lips to Fate's ears." He glanced at Lugh. "I've a car waiting to take you to hospital. Get those rope burns tended to. And you, Bethany, get the goddamn scans the medic wanted you to have."

"Scans?" Lugh glanced at me sharply. "Why?"

I waved a hand. "Just a precaution. How bad are the rope burns?"

"I've had worse." He slung an arm over my shoulders

and gently guided me out of the clearing. "Did I ever tell you about the time I was captured by Pygmies in the Cameroon Highlands forests and hauled up a mountainside so their chief could decide whether to release me or eat me?"

I laughed. "They did not."

"They certainly did. And let me tell you, I think the only reason they let me go is the fact they didn't have a rotisserie big enough."

I laughed again, and he continued to regale me with his nonsensical stories as we made our way out of the forest and headed for the hospital.

The tavern's old timbers told me Sgott was on his way up the stairs. I pulled another mug from the hooks lining the bottom of the overhead cupboards and added a few more strips of bacon to the pan. Even if he didn't want them, they wouldn't go astray. The force of the storm inhabiting my body seemed to have increased my appetite three-fold, and I was just hoping all this food was being burned off by whatever fury still lingered within rather than going straight to my hips.

Although when I'd complained to Eljin about it last night, he'd simply laughed and said it would just give him a better grip. And proceeded to show me just how delightful such a grip could be when we were both naked and I was riding him.

"Would you like a bacon butty?" I said as Sgott entered the room.

"Aye, that would be lovely."

The tiredness in his voice had me looking around. "Bad night?"

He grimaced. "Had its high points and lows."

"Was one of the high points Halak's incarceration?"

An expedited, closed court trial had been requested, and given the dire nature of the crimes he'd been charged with, not to mention the pressure being placed on the system for a quick resolution, the hearing had gotten underway yesterday. The IIT had been confident that, with the evidence they'd gathered and the confessions I'd recorded, it was basically an open-and-shut case, but I wasn't about to count my chickens until the results were in.

Sgott nodded. "He got life imprisonment, in a cell especially designed for magical killers such as him. He'll spend his life in solitary confinement, his only link to the outside world a TV and the slot through which his food comes."

"Good." I made up his butty, handed it to him, then popped more bread into the toaster for mine. "And the bad?"

"Ah, well." He leaned a hip against the counter and bit into his sandwich. Deciding what to say, I thought. Or, perhaps, how to say it.

I frowned at him. "Are they going to charge me for Mkalkee's death?"

"What? Gods no. That was justified, no question about it. Besides, a number of high-profile councilors came to headquarters on your behalf, stating your actions were a direct result of being in their employ, so if you were being charged they had best charge them too."

"The law doesn't exactly work like that," I said wryly, but was nevertheless pleased—and more than a little surprised—by their support.

Of course, I *was* currently their only hope of finding the

missing hoard, and that no doubt played a big part in their actions.

"The law," Sgott said, his voice grave but amusement creasing the corners of his eyes, "can sometimes be mighty pliable when it needs be. Or when high-profile people apply enough pressure."

My toast popped; I plucked it free and slathered butter all over it. "That's a very cynical sort of statement coming from a man renowned for following the rules."

"More so than Ruadhán, for sure, but we're both aware that I'll bend a rule or two if needs must. You, my dear woman, have been the cause of a few such bendings."

I grinned. "Sorry about that."

He waved a hand. "If I was at all concerned we were stepping too far beyond the spirit of the rules, it would not happen."

I knew that. I heaped bacon onto my toast, then dropped the pan into the sink. "So, what is the bad news you seem totally intent on avoiding?"

"It involves Cynwrig."

"Ah, Mr. Suddenly Elusive."

"With good reason, I'm afraid."

I saw the seriousness in his eyes, and my stomach twisted. "What's happened? Is he okay? Is his sister?"

"Yes, and yes."

I studied him for a long moment, the twisting in my stomach getting stronger. "It's his father, isn't it?"

Sgott nodded. "I'm afraid he died five days ago. The news only came out today, when the council announced an official commemoration would be held in his honor."

Five days placed it happening when we were leaving Cloondeash. No wonder he'd been so distant and had rushed straight home. No wonder he hadn't wanted to talk or answer any phone calls, be they urgent or trivial.

"Thought you might want to know," Sgott continued. "A Myrkálfar mourning period encompasses three to six months, depending on the situation and the stature of the person involved. It's doubtful he'll go against tradition in this matter, so you're unlikely to see him for at least three months."

I dumped my butty back onto my plate, my appetite suddenly gone.

"Thanks for letting me know. At least now I know why he hasn't been returning my calls."

"Aye, thought you might be wondering." He finished his sandwich, and I motioned him toward mine. He raised an eyebrow, silently asking if I was sure, and then when I nodded, picked it up. "I've received an invitation to the official commemoration. Thought you might like to accompany me."

I wrinkled my nose. "Would I be welcome, though? We're bedmates, Sgott, nothing more. It's not like I knew his father at all."

"No, but it never hurts to pay your respects all the same. I've known Cynwrig long enough now to know he'd appreciate the effort."

"Then go I will."

If only to see the man who turned my world upside down and had made me hunger for things I'd known could never be, one last time.

"Good," Sgott said. "I'll send you the details when I have them, but it's slotted in for Monday."

"Monday's an odd day for a commemoration, isn't it?"

"Apparently Monday has spiritual and deity significance to the Myrkálfar."

Which just proved how little I actually knew about their society.

"You want a coffee?"

He shook his head. "I'd best be heading off. I've still paperwork to cover before I can head home." He paused. "You okay?"

I smiled. "Of course. He isn't the only man in my life."

But he was the only one who'd immediately threatened my heart.

Of course, Eljin might yet get there, especially now I had at least three months to concentrate on him. But even if everything worked out between us and we did get married, I knew there'd always be a part of me hungering for what I couldn't have.

I guess I really *hadn't* moved beyond my teenage addiction to dark elves.

Sgott studied me for a second longer, then nodded and left. I waited, arms crossed, until the tavern's music told me he'd gone.

Only then did I let the prickling tears fall, and grieved for a relationship that had ended before it had ever really started.

Also by Keri Arthur

Killer's Kiss (Oct 2023)

Shadow's End (July 2024)

The Witch King's Crown

Blackbird Rising (Feb 2020)

Blackbird Broken (Oct 2020)

Blackbird Crowned (June 2021)

Kingdoms of Earth & Air

Unlit (May 2018)

Cursed (Nov 2018)

Burn (June 2019)

The Outcast series

City of Light (Jan 2016)

Winter Halo (Nov 2016)

The Black Tide (Dec 2017)

Souls of Fire series

Fireborn (July 2014)

Wicked Embers (July 2015)

Flameout (July 2016)

Ashes Reborn (Sept 2017)

Dark Angels series

Darkness Unbound (Sept 27th 2011)

Darkness Rising (Oct 26th 2011)

Darkness Devours (July 5th 2012)

Darkness Hunts (Nov 6th 2012)

Darkness Unmasked (June 4 2013)

Darkness Splintered (Nov 2013)

Darkness Falls (Dec 2014)

<u>Riley Jenson Guardian Series</u>

Full Moon Rising (Dec 2006)

Kissing Sin (Jan 2007)

Tempting Evil (Feb 2007)

Dangerous Games (March 2007)

Embraced by Darkness (July 2007)

The Darkest Kiss (April 2008)

Deadly Desire (March 2009)

Bound to Shadows (Oct 2009)

Moon Sworn (May 2010)

<u>Myth and Magic series</u>

Destiny Kills (Oct 2008)

Mercy Burns (March 2011)

<u>Nikki & Micheal series</u>

Dancing with the Devil (March 2001 / Aug 2013)

Hearts in Darkness Dec (2001/ Sept 2013)

Chasing the Shadows Nov (2002/Oct 2013)

Kiss the Night Goodbye (March 2004/Nov 2013)

<u>Damask Circle series</u>

Circle of Fire (Aug 2010 / Feb 2014)

Circle of Death (July 2002/March 2014)

Circle of Desire (July 2003/April 2014)

Ripple Creek series

Beneath a Rising Moon (June 2003/July 2012)

Beneath a Darkening Moon (Dec 2004/Oct 2012)

Spook Squad series

Memory Zero (June 2004/26 Aug 2014)

Generation 18 (Sept 2004/30 Sept 2014)

Penumbra (Nov 2005/29 Oct 2014)

Stand Alone Novels

Who Needs Enemies (E-book only, Sept 1 2013)

Novella

Lifemate Connections (March 2007)

Anthology Short Stories

The Mammoth Book of Vampire Romance (2008)

Wolfbane and Mistletoe--2008

Hotter than Hell--2008

About the Author

Keri Arthur, the author of the New York Times bestselling *Riley Jenson Guardian series*, has written more than fifty-five novels–35 of them with traditional publishers Random House/Penguin/Piatkus. She is now fully self-published. She's won six Australian Romance Readers Awards for Favourite Sci-Fi, Fantasy, or Futuristic Romance & the Romance Writers of Australia RBY Award for Speculative Fiction. Her Lizzie Grace series won ARRA's Fav Continuing Romance Series in 2022 and she has in the past won The Romantic Times Career Achievement Award for Urban Fantasy. When she's not at her computer writing the next book, she can be found somewhere in the Australian countryside taking photos.

for more information:
www.keriarthur.com
keriarthurauthor@gmail.com
https://payhip.com/KeriArthur

Printed in the USA
CPSIA information can be obtained
at www.ICGtesting.com
LVHW041658130524
780165LV00034B/270